Th
you
into time.

Can you survive
in the
Wild West?
Turn the page
to find out.

Bantam Books in the Time Machine Series
Ask your bookseller for the books you have missed

TIME MACHINE 9

Wild West Rider

by Stephen Overholser
illustrated by Steve Leialoha

A Byron Preiss Book

BANTAM BOOKS
TORONTO · NEW YORK · LONDON · SYDNEY · AUCKLAND

This book is dedicated to Ann Weil

RL 4, IL age 10 and up

WILD WEST RIDER

A Bantam Book/December 1986

Special thanks to Ann Hodgman and Martha Cameron.

Editor: Ann Weil
Book design by Alex Jay
Cover painting by Steven Leialoha
Cover design by Alex Jay
Mechanicals by Studio J
Typesetting by David E. Seham Assoc.

"Time Machine" is a registered trademark
of Byron Preiss Visual Publications, Inc.
Registered in U.S. Patent and Trademark Office.

ISBN 0-553-25180-5

Published simultaneously in the United States and Canada

Bantam Books are published by Bantam Books, Inc. Its trademark, consisting
of the words "Bantam Books" and the portrayal of a rooster, is Registered in
U.S. Patent and Trademark Office and in other countries. Marca Registrada.
Bantam Books, Inc., 666 Fifth Avenue, New York, New York 10103.

Printed and bound in Great Britain by
Cox & Wyman Ltd., Reading

0 9 8 7 6 5 4 3 2 1

ATTENTION
TIME TRAVELER!

This book is your time machine. Do not read it through from beginning to end. In a moment you will receive a mission, a special task that will take you to another time period. As you face the dangers of history, the Time Machine will often give you options of where to go or what to do.

This book also contains a Data Bank to tell you about the age you are going to visit. You can use this Data Bank to help you make your choices. Or you can take your chances without reading it. It is up to you to decide.

In the back of this book is a Data File. It contains hints to help you if you are not sure what choice to make. The following symbol appears next to any choices for which there is a hint in the Data File.

To complete your mission as quickly as possible, you may wish to use the Data Bank and the Data File together.

There is one correct end to this Time Machine mission. You must reach it or risk being stranded in time!

THE FOUR RULES OF TIME TRAVEL

As you begin your mission, you must observe the following rules. Time Travelers who do not follow these rules risk being stranded in time.

1.
You must not kill any person or animal.

2.
You must not try to change history. Do not leave anything from the future in the past.

3.
You must not take anybody when you jump in time. Avoid disappearing in a way that scares people or makes them suspicious.

4.
You must follow instructions given to you by the Time Machine. You must choose from the options given to you by the Time Machine.

YOUR MISSION

Your mission is to uncover the reason for the sudden disappearance of the Pony Express.

In 1860 the Pony Express was a daring experiment that promised to carry the mail from St. Joseph, Missouri, to San Francisco, California, in only ten days—less than half the time it took by stagecoach. Despite predictions of failure, bad weather, and hostile Indians, the Pony Express made good on its promise. The experiment made headlines and captured the imagination of people all over the world.

Yet the Pony Express was in operation for only eighteen months. Why was it discontinued so soon after it had been started? You must travel back in time to the Old West and find out. To do so, you may have to become a Pony Express rider yourself!

 To activate the Time Machine, turn the page.

TIME TRAVEL ACTIVATED.
Stand by for Equipment.

EQUIPMENT

For your mission you will wear the clothes of a cowboy—a wide-brimmed felt hat, a buckskin shirt with fringe on the sleeves and shoulders, denim trousers, and cowboy boots. You will also carry a water canteen and a map of the Pony Express route.

 To begin your mission now, turn to page 1.

 To learn more about the time to which you will be traveling, go on to the next page.

DATA BANK

These facts about the United States in the 1860's will help you complete your mission:

1) The Pony Express proved that an overland route through the mountains was superior to the southern route in the desert. Before 1860 the route through the mountains was thought to be impassable because of weather conditions and hostile Indians.

2) In the 1860's the United States government awarded contracts to private companies to carry the mail. Two freighting companies, the Butterfield Overland Mail Company and Russell, Majors & Waddell, were in competition for a $1-million mail contract in the West.

3) Starting in April 1860, the Pony Express operated for eighteen months, carrying 34,753 pieces of mail.

4) Mail and freight were carried by rail cars after the transcontinental railroad was completed at Promontory Point, Utah on May 10, 1869.

5) A stagecoach averaged 100 to 125 miles a day, whereas pony riders could cover 250 miles.

6) Relay stations on the Pony Express were 35 to 75 miles apart. Riders changed horses at each station.

7) The Pony Express mail was carried in a

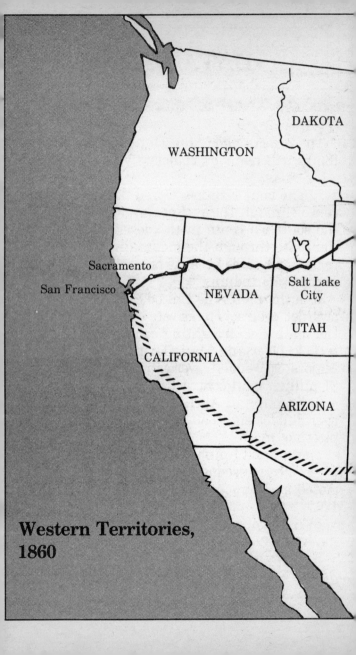

Western Territories, 1860

mochila. These leather saddlebags were fitted with four locked pouches at each corner, and were placed over the specially made lightweight saddles used on Pony Express horses.

8) The Civil War lasted from 1861 to 1865. The war began when eleven southern states—Alabama, Arkansas, Florida, Georgia, Louisiana, Mississippi, North Carolina, South Carolina, Tennessee, Texas, and Virginia—seceded from the Union and formed their own nation, which was called the Confederacy. Southern soldiers were often called rebels; Northern soldiers were known as Yankees.

9) Abraham Lincoln was inaugurated as President in March 1861. He promised to complete the construction of the dome on the Capitol Building as a symbol of preserving the Union.

10) Indians inhabited many territories throughout North America in the 1800's. Though peaceful by nature, Indians often fought with the settlers. Wyoming and Nevada were dangerous areas as a result.

11) In the late 1860's the Union Pacific Railroad hired men to battle train robbers that roamed the West. These hired gunmen often joined forces with lawmen to chase outlaws.

12) Great Britain's Royal Navy relied on the Pony Express to communicate with Britain's China Fleet via San Francisco.

13) The telegraph was invented by Samuel Morse in 1840. Morse was also the creator of the Morse code used to send telegraphic messages. In this code, letters and numbers are

represented by a system of dots and dashes (or long and short signals).

14) Plains Indians used *travois* to carry their possessions across the prairie. A travois consisted of two poles, or shafts, which were rigged to a pony. A blanket or animal hide was stretched across the shafts, and tents or other belongings were lashed to the travois.

15) A sutler was a civilian who sold provisions to soldiers stationed in the forts of the West.

16) One of the important stops on the Pony Express route was Fort Laramie. This military outpost in Wyoming provided safety from the sometimes hostile Indians.

17) The last relay station of the Pony Express was in Sacramento. From there, the mail was ferried across the bay to its final destination, San Francisco.

DATA BANK COMPLETED. TURN THE PAGE TO BEGIN YOUR MISSION.

 Don't forget, when you see this symbol, you can check the Data File in the back of the book for a hint.

ou are alone in a desert. The water canteen over your shoulder is empty, and your mouth is dry.

Far in the distance you see a cloud of dust rising toward the hot sky. You break into a run as you hear the musical clink of harness chains and the steady clip-clop of horses. Topping a hill, you see a rutted road. The sound of horses grows louder, and then a stagecoach rounds the bend.

Rolling on large spoked wheels with iron tires, the bright red coach is pulled by six horses and piled high with luggage. On the side of the stagecoach in bold gold letters are the words "Butterfield Overland Mail Company, El Paso, Texas."

You sprint down the slope to the road, raising your hand to flag the driver. He is a shaggy-bearded man whose hat and clothes are covered with fine dust. In the seat beside him is an equally dusty man cradling a double-barreled shotgun in his arms.

The driver sees you and lets out a whoop. He hauls back on the reins to bring the big vehicle

to a halt. The other man quickly raises the shotgun and aims it at you.

"Whoa!" the driver shouts to his horses. "Whoa!"

Dust settles over you as you look up into the faces of the two men and the barrels of the shotgun.

"What would your business be?" the driver asks suspiciously. "Bandits will have to answer to my partner here," he adds with a gesture to the armed man.

"I'm not an outlaw," you say. "I'm looking for the Pony Express."

"The what?" he asks. "What're you talking about?"

A passenger in the coach lifts the canvas side curtain and leans out the window. "What's the trouble, driver?"

"No trouble, sir," the driver answers quickly.

The passenger is a man wearing gold-rimmed spectacles. He looks at you and then calls up to the driver. "We're late enough as it is. All of us back here are hot and dusty. Give the youngster a lift to the next way station, and get this coach rolling."

"Yes, sir!" the driver answers. He jerks a thumb at you. "Climb on top." He raises his long-handled whip, ready to snap it over the backs of the horses.

The stagecoach is piled high with leather luggage and wooden crates. You thrust the toe of your boot into the spokes of the rear wheel

4

and step up to the top of the iron-tired rim. Just as you reach up and grasp the luggage rack, the driver lets out a shout and pops the whip. The stagecoach takes off with a sudden lurch.

Your feet go out from under you. You're hanging on to the luggage rack with one hand, dangling there as the coach picks up speed. You look down and see the big rear wheel churning dust in the desert road. Lose your grip now and you'll fall in front of that wheel!

Frantically you wave your free arm, swinging yourself up. You grab the metal bar of the luggage rack. You pull yourself up an inch at a time, as if you were doing a chin-up. Then you get a foothold on the sill of a side window. Grabbing one of the straps that secure all the suitcases, trunks, and boxes, you pull yourself all the way up to the top. You lie on top of the luggage, breathing hard.

That was close!

 Turn to page 10.

he outlaws ride away
with their gold, and the train starts up again.
The trainman's courage returns as soon as Big
Nose Phil and his gang leave. He slaps the
handcuffs back on your wrists.

"I'm not the Wyoming Kid—" you start to
explain.

"Quiet!" Pinkham, the trainman, says. "You
were identified by Big Nose Phil. That's good
enough for me, and that will be good enough
for Sheriff Carruthers in Rock Springs." He
takes you into the baggage car and shuts the
doors. This time he stands guard over you. Soon
you feel the train slow and jostle to a halt.
Shouts come from outside as the engineer reports that the train has been robbed.

Oliver throws the sliding door open. You see
a steep-roofed depot and loading platform. You
can tell that the arrival of a passenger train
is an important event in a frontier town.

People crowd around the open doorway of

the baggage car and peer in at the dynamited safe.

Oliver struts back and forth in the doorway, telling how he ran off the outlaws. "Sheriff," he shouts, "over here, Sheriff."

A tall, lanky man makes his way through the crowd. His ten-gallon hat makes him look even taller. On his vest is a brass star, and he wears a Colt revolver strapped to his hip.

"Got a present for you, sheriff," the trainman announces.

"I hear you had some trouble, Oliver," the lawman says, looking into the train car.

"We ran off Big Nose Phil and his gang," Oliver says, "but I captured this one. Recognize this outlaw?"

The sheriff looks at you and shakes his head slowly. "No, I reckon I don't."

Oliver grins. "Meet the Wyoming Kid."

The townspeople gathered behind the sheriff gasp and stare at you, wide-eyed.

"That a fact?" the lawman says.

"Sure is," Oliver says. "Big Nose Phil himself identified this one."

"I thought you ran that gang off," the sheriff says, looking past you to the damaged safe.

"Well, uh, those outlaws did manage to rob the safe," Oliver says. "They got away, but I captured the Kid."

"That's not exactly true," you say.

Oliver gives you a hard look. "Nobody's talking to you!"

"What is true—exactly?" the lawman asks you.

"I was locked inside the baggage car when this trainman found me," you say.

"That's just the way the Wyoming Kid operates," Oliver interrupts, "sneaking into train cars. Right, sheriff?"

He nods but asks you, "Just what were you doing on this train?"

"I'm looking for information about the Pony Express," you say.

Oliver smirks. "Is that the best story you can come up with, Kid? The Pony Express went out of business years ago. We carry the United States mail on the Union Pacific. And we protect it from outlaws like you!"

The sheriff takes you into town and locks you in a cell behind his office. "I hear you've escaped every jail in the territory, Kid," he says, leaning back comfortably. "My jail is the one that'll hold you." He smiles.

You sit on the bunk, suddenly tired and discouraged. You'll never complete your mission now. Maybe the Wyoming Kid would have some ideas about how to get out of here, but you don't. This cage looks escape-proof. You might as well lie down and rest.

That evening, gunshots outside awaken you and the dozing sheriff. In the next instant the door to his office crashes open. A huge man stands there, filling the doorway like a grizzly on its hind legs.

In this light you don't recognize the man who speaks until he stands outside your cell door.

"Big Nose Phil!" you say.

"I'm here to bail you out, Kid," he answers.

You watch in disbelief as Big Nose Phil takes Sheriff Carruthers's gun and then lifts the ring of skeleton keys from his belt.

"Just can't tolerate the notion of the Union Pacific sending a personal friend of mine to prison—especially when you never got a dime out of that train job. You being locked away in here just didn't seem fair. Know what I mean?"

You nod as he opens the cell door. "I didn't like the idea, either," you say.

Big Nose Phil laughs heartily and motions to the lawman. "You can stay in your own hotel tonight, sheriff."

Carruthers does as he is told, but after he is locked in the cell, he says, "You'd better ride hard and far, mister, and keep looking over your shoulder. One of these days you'll find me on your back trail."

"Being chased by a law dog as ugly as you would throw a scare into anybody," Big Nose Phil says with a laugh. "Come on, Kid."

Outside, the street is empty except for the gang of outlaws. Some are mounted on prancing horses. The masked men have their guns drawn, and you can see that they are holding the town of Rock Springs at bay. One of them, dressed all in black, looks your way as he tosses gold coins in the air.

"Want to ride with us, Kid?" Big Nose Phil asks, swinging up into his saddle.

You have to decide in a hurry. Should you stay with the outlaws, or jump in time?

 **Ride with Big Nose Phil.
Turn to page 16.**

 **Jump back in time
to Washington, D.C.
Turn to page 27.**

You sit among the suitcases and steamer trunks strapped down on the roof of the stagecoach behind the driver's seat. This is a Concord stagecoach, suspended on thick leather straps called thoroughbraces. These thoroughbraces connect the coach to the axles like shock absorbers, creating a rocking motion when the coach is underway. As you travel across the desert, you soon understand why Mark Twain called this vehicle "a cradle on wheels."

The driver shifts the reins to one hand and looks over his shoulder at you. "What's this Pony Express you were talking about?"

You wave away the dust stirred by the horses' hooves and lean closer to the driver so he can hear you. "The Pony Express carries the mail on horseback over the mountains to California."

"Impossible!" he says with a harsh laugh. "Youngster, you must have been out in the sun too long. This southern route goes from Missouri all the way across Texas and due west to

California. Freight, passengers, and mail are carried on this road year round, nonstop."

"But how long does it take for a letter to go from Missouri to California?" you ask.

"About a month," the driver replies. "I know what you're thinking—a central route through the mountains is shorter. Well, that may be true. But what about winter storms? What about that rugged country full of Indians? This southern route is the safest and the best. Get those other ideas out of your head!"

You lean back on a trunk as the driver turns his attention back to the horses. You close your eyes and rest, hoping someone at the way station ahead can give you information about the Pony Express. This driver can't help you, that's for sure.

The rocking motion of the stagecoach and the heat of the day soon put you to sleep. The sun is lower in the sky when you are suddenly awakened by a violent lurch and shouts from the driver. You sit up, grasping a strap that holds down the luggage. The stagecoach leans far to the side, almost tipping over before the driver reins in the six horses.

"Busted wheel spokes!" he says in exasperation. "Now we've got a job of work to do!"

You climb down off the top of the coach while the passengers get out and stretch their stiff legs. The driver and his partner raise the front axle with a hand jack and then loosen the wheel nut. You stand with the other passengers and watch as the wheel is pulled off the axle. Several spokes are broken, snapped like matchsticks.

"Butterfield coaches are always late," grumbles one of the passengers.

"No wonder it takes over a month for a letter to get to California," says another. "We may never get there!"

The driver straightens up and faces them. "I was trying to make up lost time for you folks. That's why we were going too fast when the wheel hit a rock. Maybe if you'd been more patient—"

The driver returns to his work, grumbling about people who do nothing but complain. You move away, looking at the barren hills of this desert country. A lizard skitters over dry leaves, and a flock of small birds flies up into the air.

"Pardon me," a voice behind you says, "but I believe I overheard you talking about a new mail route to California."

You turn around and see that the man who has spoken is one of the passengers. He is tall and thin, dressed in a dark suit and narrow-brimmed hat. He wears gold-rimmed spectacles.

"Yes, I was," you reply.

"Allow me to introduce myself," he says,

extending his hand. "My name is Rufus Haynes. I'm a newspaperman. I write for the *Courier* in St. Joseph, Missouri."

You introduce yourself and shake hands. Perhaps this man can give you information about the Pony Express.

"You have some progressive ideas," Rufus says, "just as William H. Russell does. I presume you are familiar with the freighting company of Russell, Majors and Waddell?"

"Not exactly," you say.

"Come now," the newspaperman says with a smile. "No need to beat around the bush with me. I'm acquainted with Mr. Russell myself." He adds in a lower voice, "It's no secret to me that Russell has a plan for taking the government mail contract away from Butterfield. In fact, he's on his way to Washington, D.C. right now to convince the United States Congress that he can open a new route across the West."

Rufus pauses. "But I have a feeling you know all about that, don't you?"

Before you can answer, the stagecoach driver asks for help from the passengers to lift the wheel back onto the axle. With new oak spokes in place, the big wheel is rolled to the coach. While the attention of everyone is on this job, you could easily slip away unnoticed. But should you?

You might learn something important by

going to the next way station. Or you could jump to El Paso, Texas, and try to find out more about the Butterfield Overland Mail Company.

Jump to the Butterfield office in El Paso, Texas. Turn to page 32.

Stay here and ride this stagecoach to the next way station. Turn to page 19.

You wonder what crimes the Wyoming Kid has committed. In any case, the outlaws treat you with great respect, sharing food and water as you ride across the vast prairie. After two days of hard riding, you see a change in the terrain. The land dips into a valley that is lush with green grass. A river winds through the valley, blue as the sky. Big Nose Phil takes off his hat and gives a shout.

"There's the Sweetwater River!" he says. "Time to pull off our boots and go fishing."

You and the outlaws follow his lead and gallop down into the valley to water's edge. The sight and smell of running water and knee-high grass makes this a paradise in the prairie.

"We'll hide out here," Big Nose Phil says to you, "until the Union Pacific posse get tired of sitting in the saddle all day and sleeping on hard ground all night. They'll give up. Then we can ride out of here."

That evening, while Big Nose Phil and the outlaws feast on fresh-caught trout, you ask about the Pony Express. The outlaw leader nods.

"Sure," he says, "I remember that outfit. Used to gallop through this Sweetwater country on the old Oregon Trail."

You're in the right area to find the Pony Express, but the wrong time period!

"Why did the Pony Express stop delivering the mail?" you ask.

Big Nose Phil pauses as he thinks about that. "The mail's been carried on the train for the past year now," he says finally.

"But the Pony Express went out of business years before the transcontinental railroad!" you say.

Big Nose Phil shakes his head. "You've got me there, Kid. I never was much for writing letters. My folks figured the less they heard out of me, the better. So I don't know how the mail got through the West after the Pony Express riders stopped carrying it."

The sunset turns the sky red as blood, and then a sudden explosion of gunfire threatens to shed blood on the land. A posse must have crawled through the high grass and sneaked up on the outlaws.

"This is the sheriff. We've got you outnumbered, Big Nose! Give up!"

"We'll never give up, law dogs," Big Nose Phil shouts, lying flat on the ground.

"The river's at your back," the sheriff says. "You've got nowhere to run. Not even the Wyoming Kid can help you out of this fix!"

Big Nose Phil draws his revolver. "Well then,

come and get us!" He fires several shots and then hugs the earth as the posse's bullets whine overhead.

While the outlaws are firing at the posse, you slide back toward the river and slip into the current. The swift river carries you away from the battle raging between the outlaw gang and the posse.

You were lucky to get away from the outlaws alive, but you didn't find out anything about the Pony Express. You need to find someone better informed than Big Nose Phil.

Jump back in time to Washington, D.C. Turn to page 27.

ou ride the stage-coach to the next way station. Unfortunately, you don't get a chance to talk to Rufus Haynes. At the way station a private coach is waiting for him, and he has barely enough time to wave good-bye.

This desert way station is a simple structure with a dirt roof and one small window beside the plank door. Nearby is a weathered horse barn with a corral and water trough.

A long-handled pump marks the well by the corral. The water is drawn from deep underground, and the only green patches of grass in sight are growing at the base of the pump and around the bottom of the trough. As far as you can see in all directions the land is barren, dotted with prickly cactus plants.

The door of the way station opens. You and the other passengers are greeted by a merry woman with rosy cheeks and sparkling eyes.

"Howdy, folks!" she calls out with a smile. "Name's Cora Hawkins, and I'm here to welcome you to Hawkins City." She laughs, even though she must have repeated this joke to every load of passengers that's stopped here.

You follow the others into the station house. The room is dim, lighted by an oil lamp on a long table set with plates and cups and utensils. The passengers sit on benches on either side of this table.

The meal Cora serves is simple, but filling—beef stew, beans laced with molasses, and fresh bread with butter and honey. For dessert she has made pies from dried apples.

From overheard conversation you learn that Cora and her husband are the operators of this remote way station. The stagecoach driver looks concerned about her. "You look a mite tired, Cora," he says gently.

She nods but manages a bright smile for the passengers at her table. "Reckon I am. Sam got himself kicked by a mean horse a week ago. Caring for him and doing all the chores around here is almost too much for me. I'd hire a hand, but out here in the middle of nowhere folks are always passing through. Nobody wants to stay."

In the shadows behind her you see a man on crutches. Sam Hawkins is a balding man who wears loose trousers held up by red suspenders. His right side bulges with a cloth bandage.

"I'm all right," he protests. "Come on, let's get a fresh team harnessed so you can get your passengers on to El Paso. If you're late again, Butterfield just might lose the mail contract to Russell." He moves through the room on his crutches and is followed out the door by the driver and his partner.

You leave the table and carry your dishes to

the "wreck pan"—a tin basin filled with soapy water—on the rough kitchen counter where Cora is starting to wash pots and pans.

"Was that William H. Russell your husband mentioned?" you ask her.

She turns to you. "Why, yes," she replies. "You know him?"

"No," you say, "but I've heard of him."

"Most folks have, I reckon," she says. "His freighting company is in direct competition with the Butterfield Company for the mail contract. The only route across the West is this southern route through the desert, all the way from St. Joseph to El Paso and on to San Francisco."

"Ready to roll!" shouts the stagecoach driver. The passengers thank Cora for the meal and her good cheer and file outside. You stay behind. Presently the driver pokes his head into the doorway.

"Buying a ticket to El Paso?" he asks you.

You shake your head. You got an idea when you were talking to Cora. This place might look forbidding to everyone else, but it will be a good place to learn more about Russell and that mail contract that's so important.

"If Cora will hire me," you say, "I'll stay here and work awhile."

"Well, of course I'll hire you," she says. "Welcome!"

"Looks like you've come to the right place at the right time," the driver says with a parting wave.

"I hope so," you call after him, knowing that as a time traveler you can't explain exactly what you mean.

You start to work right away as Cora sends you out to the corral where Sam is laboriously pumping water into the wooden trough. Water gushes out of the spout and flows into a plank gutter that angles down to the trough and the waiting horses. Those are the six horses that have just been unharnessed from the stage-coach.

"While they're taking water," Sam says, "go into the corral and wipe them down. Then we'll lead them into the barn and get them out of this blamed sun."

You climb through the pole corral, but as you approach the horses one suddenly rears, pawing the air. You dash back, out of the way of those shod hooves.

"Blamed jughead horse!" Sam shouts. "That's just about the way I got kicked. Good thing you can move fast. No telling when one of these critters is going to spook like that. Try him again, and see if you can make friends with him. Be careful now."

You move slowly toward the horses. The one that reared is gray with splotches of white on his back. He watches you but does not rear up as you come close.

"Talk to him in a low voice," Sam advises. You'll calm that jughead. Careful now."

You hold your hand out to the horse and then reach out and stroke his neck. The horse tosses his head once but then dips his nose to the water trough.

"You've done it," Sam says. "Now we can get on with our work."

Work is right. With all the chores around here, you work from dawn to dark. You learn to care for the horses. You feed and water them and dress harness sores so they'll be ready for the next stagecoach. But more importantly, you talk to Cora and Sam about William H. Russell.

"There's talk of a new overland mail route through the mountains," Cora says one evening after supper.

"Rumors," Sam says sourly.

"Sure, but Russell's a man with new ideas," Cora says. "I know he's trying to run Butterfield out of business, but I admire him, sort of. Newspapers are always writing about him."

"If we're out of a job," Sam says, "will you still admire him?"

Cora laughs at his joshing.

"Where will this new route be?" you ask.

"That's what a lot of folks are wondering," she says. "My guess is that it will follow the Oregon Trail across Wyoming, and then strike out through the Great Salt Lake all the way across the Sierra Nevada to California."

"That's rugged country," Sam says, "and full of wild Indians."

"From what I read in the newspapers," Cora says, "Russell has experience freighting in that part of the country. He just might be the man to pull the whole thing together."

"Then we'll have to find another way to make a living," Sam says. "The government mail contract is our lifeblood. There isn't enough money in passenger travel alone to keep this route open."

This time Cora does not laugh at her husband's prediction.

In a week Sam is feeling better. He's able to do most of the chores himself. You start watching for the Butterfield stagecoach that will take you back to St. Joseph, Missouri.

"Reckon you'll be moving on soon," Cora says one morning. "Here, I have something for you." She digs into the pocket of her calico dress and pulls out a stagecoach ticket. She hands it to you.

You turn the ticket over and see "Free Pass" printed in large letters.

"That'll take you anywhere a Butterfield coach can go," she says, looking at you warmly.

Two days later the stagecoach bound for St. Joseph pulls in. After the team is changed and the passengers fed, the driver is ready to roll. You are delayed when Cora gives you a big hug, and as the driver's whip cracks over the team, the stagecoach pulls away.

"Hurry!" Cora says, pushing you toward the door of the way station. "You can catch it!"

You run outside and sprint down the desert road after the lumbering coach. You could easily overtake it by running hard, but you decide to travel the fast way. Remembering what Cora said about the Oregon Trail, you could go there. Or you can go to Washington, D.C., and learn more about plans for the government mail contract.

**Jump ahead in time
to the Oregon Trail.
Turn to page 36.**

**Jump to Washington, D.C.
Turn to page 27.**

You shiver as you stand with a group of men bundled in heavy coats against the cold air of winter. Looking up, you see wide granite steps leading to the United States Capitol Building. The dome on top is under construction, but even so you recognize it. You're in Washington, D.C.

"I remember you!" one of the men says to you.

You recognize him, too. He's Rufus Haynes from the *Courier* in St. Joseph, Missouri. The other men in overcoats are newspapermen, too, holding pads of papers and pencils in gloved hands.

Rufus gestures to his pad of paper. You notice that he has written today's date on it: January 27, 1860. "We're here to interview William H. Russell," he tells you.

"Here he comes!" says one of the reporters.

Down the steps bounds a plump, bearded man wearing a round wool cap and heavy black coat with a fur collar. Judging from his patent-leather shoes and many diamond rings, he is clearly a man of wealth.

"Gentlemen," Russell welcomes the newspapermen, "thank you for coming out here on a cold day. This is a momentous occasion. I have just announced to Congress that I will open a new overland mail route that will connect St. Joseph, Missouri, with San Francisco, California. I will deliver the mail between those two great cities in ten days' time."

"Ten days!" one of the reporters exclaims.

"How do you propose to do that?" another asks.

"By what route?" a third reporter asks.

"Year round?" Rufus Haynes asks.

William H. Russell smiles and raises both hands in front of him. "Gentlemen, please. I will give you all the details, one at a time. First, I have printed copies of a map that will show the route I will open." He brings a sheaf of papers out of his coat pocket and hands them around.

The newspapermen fall silent as they study the maps.

"That's right, gentlemen," he says. "I'll have relay riders stationed across the West, one after the other, carrying the mail from St. Joseph to San Francisco. They'll ride the fastest horses money can buy, and they'll carry the mail like the wind!"

Russell is a dynamic speaker, and you feel the

growing sense of excitement as he describes his plan. These reporters are witnesses to a historic event. Russell says the Pony Express will begin on April 3, 1860, when the first riders leave St. Joseph and San Francisco. One will gallop west, the other east.

"After I prove that the mail can be carried on this new route," Russell says in conclusion, "the government will have to award the one-million-dollar mail contract to me!"

"Speaking of money," Rufus Haynes asks, "what about your financial backing? It's rumored that you are deeply in debt. This Pony Express will be an expensive enterprise—"

Russell's expression suddenly sours, and he interrupts, "I have been talking to Secretary of War John Floyd. The government owes money to my freighting company for army contracts, and he has promised payment."

"But, Mr. Russell," another reporter says, "if you're in debt now, how will you raise money for the Pony Express?"

"Leave that to me," Russell says curtly. "Good day, gentlemen." He turns and strides away, clearly angry.

As the newspapermen leave to file their stories, Rufus Haynes says to you, "This is a big story for the country, and especially for St. Joseph. I'm on my way to the telegraph office to send this one by wire!"

You watch him rush away. St. Joseph is the place to be, but not at this time.

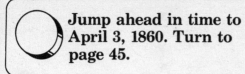

Jump ahead in time to April 3, 1860. Turn to page 45.

You move to the shady side of the street in El Paso, Texas, a frontier town on the border between the United States and Mexico. The sky is clear, and the temperature must be over a hundred degrees. Squat adobe buildings dot the street along with some red-brick structures. Few people are out at this hour. You see a mongrel dog asleep in the shade, and on the next block a man wearing a sombrero crosses the dusty street.

On a brick building ahead you see a large sign:

Butterfield Overland Mail Company
Regional Office
El Paso, Texas

You open the door marked Office and enter. A young clerk seated at a rolltop desk turns to look at you. He seems not much older than you.

"Something I can do for you?" he asks, looking up at you through the green visor perched over his eyes.

"I'm looking for information about the Pony Express," you say.

"The pony what?"

"The Pony Express," you repeat.

"Never heard of it," the clerk replies. "Dozens of express companies are operating around here. Who owns this Pony Express?"

"A man named William H. Russell," you answer.

"Russell!" the clerk says, his voice rising. "*The* William H. Russell?"

As his voice echoes through the office, a door is thrown open, banging against the wall. A man comes charging out like a bull from a chute in a rodeo.

"What's going on out here?" he demands. He wears a vest over his white shirt and black garters on his sleeves. "I'm the regional manager. What's this about Russell?"

The clerk leaps to his feet. "Russell is sending out spies now!" he reports.

"I'm not a spy—" you protest.

Before you can explain, both men advance toward you. Their expressions tell you that you'd better get out of here quickly!

You should have stayed with the coach. Rufus Haynes is the only lead you've got.

You run out of the Butterfield offices into the deserted street. You see a shaded passageway. Time to jump.

Turn to page 19.

You are sitting on a heap of canvas mail sacks inside a train car. This train is speeding across the prairie at twenty-five miles per hour. You look around and see a large floor safe. A waterfall and forest scene is painted on the door of the safe, and on the top is lettered "Union Pacific Railroad."

The wheels click rhythmically over the rails as you stick your head out of a small window. Sagebrush prairie dotted with herds of antelope is all you can see from here. The steam engine at the head of the train is pulling a coal car and a few passenger coaches. Black smoke pours out of the diamond-shaped smokestack, and cinders blow back into your face.

Quickly you turn away, blinking against the flying cinders. When your eyes clear, you look back at the yellow caboose at the end of the train. A trainman is leaning out of the window. He scowls and shakes his fist at you. You duck back into the baggage car.

The door at the far end of the baggage car swings open, and the trainman you saw in the caboose enters, still scowling.

"There's no free rides on this train," he growls. "Thought you could fool Oliver J. Pinkham, did you?"

"I'll buy a ticket!" you tell him.

"Too late for that," he says. "You just broke a federal law by sneaking into this mail car, and I aim to turn you over to the sheriff in Rock Springs, Wyoming. He doesn't like bums any more than I do. Now, turn around and cross your wrists behind you." You feel cold metal snap tight over your wrists as you are handcuffed.

"That ought to hold you, young outlaw," the trainman says with a tight smile.

With a sudden squeal of steel wheels, you and the trainman are knocked off your feet and thrown to the heaps of canvas mail sacks. The train comes to an abrupt halt.

You pick yourself up, wondering what's happened. You see that the trainman is dazed, but when you hear a commotion outside—shouts and gunshots—his eyes grow large and he sits up.

"Robbed!" he whispers. "We're being robbed!"

Outside you hear the stamping of horses' hooves and more shouting. A man with a deep voice is giving orders.

"I want this baggage car door opened right now," he says.

"But I don't have the key to that lock," a frightened voice replies.

"Shoot it!" the man with the deep voice says.

Seconds later a gunshot thunders through the baggage car. Then the door slides open. Six masked outlaws on horseback are out there, standing over a train engineer wearing oil-stained overalls.

"Well, look what we've got here!" The leader of the masked outlaws steps out of his saddle and hops into the baggage car. He stands in front of you, hands on his hips over his gunbelt.

"Please, mister," Oliver J. Pinkham says, cowering, "please don't hurt me."

"I'm not here to hurt anyone," he says, gesturing to the safe. "I'm here to make a withdrawal."

The outlaw looks at your handcuffs, then says to the trainman, "Maybe you'd better tell me what's going on here."

"This sneak thief is under arrest," Pinkham replies in a quavering voice.

"Sneak thief?" the outlaw says, taking a second look at you. He pauses. "If I remember the picture on that Wanted poster I saw in Cheyenne, this isn't any sneak thief."

"Wh . . . what?" the trainman says.

The outlaw pulls his mask down and grins at you, showing missing front teeth and a nose the size and color of a stewed tomato. "You're the Wyoming Kid, aren't you?"

"The Wyoming Kid?" the cowering trainman repeats. "I . . . I didn't know—"

"Well, now you do," the outlaw says, "and instead of sitting there on those mail sacks like

a bunny rabbit, get those wrist irons off the Kid. And after you do that, I want you to open up the safe."

Too scared to move, Pinkham only stares until the outlaw shouts, "Be quick about it!" Then the man leaps up, digging into his pocket for the key to the handcuffs.

When your hands are freed, the outlaw holds out his hand to shake. "Kid, they call me Big Nose Phil. I've heard a lot about you. We're in the same line of work, but what the heck, there's plenty of trains to go around now that the transcontinental rail line is finished. And you can bet there'll be more in the future— railroads all over the West just waiting for you and me like fruit on a tree."

Before you can explain that you aren't a train robber, the outlaw turns and grabs the trainman by the lapels of his uniform.

"I could have sworn I told you to open that safe, Oliver," Big Nose Phil says. "Didn't I politely mention that a minute ago?"

"Ye . . . ye . . . yes, sir," the trainman stammers.

"Well, you might want to get that job done before I quit being polite," he says.

"But . . . but I don't know the combination," says the trainman.

Big Nose Phil sighs. "All of you train jockeys give me the same answer." He lets go of the trainman and turns to the open door of the baggage car. "Jed, you and Mike come in here and blow the door off this safe, will you? Appreciate it."

You leave the car with Big Nose Phil, who gives Pinkham a shove out the door. The two outlaws climb into the baggage car and quickly strap a stick of dynamite on each hinge. They attach a fuse, light it, and jump out of the car.

You and the others back away while the flame sputters toward the explosive charges. Then the prairie silence is shattered by a blast that rocks the baggage car and sends the outlaws' horses rearing. When the smoke clears and the dust settles, you see the safe door ajar. Inside are sacks of gold and silver coins.

"Now there's a job well done!" Big Nose Phil says. "Let's make our withdrawal and ride."

As the outlaws climb into the car and start handing out the heavy sacks of coins, Big Nose Phil turns to you and says, "I know you had your eye on that safe, Kid. Maybe we can make a deal that will keep us both happy."

"I don't want any of that money," you say.

"I understand," Big Nose Phil replies. "And I admire you for it. I got you out of a fix with that trainman, and you figure that makes us even. I like you, Kid. You've got principles."

Big Nose Phil gestures to the horses. "I've got a spare horse, all mounted and ready to ride. Me and the boys would be plumb honored if you'd ride with us, Kid."

This is a tough choice. Should you stay here with the train? That means you'll be arrested in Rock Springs and charged with the crimes committed by the Wyoming Kid. Or you can ride with Big Nose Phil and his gang of outlaws, who will probably be pursued by a posse.

One thing is certain: that trainman will not be interested in answering any questions about the Pony Express after what has happened here. At least Big Nose Phil likes you enough to be willing to talk.

Stay on the train.
Turn to page 5.

Ride with Big Nose Phil.
Turn to page 16.

You are in the midst of a wild celebration on the streets of St. Joseph, Missouri. April 3, 1860 is a day that will live in history. Now friends and relatives can communicate by mail across the West in only ten days. Such speed is unheard of among these people.

"This man is a modern-day hero," the mayor of St. Joseph proudly proclaims as he introduces William H. Russell to the crowd. "He will get your mail from here to San Francisco in ten days, hurled by flesh and blood across two thousand miles of desolate space!"

The crowd parts at the sound of pounding hoofbeats. You watch as a Kentucky thoroughbred gallops past. In seconds horse and rider are gone, leaving behind the cheers of the excited onlookers.

You feel a tap on your shoulder. "Seems our trails cross frequently." It's Rufus Haynes! "This can't be coincidence. I still think you're working for Russell."

"No," you say, "I'm not working for him. I'm

just trying to get some information about the Pony Express."

"Hmmmm," Haynes says with a cocked eyebrow. "What sort of information?"

"When you interviewed Mr. Russell in Washington last January," you say, "he got mad when you asked him about his financial backing for the Pony Express. Does he really have enough money to keep it going?"

"The Pony Express has been a very expensive operation," explains Haynes. "Russell has borrowed money to construct relay stations and hire station masters. He's bought high-priced horses and hired the best riders. Carrying the mail even at the rate of five dollars for a half-ounce letter will never make enough profit to pay all those expenses."

And you thought mailing a letter today was expensive!

"I don't understand," you say. "He *is* trying to make money, isn't he?"

"He's trying to make a fortune," Haynes says.

"But how?" you ask.

"Once he proves the new route to California can be used, he'll start carrying passengers and hauling freight—"

"And put the Butterfield Company out of business!" you exclaim, remembering what Cora told you.

"That's right," Haynes says. "It's a bold plan. The whole thing depends on the success of the Pony Express. Which reminds me, I've got more work to do. See you later." Rufus shakes your hand and disappears into the crowd.

It's time for you to get back on the trail of the Pony Express. There's no substitute for first-hand experience.

Jump forward in time to the prairie.
Turn to page 78.

he wind-swirled snow high in the Sierra Nevada of California blinds your vision, and the cold air numbs your whole body. You are dressed for the prairie, not for winter. If you can't find shelter soon, you'll have to jump away from here before you freeze to death.

You plod through the deep snow, one lunging step at a time. You can see very little. The wind is steady, stinging your eyes like flying icicles.

The white world is briefly changed when you see a yellow spot ahead, like a warm beacon that beckons you. You struggle toward the beacon, losing sight of it as you nearly pass out. Eyes closed, you bump into a log wall.

You grope your way along the wall to the corner. That side of the building is protected from

the wind, and you see a door there. Plunging
toward the door, you open it and stumble inside.
You feel yourself falling, but as in a dream you
do not hit bottom. You fall and fall and fall. . . .

The soft, warm embrace of a bearskin brings
you back to consciousness. Wrapped in the
heavy fur, you are lying on a dirt floor strewn
with straw. By the light of a lantern you see a
potbellied stove. A crackling fire inside sends
off heat that makes your cheeks glow.

You sit up and look around. Light from that
lantern guided you here. You must have seen it
through a window in the side of this building.

From your experience working for Cora
Hawkins, you know immediately that this is a
horse barn. Stalls are on either side of the runway, and the iron stove is in the middle of the
barn, providing life-saving heat for the animals.

"Thought you were frozen solid, I did."

You turn around and see an old man striding
down the runway toward you. He is dressed in
heavy clothes, and his hair and full beard are
as white as the snow outside. He is leading a
saddled horse.

"I'm all right," you say, pushing the bearskin
away from your shoulders. "Thanks to you."

"All I did was yank your boots off," he says,
"and roll you into that bear hide by the stove."
He stops, holding the horse's reins. "At first, I

thought you were Boston Upson, I did."

"Who's he?" you ask.

"Pony Express rider," the old-timer says. "He should have been here three hours ago, but I reckon nobody's getting through today, not even mule trains."

"Mule trains use this trail in the winter?" you ask, surprised.

"That's right," he replies. "Any man who can haul food and supplies this time of year can charge five times the summer price."

"But the Pony Express riders can't make it?" you ask.

The old timer shrugs. "If any man alive can ride this trail in winter, Boston's the man." He casts a worried glance at the big double doors at the front of the barn.

"No," he goes on, "the relay riders haven't been turned back by storms in these mountains. The real trouble is with Sioux Indians in Wyoming. If the Pony Express gets closed down, that'll be the cause."

Outside you hear a muffled shout. The station keeper drops the horse's reins. He rushes to the big double doors of the barn and flings them open. Now's your chance to slip away and jump in time to Wyoming and find out if the Pony Express route will be closed by hostile Indians. Or you can stay here and find out who has arrived at the barn. If this is Boston Upson, he may be able to give you some valuable information.

**Jump to Wyoming.
Turn to page 63.**

Stay here. Turn to page 69.

At Fort Laramie you find Slim Baxter with a herd of horses. Several men are with him, and when Slim spots you, he calls out.

"I need your help!"

"What are you doing?" you ask.

"You haven't heard?" he replies. "We've got orders from Washington to do the impossible, that's what has happened!"

"Then you need more help than I can give you," you say with a laugh.

"Might seem funny to you," the dour-faced man says, "but I don't see no humor in it a-tall."

"What are your orders?" you ask.

"William H. Russell says we'll set a new record for getting the mail through to California," Slim says. "The way he's going to do it is to put a man and a horse along every ten miles of the

Pony Express route from St. Joseph to San Francisco. Can you believe it? Every ten miles!"

"That ought to set a record," you say.

"Why, sure it's easy to talk about from some fancy office in Washington, D.C.," Slim says in disgust, "but just how does a fella go about it? I've scoured the countryside for riders. I've bought a few good horses and a bunch of army plugs that might have ten miles left in them."

"What are we going to be carrying?" you ask as you pick out a pinto and swing up into the saddle.

Slim answers over his shoulder, "The inaugural speech of President Lincoln. Folks out in California are waiting to hear what this new fella has to say."

"Why?" you ask.

Slim pulls out a folded newspaper from his hip pocket and guides his horse beside yours. "Read this," he says, pointing to the front page. "Maybe you can figure out the politics back east better than I can."

You take the wrinkled newspaper and unfold it. A headline in bold type reads:

WAR BETWEEN STATES?

South Carolina, Mississippi, Florida, Georgia, Louisiana, Alabama, and Texas form a new nation to be called the Confederate States of America. California and other states may join. What will President-elect Lincoln do?

A second headline catches your eye:

PONY EXPRESS ATTEMPTS RECORD RUN

William H. Russell promises to deliver Lincoln's inaugural address to California in the record time of one week. The eyes of the country will be watching as this seemingly impossible feat is attempted by the flamboyant Russell.

If the Pony Express gets Lincoln's inaugural message across the country in time, perhaps California won't join the Confederate States.

Slim takes a deep breath. "Well, are you with me, or not? I can't stand out here all day. I have to get back to the Horseshoe station."

With all the excitement here, it would be easy to slip away and jump to Washington to see Abraham Lincoln in person as he gives his inaugural speech. The whole nation is eager to learn what he will say—especially California, as that state considers whether to stay in the Union.

Decide quickly. Slim is waiting for your answer.

 Jump ahead to Washington, D.C. Turn to page 86.

 Ride with Slim. Turn to page 73.

he tent is real! As you
approach, you hear voices. The tent is open on
all four sides, and now you see a group of men
sitting on folding chairs around a camp table
covered with a white linen cloth. The table is
set with silverware, a gleaming silver teapot
with matching sugar bowl and creamer, and
porcelain cups and saucers.

"I say, who goes there?" one of the men asks.
He has a British accent. The other four turn
their gaze toward you, too.

You wave hello and introduce yourself as you
enter the camp. This is very strange. Out here
in the middle of this flat prairie, five proper
Englishmen are drinking hot tea and eating
muffins with marmalade. Each man wears
starched white clothes and polished black boots.
All are freshly shaven, with short, neat hair-
cuts—nothing like the pioneers and frontiers-
men you have seen in the West.

You step into the shade of the tent. In a gun
rack on the other side you see half a dozen high-
powered rifles. Beyond the tent several buffalo
heads lie on the ground. Trails of blood lead

back to the headless bodies. The buffalo are too heavy to move; the hunters take only the heads as trophies.

Now you understand. This is a hunting party. These Englishmen have come to the American West on a "safari" and have collected their trophies from that large herd.

"Quite a run, wouldn't you say?" one of the men asks as he unfolds a chair for you and pours you a cup of tea.

"Run?" you ask, sitting at the table.

"Stampede, I believe you Americans call it," another says, offering you a biscuit from a tin with a hinged lid. "We shot several of the biggest bulls, and the herd began to run. Quite a sight, indeed."

You nod agreement, sipping tea. Quite a sight—especially those hooves flying overhead, inches from your face.

"We've seen hundreds of thousands of the brutes out here on this wasteland," one of the mustached Englishmen says. "I daresay there isn't enough ammunition in the whole country to shoot them all."

The others laugh in agreement, but you know better. In the next ten years, over four million buffalo will be killed and their bones shipped east for fertilizer. In just one decade the great herds will be gone, and the Plains tribes of native Americans will be starving.

"You're not lost, are you?"

You look at the Englishman who spoke and

see an expression of concern on his face. You realize that your being alone out here is as strange a sight to these men as they are to you.

"No," you say, even though you are not exactly certain where you are. "I'm looking for the Pony Express."

"I say!" he exclaims. "The Pony Express!"

"You've heard of it?" you ask.

"Indeed we have," he replies. "The Pony Express is vital to the war effort."

You are surprised to learn this.

"We are at war with China," he explains, "and our government in London uses your relay riders to send messages to San Francisco Bay and on by ship to our China Fleet."

"Speed is of the essence," another man comments, and the others agree.

You knew that the Pony Express has been reported in many parts of the world, but you didn't realize that it was actually used by a foreign government. Just think! Secret orders for a whole fleet were carried in a locked pocket of a mochila carried by Pony Express riders!

A moment later the Englishmen forget their quiet reserve when they sight a lone rider on the prairie. They jump up from their chairs and rush from the tent to watch the galloping rider pass by from east to west.

"Look at that chap ride!" one shouts.

"On Her Majesty's service!" says another with a wave of his hand.

After the Pony Express rider has disappeared

from sight, you say good-bye to these men. You have found the Pony Express and discovered another obstacle—stampeding buffalo. But would that be enough to stop Russell's entire enterprise?

You should check other parts of the Pony Express routes to see what obstacles are there.

 Jump to Fort Laramie, Wyoming. Turn to page 63.

 Jump to the Sierra Nevada in California. Turn to page 49.

n Fort Laramie, Wyoming, you are standing in the shade of the enlisted men's barracks when you see soldiers gathering on the parade ground by a tall flagpole. A door to this building opens and a private steps out. As he heads for the parade ground, you catch up with him.

"What's going on?" you ask.

"Pony Express rider's coming in," he replies. "At least, he's due."

"You think he won't make it?" you ask.

The soldier glances at you without breaking stride. "New out here, aren't you? This is spring. The Sioux are out in force this time of year. No telling what kind of mood they're in."

You look around as you walk beside the private. Fort Laramie, alone on the grassy plains of Wyoming, is impressive. Around a rectangular parade ground the size of a football field are rows of buildings and tents—a large bakery, sutler's store, officers' quarters, barracks for infantry and cavalry, and administration buildings. Beyond the buildings the Laramie River lazily winds past this prairie fortress.

This is a part of the Oregon Trail, and over the years many fur traders and pioneers have passed this way. At first this was only a small outpost and meeting ground for trappers, but now it's an important fort for the army.

Drumming hoofbeats turn the heads of the gathering soldiers and a few civilians. Over a grass-covered rise to the east comes a lone horseman, traveling at full gallop toward the fort.

"That's Hank Avis!" a corporal shouts. "He made it from the Torrington station!"

The pounding hoofbeats grow louder as the rider draws near. You see that the brim of his hat is blown back by the wind, and on his belt he wears two revolvers. When he reaches the edge of the parade ground, he reins the horse to a halt, and in one smooth motion he steps out of the saddle. One of the civilians brings a fresh horse, and the rider quickly transfers the mochila. He thrusts a boot into the stirrup and swings up, settling easily into the saddle.

"Not so fast."

Everyone turns to see that the man who has spoken is a colonel in neat full-dress uniform. Beside him is a man dressed from head to toe in wrinkled buckskin.

"Before you ride out of here," the colonel says, "you'd better listen to what I just heard from this scout."

"No time for a long story," Hank says, pulling back on the reins of the prancing horse. "I've got a schedule to keep!"

"You've got time to hear this, mister," the army officer says. "Sioux hunting parties are out there. By now they've probably closed the Oregon Trail."

"I'll find out for myself, Colonel," Hank says.

"You shouldn't go out there alone," the colonel says.

Hank laughs. "Anyone who can keep up with me, come on!"

No one volunteers, and you see your chance. "I'll ride with you," you say.

Hank looks at you in surprise. "I had in mind an experienced rider."

"I've worked with horses at a stagecoach relay station in Texas," you say.

The colonel chuckles sarcastically. "Sounds like we've got an experienced rider here, Hank."

Hank looks at you approvingly, though. "Maybe this rider is right for the job. All that's needed is a horse that can keep pace with mine."

The colonel pauses at this challenge. "Mine's ready to ride. I was getting ready to inspect the cavalry when you rode in, and my horse could use a good run."

A moment later Hank Avis rides out. You follow, galloping to keep up. The colonel's horse is very fast! You soon catch up with Hank, and the two of you gallop side by side for a distance. Then Hank reins in his mount to a high lope, and you do the same.

"We'd better save their strength," he says, rubbing his horse's neck, "in case we need it later." You and Hank head for the Horseshoe relay station, less than ten miles away now.

The land flattens out into a treeless plain. On the trail ahead you see a dozen Sioux hunters on horseback. They carry bows and arrows as well as a few old rifles. When they see you, they halt and wait.

Hank glances at you. "Act friendly," he says, "and hope they are."

You ride side by side to the hunting party. Hank raises his hand in a gesture of peace. But the Indians aim their rifles at you! Several draw back their bowstrings, pointing flint-tipped arrows at your chest.

This is scary. None of the Indians shows any emotion. They only stare as you come closer to them.

"Howdy!" Hank calls out as though he's greeting old friends. "How's the hunting this season?"

When the leader of the hunting party only stares at you over his rifle barrel, Hank goes on, "Nice day for a ride, isn't it? We ought to get together for a picnic. What are you fellows doing next week? We can roast a couple of turkeys, squeeze out some lemonade, and have a mighty good time."

Hank's smile and the friendly tone of his voice makes the leader lower his rifle. He utters a command to the others, and they follow his example. Then the leader raises his hand.

"Whew!" Hank whispers to you.

You pass within a few yards of the Indians and ride on. A glance over your shoulder shows that the Sioux are staring at you curiously.

"Did they understand what you were saying?" you ask.

"Nope," Hank replies with a laugh. "I just kept talking until they knew I wasn't out to do them any harm." You'll have to remember that trick!

"Wait until the colonel hears about our encounter." Hank says, laughing again. "Come on. Let's make up for lost time! Meet you at the Horseshoe station." Hank touches his heels to the horse and takes off in a gallop.

In a few minutes, Hank is out of sight around a bend. Should you ride on with him, or jump in time?

You remember that Russell had a lot of trouble financing the Pony Express. Perhaps you should go to Washington, D.C., to see if Russell ran out of money after all.

 Ride on to the Horseshoe station. Turn to page 82.

 Jump to Washington, D.C., in 1861. Turn to page 86.

Pony Express rider guides his tired horse into the barn.

"Boston!" The station keeper closes the big doors after him.

Crusted snow falls to the dirt floor when Boston Upson stiffly dismounts. His face is covered like a mummy's, and you watch as he unwinds a heavy scarf that conceals his face and neck. The man who appears is grinning.

"A bit stormy out there today," he says. "Or is it night?"

"No way to tell in this blizzard," the old station keeper replies. "Boston, you'd best hole up here until this storm breaks. A few more hours' delay won't hurt."

Boston gestures to the fresh saddle horse. "Now, you know I'm not going to take that advice. I'm paid to get this mail through, and that's what I'll do."

"Figured you'd say that," the old-timer says. He turns and moves to the stove, where he lifts a battered coffee pot and pours steaming black brew into a tin cup. "Stay long enough to drink this, anyhow."

"According to regulations," Boston says with a grin, "I can only stay two minutes at each relay station."

"Stay ten minutes," he says, "and get warmed up. I won't report you to Mr. Russell."

Boston laughs and pulls off his heavy mittens as he comes to the stove. He grasps the steaming tin cup in both hands and raises it to his mouth.

After Boston takes a long swallow, you introduce yourself. He shakes your hand in a strong grip.

"How will you make it through the snow drifts to the next station?" you ask.

"A mule train is headed this way," Boston replies. "Nothing like a line of big, strong mules to bust open a snowbound trail. Soon as I meet up with them, I'll have an easy ride."

"Easy!" the old-timer repeats, shaking his head.

Boston Upson laughs. You can tell that he's courageous—he takes chances, yet he is not reckless. You ask him how you can become a rider for the Pony Express.

"Just about everybody in the state of California who can ride wants this job," he replies, taking a last swallow of hot coffee. He walks to his horse and pulls off the mochila. He throws it over the saddle of the fresh horse and then puts on his scarf and mittens. Before he covers his mouth, he adds:

"I hear riders are needed out in Wyoming, but that's Indian country."

Boston covers his face and swings up to the saddle. The old station keeper hurries to the double doors, and at a wave from Boston, he throws them open. You watch as the rider gallops into the swirling snow, and a moment later the doors are pulled shut.

You get permission from the old-timer to spend the night in the barn. When he takes his lantern by the handle and returns to his cabin, you're alone. No one sees you jump in time.

Jump to Wyoming
Turn to page 63.

'll ride with you," you say to Slim.

He manages a slight smile. "Well, that's the first piece of good news I've had today. Grab ahold of one of these horses, and come on!"

Slim signals the others with a wave of his arm. "Let's get these horses out on the trail. We don't have a minute to spare!"

You and the other riders follow Slim as he rides out to the trail used by the Pony Express. Slim leaves you on the high plains and rides off. You'll wait here for the relay rider from the east who will bring the mochila with Lincoln's inaugural address.

Alone here, you look around. The blue, cloudless sky stretches endlessly over the high plains of Wyoming. That sky seems to cast a deep silence on the land.

You think about how exciting the Pony Express is to the people of this time. Before the Pony Express, letters from friends and relatives took a month or more to reach their destinations. Sending a letter in only a week is as exciting to these people as space travel is to you.

You turn to face the east, your attention drawn by the drumming hoofbeats of a running horse. On the far horizon you see a man on horseback, riding hard.

Your horse is grazing in the high grass. You catch his reins and check the saddle cinch once more. The mustang tosses his head and whinnies at the approaching rider.

You give your hat a tug and get ready to transfer the mochila to your horse. Hoofbeats are growing louder. One hundred yards away now, the lone horseman is coming fast.

He is young, his blue eyes bright with excitement. A dozen paces away, he reins his galloping horse to a halt and leaps to the ground. Snatching the mochila off his saddle, he quickly hands it to you with an eager shout: "Ride!"

You toss the mochila over your saddle. Your mustang prances with excitement. You grab the saddle horn on the run and throw a leg over the saddle. In the stirrups, you give the mustang the signal he wants—a tap with your boot heels—and he races away at full speed.

The galloping mustang follows this trail across the high plains. You bend low over his neck, feeling his muscular strength with every step. Warm air brushes your face as you watch the trail ahead.

The tracks you see here mark the old Oregon Trail—a trail of history in America. Trappers, prospectors, and settlers have passed through here, and more will come. You are racing into history, carrying in a locked pouch the inaugural address of President Abraham Lincoln.

No horse can run at full speed for ten miles, but every spirited horse will try it. You rise up in the saddle and slow this mustang down to a high lope. You'll save his strength and cover as much ground as you can at this speed, then let him run the last mile.

This is near the spot where you and Hank Avis encountered the band of Indians. In these hills you see no sign of them today. They may have moved on, maybe to get farther away from the white settlers who have invaded their hunting grounds.

You make good time through the hills, coming out on the plains again. The Horseshoe station is not far ahead. As if sensing that, the mustang breaks into a gallop, his hooves pounding the earth. You let him run.

Slim Baxter is waiting by the barn with a relay rider and a horse. They are ready to go, and when you rein up and leap out of the saddle, Slim grabs the mochila. He throws it over the saddle of the fresh horse, gives a shout of encouragement as the new rider mounts, and rides off, heading westward toward California.

"We're going to set a record," Slim says excitedly. "We sure are!" He jumps up and down, waving his arms.

You have to laugh. This is the first time you have seen him smile, and this may be the first time he has ever been excited about anything in his life.

You shake hands with Slim and say good-bye. He looks at you and blinks rapidly.

"I'm going to miss you," he says.

"I'll miss you, too," you say.

"Where are you headed from here?" he asks.

"I want to see another section of the Oregon Trail," you reply. You like Slim, but you can't stay here. The only way to succeed in accomplishing your mission is to keep searching. You may find what you're looking for on another part of the trail.

"Well, so long," he says, and waves as you walk away.

As soon as you're out of sight, you can jump to the Oregon Trail.

 Turn to page 93.

On prairie land flat as an ironing board and nearly as hot as an iron, you see a huge cloud swelling up on the far horizon. From here the horizon is a straight line between land and sky. The only sound you hear is deep and distant thunder.

At least you think it's thunder. But as the rumbling sound grows louder, the earth under your feet starts to shake. An earthquake? No, but as you look at the swelling cloud again you see that it isn't a storm cloud. That's dust rising into the sky. The dust is stirred by a moving brown mass. That mass is heading toward you!

Shaggy, horned heads are bearing down on you, coming at you with surprising speed. The brown mass is a herd of buffalo—hundreds of them! They're in full stampede!

You angle to your right, running hard through the grass and sage, hoping you can reach safety at the edge of the great herd. But the shaggy-headed giants are rapidly gaining on you, their short, curved horns glistening in the sunlight.

You jump over a small ridge and fall into a gully. You roll against the bank, looking up in time to see one buffalo after another leaping over you. Hundreds of them jump this gully, their hooves flying inches above your head.

Then they are gone, and the land is still again.

You stand up, shaking. The land looks different. As far as you can see, the soil is churned up. Everything is trampled—every blade of bluestem grass, every sunflower, every clump of sage is flattened to the ground.

You climb out of the gully and walk toward the horizon, where the stampeding buffalo came from. Presently you see another strange sight on this flat prairie: a white canvas tent with a group of people sitting inside. Is this a mirage? You haven't had a drink of water in several hours, and almost getting crushed by a herd of buffalo hasn't improved your state of mind. Maybe you should jump out of this prairie and look elsewhere for the Pony Express. The map you got from Russell shows that the Pony Express traveled through the Sierra Nevada in California. It would certainly be cooler there!

 Stay here and investigate the tent. Turn to page 57.

 Jump to the Sierra Nevada. Turn to page 49.

n a few minutes you and Hank Avis reach the Horseshoe station. You decide to stay at the station while Hank rides to the next relay station on the Pony Express route.

You wait with the station keeper, Slim Baxter, for the eastbound Pony Express rider, who is long overdue. Slim is a worrier. He leans against the barn door, offering reasons why the rider hasn't come.

"Throwed from his horse and bit by a rattler," Slim says sadly. "That's what must have happened to him."

A while later, a single gray cloud floats by. "Struck by lightning, poor devil," Slim says. "Painful way for a man to die."

When the cloud drifts on, Slim says, "Indians got him. Yes, sir, Indians run him down and lifted his hair. Must have left him staked to an anthill, yes sir."

You hear hoofbeats in the distance—not the pounding of a fast horse at full gallop but the clip-clop of a walking horse. You leave the shade of the barn with Slim and see the lone rider

coming. The Pony Express rider is bent over the saddle, barely hanging on.

You and Slim run out to meet him. Slim thinks he sees an arrow sticking out of the man's back, but when you reach him, you see that he is unhurt.

"Sick," the rider mumbles. "Never . . . never been . . . so sick . . . in my blamed life."

"What's the matter?" Slim demands, helping the rider down from the saddle.

The Pony Express rider is young, with curly black hair and a face as pale as a bedsheet. "Ate some tainted food, I guess." He draws a deep breath. "I'm as weak as a cat."

Slim's face was lined with worry before the rider came; now he looks stricken. "You're in no shape to ride, that's for sure. How are we going to get that mochila to Fort Laramie?"

"I'll take it," you say.

"You're not an authorized rider for the Pony Express, are you?" Slim asks.

"No," you say. "But I know the trail, and I've got a fast horse."

Slim pauses, then nods once. "Well, that's the way it's going to have to be. I'll meet you there as soon as I can. Now get that black horse out of the barn, and ride!"

Mounted on the colonel's horse, you make a fast ride across the prairie back to Fort Laramie. In the hill country you follow the example set by Hank Avis and scout valleys from hilltops. You see no Sioux hunting parties, and before nightfall you ride into the parade ground of Fort Laramie.

A Pony Express rider is waiting there, and in a fast exchange he takes the mochila and rides east.

The colonel congratulates you on the ride you made, and you thank him for the use of his horse. He runs his hand over the animal's shoulder.

"I'll be taking this one back east," he says, "when I'm transferred."

"You're leaving Fort Laramie?" you ask.

He nods. "And a lot of these soldiers are going with me. There's talk of war."

War? Of course—he's talking about the Civil War. You hadn't thought of it before, but the war must have had an effect on the Pony Express. For one thing, there wouldn't be as many soldiers in the West to protect the riders.

Could this be the reason behind the failure of the Pony Express? You should go back east yourself to find out!

 Jump to Washington, D.C. Turn to page 86.

ou are in Washington, D.C., in March 1861. You make your way to the front of the crowd gathered along Pennsylvania Avenue near the Capitol. A military parade passes by, and then you see a low-slung carriage draw up.

Seated in the glistening black carriage are two men wearing dark wool overcoats and silk top hats. They climb out, bowing to scattered applause among the onlookers. One man is tall and angular with a dark beard. The other man leads the way. He is white-haired and looks tired.

You recognize Abraham Lincoln, but not the other man. You turn to a bystander wearing a top hat and overcoat.

"Who's that?" you ask.

"Why, that's President James Buchanan of course," he replies. "Or I should say, former president. Abraham Lincoln is assuming office today."

"There go the exhausted energies of the old," another bystander says, watching the historic scene, "followed by the vigorous strength of the

new. If anyone can keep us from civil war, Honest Abe Lincoln's the man." You nod in agreement, even though you know it won't work out that way.

You watch as Lincoln is sworn in as the new president of the United States. Surrounded by solemn dignitaries, he delivers his inaugural speech in a strong voice. You listen closely as he finishes his speech:

"I have the most solemn oath to preserve, protect, and defend the Union. We are not enemies, but friends."

You realize these words are aimed at the states who have left the Union and others who might be considering the idea of joining the Confederacy in the South.

"Well, that settles it," the bystander next to you says. "If the Confederates want a fight, they'll get it."

Other people nearby loudly agree. "If blood is to be shed, let's get on with it—now!"

The crowds move away, and you spot William H. Russell. You move closer and hear him speaking intently to a group of senators. "A horse and rider every ten miles of the Pony Express route. Within the hour the first relay rider will gallop westward, and the words we just heard will be in San Francisco within a week. Think of it, gentlemen—a week's time!" He adds, "Then no one in the House or the Senate will be able to deny my claim to that mail contract."

"You make a strong case," one of the senators says, "but we cannot overlook your declaration of bankruptcy. The firm of Russell, Majors & Waddell is broke!"

"But I still have the Pony Express," Russell insists, "and I intend to use it to show that my route through the mountains is the best in the land. One day all westbound freight will be using my trail."

"Perhaps," another senator says, "but time will tell. Time will tell."

You've learned one thing here. Russell is broke. All of his hopes now are tied to the success of the Pony Express.

You wonder what's happening in the West. The riders are brave men on fast horses, but how are they surviving against bad weather and hostile Indians?

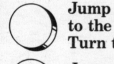
Jump ahead in time to the Oregon Trail. Turn to page 93.

Jump to Fort Laramie to ride with Slim. Turn to page 73.

A group of people is standing on the plank boardwalk in the frontier town of Salt Lake City, in Utah Territory. The date is October 24, 1861.

You move closer and see that workmen have dug a hole on the edge of the hard-packed dirt street. They lift a telegraph pole and set it down into the hole.

Another man climbs the pole and connects two wires at this pole. One wire comes from a line of poles that stretches out to the west. The other wire comes from the east.

A cheer rises from the onlookers, and they applaud as the crewman waves and comes down from the pole.

"Now this country can send telegrams from coast to coast!" he says, jumping to the ground.

A second man pulls a large pocket watch from his vest pocket. "The first telegram should be going over the wire from San Francisco to Washington, D.C., right at this moment."

The contents of that first message have been made public, and this man reads it aloud. The message is from California Chief Justice Stephen Field to President Lincoln. The chief justice congratulates the President on this achievement and pledges his state's loyalty to the Union.

The gathered onlookers applaud again. You move away from the crowd. This is an important event in the history of the country, but it's not as exciting as the Pony Express. The relay riders did more than carry mail across the western frontier. They opened a new route, one that the telegraph line now follows.

You remember the excitement felt across the country when the first Pony Express riders left St. Joseph and San Francisco. No one knew if they would reach their destinations, and people waited eagerly for news.

Now, with the telegraph line stretching across the open spaces of the West, messages can be sent and received in a matter of minutes. You wonder what effect this single strand of electrical wire will have on the Pony Express.

The best way to find out will be to jump ahead a few years and find out what has happened to a Pony Express relay station.

 Turn to page 116.

he air is cool with gray clouds overhead, and the vast field of grass where you stand is dried to the color of buckskin. This is the autumn season on the Great Plains. Soon cold wind and snow from the north will hold this land in winter's icy grip.

A pair of deep ruts left by the iron wheels of heavy wagons tells you this is the Oregon Trail. You turn around, your attention drawn by the smell of smoke. There's a grass fire in back of you!

A lone deer, brown eyes wide with fear, leaps out of the wall of smoke and bounds past you. You'll have to run, too.

You turn and sprint away from the racing prairie fire. Heat from the flames hits your shoulders and back. Acrid smoke fills your nostrils.

Then, as the breeze shifts, you're suddenly surrounded by billowing clouds of smoke. Flames crackle at your feet, and now your clothes are so hot that they burn your skin.

You dash one way, then another. You find a patch of dried grass, but the fire quickly eats away at it. You're trapped. Your face feels as if it's on fire. Tears roll from your eyes, and the bitter smoke engulfs you.

You're about to jump away from here when you hear a man's voice. The voice comes from far away, but you answer with a shout. The reply is louder. "Over here!"

You turn in that direction. Through the smoky haze you see a strange sight. In the middle of this prairie, a man is sitting on top of a tall pole.

You burst through the smoke and jump over the racing flames. Heat comes through your clothes, and for a moment you think you won't make it through the wall of fire.

"Over here!"

You look in the direction of the shout. Your eyes have not deceived you. A man *is* sitting on a pole, and he waves at you.

"You all right?"

You wave back and run toward him.

"That was a close one!" he exclaims, climbing down from the pole to greet you. Holding out his hand, he says, "I wouldn't have seen you if I hadn't been stringing wire."

"Stringing wire?" you ask. You look up at the pole and see a glass insulator and loop of wire. The line runs to another pole thirty yards away, and another beyond that one. A wagon loaded with poles is there. You see two other men with the wagon, both armed with rifles.

"We're putting up a telegraph line," the man

says. "Sioux Indians started that grass fire. They don't like the idea of a wire and poles going through their hunting grounds. We're lucky the breeze changed directions when it did. So are you!"

Arrows whiz overhead, and gunfire comes from behind the wagon. The two men there duck down and start shooting.

"Come on!" the telegraph crewman says. "Run for it!"

The gunfire is deafening, mixed with shouts and war whoops, and soon the air is filled with smoke again. The crewman becomes a ghostly figure sprinting for the wagon. You realize the Indians moved upwind and started another fire.

You lose sight of the crewman. Moments later you hear the sounds of a team of horses whipped to a run. The sound fades away, and the shooting stops.

The danger now is not so much from this smaller fire, but from being discovered by the warriors. That war whoop was terrifying, and you'll never forget the sight of arrows zipping through the air.

You run blindly, trying to put as much distance between you and the Indians as possible. The ground drops away from under you, and you run into a small valley with a creek meandering through the bottom. With the billowing smoke behind you, you stop and take a deep breath of fresh air. You wonder if you should stay here to find out more about the Oregon Trail, or jump in time to learn the effect of the telegraph on future communications.

 Stay here. Turn to page 111.

 Jump ahead in time to learn more about the telegraph. Turn to page 105.

Remembering how Hank Avis acted when you met Sioux hunters on the Pony Express route near the Horseshoe station, you raise your right hand in a gesture of peace and speak cheerfully to them. It worked with Hank; you hope it works for you too!

"How are you folks today?" you say, smiling. "Nice weather we're having, isn't it?"

The women and children of the tribe stare at you in silence for a long moment. Then they begin talking to one another and gesturing toward you. It seems that they are discussing what to do with you!

A square-faced woman in a buckskin dress steps forward and gestures for you to follow as she turns and leads the others to the far side of the encampment.

In the dried grass beyond the tepees you see a pair of footpaths. The paths are about fifty yards long, side by side in straight lines. The woman utters a brief command. Boys and girls of the tribe form two lines and line up behind the footpaths.

At a second command from her, an Indian
boy and girl at the front of the lines race one
another to the end and back again. Then the
second pair takes off, running hard. You watch
as the winners return to the back of the line.
The losers drop out and move to the side of the
paths, where they cheer on the runners.

You understand what is happening. Only the
strongest and fastest runner will be left when
the competition is finished.

Soon only one boy and one girl remain. With
a barked command from the stern woman, they
leap away from the starting line. You see that
the boy is ahead as the runners turn and come
back. Cheers rise up from the women and children beside the paths, and the girl puts on a
burst of speed. For several seconds the two run
neck and neck, faces straining with their ef-
forts. When they cross the finish line, the girl
is half a step ahead of the boy. After the girl is
given a chance to rest, she returns to the starting line. The square-faced woman turns and
points to you. She gestures toward the other
footpath.

You are caught by surprise. The woman is
obviously telling you to move up to the footpath
beside the girl. The Indians expect you to race
their best runner.

The woman impatiently repeats her gesture,
this time speaking harshly to you. You move
toward the starting line. You are not prepared
for a race, but you'll have to do your best. You

wonder what will happen if you lose—or if you win!

You pull off your boots and step up to the line. The woman quickly barks out a command, and the girl at your side leaps away, bursting into her long-legged stride.

You run after her, wishing now that you had taken a few minutes to warm up.

But you do have one advantage. You are rested, and the girl has just run a marathon of foot races.

You see the girl reach the end of the footpath. She turns, and in the moment when she passes by, you see the strain of this race on her face.

You make the turn quickly and run back toward the finish line.

You start to gain on the girl. Cheering from the sidelines echoes in your ears. Ten yards behind now, you try to kick out your stride to close the distance. The smooth stride of the Sioux girl falters.

With the finish line rapidly approaching, you move up behind her. Two paces. One pace. Then you are running even with her. Both of you leap across the finish line.

You slow down and then stop, breathing deeply and bending down to brace your hands on your knees. You couldn't tell who won. Back in your time period, this race would have been a photo finish. You know one thing. If that Sioux girl had been rested, she'd have won that race. She's fast!

When you've caught your breath, you straighten up and look around. The women and children have left. You turn and see them hurrying to the other end of the camp. You pull on your boots and slowly follow.

You see two men riding double on an Indian pony. When they reach the edge of the camp, the second man dismounts. He walks straight to the pony you rode into camp and carefully checks the animal over. Then he looks at you. The other members of the tribe follow him when he comes toward you.

You hold your ground and smile, remembering once again how Hank Avis acted when you encountered a band of Sioux hunters on the Pony Express route.

"Howdy," you say. "How's the hunting this fall?" None of the Indians understand a word you're saying, but your manner and tone of voice are what counts. At least you hope so.

The leader stops a few feet away from you. The others gather around. All of them stare at you soberly.

You introduce yourself, still smiling. "Nice weather we're having these days, isn't it?"

Still no reaction. One advantage Hank Avis had when he talked his way past the Sioux hunting party was that the horse he rode did not belong to the Indians. Horses are important to these Plains tribes.

You are taken to a tepee and shoved inside. The flap is closed behind you. This tepee smells of leather and smoke. It's empty except for a furry hide on the ground. You hear chatter and laughing outside, but no one can see you in here. Time to jump out of here.

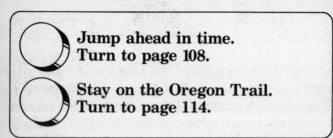

Jump ahead in time.
Turn to page 108.

Stay on the Oregon Trail.
Turn to page 114.

Outside a telegraph office on Pennsylvania Avenue you see a familiar figure. As you cross the wide street, this man sees you. He looks surprised and puts his hands on his hips.

"You again," Rufus Haynes says. "Another coincidence, I suppose?" He moves to the doorway and peers through the window of the telegraph office. "Soon as the wire is clear, I'm sending a war story to the *Courier.*"

"War story?" you say.

"Haven't you heard?" he asks, turning to look at you. "There was a battle at Bull Run today. It's the biggest story since the rebs fired on Fort Sumter—maybe bigger. From what I hear, the Union troops took a thrashing."

"I've been doing a few other things," you say. "And I've still got a few questions about the Pony Express and William H. Russell."

"Questions," he says. "Is that all you ever do—ask questions? The famous Mr. Russell is lucky to be out of jail. He's a ruined man."

"What happened?" you ask.

"Turns out he financed the Pony Express on

illegal government vouchers from the Secretary of War, John Floyd," Haynes says.

"But isn't the Pony Express still in operation?" you ask.

"Yes," says Haynes, "because the federal government needs it. Another man was appointed to run the Pony Express under a government contract. The Butterfield Overland Stage Company is using the new route."

So now the Pony Express is fully supported by the government. It has not been stopped by bad weather, hostile Indians, civil war, or Russell's bankruptcy. Your question is still unanswered.

As soon as you can slip away, you'll go out West again. This telegraph office has given you an idea.

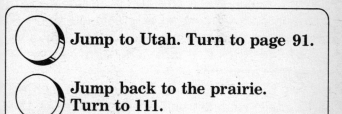

Jump to Utah. Turn to page 91.

Jump back to the prairie. Turn to 111.

■t's early on Sunday morning of December 7, 1941, and you're in Denver, Colorado. A woman comes down the empty street and hurries past you into an office. She is in tears. The sign on the glass door of the office reads Western Union Telegraph.

You look in and see that the telegrapher is asleep at his desk. He jumps up when the woman cries out, "Pearl Harbor has been bombed!"

You listen as she goes on. "I want to send an urgent message to the Navy Yards in San Francisco. My husband is stationed there. I have to see him before he goes off to war. The telephone lines are jammed. Can you get a message through?"

"Yes, ma'am," the telegrapher says, reaching for the telegraph key on his desk. You notice the key is connected to an electrical wire. As the woman gives her message to him, the telegrapher taps it out in Morse code.

That's a quick way to send an important message. You remember seeing the telegraph wire crew working on the high plains of Wyoming back in 1860. You can jump back there and find out more about them, or you can jump back to Fort Laramie. You still have more to learn about the Pony Express.

 Jump back to Fort Laramie. Turn to page 53.

 Jump back 80 years to Wyoming. Turn to page 114.

alking along the prairie, you see twelve or fifteen ponies ahead. These are Indian horses, all hobbled to prevent them from running away. No guards are here. The ponies can't go far, but with the smell of smoke in the air from the grass fire, they are restless. They keep trying to get away from you.

You finally catch one by grabbing his Indian bridle—a single rein of braided horsehair tied to the animal's jaw. Holding the rein, you bend down and untie the hobbles.

Freed, the pony tries to run, but you grab his mane with your other hand and throw a leg over his back. Riding bareback isn't easy, and when the pony bucks, you're nearly thrown. But you hang onto a handful of mane and pull back on the rein.

The pony is well trained. He comes to a quick halt. You soon discover that you can turn him by nudging him with either knee, and a light tap of your heels makes him run at a fast canter. Another tap, and he'll run like the wind.

You ride out of the shallow valley and look for the wagon of the telegraph crew. It is nowhere to be seen from here, and neither are the wheel ruts of the Oregon Trail. You're lost!

Suddenly the pony tosses his head and gallops up a hillside. You try to rein him in, but he fights and prances to the crest of the hill. When you look down into the next valley, you understand why the pony is acting this way. He wants to go home!

The wide valley is lined with tepees. This is probably an autumn hunting camp of the Sioux. No telling if this tribe is friendly. The band you and Hank Avis met weren't hostile. But many of these Indians have been setting grass fires, unhappy that their lands are being invaded by outsiders.

Better get out of here, you think, before you are seen on this hilltop. You pull back on the rein and nudge the pony with your knee. But this pony has other ideas. Instead of turning back, he breaks into a full gallop and heads for the Sioux encampment.

You pull back on the reins with all your strength, but the pony simply runs at full speed while fighting the bridle. Ahead you hear shouts and a chorus of barking dogs. You look up to see everyone in the village gathering to meet you.

You lean forward and swing a leg over the pony's back. You let go of the rein and roll, falling to the ground, and come to rest against a clump of sagebrush. The wind is knocked out of you, but you're all right. You hear the shouts of the Indians running toward you.

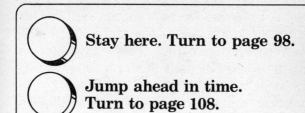

Stay here. Turn to page 98.

Jump ahead in time.
Turn to page 108.

You're back in Wyoming in 1861. You walk along the bank of the creek, seeing trout dart into the shadowed water near the edge. Ahead you see a sturdy cabin and horse barn. In the corral are several handsome saddle horses. That's a Pony Express relay station, all right.

As you approach, the cabin door opens. A woman steps outside and shakes out a tablecloth. Something about her looks familiar. You walk faster and then wave frantically. "Cora!" you yell. "Cora Hawkins!"

She lowers the white tablecloth and looks at you. Then her eyes widen in amazement. She lets out a shout and runs across the yard toward you, grabbing you in a big hug. When she lets go, you both ask the same question at the same time: "What're you doing here?"

You both laugh. "You tell me first," she says.

"No, you go first," you say.

She takes a deep breath. "Well, we had to leave Texas."

"Why?" you ask.

"Where have you been?" she asks. "Texas

joined the Confederacy, and they cut off the southern route to California. Soon Butterfield stagecoaches will use this central route. Sam and I are keeping this Pony Express relay station open, but when the wagons roll, life will be busy around here."

That's good news for Cora, but bad for William H. Russell. He has lost out to his competitor. To find out what's happening back east, you'll have to travel to Washington, D.C.

After a bath and one of Cora's meals, you say good-bye and slip out back.

**Jump to Washington, D.C.
Turn to page 105.**

The line of telegraph poles runs past the Pony Express relay station operated by Cora and Sam Hawkins. In the corral you see stout horses like the ones used to pull stagecoaches—not the fleet, slender horses owned by the Pony Express.

The weather now is different, too. The sky is gray with clouds. A cold wind blows out of the north. You hunch your shoulders and walk hurriedly to the house.

Your knock on the door is answered by Cora. Her face brightens with delight. "I never will get used to the way you appear out of nowhere!" she says. "Come in out of the cold."

The interior of this small house is plain, with bare plank walls, the same table and benches you saw in her desert way station, and a large black cookstove on the far wall. Now that stove is sending off heat. You welcome the warmth and rub your hands together in front of the stove.

"Sam's out in the barn with the horses," she

says, "but he'll be in for dinner soon. Are you just passing through, or can you stay a spell?"

"I'm passing through," you say, "but I wanted to see you before I left."

Cora smiles. "That makes me happy." She adds, "I need something to be happy about."

"What do you mean?" you ask.

She opens a door to a back room and shows you a small desk with a telegrapher's key on it. "We receive and send messages for home-steaders out here. Folks are getting news of the war back east, and it's mighty sad. Americans are fighting Americans."

From outside comes a shout. You recognize Sam's voice. "Cora! Cora, we've got trouble out here!"

You follow as she rushes to the door and flings it open. The yard is filled with Indians. A whole tribe of Sioux men, women, and children are gathered here—fifty or sixty of them. Some are mounted on horseback, but most of the spotted ponies are used to pull travois loaded with their possessions.

The Indians on foot are wrapped in blankets and animal hides to ward off the cold. Several of the men hold rifles in the crooks of their arms. They are staring at Sam.

Sam is wild-eyed with fear. In his hands is a shotgun, and he holds it shakily. "You savages get out of here," he says.

You step out of the house. You recognize a horse and rider—the chocolate-brown pony with a white head and rump. You raise your hand to the rider who turns toward you.

Cora calls out for you to come back into the house. Sam does the same.

"If there's going to be shooting here," he says, "let me handle it!"

"I don't want any shooting," you say. "I'll try to find out why they're here." You raise your hand to the Sioux leader and smile. "Howdy! We meet again."

He is startled by your presence. His expression slowly changes, and he smiles. You have shown bravery by facing the whole tribe and have earned his respect.

"Going south for the winter?" you ask, pointing in that direction.

He nods. Then he turns and gestures to the ponies. You see that they are thin and tired, heads drooping. This time of year the grazing land is sparse, made worse by the prairie fires.

You turn to Sam. "Put the gun down. These Indians need help."

Sam is still obviously frightened. His hands shake and his eyes are stretched wide open. But he lowers the shotgun.

"Do you have any extra grain for their ponies?" you ask.

"Well, I reckon I do," he says slowly. "Is that

all they want? I thought they were here to scalp us."

"Their horses need to eat," you say, "so they can travel to their winter range."

"I'll be durned," Sam says, grinning. "Say, I've got fifteen or twenty sacks of oats left over from the Pony Express horses. They can have it all." He turns and goes into the barn.

Among the Indians you see a pair of familiar faces. One is the square-faced woman who first met you when you came into the Sioux encampment. She looks at you now without showing any sign of recognition.

The other face belongs to the girl you raced against. She smiles at you.

The Sioux are proud people, but they welcome the gift of these burlap sacks filled with grain. Now they will be able to travel to their winter hunting grounds.

After the tribe has left, Cora says to you, "You helped us out again. Funny how you have a way of showing up when we need a hand."

You smile at her as you return to the warmth of the house.

"Sam," she calls over her shoulder, "come in for dinner!"

Sitting down at the long table with Cora and Sam reminds you of the first time you met them in the remote desert way station. They always ate just before the noon stagecoach rolled in.

When the hungry passengers arrived, the house smelled of freshly cooked food. That was how Cora, with a smile and a joke, liked to welcome her guests. .

"You've got a faraway look in your eye," Cora says to you as you take a bite of apple pie.

"I was thinking about the first time we met," you say.

"I remember that well," she says. She glances at Sam. "He was hurt, and we were both worried that Butterfield would go out of business and leave us without a job."

"Instead, we were transferred up here," Sam says. "Best thing that ever happened to us. This is fine country, and with your help today I believe we'll get along with the Sioux. We're neighbors with those Indians and with new settlers building homesteads in these parts. The West is changing fast."

"Too fast, I reckon," Cora says.

"Now, Cora," Sam says, "you can't stop progress."

"I know," she replies. "But sometimes I get a feeling that time is passing by too fast. Ever get that feeling?"

You nod. As a time traveler, you sure do!

"Machines are taking over for human beings," Cora says. "Take the telegraph—"

Sounds of hoofbeats and clinking harness chains brings Sam to his feet. He heads for the door.

"You take the telegraph," he says to her with a grin. "I've got a stagecoach to take care of."

You go outside and help Sam with the team. The tired horses are unhitched and herded into the corral, and fresh horses are put into harness. After the passengers have eaten Cora's noonday meal, they climb back into the stagecoach.

You see Sam toss a gray canvas bag up to the driver. He drops a similar one down to Sam. The black stenciled letters on the bag read U.S. Mail.

With a shout and a snap of the whip from the driver, the stagecoach rolls away, headed east. Cora stands at the open doorway of the station and waves good-bye.

Now you realize what Cora was talking about when the stagecoach came in. "Mail from the local homesteaders travels by stagecoach now."

Cora nods. "Those letters to relatives are the lifeblood of the pioneers out here. News from home, even when it's war news, is eagerly awaited by our neighbors."

"But if anyone needs an urgent message," you say, "the telegraph is used. That's why the Pony Express went out of business. No one on horseback can keep up with the telegraph!"

"That's right," Cora says. "And that's what I meant when I said machines are taking over for human beings. When the mail was carried across the West by riders, the whole nation cheered them on. The whole nation worried about those young riders during winter storms or when Indians were hostile. People all over the world were fascinated by the Pony Express."

She points to the line of telegraph poles that carry the wire across the continent now. "Nobody worries about that wire."

Sam says, "It's a modern miracle."

"So was the Pony Express," Cora says with a smile touched by sadness.

You agree with Cora. For eighteen months in 1860 and 1861 the Pony Express provided a link of communication across the West. Day and night the relay riders carried mail to people who had no other means of communicating with loved ones. That was a part of the development of the West that would never be forgotten, a brief period of history when a man named William H. Russell saw his dream come true.

"There will be other miracles to come," you say.

Cora turns to look at you. "Sometimes you act as if you know what's in the future, the way you have of showing up at just the right moment."

"See into the future?" Sam says with a smile. "Now, that's funny, Cora. Very funny."

You laugh out loud, and after a moment so does Cora.

If only you could tell her how close to the truth she is!

MISSION COMPLETED.

DATA FILE

About the Contributors

STEPHEN OVERHOLSER's first novel, *A Hanging in Sweetwater,* won the Western Writers of America's Spur Award of 1974. Since then he has written nine novels and numerous short stories. His recent books include a Bantam Books series featuring the heroine Molly Owens, set in the intermountain West of the 1890s. He lives in Boulder, Colorado, with his wife and son.

STEVE LEIALOHA, illustrator, spends most of his time writing, drawing, and inking comic books, with occasional forays into advertising, film production, and book illustration. He is a native of San Francisco, where he lives in a Victorian house with several artists.

TIME MACHINE

Incredible Love for *L*

'Silvey has created a fresh and
charm and tenderness. A be
time and fate, guarante
Holly Miller, internationally bes

'A beautifully crafted love story on the nature of fate
and free will, delivered with huge charm and warmth'
Laura Jane Williams, author of *Our Stop*

'Clever, warm and moving – I loved it'
Holly Smale, author of *Cassandra in Reverse*

'A novel every bit as smart, tender, and intriguing as its title. Part
time-travel narrative, part epic love-story, and a fully realised
exploration of what it means to live in the present while also
acknowledging the million futures that might lie ahead of us all, I fell
head-over-heels for Joe, Esi and their world. I know readers will too'
Abbie Greaves, author of *The Silent Treatment*

'Hugely charming, funny, and philosophical, *Love & Other Paradoxes*
is a timey-wimey Cantabrigian love story for the ages. Silvey is an
absolute master of witty banter, and it's impossible not to root for
Joe and Esi as they fumble their way to finding themselves'
Julie Leong, author of *The Teller of Small Fortunes*

'Stunningly clever, sweepingly romantic and so beautifully crafted.
Catriona has created story magic by taking the intricate topic of
time travel and making it an effortless and joyful read. Truly, one of
the most interesting novels I've read all year! I absolutely adored it!'
Helly Acton, author of *Begin Again*

'Combining Y2K nostalgia, swoony romance and big questions
about destiny, *Love & Other Paradoxes* is a funny, tender time
travel romance that will delight readers. I loved it!'
Zen Cho, award-winning author of *Sorcerer to the Crown*

'Like Cyrano de Bergerac filtered through *Back to the Future* and a 2000s coat of paint, *Love & Other Paradoxes* is a fun and surprising dive into love and destiny – or lack thereof. Joe and Esi jump off the page, grounding sci-fi twists with humour and humanity, all with a brilliantly fresh take on time travel. Catriona Silvey is an absolute must-buy author for me'
Mike Chen, *New York Times* bestselling author of *A Quantum Love Story*

'An utterly charming and completely unique love story. With irresistible mid-aughts nostalgia and the perfect blend of romance, wit, and speculative twists, *Love & Other Paradoxes* will have readers both swooning and contemplating what it means to follow one's destiny. I couldn't turn the pages fast enough to find out what happened next!'
Holly James, author of *The Déjà Glitch*

'A thrilling, thought-provoking gem of a love story, sparkling with wit and whimsy. I was drawn in by the intriguing premise of a time-travelling romance, then hooked by the twistily compelling plot and irresistible charm of Joe and Esi. The way in which the story came together at the end left me dazzled, answering brilliantly the conundrum of whether there's just one future mapped out for us or whether we can alter our destiny. Fabulous fun from start to finish!'
Sarah Haywood, *New York Times* bestselling author of *The Cactus*

Love & Other
Paradoxes

ALSO BY CATRIONA SILVEY

Meet Me in Another Life

Love
& Other
Paradoxes

CATRIONA SILVEY

HARPER
Voyager

Harper *Voyager*
An imprint of HarperCollins *Publishers* Ltd
1 London Bridge Street
London SE1 9GF

www.harpercollins.co.uk

HarperCollins *Publishers*
Macken House,
39/40 Mayor Street Upper,
Dublin 1
DO1 C9W8
Ireland

First published by HarperCollins *Publishers* Ltd 2025
1

Interior text layout design by Diahann Sturge-Campbell

Catriona Silvey asserts the moral right to
be identified as the author of this work.

A catalogue record for this book is available from the British Library.

ISBN: 978-0-00-840841-1 (PB)
ISBN: 978-0-00-840838-1 (TPB)

This novel is entirely a work of fiction.
The names, characters and incidents portrayed in it are
the work of the author's imagination. Any resemblance to
actual persons, living or dead, events or localities is
entirely coincidental.

Printed and bound in the UK using
100% Renewable Electricity by CPI Group (UK) Ltd

MIX
Paper | Supporting
responsible forestry
FSC™ C007454

This book contains FSC™ certified paper and other controlled
sources to ensure responsible forest management.

For more information visit: www.harpercollins.co.uk/green

To the class of 2006:
I hope your futures
turned out delightfully unexpected

Chapter One

Joe stood in the hush of the Wren Library, looking up into the marble eyes of the poet.

The poet was lounging on the ruins of an ancient Greek temple, foot drawn up to rest on a broken pillar. One elegant hand pointed a pencil to his chin; the other held a finished book of poems. The poet's handsome brow was furrowed, his eyes fixed on the middle distance. Joe found himself unconsciously mimicking the pose: raising one hand, setting his jaw, staring across the black-and-white tiles of the library floor. A girl sitting in an alcove looked up and met his eyes. Thinking he was looking at her, she smiled. He was about to smile back, then remembered he was supposed to be looking intense and poetic. He frowned, shifting his gaze to the stained-glass window. When he glanced surreptitiously at the girl, she had gone back to reading.

'Lord Byron,' said someone behind him. 'He was a student here, you know.'

Joe flinched in surprise, then fell back into his usual apologetic slump. The speaker was one of the black-uniformed men who were an everyday feature of Cambridge life. They were called things like *porter* or *proctor* or *praelector*, and seemed to appear from nowhere. He had a theory that they seeped spontaneously out of the marble whenever you stood still for too long.

'I know,' he replied. That was why he was here: to remind himself that Byron had once stood where he stood, which meant that achieving his own destiny as a great poet was not completely out of reach. Byron, of course, had not been looking up at a statue of himself, unless, alongside writing poetry and having sex with a lot of people, he had also invented time travel.

'Kept a bear in his room,' said the black-uniformed man. 'Legendary lover, of course,' he added.

Joe felt a laugh creep up inside him. 'The bear?'

The man was looking at him with a mixture of pity and disappointment. 'Are you a member of the college?'

He tensed, confronting the spectre of not-belonging that had haunted him for the past two years. 'No. I mean, I'm a student, just – not at Trinity.'

The man patted him heavily on the shoulder. 'Then I'm afraid I'll have to ask you to leave.'

Outside, the autumn sun glinted off the dew-damp grass. A chill October wind blew up from the river, cutting through his cheap coat. He hurried through the insane, stage-set grandeur of the college, so different from the squat fishermen's cottages he had known for the first eighteen years of his life. Now, at the beginning of his third year as a student, he had almost stopped noticing it. It only came clear to him at moments like this, when he confronted the reality that in eight short months, he would be graduating. He would be cast out, like an orphan stumbling from Narnia back into wartime England – or in his case, rural Scotland, back to his job at the village pub, with no proof that his time here in the other world had been anything but a dream. Unless he could find a way to prove that he had always belonged here, among the historymakers; that letting him in had not been a terrible, embarrassing mistake.

As he left Trinity through the vaulted archway of the Great Gate, he was so lost in thought that he walked straight into someone.

'Sorry,' he blurted, looking at the person he'd almost knocked over. A girl, pale-faced, with unusual light green eyes. She had swept her dark hair to one side, in the way all the posh girls here did, as if they were in a strong wind no one else could feel. Something about her was familiar. He couldn't understand why until he saw what was printed on her hoodie. *Macbeth 2004*. He had seen that show, last year at the ADC Theatre. She had played Lady Macbeth. He remembered her being blazingly, shockingly good, outshining the other actors like candles to her sun.

She raised an elegant eyebrow. He sensed the chance to say something, to change the future of this moment, but he couldn't think of anything clever enough. The girl threw him a disdainful look and walked on.

He folded into himself, grimacing. 'Byron wouldn't've just stood there like a numpty,' he muttered. 'Byron would've said something.' Out on Trinity Street, the late-morning light slanted down, turning the fallen leaves to splashes of gold. The back of his brain filed the details away to use later, even as the front of his brain brooded over the fact that he hadn't finished a poem since he'd started his degree.

By Great St Mary's church, the usual tour groups were craning to look up at the tower. He was edging his way past when he saw with alarm that one of the groups was staring straight at him.

He stared back. Most of them looked away. One met his eyes and stepped forward. A girl with a strange, asymmetric haircut, dressed in the thousand-pocketed combat trousers that had been fashionable about five years ago. She was gazing at him in slack-jawed disbelief. He immediately worried that he had toothpaste around his mouth. As he went to scrub it off, someone pulled the girl away – an olive-skinned woman in her late twenties, brown hair tied back in a ponytail, wearing a tabard that marked her out as the tour guide.

'Time's up.' She corralled the group together and ushered them away. He watched them dwindle down King's Parade, the girl in the combats casting surreptitious glances over her shoulder. He made a mental note to look in a mirror as soon as he got back to his room.

Inside the stone walls of his own college, no one gave him a second glance. Reassured, he went by the post room to check his pigeonhole. Usually, it would have contained nothing but free con-doms and flyers from the Christian Union, but lately, he had been finding it full of strange gifts. A single white rose; a fountain pen; a keyring with a quote from a poem that, when he looked it up, didn't appear to exist. Today, there was a scribbled note that said simply, *Thank you*. With growing unease, he crumpled it into the recycling bin and headed up the stairs.

College had a strict rule that shared sets of rooms were for friends, not couples, on the grounds that student romances were too unstable to last the nine months of the lease. Joe couldn't fault their logic. He and Rob had been friends since first year, outliving his longest relationship to date by a factor of nine.

He climbed the staircase two steps at a time: after a summer on his feet serving endless pints to seaside tourists, he could reach the top without getting out of breath. He unlocked the door, blink-ing in the sun that spilled through the high windows. He loved his and Rob's rooms, fiercely and completely. He loved the living room, with its sagging sofa and its blocked-off fireplace stacked with bottles of cheap wine; he loved his bedroom, with the window that opened onto a tiny stretch of battlements, the closest he would ever get to living in a castle. By inching along a narrow ledge and scaling a drainpipe, you could supposedly get to a secret terrace with a view of King's College, but he had never tried: he was haunted by visions of falling, to be memorialised only by a snippet in the local paper lamenting his wasted potential.

Rob was technically studying physics, but his true passion was the mock-combat game known as Assassins. As Joe came in, he was fashioning a trebuchet out of old copies of the student newspaper, pink with concentration, sandy hair flopping over his face. 'Morning, Greeney,' he said without looking up.

Joe muttered in nonresponse and went straight through to his bedroom. Flinging open his desk drawer, he threw out the toy Highland cow his Scottish mum had got him so he wouldn't forget his roots, the toy London bus his English dad had got him in retaliation, and the toy penguin his sister Kirsty had got him because 'it reminded me of you'. Hidden underneath was a pile of notebooks scrawled with poems. He combed through them, searching for something he already knew he wouldn't find. None of them – the epics he'd feverishly scribbled as a teenager, the fragments he'd forced out word by tortured word since coming to Cambridge – were remotely good enough. There was a fire in his brain, white-hot and unrelenting, but not a single spark had made it onto the page.

He groaned, burying his face in his hands.

'What are you moaning tragically about?' Rob called from the living room.

He staggered out of his bedroom and collapsed face down onto the sofa. 'I'll never be a great poet,' he said into the cushions. 'I might as well just sit in a bin and wait to die.'

'Surely there's some middle ground between "great poet" and "dead in a bin". What about a nice job in the civil service?'

'I'd rather be dead in a bin. Anyway, you need a good degree to get a job in the civil service, and according to Dr Lewis, I'm not getting one of those.' He winced, anticipating what his Director of Studies would say tomorrow morning when they met for their weekly supervision. Failing out of his degree was a real and ever-growing possibility. He had nightmares about it sometimes: going home to face his parents' poorly hidden disappointment, the smug vindication of everyone who'd thought he was an idiot for even applying.

'This is a radical suggestion, Greeney, but – why not take her advice? This is the only year that counts towards your final mark. Maybe it's time to drop the poetry and focus on what you're here for.'

Joe rolled over and stared at the ceiling. His family's expectations, his diminishing overdraft, the loans he would somehow have to find a way to pay back, all agreed with Rob: the important thing was to graduate, so he could get a job and not have to live, or indeed die, in a bin. But he had only ever really wanted one thing, and the fact that it currently seemed impossible didn't make it any less vital. 'What about you?' He turned the question back on Rob. 'Why don't you stop pretending to kill people and focus on what *you're* here for?'

'You know why, Greeney. Because I have to defeat my nemesis.'

'Aye, of course. The Deadly Mr Darcy.' Joe had never actually met Rob's nemesis. He only knew that they had fought a duel at the end of first year, which had ended in Rob's death by blue confetti. 'What's your pseudonym again?'

'Entropy.' Rob struck a pose. 'It's going to get you in the end.'

'It's not funny if you have to be a physicist to understand it.'

'Stop changing the subject. The point is, you don't have a nemesis. What's your excuse?'

He thought about looking up at the statue, a hundred and eighty years after the poet had taken his final breath, and the answer came easily. 'I want to be remembered.'

It was a ridiculously grandiose thing to admit to. But Rob just nodded, as if it made sense. 'Okay. So, be memorable. I thought you'd already started. Didn't you win the Tartan Limerick contest, or whatever?'

'The Scottish Young Poet award,' Joe corrected him. 'When I was fifteen. And what have I done since? I submitted a poem to *The Mays* in first year, and they rejected it for being "naive".' That note still rang in his ears every time he sat down to write. 'And see what I'm up against.' He grabbed a copy of *Varsity* from Rob's pile and leafed through at random. 'Here. Someone in second year who's already been commissioned by the BBC.'

'Overachiever,' Rob scoffed. 'Ignore them.'

'I can't afford to ignore them. I'm the first kid from my school to go to Cambridge since anyone can remember. Everyone back home's expecting me to, I don't know, invent the moon or something.'

'Moon's already been invented, Greeney. You'll have to think of something else.'

'And poetry has always been my thing,' he went on. 'It's what I do. It's like – like . . .'

Rob placed a hand dramatically on his heart. 'Like *breathing*.'

'No. It's not like breathing. Breathing is boring, and easy, and everybody does it. Poetry is – it *used* to be fun, and hard in the best way, and it made me feel more like me than anything else.' He flushed: if he'd been talking to anyone but Rob, he would never have let the conversation get to this level of honesty. 'I applied here because I thought it would turn me into the poet I'm supposed to be. But it's the opposite. I think about all these great poets who came here before, and all I can see is how I just don't measure up.'

Rob cleared his throat. 'Greeney. Do you remember what happened when I joined the Assassins' Guild in first year?'

'Someone shot you at point-blank range with a banana.'

'That is correct.' Rob steepled his fingers. 'And how did I respond?'

Joe scrunched up his face. 'Am I a bad friend if I don't remember?'

'I read the reports of every Game since Lent 1993, consulting the same hallowed archives in which I hope to one day be enshrined as a Master Assassin. I learned the Game's most important principle: make yourself hard to find. And, crucially, *I kept playing*. The result? While I've yet to win, I've survived till at least week five in every Game I've taken part in since.'

'Was there a point to this story?'

'The point is, you submitted to one pretentious student anthology and you didn't get in. Big deal. Keep trying.' Rob reached in his pocket and took out a pink sheet of paper. He scrunched it into a ball, loaded it into his trebuchet, and fired. It hit Joe in the face and bounced off into a gap between the sofa cushions.

'Ow,' said Joe pointedly. He fished the ball out and unrolled it.

It was a flyer for a poetry competition. The title, surrounded by hearts, was Love Poems for Tomorrow. The idea was to pair emerging student writers and actors, who would perform the winning poems at an event on Valentine's Day.

He imagined the hush of the ADC Theatre, his words echoing out from the stage. He visualised his future unfurling from that moment: a life of art and glory, where people knew his poems and treasured them, passing them down the years until the mess of his existence was overwritten by the perfect things he'd created.

'So?' Rob prompted him.

He sighed. 'When's the deadline?'

'Didn't look. Must be on there somewhere.'

He found it at the bottom of the flyer. The first of November 2005. Tomorrow.

The perfect, imaginary poem evaporated, leaving behind the terror of a blank page. Who could he write a love poem about? His first-year girlfriend, who had dumped him after three months when they had run out of things to say to each other? The girl he had kissed outside the toilets last time he went clubbing, who had slurred something in his ear about how much she loved *Braveheart*, passed out on his shoulder, and never called him back?

'Oh no,' said Rob, recognising the expression on Joe's face. 'You're having a Thought, aren't you?'

The revelation built itself like a poem, elegant and inescapable, the end contained in the start. 'This whole time, I was thinking, *I can't believe Rob is comparing my poetry to being in the Assassins' Guild*. I mean, you pretend to kill people, with banana guns and wee paper swords. It's playacting. It's a cheap, brazen mockery of anything real.'

'All right,' Rob muttered. 'I don't judge your hobbies.'

'And my poetry is exactly the same.' He spread his hands. 'I've been sitting here trying to make a trebuchet out of old newspapers. Because I've never been in love.' It felt like looking up at the statue, recognising the immense gap between who he was and who he wanted to be. 'That's the problem.'

'No. That's not the problem. The problem is that you've let this place get to you. I mean, you're trying to write poetry while literally being stared at by the ghost of Lord Byron.'

He started. 'How did you know?'

'You've got ink on your chin. You were doing that pen pose again, weren't you?' Joe licked his finger and scrubbed. 'Greeney. Stop reading *Varsity*. Stop staring at statues of insane aristocrats who had inappropriate relationships with their sisters.' An idea lit Rob's face. 'In fact, why not get away from the university? Go somewhere completely unexpected. Say . . . Mill Road.'

'This is starting to sound really specific.'

'Fine.' Rob tapped the wall chart that tracked his progress in the Game. 'Truth is, I've got a target out at Hughes Hall, and I don't want to walk there on my own.'

Joe sighed. 'All right. But then I'm coming straight back to sit in a bin and wait for death.'

'Deal.' Rob checked his watch. 'Oh. Give me a second.' He disappeared into his bedroom, emerging a few minutes later in a green waistcoat and straw hat.

Joe looked him up and down. 'Is that your fancy murder outfit?'

'Got a shift on the river at quarter to one. I won't have time to change.' Rob had a technically forbidden part-time job as a punt guide, poling tourists along the river while telling them outrageous lies about the famous people who had attended Cambridge in the past. He clapped his hands. 'Chop chop, Greeney. Those poems aren't going to write themselves.'

Joe pocketed a blank notebook and the flyer and followed Rob out of college. Across the street, the woman in the tabard was watching him with bored intensity. As Joe turned left, she directed her group in parallel along the opposite pavement.

He leaned towards Rob, keeping his voice low. 'See that woman?'

'What woman?' Rob turned.

'Don't *look*!'

'You want me to see without looking? I thought you were a philosopher.'

'And I thought you'd spent the past two years working on your stealth skills.'

Rob sighed as they turned up Pembroke Street. 'I know you've just decided the crux of all your problems is that you've never been in love. But fixating on the first woman you see in the street is not a solution.'

'I'm not fixating. *She's* fixating. She's been following me around. Look! She's got a whole group with her!' One of them raised a disposable camera and flashed a photograph. 'They're taking pictures of me!'

'Greeney, I'm not saying you're delusional. But we live in one of the busiest tourist spots in Western Europe. Is it possible that instead of taking a picture of you, a random undergraduate, they were instead taking a picture of the stunning twenty-fourth-century court of Pembroke College, which is directly behind you?'

'Fourteenth century. I'm not on one of your tours; you don't need to lie.' Still, he couldn't shake the paranoia. 'This, and all the weird stuff in my pigeonhole – there's definitely something going on.'

Rob looked at him sideways. 'Maybe I signed you up for Assassins without telling you and now everyone is out for your blood.'

'I can't tell if you're joking.'

'Course I'm joking,' Rob scoffed. 'That would be absurd.'

He eyed the newspaper trebuchet under Rob's arm. 'Aye. *That* would be absurd.'

They crossed the grassy expanse of Parker's Piece. With no sea to frame it, the sky felt too big, like a huge eye staring down at him. Only when they passed the lamppost known as the Reality Checkpoint, where the university gave way to the rest of town, did the feeling of being watched start to ease off.

'This is me.' Rob turned down a side street.

'Good luck with the murder,' Joe shouted encouragingly. Someone walking past did a double take.

'Keep it down, Greeney. We're in the real world now.' Rob turned back. 'Don't forget, it's Halloween Formal tonight! Don't come as some poet no one's ever heard of.'

'Don't worry, I will.' He turned, fingering the competition flyer in his pocket. A day and a half to write a love poem so unprecedented it would determine the course of his future. The thought made him quail with inadequacy. He walked on up a street that could have been anywhere, lined with convenience shops and run-down cafés: hardly the stuff of poetic inspiration. He was on the point of turning back when something caught his eye.

It was a Halloween display in a café window. It depicted a sack of coffee beans that was under attack from espresso cup vampires. The vampires had googly eyes and drawn-on pointy teeth, and they were swarming the poor beleaguered sack, spilling its blood in gushing coffee-bean rivers. The sack had distressed eyebrows and a mournful, gaping mouth. The overall effect was so charming that he caught his reflection smiling. He brushed his chronically messy hair aside and frowned, leaning closer. The Joe in the window didn't look like the sort of person anyone would want to turn into a statue. He looked pasty, and dishevelled, and tired. Maybe a coffee would help.

He went inside. The café was cosy but shabby: the chairs, the tables, and indeed the entire structure appeared to be held together with duct tape. He edged past the bookshelves to the counter, where a girl with high cheekbones and warm dark brown skin was cleaning the espresso machine, her short braids swaying as she filled up the water tank. 'With you in a second,' she said without looking.

'No bother, take your time.' He looked around: a couple holding hands across a table, a teenage girl frowning over her laptop. No one was paying him the slightest bit of attention. He felt ashamed. Stupid to think the tour group had been following him. Rob was right: he was just a random undergraduate, of no interest to anyone.

'Sorry about that,' said the girl behind the counter. 'What can I get—'

He turned round. For a moment, he was lost in her wide-spaced, deep brown eyes. Then he realised she was staring at him, and not in a way that suggested she was lost in his. She was wearing an expression of utter, consuming horror.

'*You*,' she said, like the universe was about to end and it was all his fault.

Chapter Two

'**W**hat?' said Joe.

The girl flinched, like he was a timer on a bomb that had just ticked down to zero. When he failed to explode, he saw her rethink. 'What?' she echoed.

He groped for the source of his confusion. 'You said, "*You*." Like – like—' He couldn't find the words. 'Like I'm the last person you wanted to see.'

'No, I said, "What can I get *you*"?' Her fingers were clenched so tight on a napkin that she was tearing a hole in it. 'So? Are you going to order?'

'Uh – yeah.' He scanned the chalkboard behind her, barely registering the options. 'Can I get a latte, please?'

She punched some numbers into the till with trembling fingers. He paid – it took a while, as she seemed confused by the coins he gave her – and waited awkwardly for his coffee. When she saw him hovering, she shooed him away. 'I'll bring it over.'

Still reeling, he sat down at the table that looked least in danger of immediate collapse. He took out the Love Poems for Tomorrow flyer and opened his notebook to a blank page. He sat and stared at it, pen in hand, but he couldn't get the girl at the counter out of his head. She had looked at him like he was something dangerous, something vital. He glanced up, expecting her to be watching him like the tour guide, but she was steadfastly ignoring him, head bent over the espresso machine, braids parted around her slender neck. She looked around his age: he would have assumed she was a student, if having a job during term time wasn't forbidden for undergraduates.

She was coming over. He looked away. As she leaned to put the coffee down, he reflexively closed his notebook.

She swallowed a laugh. 'Don't worry, I'm not trying to read your poetry.'

He looked up in surprise. She flinched, like she was afraid of his attention. He felt wounded, and compelled, and so curious he could barely stand it. 'You don't like poetry?'

She hovered, leaning back towards the counter. He got the impression that she wanted to get away from him as quickly as possible. He got the second, conflicting impression that she couldn't resist answering his question. 'I don't know,' she said finally. 'There's this one guy I had to study at school, and I thought he was so overrated.'

'The stuff they make you learn in school is always the worst. I think there's some kind of rule. Only shite poets end up on the syllabus.'

'Mmm.' Her cheek was trembling, like she was fighting some strong emotion.

'But you shouldn't let him put you off,' he continued. 'There's some great stuff out there.'

'Oh yeah,' she said in the same unreadable tone. 'I bet some of the best people haven't even been published yet.'

He tilted his head, unsure if she was mocking him. 'Right.'

Her cheek twitched again. She looked away, briefly closing her eyes. Seeming to recover, she cleared her throat. 'I guess I don't get the point of it. Poetry, I mean. Like, why not just write a song?'

'You wouldn't be asking that if you'd ever heard me sing.'

Her smile, mobile and generous, transformed her face. She crossed her arms over her shapeless black sweater. 'Okay. So poets are just tone-deaf songwriters?'

He leaned back in his chair. 'I mean, I could go off on one about how lyrics are always parasitic on the melody, and how in poetry, the music comes from the language itself. But that would be a boring, pretentious rant, and no one wants to hear that.'

'Right.' The gap between her front teeth gave her smile a conspiratorial sweetness, like they were sharing a private joke. 'That's why you're not going to say it.'

'No. And also, because it's not really the point.' He leaned forward, no longer conscious of his body, following the pull of her thoughts on his. 'The point is, when I'm feeling something, poetry is how it comes out. And when it goes right, it doesn't feel like I'm trying,' he went on, aware he was describing something he hadn't experienced in years. 'It just feels like it happens.'

She was watching him with wide-eyed attention. He couldn't tell if she was fascinated or appalled. He scrubbed a hand through his hair, laughing. 'I'm sorry. I probably just sound mental.'

Her face relaxed. She turned to the window. 'No. I get it,' she said, sounding surprised. 'I mean, it's not poetry or anything, but I – make stuff.'

'Really? Like what?'

She indicated the window display.

He looked back at her, delighted. 'That was you?' She nodded, that smile still playing around her mouth. 'No way. I mean – that's the reason I came in here.'

'Of course,' she said with strange brightness. 'Because of all the cafés in all of Cambridge in the blessèd year two thousand and five, you had to come and write your poetry in the exact one I happen to be working in.'

He laughed uncertainly. She laughed back, her eyes wild. It was clear there was a joke he wasn't getting, but he wasn't sure if he cared. Smiling, he looked down to his notebook. He had moved his pen unconsciously, making a mark on the otherwise blank page.

'Wait.' He looked up. 'How did you know I'm writing poetry?'

A flash of panic. She twisted a braid between her fingers. 'You just – seemed like the type.'

'Really?' His visit to the Wren Library must have paid off: clearly, he was projecting Byron from every pore. 'What makes you say that?'

She looked him up and down. 'The hair.' Her fingers made a *chaos* gesture that moved downward. 'The coat that looks like you slept in it. The – I don't even know what to say about the jumper.'

It had been a Christmas present from his auntie: hand-knitted, with a naive seascape of boats and little clouds. 'Okay,' he said. 'Jesus.'

'Sorry. You asked.' She said it with familiar ease, as if she had known him for years and was frankly a little exasperated with him by now. It was jarring, and inexplicable, and he didn't entirely dislike it. 'Anyway. Enjoy your coffee. I'm going to . . .' She made a vanishing gesture.

Before he could think of anything to say to keep her there, an older woman appeared behind the counter. 'Esi,' she called. 'How long has the till been out of paper?'

Esi cast a comically adrift glance at Joe, as if the question was ridiculous. 'It needs paper?'

'Of course it needs paper! How else is it supposed to print re-
ceipts?' The older woman shook her head, retreating into the back
office. 'Honestly. You seemed so articulate when I hired you, but
you don't know the most basic things.'

Esi's jaw clenched. 'Right,' she muttered under her breath. 'I'm
sorry I didn't notice we'd run out of dead trees to squeeze crushed-
up rocks onto, so when we put the shiny tokens into the counting
machine, people can take home a physical reminder of how much
their coffee cost.' She marched behind the counter and picked up a
battered shoulder bag. The other barista, a girl with close-cropped
Afro hair and a Homerton MCR T-shirt that identified her as a
postgrad student, rolled her eyes in solidarity, but Esi didn't ac-
knowledge it.

'Make it fast,' called the manager from the back. 'And less of
the attitude.'

Esi stared at the office, murder in her eyes. Then she walked
out, pulling the door neatly closed.

Joe didn't think. He shut his notebook, downed the rest of his
coffee, and went after her.

She whirled on him, looking panicked. 'Why are you following me?'

He stepped back. 'I'm not following you. I mean – I am, but I
was just . . .' He took a breath, began again. 'I'm heading back to
town, so I thought we could go together.'

She sighed, closing her eyes. 'Deev.'

'What?'

'Um. I said – good. It's really unbelievably *good*, *fantastic*, and
brilliant that you of all people have decided we should *go together*.'
She looked anxiously over his shoulder. 'What's the time?'

He checked his watch. 'Half twelve.'

'Lunch break,' she said under her breath. 'Fine. Let's make it quick.' She set off, keeping a few paces ahead.

He faltered. 'I'm sorry. I don't know what I did, but – I get the message. I'll leave you alone.'

She stopped. He could see the tension in her, a taut line running across her shoulders. 'You didn't do anything.' She waved a hand at herself. 'I do this. Take shit out on people when it's not their fault. It's one of the many things wrong with me.'

He took a step closer. 'Are you okay?'

She turned to face him. 'No,' she said, with a hoarse laugh. 'No, I'm really not.' Her eyes focused, as if she was seeing him for the first time. 'Thank you for asking.'

'Esi, is it?' She nodded. 'I'm Joe.'

'Hello, *Joe*,' she said, with a strange, desperate smile.

She really was extremely odd. He was relieved. It took the pressure off him to be normal. 'So, can I walk with you?'

'Sure.' She made an extravagant gesture of surrender. 'But if you're anywhere near me in half an hour, I'm making a run for it.'

He couldn't tell if she was joking, but he was starting to get used to that feeling. 'So, was that your manager?' he asked, doing a fair impression of a person who fell into conversation with attractive strangers all the time.

'Yup,' she said, the syllable loaded with distaste.

'She shouldn't treat you like that.'

'She's doing me a favour. Giving me a job off the books, paying me in cash.' She looked away. 'I'm not exactly here legally.'

'Really? You sound like you're from London.'

'I will be, if you wait around long enough.'

He blinked. 'I'm sorry?'

'No, *I'm* sorry. Ignore me.' He couldn't have ignored her if he'd tried. She was a flutter of nervous motion: eyes darting, head turning, like the world might end if she stopped paying constant attention.

'So how long have you been in Cambridge?' he asked.

'A few weeks.'

'How do you like it so far?' He cringed even as he said it. He sounded like a phrase book.

'Honestly? People are kind of rude. And everything's expensive. But it's okay. I'm not staying.' She paused to peer through the window of a whole foods shop; apparently disappointed, she kept walking. 'I'm here till the twenty-third of June. Then I'm gone.'

He wasn't surprised. It put words to the way she carried herself: unanchored, like her feet weren't touching the ground. 'What's happening on the twenty-third of June?'

'Something important.' Her eyes glanced off him. 'Family stuff. Okay? It's not actually your business.'

'Okay,' he said, chastened. 'Sorry.'

In silence, they passed the Reality Checkpoint. Esi seemed to get more tense as they approached the centre. He said goodbye to her in glances: her eyes, seeming to take in everything and everyone; her hands, fidgeting with the ends of her sleeves; her bag, almost sliding off her shoulder. Pin badges dotted the strap. Most of them said *The Swerves*.

'What are they, a band?' he asked.

She smirked. 'Yeah. You won't have heard of them.'

It stung: a strange, cooler-than-thou thing to say. 'All right.'

She realised how it had come across. 'Oh. No, I didn't mean it like that. I mean, it's literally impossible for you to have heard of them, because they don't exist.'

He gave her a look. 'You're a fan of a band that doesn't exist.'

She winced. 'Yeah?'

'You're really odd.'

'I know. Sorry, I—'

'It's a compliment,' he said, with a frustrated laugh.

She stopped. 'Look. Joe.' The way she said his name was a puzzle he could have worked on for years: weary, exasperated, like an in-joke too complex to explain. 'You seem nice. Like, surprisingly nice. Honestly, I thought you'd be an entire . . .' She closed her eyes, put a finger to her lips. 'This has been fun. I'm sure I'll laugh about it one day, before I forget any of this ever happened, because it won't have. But there's something you should know about me.' She leaned in, her voice dropping to a whisper. 'I'm a disaster. Like, a full-on bomb crater of a person. So if we never see each other again, which we won't, just know – you're not missing anything.'

He shook his head, bewildered. 'I don't think that's true.'

'You have no idea. You just met me. And now, we're going to un-meet.' She pointed at the ground, marking the moment. 'This is where I walk away.'

He spread his hands, helpless. 'Okay.'

She turned towards WH Smith. Off to buy a roll of dead trees for the counting machine. He watched her go, feeling strangely bereft. Then someone walked into her. She stumbled, and her bag slipped to the ground. '*Shit*,' she yelled in disproportionate panic, as something fell out. It was a small hardback book. She lunged to pick it up.

'Let me,' he said.

'*No*,' she protested, but it was too late. He had already seen his name on the cover.

He picked it up, holding it out of her reach. He read the title. *Meant to Be: Poems for Diana.* By Joseph Greene. Above his name was a picture of a dark-haired man and woman embracing. Aside from the fact that the man was in his thirties, it was recognisably him.

His mind thundered with wild noise. 'Explain?' he said weakly.

The expression on her face mesmerised him. It was one he had never seen before on anyone's, and on hers, it was extraordinary. 'It's a joke,' she said desperately. 'A stupid prank. Your friends put me up to it. Let me . . .' She tried to grab the book.

He stepped away, slow as a fly in honey. 'If it's a joke, why aren't you laughing?'

Her face contorted, a terrified, pleading parody of a smile. 'It has to be a joke, right? That's the only way it makes sense.'

'No.' He ran back over their conversation: the band that didn't exist; the way she'd responded when he'd asked if she was from London. *I will be, if you wait around long enough.* Barely believing himself, he said it. 'You're from the future.'

She should have laughed. She should have called him an idiot and sauntered away. Instead, she fixed her eyes on the book in his hands with a look of utter despair. 'There's this company. Retroflex. They run tourist trips back in time, to see famous people when they were young.'

His brain was in freefall. 'I'm going to be famous. For my poetry.'

'Yeah. For some reason, you are.' She was looking in panic over his shoulder. 'And in five minutes, the tour guide's going to be off her lunch break and bringing more people here to stare at you, which means . . .' She reached out. 'You need to give me that back. *Now.*'

She grabbed the book. He pulled. She clung, her fingers tightening.

A bike bell rang, shrill and close. They jumped apart to let it through. The book was in Joe's hand.

Their eyes met across the narrow street.

He ran.

Chapter Three

He pelted away, Esi's footsteps ringing behind him. He sprinted past Great St Mary's, narrowly avoiding a crocodile of tourists who were staring up at the tower instead of watching where they were going, and skidded down the narrow alley of Senate House Passage. High walls closed him in: if she caught up with him here, he'd have nowhere to run. He slalomed through a gauntlet of bikes, dodging a group of first-years in college scarves who were walking four abreast. He risked a glance over his shoulder. Esi was closing in, pacing relentlessly through the gap his chaotic flight had made. He burst out of the passageway, slicing right then left, where chalk scrawled on bricks read, *TO THE RIVER*.

The twists and turns had slowed her: she didn't know this part of town like he did, and he used it. Instead of crossing the humped bridge, he slipped down the jetty on the right, hoping she would race on across the river. But he had misjudged her. Before she charged onto the bridge, her head turned in restless, searching attention, and her eyes locked with his.

He was trapped between her and the green water. He could jump in and swim for it, but the book would get wet. He looked frantically between it and the river.

'And this,' he heard from his left, 'is Garret Hostel Bridge. Named, of course, after Dr Garret Hostel, the original inventor of the swan.'

His heart leapt. Rob, in his green waistcoat, poling a shallow wooden boat along the sluggish river. Nestled under blankets inside was a group of tourists who seemed unmoved by his invented facts.

'Rob!' he yelled. 'Can I get a lift?'

Rob nearly fell off the punt. 'Greeney! Um, normally, yes, but these people have, you know, actually paid for a tour—'

He didn't wait. He flung himself out like Frodo at Bucklebury Ferry and landed heavily in the boat, one foot squashing a punnet of strawberries. He staggered to the front and sat down, as the punt rocked madly and the passengers shouted and Rob steered them out from the sudden embrace of a willow tree, announcing loudly that everything was fine.

Joe looked back at Esi leaning over the water. For a second, he thought she would jump in and swim after him. But she just stood, chest rising and falling, hands balled into fists at her sides. As the punt crawled away up the river, he had the time to see that she didn't look angry: she looked terrified.

'And what's this?' Rob resumed in his tour-guide voice, as if nothing had happened. 'A spooky Halloween treat for us all. A visit from Joseph Greene! Who, while he may appear to be a living, breathing undergraduate, is in fact *dead to me.*'

Joe smiled uncertainly at the tourists. 'Can you drop me off at the Mathematical Bridge on the way back?' he asked Rob in a stage whisper.

Rob ignored his request and pulled directly into the bank. He prodded Joe with the wet, dripping end of the punt pole until he stumbled out. 'Begone, foul spirit!' Rob shouted, propelling the punt smoothly back into the middle of the river.

Joe straightened up, hugging the book, and ran.

He took an indirect route back to college, checking constantly over his shoulder. The book was a burning coal against his chest; he didn't dare look at it, in case what he'd seen had been nothing but an illusion, his mind inventing the future he had dreamt of. As he climbed the staircase, he kept going back, like a talisman, to Esi: her quick, desperate breaths, the terror in her eyes as she had watched him drift out of her reach. If she cared about the book that much, it had to be exactly what it seemed.

By the time he got to his bedroom, his brain was a fuzz of static. He placed what was in his hands down on the desk in front of him.

Poems. By Joseph Greene. His eyes skittered off the words, then came back to rest on them. He felt them settle at his heart, sparking a tiny, glowing light. He lingered on the face of the man on the cover, familiar and uncanny at once: the dusting of silver at his temples, the frown lines between his brows. The eyes of the poet – he couldn't yet think of them as his own – were focused with single-minded intensity on the woman in his arms. Joe had never looked at anyone like that. It was unnerving, like seeing a picture taken while he was possessed, consumed by a feeling he couldn't remember.

He touched the slim hardback. It seemed to vibrate, with a potential frantic and invisible as radioactivity. The cover was a promise, but he didn't know how it would translate into reality. Until he opened the book, everything was possible. He had the strange, superstitious urge to fling it out of the window. But he already knew he wouldn't. From the moment he had seen it lying on the road, the only future that existed was the one where he read it.

He took a breath and turned to the first page.

The book began with an Introduction. It was the kind of thing he would usually have skipped – overwritten, academic, promising to 'put the poems in context' – but right now, he felt like he needed all the context he could get.

Meant to Be was a collection of poems about someone called Diana Dartnell. She was an actress, the Introduction told him, the most celebrated of her generation. And she and Joe had been – were going to be – lovers. Epic, till-death-do-us-part, legendary lovers. They would adore each other, and the words he wrote to immortalise that passion would be read, shared, recited at weddings, taught in schools. Remembered. He skimmed over the words, hardly daring to believe it, wanting to with every fibre of his soul.

He turned back to the cover, to the woman who was destined to be his muse. Her graceful black-and-white profile was somehow familiar, as if their souls had already met.

He read on with strange vertigo. The Introduction was a portrait of his life seen from the air, rendered flat and distorted. It talked about a childhood he didn't recognise, spent in poverty (his parents were solidly lower-middle-class), where his only solace was to roam the Scottish Highlands in search of inspiration (he was from the East Neuk of Fife, sixty miles from the nearest real mountain). It sketched his time at Cambridge with the breathless exuberance of a prospectus, but made no mention of Rob. Diana, of course, had gone to Cambridge too; she would graduate with a 2:2, while he would somehow manage a 2:1. He felt a mixture of surprise and relief. The only other person from their student years who merited a mention was Diana's ex-boyfriend Crispin, to whom she would later be briefly and unhappily married. The implication, that the perfect love story would be interrupted by a breakup and a marriage to someone else, struck a strange, sour note. Reminding himself that the course of true love never did run smooth, he kept reading, scouring the pages to find out when he and Diana would meet – today? Next month? After exams, in the delirious sunshine of May Week? But the Introduction was frustratingly short on details, as if their story was so well-known it didn't need to be told.

He turned the page to a spread of photographs. Here he was as a student, on crutches with his right leg bandaged. The caption told of a collision with a bike that would happen in his third year (*This year*, he thought, with a shiver of foreboding), leaving him with a permanent scar. Here, in another photograph, was Diana, the same age or a little younger, arm in arm with a friend at a party. The other girl caught his attention – her expression anxious but determined, the camera flash picking up the dark shine of her skin – but he soon moved on to the last picture, which was of him and Diana together. They were older now, in their mid-thirties, but their eyes were locked, their hands entwined, as if they were still in the first flush of new love.

He raced through the rest of the Introduction in feverish haste: how his poetry about Diana had catapulted him from relative unknown to national treasure; the awards and honours that had followed; the poems' enduring legacy as a testament to obsessive love, taking their place in the canon alongside the likes of Shakespeare and Byron (he reread this part several times). Finally, he was heartened to learn that their love story had a happy ending: at the time of writing, he and Diana were still living together in London.

The time of writing. He flicked back to the copyright page. *Retroflex Special Edition*, it said, with a logo of a capital *R* that looped backwards to draw a second, faded *R* behind it. The year of publication was 2044. He did some quick arithmetic. 'Sixty,' he murmured. Here and now, his heart hammering, his blood fizzing in his veins, the idea that he could ever be that old seemed impossible.

He had finished the Introduction. Overleaf were the stark words:

THE POEMS

He turned the page, his heart beating like a countdown.

Those poems aren't going to write themselves, Rob had said, an hour and several lifetimes ago. But they had. Here they were, laid out on page after page in neatly printed stanzas. And they were good. They were better than good: they were the poems he wished he could write, the ones that always disintegrated somewhere between his mind and the paper. These, miraculously, had made it there intact. The more he read, the more he forgot what he was reading and sank into the poems' reality: a reality centred around one woman, her beauty woven so vividly through the words that by the end, he longed for her with the rich, impossible yearning you feel for a character in a book.

He closed *Meant to Be* and sat in the afterglow. He had never been in love, but now he knew how it would feel, and why he needed that experience to write the poems that would realise his potential. The poet wrote about love as a transformation, a tearing apart of the self and remaking it as something infinitely better. He wanted to step into the furnace of that feeling and come out changed into everything he had longed to be.

He opened the book and read the poems again. And again, and

again, until he no longer had to look at the words to hear them resonating inside his skull, as if they had always been there. He wondered if he was the first poet in history to learn his work by heart before even writing it.

And the worry crept in, starting in his gut and working its way up to his fingertips, tingling where they touched the pages. Wasn't that a paradox? Shouldn't the space-time continuum be collapsing right now? He lowered the book, half expecting to see the walls dissolving, but they looked as solid as ever. It wasn't until he caught sight of himself in the mirror, so different from the suave figure on the book's cover, that he thought of something even worse. By reading about his future, had he inadvertently changed it?

Horror rushed through him. He flung the book away. It hit the edge of the bed and rebounded, falling open. A leaflet fluttered out.

He picked it up. At the top was a drawing of a friendly hourglass with googly eyes, and the heading *FREQUENTLY ASKED QUESTIONS*.

—Is it really safe to travel through time?
    Yes! Stick with your tour guide and follow the terms and
    conditions, and you'll be just fine.

—What if I cause a paradox and become my own
grandfather?
    That's between you and your grandmother!! But
    seriously, don't worry – it's impossible for anything you
    do in the past to cause a paradox, because *anything you
    do in the past has already happened.*

—So I can't step on a butterfly and accidentally change the future?

No! It's pretty deev if you think about it. You were always meant to go back in time. In a way, you already have. And once you're done, you'll return to the same future you left. Simple!

He fell backwards onto the carpet, drowning in waves of relief. The future he'd read about was safe. Nothing could change it.

When his heart had slowed its pounding, he got up. He paced to the mirror and stared at his reflection: flushed, wide-eyed, like he had woken up from a dream to find it was still happening. He held the book up next to his face, mirroring the image of the poet. He turned his head to match the angle, arms awkwardly open to embrace an invisible Diana. The resemblance wasn't perfect: aside from the obvious problem of the missing muse, there was something in the depths of the poet's eyes that he couldn't replicate, no matter how he squinted. Not *the poet*, he reminded himself. 'Joseph Greene,' he said aloud, imbuing his name with an English-accented gravitas that matched the serif font on the book's cover.

Like tilting a hologram, his perspective shifted. He saw himself from the outside, and what he saw was hilarious. He burst out laughing, falling onto his bed, pressing the book to his face. 'It's fucking real,' he said into the pages. 'It's going to happen.' He laughed and laughed, a joyous convulsion that took all the coiled-spring energy the poems had wound into him and flung it back out into the world.

When the laughter was over, he sat up. He took in the familiar

detritus of his room: the Highland cow, the bus, and the penguin
scattered across the floor; the philosophy books sitting unread on
the windowsill; his threadbare coat, hanging where he had flung
it over the back of his chair. Something pink was sticking out of
the pocket.

It didn't feel like a decision. And, after all, it wasn't. *Anything
you do in the past has already happened.* He got up, his body moving without his direction, and spread the flyer out on his desk.
Love Poems for Tomorrow. He had imagined the audience in the
ADC Theatre, sitting rapt as they witnessed the beginning of his
future. He had given that vision up because he hadn't experienced
a love worth writing about. But his future self didn't have that
problem. He had fallen in love and risen out of it better, more interesting, ready to write the poems he was always meant to write.

He opened the book again. He leafed through, considering each
poem, finally settling on one about a kiss, exuberant without being
juvenile, sensual without being embarrassing. He opened his laptop, minimised the MSN Messenger window he mainly used for
asking Rob to make him tea, and brought up his university web-
mail. In the body of a new email, he typed out the poem, word by
word, constantly checking to make sure his imperfect younger self
hadn't introduced an error. It was a strange, meditative process,
flicking back and forth between the printed page of the future and
the glowing screen of right now. He felt the words passing through
him, like he was a conduit for something greater, taking dictation
not from the muse but from a better version of himself.

He read it through and nodded in satisfaction. In the 'To' field,
he typed the email address on the flyer. As he hovered over the Send
button, a tremor of doubt assailed him. He tried to reassure himself.
They were his poems. The fact that he hadn't technically written

them yet was beside the point. But he couldn't shake the idea that he was doing something wrong, if not morally, then metaphysically. His gaze flicked to the philosophy books on the windowsill. Maybe if he had actually read them, he would have a better idea of the implications of what he was about to do.

The living room door banged, announcing Rob. 'Greeney, what have I said about hijacking the punt when I have paying customers? I had to tell my manager you were a tragic wild boy raised by swans or she would have sacked me.' His footsteps came closer. 'What are you doing back there? Are you actually working? This I have to see.'

Joe panicked, closed his eyes, and clicked Send.

Chapter Four

He shut the laptop and lunged to hide the book under his pillow. By the time Rob peeked around the door, he was poring over a philosophy textbook in a way that almost certainly looked suspicious. 'Sorry,' he said absently.

'Ah, no harm done. Only one person complained. The rest of them lapped it up. I spun it into a whole story about how you were the ghost of a student who drowned himself after failing his exams.'

'Hey,' Joe protested weakly.

'It was very moving. Especially the part where I mimed your floating corpse.' Rob paused, looking at him closely. 'Yes. That's exactly the expression. Uncanny.'

He needed to get his face under control. He closed the textbook and spun round in his chair. 'For your information, I'm going to get a 2:1.' Saying it aloud brought home what it meant: he no longer had to worry about failing. The crushing pressure lifted from his chest, finally letting him breathe.

'Great news,' said Rob. 'Happy for you. Is that what you're wearing for Halloween Formal?'

He looked down at himself. 'No. But that's not till this evening.'

Rob indicated the darkness outside. 'Through the magic of time travel, this evening is now. So come on, get spooky. We have to be there in five minutes.' He tapped the door frame and disappeared into his own bedroom.

Joe stared out at the fingernail crescent moon hanging over the battlements. Hours had passed in the present while he had been wandering the pages of the future. He got changed into his costume, but his heart wasn't in it. He felt like he was his older self, playacting at being a student again.

When he emerged, Rob was baffled. 'Why do you have a toy train hanging off your jumper?'

He indicated the bridge motif knitted into the jumper, and the deliberate rip he'd made down the middle. 'I'm the Tay Bridge Disaster.'

Rob made a face. 'Isn't that a bit tasteless?'

Plucking at the jumper for emphasis, he explained, '"The Tay Bridge Disaster". By William Topaz McGonagall.' He searched unsuccessfully for recognition in Rob's eyes. 'Worst poem ever written? Rhymes "buttresses" with "confesses"?'

Rob shook his head. 'Greeney, you're supposed to wear a costume someone other than you would have a chance in hell of recognising.'

Joe looked Rob up and down. He was dressed as usual for Formal, in a shirt and black jacket under his gown. 'What about you? Who are you supposed to be?'

'I'm Future Rob,' he said, leading the way down the stairs. 'Rob from the future.'

Joe stared at his roommate. Had he sneaked a look at the book while his back was turned? Trying to be casual, he said, 'You're still going to be wearing your undergraduate gown when you're sixty?'

'Who says I'm sixty?'

'Okay,' said Joe with exaggerated patience, 'how far in the future are you from?'

'Ten minutes.' Rob took the last flight of steps two at a time. 'I've come back to tell you the starter was *delicious*.'

They headed into the college dining hall, where the long tables were lined with dripping candles and grinning pumpkins. Joe sat opposite Rob at the edge of their group of friends. Two of them asked about his costume, and he answered mechanically, barely hearing himself over the poetry singing wildly through his head.

Some time later, Rob clapped his hands in Joe's face. 'Greeney, you're miles away. What's up?'

Through the haze of wine, Joe focused on his friend. He wanted to tell Rob. He was desperate to tell Rob, because Rob was the person he talked to about important things, and this was by some orders of magnitude the most important thing that had ever happened. But Rob was also a physicist. Joe didn't know much about physics, but he suspected that if he opened the conversation with the fact that time travel was real and he had the proof under his pillow, Rob would have trouble getting past that to discuss the vastly more interesting topic of Joe's future poetic greatness.

He had to tell Rob. There was no way in a million years he could tell Rob. He hovered, torn between two incompatible compulsions, until his mouth opened of its own accord and an inarticulate noise came out.

Rob leaned across the table. 'What?'

He could test the water. Pitch it as a hypothetical, then decide on the basis of Rob's reaction whether to make it true. 'Could time travel be real?'

Rob gave him a warning look. 'Do you really want to get into this? You've had most of a bottle of wine.'

He was offended. 'You saying I can't keep up?'

'I'm saying nothing. I'm just reminding you that last time I tried to talk to you about physics, you hid under the pool table and sang The Proclaimers until I went away.'

He let that pass. 'I mean it. I want to know.'

Rob's face lit up. 'Okay, so, general relativity allows for closed timelike curves. And the most intuitive solution that gets you a space-time with CTCs is a traversable wormhole of some kind . . .'

He tried to listen, but the technical jargon paled to the wonder of having seen his future, printed in black and white. He imagined what his and Diana's house in London would be like. Huge, probably: she was a successful actress, and *Meant to Be* must have sold a fair number of copies. No one went into poetry for the money, of course, but love was very marketable, and he prided himself that the poems were written in plain, unpretentious language, accessible without being dumbed down. He would be a poet of the people, opening the genre up to a whole new audience. Young poets from underrepresented backgrounds would write to him, thanking him for making their art possible.

Rob was still talking. 'So to make a traversable wormhole, you'd need some amount of negative energy, which is a challenge because, at least at the moment, that's a purely hypothetical construct . . .'

Joe's attention drifted up the room to the dais, where the Master and Fellows sat with their guests at High Table. Famous alumni were sometimes invited back to dine. He imagined himself and Diana up there, exchanging witty repartee with his former professors. 'Mr Greene was, of course, the first student from his school to be admitted to Cambridge,' the Master was saying as Diana affectionately squeezed Joe's arm, 'making his achievements all the more remarkable . . .'

Rob's voice rose in excitement. 'But if you ask me, the only model that makes any actual sense is Deutsch's account, which relies on the many-worlds interpretation of quantum mechanics . . .'

They would probably both get OBEs. Or Diana would be a dame, and he would get a knighthood. He didn't approve of the British Empire or the Royal Family, but he was pretty sure he would sell out on his principles if it meant he got to be called Sir for the rest of his life. *Sir Joseph Greene.* He mouthed it silently. It had a ring to it, but it did mean he'd have to go by his full name from now on. 'Joe' was right out.

'. . . Does that answer your question?'

He snapped back to the present. Rob was looking at him earnestly.

'So you're saying,' he said, working more from Rob's tone than from his words, 'that if someone discovered time travel, it would be big news. Physics-wise. Like – folk who are into physics would want to talk about it.'

'Are you kidding?' Rob laughed. 'They'd never want to talk about anything else.'

His heart sank. 'Okay.' He tipped back the last of his wine. 'Thanks for clearing that up.'

'No problem.' People were starting to leave, drifting towards the bar for the party. 'Since when have you been interested in this stuff?'

He flailed for a lie. He gestured at Rob's conspicuous lack of a costume. 'I was wondering if Future Rob could ever pay us a visit for real.'

'What are you talking about? Future Rob *is* real. I'll prove it.' He put a hand to his temple, closing his eyes. 'I have come back from the party to tell you that they're about to play "Thriller".'

As they left the dining hall and descended the steps towards the bar, a familiar bassline started up. 'Wow,' said Joe, with drawn-out amazement. 'Sorry I ever doubted you.'

In the bar, the party was already in full swing, the tidemark of sweat rising up the walls. Vampires, devils, and a sexy Magna Carta were tearing up the small square of carpet that passed for a dancefloor. He made a half-hearted effort to join in, but he was too hot in his jumper, and, more importantly, his brain was on fire. He pushed his way out of the bar and stood at the side of the court, staring up at the slender moon. His soul itched with impatience to fast-forward the present and land cleanly in the future.

Someone collided with his shoulder. Rob, sweaty and euphoric, surrounded by a gang of their friends. 'Greeney! You're coming to the Kambar. No arguments.'

The Kambar was the least terrible of Cambridge's collection of terrible clubs, in that it played indie instead of endless loops of 'Build Me Up Buttercup', and also had beanbags. Joe tailed Rob and his friends up Bene't Street, lagging farther and farther behind until he was alone. Laughter drifted back to him like radio signals from a distant planet. He visualised the next few hours: going through the motions of enjoying a night out, pretending to exist in the moment when his entire being was straining beyond it.

He turned towards the market square. The street seemed to stretch out forever, the roof of the Guildhall pointing the way to infinity. Outside the Cambridge Arts Theatre, a group of girls stood in a circle, hugging themselves against the cold. One of them was dressed as an angel. She wore a white silk gown, and a tinsel halo nestled in her dark curls. She laughed at something he couldn't hear, then stared away over her friends' shoulders, like she was looking through the present to see what was on the other side.

'Greeney!' Rob yelled. 'Come on!'

The girl was swaying, her gown shadowing the impossibly graceful movement of her body. Something about her was intensely familiar. He stepped closer, trying to work out where he knew her from. Not college; not a seminar; not the awkward charity blind date that had ended with him and his match agreeing she should get back together with her boyfriend. No, what he felt when he looked at this girl was both more distant and more intimate, as though they had spent lifetimes together in a dream.

She turned her head, looking up at the moon. For an instant, her profile was caught in a streetlight. His heart did a somersault.

'Greeney!' Rob had been shouting for a while. 'Last chance, or we're leaving you behind!'

Joe didn't answer, because he had just realised the girl was Diana.

Chapter Five

At first, he didn't believe it. She was an idea from a book: she couldn't be here. Had he somehow willed her into existence, constructed her like a mad scientist out of words and desire? But as he moved closer, it became undeniable. Those were her eyes, her pale green eyes, *like chips of sea-glass*; that was her smile, the enigmatic, shifting smile he had compared to *a windblown shadow*. He walked on like she was his destination, like his whole life had been a long, slow trudge towards her.

Just before he reached her, a flicker of doubt assailed him. The book didn't say exactly where and when they had first met. How could he be sure this was the right moment?

The hesitation lasted until he remembered the leaflet. *Anything you do in the past has already happened.* He wouldn't be here, inches from her, unless this were meant to be. A beatific smile spread across his face. *And on that fateful night*, a voice like the Introduction said in his mind, *Joseph Greene would meet his eternal muse, his one great love.*

'Diana Dartnell.'

The shock of her attention paralysed him. It was as if he had been standing in a gallery, admiring a portrait of some long-dead beauty, only for the subject to lean out of the frame and beckon him closer. But when their eyes met, he realised he had seen her before. In fact, he had collided with her, on his way out of Trinity after his visit to the Wren Library. The sense of rightness, of destiny, swelled in him like a crescendo. His muse had appeared exactly when she was needed; he just hadn't had the sense to recognise her.

She looked at him curiously. 'Yes?'

And he froze. His first chance to talk to the love of his life, and he had no idea what to say. He prodded his brain to think of something, but his brain was for some reason fixating on her costume, and just kept repeating the same stupid chat-up line about whether it had hurt when she fell from heaven. He was about to walk away, pretend it had all been a misunderstanding, when something came into focus like the sun through a magnifying glass. He didn't need to find new words to say to her: he already had a book full of them. He cleared his throat and recited from memory:

> *No one who had seen her*
> *dressed as the night, the moon caught in her hair*
> *could say: I do not know beauty.*
> *For beauty*
> *demanding to be known*
> *spilled out of her, like blood-dark wine*
> *from the shattered glass of her heart.*

She stared at him in utter confusion. 'I'm sorry, what?'

He felt like he had stepped onto a bridge that had crumbled. The air yawned beneath him; the waves clamoured for his bones. He sank down into himself. 'It's – it's poetry.'

'Yes, I am familiar with the concept.' Her voice was low, her accent brittle glass. She glanced downward, her immaculate brows knitting in a frown. 'Why do you have a toy train hanging off your jumper?'

'I'm "The Tay Bridge Disaster",' he explained, confident she would get it.

She shot a look at one of her friends. 'Isn't that in rather bad taste?'

'No, it's – the poem—' He ran a hand through his hair. 'Mc-Gonagall? "For the stronger we our houses do build / The less chance we have of being killed"?'

She studied him for a moment with perfect disdain. 'I preferred the first one,' she said, and turned back to her friends.

'We should go,' one of them was saying, as if Joe hadn't spoken, as if he weren't falling screaming into icy water. 'Cindies is only free entry till ten.'

Diana sighed. 'And what a tragedy it would be to miss out on Cindies.' Under the performative ennui, he caught a longing for something else, a desire for the transcendent that he recognised.

Diana's friend nudged her, a knowing look in her eyes. 'Crispin's already there.'

The name ricocheted through Joe's drunken brain. Crispin. Diana's future briefly-husband: the one blip in their perfect love story. Unless she knew multiple people called Crispin, which, given that she was at Trinity, wasn't completely outwith the bounds of possibility.

The name had an effect on Diana too. She stood taller; one hand went faux-carelessly to her hair, adjusting her halo. 'Fine,' she said in a clipped tone. 'Let's go.' She swept away, a queen trailed by her ladies-in-waiting. Joe watched her go with barren disbelief. They had just met. She couldn't possibly be leaving.

'Diana,' he called after her.

She turned, staring at him with a mixture of puzzlement and annoyance. 'I'm sorry. Do I know you?'

'Not yet.' He tried to look compelling and mysterious. He hoped he was doing it right and not just squinting. 'But you will.'

Her smile made his whole body melt with relief. 'All right, Train Boy. I'll bite. Why am I going to know you?'

He walked up to her. The closer he got, the more real she became: the light pink flush under her pale cheeks, the almost-invisible freckles dusted around her eyes. He reached out, brushing his hand against her tinsel halo. 'Because we're meant to be.'

One of her friends gasped.

Diana's hand reached up to his. Their fingers touched for the first time. Electricity wasn't a good enough metaphor: he experienced it as alchemy, his entire substance disassembled and rearranged.

'That is' – her eyes wandered over his face in fascination – '*incredibly* creepy.' With a quick, cool shove, she pushed him away. 'Goodbye forever.'

She swept past him, her friends moving in protectively on either side. He watched, not quite understanding what had happened, as his future walked away.

HE WENT TO the Kambar. He didn't know what else to do but try to exorcise the humiliation through angry dancing and cheap cider. Somewhere along the way, he accidentally flushed the toy train down the toilet. The last thing he remembered was trying to explain to a girl dressed as Socrates that this was completely appropriate, since McGonagall's poem clearly stated that 'down went the train and passengers into the Tay', but she didn't seem very interested.

He woke slumped over his desk.

He sat up, snort-coughing. Something was stuck to his cheek. He prised it free. It was one of his poetry notebooks, the open page scrawled with words. Most of them were unreadable; with some effort, he deciphered *scintillating*, *limerence*, and, puzzlingly, *banana*. This, he had underlined three times, with a note in the margin saying *rhymes!!*

Like a machete moving through honey, his brain cut through the confusion. He had been trying to write a poem about Diana.

The events of the previous night sluiced in, drowning him. He closed his eyes, reliving every awkward millisecond: the way she had looked at him after he quoted the poem, that awful mix of bafflement and pity; how she had left, and he had ceased to exist. But the image that haunted him was her face just before she had walked away: scornful, affronted, maybe even a little horrified.

When he finally opened his eyes, he saw his laptop was open. A new dread pooled in his guts. Had he tried to send her an email? He felt a flash of resentment at all these other versions of him – the future poet, the past drunk – who kept making decisions without him being present to approve them. He lunged for the laptop, pulling it towards him. There was nothing new in his sent items, but there was an unread message at the top of his inbox. It wasn't from Diana. It was from someone called LPFT, and the subject line was *Re: submission*.

Dear Joseph Greene,

We are pleased to let you know that your poem 'A Taste of Stars'
has been selected for inclusion in Love Poems for Tomorrow.

His heart burst. This was it: his first step, proof that all the
dreaming and longing and wanting hadn't been in vain. He experienced a moment of pure, uncomplicated happiness. Then he
read the next line:

The actor you have been paired with is: Diana Dartnell.

He felt hot, then cold, then sick to his stomach. It was perfect
and it was terrible, all at once. Stars floating in his vision, he read on:

You and your partner will workshop the performance of your
piece to ensure it reflects your creative intent. Please attend a
preliminary meeting of all writers and cast at the ADC Theatre at
5pm on Friday, 4th November.

Three days from now, he had to walk into a room with Diana
Dartnell and convince her that he was not a creepy stalker with a
train fetish, but was in fact the man of her dreams.

He projected the moment in his mind's eye: Diana sitting on
the stage, still in the white dress and tinsel halo, as he walked
up the aisle towards her. He tried to imagine meeting her eyes,
seeing her recognise the deep kinship between their souls. But
her expression kept changing, morphing into the horror-tinged
contempt she had worn last night.

He got up too fast, blood rushing from his pounding head. He groped under his pillow for the book of poems. He was half-afraid it would have disappeared or turned into gibberish, but when he pulled it out, it was unchanged: his name, the title, the photograph of him and Diana on the cover. He pulled out the leaflet and reread it, going over the questions and answers until he started to calm down. It was right here in black and white: the past couldn't change. However much of a mistake it seemed, last night's meeting with Diana had been the way it was meant to happen.

He slumped down against the side of the bed. He had wondered why the Introduction didn't tell the story of how they met. Now he knew it was because their first interaction had been a disaster. She would forgive him – she had to, for the future to happen – but he couldn't imagine how. The gap between who he was and who he was meant to be yawned like a chasm, and he had no idea how to cross it.

His room closed in on him: the Highland cow and the bus abandoned on the floor, the penguin staring up at him like a goofy reflection. Everything reminded him of who he was now, the mess and embarrassment of his current self. He had to get out. He slipped the book into his coat pocket and left, slamming the door behind him.

Outside, the Chapel clock told him it was already midday. As he crossed the threshold of college, squinting in the pale sunshine, Esi stepped into his path. 'Give me the book back.'

The sight of her was a shock to his heart. He had forgotten, in the chaotic whirl of revelation that had consumed the past twenty-four hours, that it had all started with her. He had met her as a stranger, but she had known who he was from the beginning.

With a peculiar lurch, he saw her mocking, familiar manner in a new light. 'Why did you even have it? You that much of a fan?' He saw her flinch, and he pursued it. 'See that poet you had to study at school. The one you thought was overrated. That was me, wasn't it?'

She ignored his last question. 'The book was a free gift. I need it back because . . .' She took in a ragged breath. 'I'm here in the past to change something, and if you start making other changes because you know stuff you shouldn't, then you could undo my change, and I—'

'Wait,' he interrupted, his heart imploding. 'You're saying the past can change?'

Chapter Six

'I don't understand,' he went on. 'The leaflet says—'

'I know what the leaflet says.' She looked over his shoulder. 'Just – please tell me you haven't read the book.'

He laughed in her face. 'Of course I have! You're telling me if someone gave you a book about your future, you wouldn't read it?'

'I didn't give it to you. You took it.' She closed her eyes in despair. 'Yeah, I'd read it,' she added quietly.

The wind spiralled, sending red leaves skittering around their feet. 'Look,' he said. 'Can I get you a coffee?'

She looked at him like he'd offered to get her a hamster. 'What?'

'Just – my friend Rob says I'm the worst person to talk to about time travel in the best of circumstances. And this is not the best of circumstances, because I'm extremely hungover just now. So ideally, I'd want some caffeine in my system before we get into closed timelike whatevers. If that's all right with you?'

'I guess I can't just let you walk away with all that future stuff in your head.' She hesitated. 'Fine. Let's get a coffee.'

He dithered over where to take her, until he remembered she wasn't his destined beloved and he could take her anywhere he liked. He decided on Indigo, a tiny café up the narrow side street of St Edward's Passage. 'This is on me, by the way,' he said as they stood at the counter. 'Least I can do for my biggest fan.'

Stone-faced, she scanned the price list. 'Large mocha,' she said, 'extra marshmallows,' and stamped away upstairs.

He ordered a latte for himself, and carried the drinks up the creaking steps. The tables were proportionally tiny: when he sat down opposite Esi, he was startled by her closeness. She leaned in farther, her eyes flickering down to his cheek. His heart stuttered.

'You've got something . . .' She squinted, her finger hovering near his face. 'It looks like *banana* written backwards?' He flushed, rubbing at his cheek. She was trying unsuccessfully not to laugh. 'The Shakespeare of our time,' she murmured.

He cleared his throat, feeling as awkward as if he were on a first date. 'So. See this.' He took the book out of his pocket and extracted the leaflet. 'It says, "anything you do in the past has already happened".'

'Sure. That's the official line.' She leaned back in her chair. 'I think it's bullshit.'

'Okay,' he said, trying to keep his voice calm. 'Why?'

'The terms and conditions.'

He laughed. 'I was expecting something a wee bit more dramatic.'

A brief smile lit her face. 'Stay with me. It gets good. So, here's what they make us agree to.' She counted on her fingers. 'Time travellers may not carry any future technology. Time travellers must stay with the tour guide at all times. Time travellers may only enter the wormhole between local hours of nine a.m. till twelve p.m., and one p.m. till five p.m. each day—'

'Wormhole?' he interrupted. 'There's a wormhole?'

She gave him a deadpan look. 'What did you think, we got the bus?'

He spluttered out a laugh; she looked pleased despite herself. 'Give me a break!' he protested. 'I'm still trying to process the fact that I'm a tourist destination.' He took a gulp of coffee. 'So where is it, this wormhole?'

Esi picked a marshmallow off the top of her mocha and popped it in her mouth, briefly closing her eyes. 'King's Lane.'

King's Lane was a concrete alley, attached to the Gothic splendour of King's College like a tin can to a thoroughbred's tail. No one went down King's Lane for any reason but to relieve themselves at the end of a night out. 'I'm sorry. You're telling me there's a wormhole to the future, and it's in *Piss Alley*?'

She glanced over her shoulder. 'Sure, just announce it to everyone.'

'It's fine. This is Cambridge. They're just going to assume we're rehearsing a play.' She rolled her eyes, and he smiled. 'Why, are you worried folk might try and walk through?'

'They can't,' she said impatiently. 'It's hidden. There's a password you have to say to reveal it. And no, I'm not telling you what it is. I'm not even going back through myself until I'm done making my change. Anyway, can I get back to my point?'

'Right. Sorry,' he said graciously. 'You were reciting the small print.'

'A lot of it's about the target. That's you,' she explained, wiggling her fingers at him. 'Time travellers may not follow the target into any private premises, or beyond the radius of 0.5 miles of the wormhole. Time travellers may leave gifts for the target, but said gifts may not contain any text or media originating from the future. Time travellers may not interact with the target directly—'

'Sorry, just to check,' he interrupted her. 'You agreed to these terms and conditions?'

'Obviously. Otherwise they wouldn't have let me on the trip. But I ran away from the tour guide the first chance I got, and now I'm just trying to stay out of her way.'

'And the company – they haven't sent out a search party? They're okay with you just disappearing?'

'I don't know if they're okay with it. Honestly, I don't care. That's not the point. The point is . . .' She leaned across the table, her gaze locked on his. 'They don't want us getting anywhere near you. It's like they're trying to stop us doing anything that might change your future. But if the leaflet's true, nothing can change your future. So why do they need us to agree to all that?'

He followed her logic. 'So you think time travel *can* change the future, they're just pretending it can't?' She nodded. 'But – that can't be right. People would know if the future was changing. They'd *notice*.'

'Would they?' She lifted her chin. 'What if it was changing all the time, but our memories were changing too? No one would even realise it was happening.'

He felt a hallucinatory lurch at the thought. If she was right, his entire life could be being rewritten from moment to moment, his sense of a persistent self nothing but an illusion. And it was worse than that. His glorious future could dissolve at any second.

It wasn't true. He couldn't let it be true. He sat back, crossing his arms. 'Nah.'

She looked affronted. 'What do you mean, "nah"?'

'I mean, nah, I don't buy it. There's plenty of other reasons they might have those terms and conditions. Maybe it's about respect.

Maybe they just want to give me a wee bit of privacy. It doesn't have to be a conspiracy theory.'

She choked out a laugh. 'Conspiracy theory?'

'And no company would do that. Imagine, if time travel could really change the past and they knew it. They'd never take the risk. They could write their customers out of existence. They could write *themselves* out of existence. Flimsy terms and conditions aren't going to be enough to protect against that.'

She made a soft, frustrated sound. 'You're sitting there with a book of poems you haven't written yet, and you're seriously trying to tell me time travel can't change the past?'

His coffee was starting to get cold, but he didn't care: he was too absorbed in their argument. 'No, I get it. I had the same thought. But think about it. What if you were always meant to come back in time?' He leaned across the table, holding her gaze. 'You'd always have dropped the book. I'd always have read it. It would always have been part of my story.'

She didn't lean away. 'What are you saying?'

'I'm saying – maybe it doesn't change the future. Maybe it creates it.' He laid his hand on the book. 'Honestly, before, I never really believed all this stuff was possible. I wanted it – Jesus, I *really* wanted it – but did I actually think I could get there? Not in a million years. Now? I know I can. Because look. It happened.' She was watching him intently, but he didn't register her expression; he was in full flow, as if he were in a supervision with his Director of Studies but it was going well for a change. 'So the company line makes sense to me. And it's not miles off from how some philosophers have thought about time travel. The past can't change,' he finished triumphantly, 'because any attempt to change it would always already have happened.'

Her face crumpled. She covered her mouth with her hand, her eyes filling with tears.

He reared back. 'Jesus. Fuck, I'm sorry. Did I— What did I say?'

A tear spilled from her eye, and she dashed it away. 'You know it all, don't you? This was stupid. I should never have talked to you.' She got up, chair screeching across the floorboards.

His mind raced, trying to understand. She was here to change something: something so important she had almost jumped into a river to stop him from messing it up. 'Esi, wait.'

She turned, red-eyed. He felt the trembling weight of the moment: what he said next could hold her here, or push her away. He made a wild, desperate guess. 'You're here to save someone.'

She closed her eyes. The tears spilled over as she nodded. He watched her carefully as she came back to the table. 'Who?'

'My mum.' She sat down, scrubbing wildly at her eyes. 'I told you I was a bomb crater, right? She was the bomb.'

He swallowed. 'What happened?'

'Car accident. She was driving, and a truck sideswiped her. Wrong place, wrong time.' She looked down, picking at the backs of her hands. 'I was eight. Old enough to understand she was gone, not old enough to handle it.'

He shifted in his seat. 'I'm sorry.'

'Yeah. Everyone's sorry.' She rubbed her sleeve across her eyes. 'My sisters, they were younger. After a while, they didn't even remember her. I ended up being more of a mum to them, in the end. Well, me and my aunties. And my dad – he grieved, but his friends from church carried him through. Me – it broke me.' She looked up, and he felt for an instant the full force of her loss. 'People throw that word around, but I mean it. When my mum

died, the person I was meant to be died too. And all that's left is –
this.' She made an angry gesture at herself.

He wanted to say something – that she shouldn't talk about herself like that, that her mum would have wanted her to move on – but
in the face of her grief, all his words sounded useless. 'But – that's
got to still be in the future, right? The book's from 2044. If that's
when you're from, there's no way you're eight in the present.'

'No. I'm not even born.'

'So why come back to now?'

'When it happened . . .' She took a breath. 'She was driving back
here. Back to Cambridge, for the twenty-fifth anniversary of an
award she'd won on the twenty-third of June 2006.'

He saw it like a warped perspective coming into focus. 'She's a
student here.'

She nodded. 'Same year as you. When Retroflex said they were
launching a trip to see you, I knew that was my chance. Right
place, right time.' She pressed her palms to her cheeks. 'So. What
they say, about how the past doesn't change? I can't think like that.
What happened to her – what's going to happen . . .' Her eyes met
his, burning. 'You can't tell me that was meant to be.'

He looked down at the leaflet. He wanted to believe it for himself so badly. Now he understood why she was so desperate to believe the opposite. 'I'm not saying it's *meant to be*. I don't think
it's right, or that God wants it, or any of that shite. I just think –
maybe it's how the universe works. What's going to happen happens, and we can't change it.'

Her red-rimmed eyes met his. 'Do you know that for sure?'

'Fuck no.' He laughed. 'I'm a philosopher. Knowing stuff isn't
our strong suit.'

She swirled the dregs in her mug. 'And I don't know the future

can change. But I believe it. Because I have to. I'll find her, and I'll
do whatever it takes to stop her winning that award, so she's got
no reason to come back here on that day.'

'And then what? You go back through the wormhole into the
future?' He rubbed his temples, wincing. 'But – a different future
from the one you left?'

'A better one. The future me and my family were supposed to
have.' She looked down at her hands. 'And I'll be the me I was
always meant to be.'

'Okay.' He sat back. 'So do it. I might not agree that it's possible,
but I'm not going to stop you trying.'

She shook her head. 'It's not that simple. Have you heard of the
butterfly effect?'

'Aye, it came out last year. The guy who goes back in time and
rewrites his childhood, but he keeps making everything worse?'
She looked at him blankly. 'Oh. I thought you meant the film.
Guess that one didn't stand the test of time.' He frowned. 'The
butterfly effect. What, a butterfly flaps its wings and ends up causing a hurricane?'

'Tiny changes build up.' She interlocked her thumbs, spreading
out her fingers. 'I need to stop my mum winning that award. But
I can't change anything else. If I make the wrong change, even a
small one, the consequences could be huge. She might not meet
my dad. She might stay here and do a PhD, or she might move back
to Ghana, or – or some other accident might happen that I can't
save her from.' She looked at him, her expression solemn. 'Since I
got here, I've been trying to stay out of people's way. Affect as little
as possible. This' – she gestured between the two of them – 'this is
a huge risk. I could be making a million tiny changes, just by talking to you. But I had to make sure you're not going to do anything

differently because of the book. You have to act like you never read it. Do whatever you were going to do before.'

He rubbed his face, smearing the words from his drunken poem. 'Uh-huh.'

She was looking at him uneasily. 'What?'

He gave her a slightly edited rundown of the events of the previous night. Her face steadily fell, until she looked almost as appalled as when she'd first seen him in the coffee shop.

She pinched her forehead. 'I'm sorry. I want to make sure I understand. You walked up to Diana Dartnell dressed as a railway accident and told her you're her destiny?'

Through her words, he saw himself from Diana's perspective: a drunken imbecile, acting like she owed him her attention. He winced. 'I truly wish that summary was less accurate.'

Esi made a grinding noise in her throat. 'This is exactly what I was afraid of. All I had to do was come here and change one thing, and now it's fucked and it's all my *fault*—' Her head snapped up, braids flying. 'You've got to fix this.'

Her terror cut through his shame. 'I don't understand. Why would anything I do affect your mum?'

She grabbed the book and opened it, turning to the page with the photographs. She tapped the girl with her arm around Diana. In a rush, he saw past the differences – the cool tone of her complexion where Esi's was warm, the shining fall of her straightened hair – to the likeness in her cheekbones, her eyes, her nervous smile. 'Because they're friends. Her and Diana Dartnell. Not in the future, but – here and now.' She looked up in desperation. 'If you and Diana don't get together when you're supposed to, that changes Diana's path. Which changes my mum's path.' She mimed an explosion with her fingers. 'My one change gets butterfly-hurricaned into nothing.'

Chapter Seven

He stared at her across the table. Her vision of the universe – unstable, rewriteable, constantly in flux – possessed him. Could she be right? By walking up to Diana last night, had he knocked his entire future off course?

'Me and Diana,' he said, trying to stay calm. 'Do you know for sure that's not how we first met?'

She made a face. 'Of course it's not how you first met. That'd be ridiculous—'

'Do you know for sure?' he interrupted. 'Come on, you must know how we got together. You had to study me in school, for fuck's sake.'

'Honestly, I tuned most of it out. But no. I don't think they ever told us how you met.' She stared at him thoughtfully. 'Did you even get together at Cambridge?'

'You're asking *me*?'

She bit her lip. 'You must've done. That's how all the fancy people end up knowing each other, right?'

'Right,' he agreed. 'Where else would I have met someone like her?'

'Okay. So you met here. But there's no way you were supposed to just walk up to her in the street and tell her you're meant to be.'

'How do you know?'

She spluttered. 'Because I know! No romance in history has ever started like that.'

'And you're an expert?'

'Actually, yeah. I read a lot of romance.' She sat back, looking embarrassed. 'And no, I'm not accepting any comments on that.'

Something clicked in his mind. He started laughing. 'It all makes sense. Don't you see?' He leaned across the table, beaming. 'You're going to help me and Diana get together.'

Her face was a picture of confusion. 'I don't get it. Why do you think you need help, if you believe it's meant to be?'

'Because it's all meant to be. All of it. You were meant to come back in time. You and your – romance expertise, and your knowledge of the future, and . . .' He shook his head, delighted. 'Now I see it, it's obvious that's the only way it could happen. Diana's way out of my league. Or that's what I'd think, if I didn't know I was going to be with her.'

Esi's smile started small and grew until it was wide and dazzling. 'You,' she said, shaking her head, 'are crazy.'

'They didn't teach you that in school?'

'Maybe. Told you, I wasn't listening.' Her smile faded. 'But – I can't think like that. Like everything's going to turn out the same no matter what.'

'That's fine,' he insisted. 'We don't have to agree on how this all works. What matters is, we both want me and Diana to get together. Right?'

She nodded slowly. 'Right.'

He tapped the photograph. 'And while you're helping me with that, I can help you find your mum.'

She looked suspicious. 'Why would you help me find her if you don't think I can save her?'

He shrugged. 'You might as well try. Worst case, you get to see her one last time.'

Her eyes flicked up to the ceiling. 'Okay,' she said. 'Deal.'

She slid her hand into his. She had already affected his life so profoundly that it was strange they hadn't touched until now. Her palm was cool and soft, as lightly anchored to this moment as the rest of her. He could almost feel the gulf of time stretching between them. It made him a little dizzy.

She coughed, drawing back her hand. In search of somewhere to look, he focused on the photograph. He felt ashamed of how quickly he had turned the page, more interested in his own story. Now, knowing how this girl's story ended, there was a haunting quality to the picture: her lifted chin, her tense, bare shoulders, the sea of white faces behind her. 'Do you know what college she's at? Or what she's studying?'

Esi shook her head. 'She never really talked about her time here. It wasn't easy for her. She never felt like she belonged, and she had to work twice as hard as the white students to get half as far. I guess she didn't want to relive that.' She shrugged. 'I went through the stuff she left behind, but either she got rid of anything from here or she never kept it in the first place.'

'But she still came back twenty-five years later. So whatever she got the award for must have been important to her.' He tapped the table, thinking. 'You could try asking at student registry. They should have a record of everyone who's studying here.'

'Already tried. They wouldn't tell me anything. Data protection, apparently.' She folded her arms grumpily. 'Didn't know you had that back here in medieval times.'

'Okay, so we bypass the official channels. We've got her picture. We can make photocopies.'

'Photo – copies?'

'Come on, the clue is in the word.'

'Oh. Right.' She frowned. 'You mean, like, put posters up?'

'Aye. And we can ask around. Someone's bound to know someone who knows someone who—'

'No,' she interrupted. 'No asking around, no posters. I told you, I don't want to affect anything else in her life. Getting everyone talking about her, sticking her face up all over town? Can you imagine the changes that might set off?' She shook her head tightly. 'I want to find her quietly. If I do it right, she'll never even know I was here.' In her guarded posture, he sensed something she wasn't saying. But the same intuition told him not to push it. 'I need to focus on the award. If I can find out what it is, I can try and change who wins it.' Catching his look, she added, 'I know you think that's impossible. Just humour me.'

'So was it an academic thing, a sports cup – what?'

'It would've been something academic.' She fiddled with her braids. 'She was so smart, so focused. I can't see her caring that much about anything else.'

'So we're looking for academic awards that get given out on the twenty-third of June. I can ask my Director of Studies,' he offered. 'She knows about all that stuff.'

Esi nodded. He sensed a change in her bearing, as if a deep, thrumming tension had been released. He remembered what she'd said. *I've been trying to stay out of people's way.* Until now, she'd been alone in this. 'Okay,' she said decisively. 'Now we need to figure out your next move with Diana. I'm guessing you haven't seen her since . . .'

'Since our legendarily romantic first encounter?' She smirked. 'No. But the good news is, I've got a reason to see her again. I got into this poetry workshop, and she's the one performing my poem. Which means I'm going to meet her at the ADC Theatre on Friday.'

'Friday as in three days from now?' She looked him up and down, as if calculating how long it would take to transform him into someone Diana might find appealing. She sighed. 'Let's be clear about what I can offer. I can't give you any inside information. I probably know less about you and Diana than anyone else on this trip. But I can help make sure the next time you see her, you don't act like such a nozz.'

'Nozz?'

'You know what you did. Figure it out.' She hid her smile. 'The good news is, Friday's my day off. What time's your poetry thing?'

'Five p.m.'

'Let's meet a couple of hours before to talk it through. And get you some better clothes. What kind of budget are we working with?'

A laugh escaped him. 'Basically none?'

'That might be a problem. If you're going to impress her, we need to go high-end.'

'What about charity shops? My friend Holly's always talking about finding cheap designer stuff on Burleigh Street.'

Esi looked sceptical. 'Guess we can give it a try. In the meantime, we should stay in touch. Do you have a phone?'

'*Do I have a phone*,' he scoffed, taking it out. 'Come on. It's 2005.' Like all his phones, it was a hand-me-down from Kirsty, but she had got bored of it faster than usual, so it was surprisingly up-to-the-minute: a Motorola flip model with an etched keypad and a second screen on the outside. He was quite proud of it. Esi's was a chunky, old-fashioned Nokia, the kind he used to have in high school. 'Wow,' he said. 'Vintage.'

She looked at her phone, then at his. 'I literally can't see the difference.'

'Mine has a colour screen,' he protested.

'Wow. Are you sure it's not you who's from the future?'

They exchanged numbers, Esi grumbling about the stupidity of devices with physical buttons, and left the café. At the corner of Bene't Street, she turned left. 'See you Friday.'

'See you.' Something occurred to him. 'Wait. What about the time travellers? Won't the tour guide freak out if she sees us together?'

'She won't. Burleigh Street's outside her range. 0.5-mile radius, remember?'

He shook his head, smiling. 'For someone who doesn't respect the terms and conditions, you certainly have them memorised.'

She hissed, drawing back into the shelter of the cash machine. 'Not well enough. Looks like I overshot lunch break.'

He peered round the corner. The woman in the tabard was waiting outside the entrance of college, looking as bored as usual.

'That's Vera,' said Esi. 'The tour guide.'

'*Vera?*' He did a double take. 'All the Veras I know are over a hundred.'

'Guess that means it's due for a comeback.' Behind Vera, a girl in a cropped Fair Isle jumper and a boy in wide, flapping trousers were anxiously watching the gate. Esi shook her head. 'I'll leave you to your fans. Bye, Joseph Greene.'

The formality of his full name made him laugh. 'Bye.'

As she sidled away up Bene't Street, he went on towards college.

He tried to compose his face into a poetic expression, but he was so conscious of the time travellers staring that it made him forget how to walk. He tripped, catching himself on the steps. Cheeks burning, he scrambled up and hurried through the gate. So much for living up to his own legend.

He checked his pigeonhole, finding a green feather, a paperweight in the shape of a cat, and a scribbled note that said *LOVE*. Before, he would have binned them or left them in the blank pigeonhole of a student who'd dropped out, but now, they were precious mementos of his future. He pocketed them and headed up the staircase, past a man running down with a plastic sword and a look of bitter disappointment. Joe entered the living room to find Rob posing for a picture, a Highland cow in one hand and a London bus in the other.

He stared. 'What are you doing with Hamish and Clive?'

'Celebrating,' said Rob with a grin. 'These two just helped me foil an attempted assassination.'

'How?'

'Stunned him with the Highland cow and then ran him over with the bus.'

'Great. Congratulations.' He looked back, reconfiguring his impression of the man on the stairs. 'So that was your nemesis?'

Rob snorted. 'You think I could get Darcy with a basic combo like that? No. Next time we meet on the battlefield, I'm going to have to whip out something truly unprecedented.' He threw Hamish and Clive at Joe, who completely failed to catch them. 'How about you? Did you submit to that poetry thing I told you about?'

'Aye, I did.' He went on into his bedroom.

Rob followed him expectantly. 'And?'

He let himself smile. 'I got in.'

Rob's face lit up. 'Nice one, Greeney! So who did you write a poem about?'

'Oh. Uh – just this girl.'

'"Just this girl",' Rob proclaimed, hand on his heart. 'There's the competition-winning eloquence I'd expect from our future poet laureate.' He went to sit on Joe's bed. 'Does "this girl" have a name? Or does her perfection defy our mortal labels?'

Joe smiled dreamily as he sat down to check his email. 'Her name's Diana.' There were no further communications from Love Poems for Tomorrow, but there was one from Dr Lewis, his Director of Studies. The subject line was a question mark. The body of the email was empty. 'Why is Dr Lewis sending me blank emails?'

Rob looked over Joe's shoulder. 'Maybe she's wondering why you're not at your supervision.'

'What?' His heart skipped. He checked his watch, cross-referencing against his crumpled mental timetable. Rob was right: he had been supposed to meet Dr Lewis forty-five minutes ago.

He leapt up from the desk, banging his knee. 'Fuck! How do you know my schedule better than me?'

Rob watched him scramble to gather the neglected philosophy books from the windowsill. 'I'm an Assassin. It's my job to know everyone's schedule.'

'Assassin's not a job,' he retorted, running for the door.

'Neither is poet!' Rob shouted after him.

He thundered down the steps, then ran through to the next court and up another flight of stairs to arrive panting by the door marked *Dr J. Lewis.*

'Don't waste more time knocking,' a resonant voice said from within. 'You're already late.'

He stepped inside. Dr Lewis's rooms were like an eccentric,

disorganised museum: from her collection of replica Benin Bronzes, staring regally down from sixteenth-century West Africa, to her sousaphone, which she played in a jazz band on the weekends, to the bust of Wittgenstein with a suction cup dart affixed to one side of his face. In a throne-like armchair sat his supervisor, her usual brightly patterned dress contrasting with an expression of steely disappointment. 'What happened?'

His insides cramped with guilt. Dr Lewis knew better than him what it was like to come to Cambridge from a nontraditional background, and it meant she was usually willing to cut him some slack. But today, it looked like her patience had run out. He fumbled for an excuse. *I was having coffee with a time traveller*, while valid, would pose more questions than it answered. A fragment of his conversation with Esi came back to him, along with a vivid image of her face. *We can't change it.* 'Determinism.'

Dr Lewis pushed back her salt-and-pepper locks. 'That's your excuse for missing our appointment? Determinism?'

He nodded.

She took off her glasses. 'Aristotle save me,' she murmured. When she looked up, her eyes were bright with anger. 'You know what my problem with this place is? Well, one of my many problems. Students who think they have the right to waste my time. Worse, the ones who try to look clever while doing it.'

He panicked. 'No,' he blurted out, 'it's not an excuse. I – I saw something that proved to me that the future is already written.'

She sat back, like she was taking what he said at face value. 'Okay. And, what, that means you were predestined to be late today? You had no control over your actions, so you can just chalk it up to fate?'

He squinted, sensing he was walking into a trap. 'Yes?'

'No. This is typical of you, Joe. You have a tendency to make leaps of logic that aren't justified by the evidence.' She cleared her throat. He recognised the signal that his line of thought was about to be vivisected. 'Imagine you know your future.'

He resisted the urge to scream with laughter. 'Okay.'

'Now, imagine that future includes you graduating with a First.'

'2:1,' he corrected her.

She frowned. 'If you insist. *Great*, you think, *I'm predestined to get a 2:1*. Now, how do you respond? Do you think, *Well, fate's got this covered, looks like I can relax?*' She leaned forward. 'No. You can't. Because hard work is the only mechanism that's going to get you there. Determinism isn't going to take control of your legs and march them to the library. It's not going to read the books for you, or put in the long, hard, deliberate effort that turns reading into original thought.' She waved her hand in parenthesis. 'Not to mention, unless you're a white man who went to Eton, the much greater effort of persuading everyone else to take you seriously.'

He stared over her shoulder, the cogs in his brain turning. 'You're saying, even if you're destined for success, you still have to do the work.'

'I'm saying more than that. I'm saying determinism makes the work necessary.' He looked at her blankly. She sighed. 'I see too many students here who think they know the future. They think a good degree is something they're entitled to, not something they have to work for. You know what happens to those students?' She handed back his essay, covered in red pen. 'They fail.'

He knew what she was trying to say. But he wasn't like those students. He didn't think he was entitled to a good degree because he'd gone to the right school, or because his parents had a lot of money. He *was* entitled to one because of the physical laws of the universe. It was a completely different situation. 'No, I get it,' he said. 'I'll do better.'

'Glad to hear it. Any other questions?'

He remembered what he'd promised Esi. 'Yeah, actually. Are there any academic awards that get given out on the twenty-third of June?'

Dr Lewis looked bemused. 'The twenty-third of June?' She leaned over to her side table and leafed through an academic calendar. 'That's in May Week. Too early for any university-level awards.' She pursed her lips. 'I suppose some societies might give out awards then.'

'Societies. That's a good idea. Thanks.' He folded his essay in half and left.

'Aren't you getting a little ahead of yourself?' Dr Lewis's voice followed him down the stairs. 'Work first, Mr Greene. Awards later.'

Chapter Eight

If he had still been living in linear time, he would have heeded Dr Lewis's advice and spent the next few days in the library. But his 2:1 was guaranteed: if he didn't put the work in now, he was bound to put it in later. Instead, he spent the time reading and rereading the poems, daydreaming about falling in love with Diana.

On the day of their fateful reunion at the ADC, he headed out to meet Esi. As he left college, he saw Vera across the street, surrounded by his oddly dressed devotees. They tailed him through town, muttering just out of earshot, leaping comically into the shadows whenever he turned around. He tried to remind himself that these people had come here from decades in the future because his poetry meant something to them. Their presence was the ultimate realisation of his dream. But the close, prickling attention made him feel like he was back in high school, marked out and picked on. He hunched his shoulders and walked faster. As he crossed the grass of Christ's Pieces, the muttering subsided. He turned back from New Square Park, pretending to crouch and admire the autumn leaves. The time travellers were standing in a line on the other side of the road, forlorn as puppies peering through a stairgate.

'Good,' he said under his breath. 'At least some of you are taking the terms and conditions seriously.'

He went on towards the Grafton centre and turned right onto Burleigh Street. Esi was leaning against a bike rack in black leggings and an oversized grey sweater, working her way through a box of chips.

'The chips are *better* here,' she said, offering them. 'How did we manage, as a society, to make chips worse?'

After the breathless awe of the other time travellers, her total unimpressedness with him was a relief. He took a chip. It was perfect: hot and greasy. 'You're telling me in return for poetic greatness, I have to accept substandard chips?'

'These are the sacrifices we make, I guess.' She wiped her hands and threw the empty chip box in a bin. She looked briefly over his shoulder, following someone in the crowd, before focusing back on him. 'So. Joseph Greene.'

'So,' he echoed. 'Esi . . .' He laughed. 'I don't know your surname.'

She smiled. 'It's Campbell.'

'Oh! Scottish connection?'

Her smile froze. 'I guess? My dad's family is Jamaican, way back. It's a pretty common name there.'

'Ah. So not the fun kind of Scottish connection.' He winced. 'Sorry.'

She looked at him sideways. 'I mean, according to you, all that was just destiny, right? How sorry can you be, if you think it was meant to happen?'

She was teasing him, and she wasn't, something serious behind her eyes. 'That's not how it works,' he said, remembering his conversation with Dr Lewis. 'Even if our actions are predetermined, that doesn't mean we're not responsible.'

Her smile broadened, showing her tooth gap. 'Deep, Joseph Greene. You going to put that in a poem?' Before he could react, she winced. 'I'm doing it again. Sorry. I didn't want to interact with anyone in the past, and now I'm here talking to you of all people, and it's a mess, but it's the only way to fix the even bigger mess I've made already, and I'm just—'

'You're fine,' he interrupted, laughing. 'Do you think I'd be standing here asking you to help me impress Diana Dartnell if I took myself that seriously?'

She looked quietly surprised. 'I guess not.'

'Okay.' He spread his arms. 'So. Where do we start?'

'Where every good romance starts. With a makeover.' She stepped back, her eyes moving over him. 'We need to overhaul your look.'

'My *look*?' He blinked. 'I wasn't aware I had one.'

She waved her hand at him. 'What else do you call this whole messy-hair tatty-jumper aesthetic you have going on? We can lean into it, but it needs work. We need to make you look more – arty.'

'I am arty!' he protested.

'Arty like *my dad owns a gallery*, not arty like *I got rashed at the library then fell asleep in a bin.*'

'Rashed?'

'Use context, Joseph Greene. You can figure it out.' She turned, beckoning him to follow. 'Come on. Time to dress you up in the finest vintage early 2000s fashion.'

'Can you stop calling now "vintage"? It's making me time-sick.'

Reluctantly, he followed her into Oxfam. She sorted through

the racks, pausing on a pale blue fitted shirt. She examined the label, then the price, and whistled. 'Okay, your friend has a point.'

Her surprise made him curious. 'Do you not have charity shops in the future?'

'Yeah, but they're expensive. Only rich people shop there.'

'That doesn't seem right.'

She threw him an amused look. 'No one said things only get better.' She lifted the shirt from the rack. 'To bring out your eyes,' she said, glancing briefly into them.

'Uh – okay,' he said, feeling a little flustered.

She moved through the racks, gleaning clothes like a magpie, then dropped an armful on him and steered him for the changing room. 'Transform, butterfly, transform.'

There was a gap in the curtain that wouldn't close. Through it, he could see Esi looking at her phone. She appeared to be playing Snake. 'What difference is this going to make?' he complained, pulling off his jeans. 'It doesn't matter how I look if I don't know what to say to her.'

She turned. Down to his boxers now, he hid behind the curtain. 'Patience, Joseph Greene. This is Phase One. The goal of Phase One is to maximise the chances she'll actually let you near her.'

'I see. Which she's unlikely to do if she recognises me as the guy who – how did you put it? Walked up to her dressed as a railway accident and told her I'm her destiny?'

The corner of her mouth twitched. 'Look at Joseph Greene quoting me.'

He caught his own smile in the mirror as he buttoned his shirt. 'So what's Phase Two?'

'Don't rush me.' She looked airily back to her phone.

The shirt was tighter than he would usually have been comfortable with. He pulled on a pair of black boot-cut jeans and a long black trench coat. He tried to fix his hair, which had got all messed up in the process of taking off his jumper, then sighed and gave up. 'All right. Coming out.'

Esi's snake crashed into itself and died. She reached up and smoothed out his collar, breaking into a grin. 'This is – wow. Not terrible, actually. Can you take the coat off for a second?' He obliged, and she stepped back, appraising him with frank attention. 'The shirt was a gamble, to be honest. I couldn't tell what you were shaped like under all those jumpers. But turns out, you've got nice arms.' She clapped. 'Buy it. Buy it all.'

He bought it all, for a surprisingly small amount, and met her back outside the shop. 'Now we need to do something about the hair,' she announced. 'Do you use any product?'

'What kind of products?'

She sighed and took him to Boots. Armed with a tub of blue goop, she dragged him into the shopping centre toilets and stood him by the sinks. 'Stand still,' she commanded, and started dolloping the goop into his hair.

At first, he was uncomfortable. Then, the feeling of her hands in his hair started to be almost relaxing. She was humming a soft melody, a little furrow of concentration between her brows. He became acutely aware of her breath and his, touching in the space between them.

She met his eyes. Surprise, and a flicker of something else. 'There,' she said, stepping back.

He looked in the mirror. His hair was swept into an artfully tousled faux-bedhead. 'I look like I have a trust fund.'

'Exactly.' She grinned. 'Phase One complete.'

He stared at the man he was pretending to be. An uncanny fear swept over him, that his reflection was going to walk off without him into a successful future, leaving him floating in the Grafton centre toilets like a sad and unsanitary ghost.

Esi was already leaving. 'So,' she said as he hurried to catch up. 'If Phase One was about giving you a chance to talk to her, Phase Two is about what you're going to say.'

'Right.' He stepped out into Burleigh Street. A bike bell rang, and he jumped back.

She looked at him quizzically. 'Why are you acting like the road is made of lava?'

He glanced nervously down the street. 'The book says I'm going to get run over by a bike this year.'

'I see,' she said innocently. 'So if it's meant to happen, why bother trying to stop it?'

He opened his mouth to retort, but she had him. Even though it was impossible, he couldn't repress the impulse to thwart the future.

She looked away with a smile of satisfaction. 'The first thing you need to say to Diana is *sorry*. She's going to ask you for an explanation, but that's not what she really needs. She needs to know you realise what you did was bad, and creepy, and invasive, and you're never going to do anything like it ever again.'

'Got it,' he said. 'Bad, creepy, invasive, never again.'

She narrowed her eyes.

'No, I'm not taking the piss,' he said. 'I'm making mental bullet points. It's a revision technique.'

She sighed. 'Then, you need to focus on her. And I don't mean, like, brainstorming the next poem you're going to write.'

'But she's going to be my muse,' he protested. 'Having poetic thoughts about her is the whole point.'

'I'm not banning you from having poetic thoughts. I'm just saying, don't pay more attention to them than to what she's actually saying.'

'Okay. Fine. What else?'

'Don't think about the future. And whatever you do, don't talk about your destiny.' She turned round, facing him as she walked backwards. 'Listen to her. Be present in the conversation. And don't be afraid to be vulnerable. Women like it if you're not always trying to look like a winner.'

'That shouldn't be hard.' He scratched his head. 'Anything else?'

She shrugged. 'She's a person, Joseph Greene. Treat her like one.'

He felt oddly disappointed. 'Doesn't sound that complicated.'

'It isn't. But honestly, the bar is so low that if you can manage it, she's going to think you're some kind of wizard.'

The sun had sunk below the buildings. He checked his watch. A surprising amount of time had elapsed. 'Fuck. I have to be at the ADC in fifteen minutes.'

She nodded. 'I'd walk you there, but, you know. The adoring fans wouldn't like it.'

'Guess not.' He looked down the road towards town. 'Actually, it's been nice not to be followed around for a while.'

She looked surprised. 'You don't like the attention?'

He laughed. 'Do I seem to you like the kind of person who enjoys being stared at?'

Her keen gaze took him in. 'Why do you want to be a famous poet, then?'

It took him a while to articulate his answer. 'I want to make something that matters. I don't want to *be* the thing that matters. Does that make any sense?'

She looked at him for a long time, then laughed. He liked her laugh. It was warm and chaotic. 'What?' he asked, smiling.

'Nothing. You just keep being the complete opposite of what I expected.' The traffic lights ahead of them changed, and a car roared off down East Road. She jumped at the noise, briefly clutching his arm.

'You okay?' he said, his heart beating strangely.

She let him go. 'Yeah, I'm fine. Just – cars are so loud here.'

He nodded sagely. 'Guess you usually can't hear them because they're so high up.' She gave him an uncomprehending look. 'Flying car joke,' he explained. 'Because you're from the future.'

She stared at him, then burst into a laugh. 'You are such a goob.'

He should have been practising his serious poetic persona, but he couldn't regret making her smile. 'I thought I was a nozz.'

'Maybe. Maybe not. I haven't decided.' She swayed closer to him, then seemed to become aware of herself. She stepped back, crossing her arms. 'Did you find out anything about the award?'

'Oh. Right.' He cleared his throat. 'My supervisor said the twenty-third of June's too early for it to be something academic. But she thought there might be societies who give awards out then.'

'Societies?'

'Like, extracurricular stuff. Sports, drama, that kind of thing.' A thought struck him. 'Drama might actually be a good shout. If she's friends with Diana, maybe she's part of the ADC crowd.'

'An actor?' She looked sceptical. 'I can't see it.'

'Still. If I spot her, I'll text you.'

'Text me either way. I don't want to be waiting and hoping.' Another piece of her, offered up like a clue in a treasure hunt. He suspected that if it had been him, he would have wanted to hold on to hope as long as he could. She headed across the road.

'You not going to wish me luck?' he called after her.

She turned back. 'Luck isn't enough. You have to make this work.'

In the dying light, solemn as a priestess, she was an image of frozen grief. It brought home what she had to lose: what she had already lost. In that moment, he felt the responsibility like a weight he had no power to lift. Strange, that he wanted so much to help her when he knew what she longed for was impossible.

'I will,' he promised.

Chapter Nine

He followed his future towards the ADC. His hair felt like something had nested in it, and the trench coat lay heavy across his shoulders. He shrugged, trying to get comfortable in the new self he was wearing. Strange, how he could feel so certain about the future, and so terrified about the next half hour. He and Diana were destined to be together: whatever Esi said, he still believed that. But any number of disasters might stand between them and happiness. And it wasn't as if he could just wait them out. He had to keep trying, hoping each time that this would be the turning point. It was like Dr Lewis had said. Determinism was nice in theory, but it didn't actually save you any work.

He pushed through the glass doors into the lobby. His vision of Diana sitting onstage had been a fantasy: signs informed him that the meeting was upstairs in the bar. As he entered, a man in a velvet blazer was talking about how the potential collected in the room could power a thousand nuclear reactors, or something equally unscientific that would have made Rob cry. Joe looked around for Diana. *Soon, he would see her,* said the narrator in his head, *gleaming through the crowd like an emerald amongst the—*

He couldn't find her. He searched again, lingering on every dark-haired woman. Finally, he saw her at the bar, severe in a black turtleneck, hair pulled up into a bun. He was disturbed that he hadn't recognised her. Surely her soul should have called out to his, regardless of how differently she was dressed? That thought lasted until he touched his goop-covered hair and remembered he was effectively wearing a costume.

He wiped his hand discreetly on his jeans and turned to his secondary objective, to look for Esi's mum. That was easier: he ascertained at a glance that everyone in the room was white. He usually wouldn't have noticed; now, he couldn't unsee it. His feeling of accomplishment took on a sour aftertaste, like spoiled wine.

As the velvet-blazered man started introducing the actors, Joe texted Esi.

> She's not here. I'm sorry.

A few seconds later, her replies came through.

> that's ok

> knew it wouldn't be that easy

He flipped his phone closed as the man in the velvet jacket finished his introductions. 'Poets, you should already know who you've been paired with.' He clapped his hands. 'Tomorrow begins today!'

Joe took a deep breath and walked towards Diana.

She was scanning the room, looking for the person his words had made her imagine. When their eyes met, he tried to feel the weight of the moment, but he was too busy panicking that she would recognise him. She took him in, a roving, interested glance. She didn't gasp, or flee in terror. Esi's magic had worked. He thanked her wordlessly for giving him the second chance to make a first impression.

'So,' Diana drawled, putting out her hand. 'Joseph Greene. The genius behind "A Taste of Stars".'

And it all went to pieces. Esi had dressed him up, arranged his hair, told him what to say, but she hadn't told him how to act normal when the future love of his life called him a genius. His shoulders caved; his hand went automatically to the back of his neck. 'Uh – yeah,' he said with a nervous laugh. 'That's – that's me.'

'No.' She reared back. Her eyes narrowed. 'It's *you*.'

His heart was hammering. 'What?'

She pointed at his chest emphatically. 'Train Boy! Is this some kind of joke?' She held up a printout of the poem. 'Did you even write this?'

'It's not a joke. I . . .' *I did write this.* He couldn't say it. He searched for a way to claim it that was true. 'That's my poem. I'm Joseph Greene.'

She looked at him, then back at the poem. She took a breath. 'You should know that the only reason I'm not walking out right now is because I am a consummate professional.'

He exhaled in heart-stopping relief. 'Thank you. I—'

'And because your poem is, I grudgingly have to admit, very good.' Her attention pinned him in place. 'Who's it about?'

His brain short-circuited. 'I'm sorry?'

'The poem,' she said, with fraying patience. 'Who inspired it?' When he still failed to reply, she rolled her eyes. 'Oh my God. Do I have to spell it out for you? *Who were you kissing?*'

'Just – this girl.' Rob's words echoed. *There's the competition-winning eloquence I'd expect.* He had to do better. 'She's—' And as he said it, he realised his dilemma. The poem had been written by someone deeply in love. But he couldn't have Diana thinking he was taken. 'She was the love of my life.'

Cliché. He winced internally. Diana raised an eloquent eyebrow. 'Was?'

She died. He rejected the lie with the same instinct that rejected the wrong word when he was writing a poem. Another cliché, not to mention it was in bad taste, not to mention he'd have to think up something his imaginary girlfriend could have died of and keep that straight for the entirety of his and Diana's future together. 'It didn't work out.'

She looked at him knowingly. 'You mean she broke up with you.'

He felt the self-protective urge to deny it. Wouldn't it make him look more desirable if he'd been the one to end it? Esi spoke softly in his ear. *Don't be afraid to be vulnerable.*

'Yes,' he said, with a quiet laugh. 'She did.'

Diana nodded sagely. 'You couldn't have written this poem otherwise. The pain, the loss – that's what drew me to it. All that longing, all that desire for what can no longer be, it's there in every word.'

'Aye – yeah, that's exactly what I was going for,' his mouth said, while his brain protested, *What the hell is wrong with you?* How could she read the poem as a lament for love lost, when it was clearly a celebration of love everlasting?

She threw him a sly glance. 'Is this what all that nonsense was about the other night? You knew I was involved in Love Poems for Tomorrow, and you were – what, auditioning?'

He remembered what Esi had said. *She's going to ask you for an explanation, but that's not what she really needs.* 'It doesn't matter. I should have realised going up to you like that was creepy and invasive. I'm sorry. I won't put you in that position again.'

She looked taken aback. He wondered uneasily if she wasn't used to men apologising. The idea of Crispin floated into his mind. Her unhappy, inevitable marriage loomed on the horizon, a shadow she was doomed to walk through.

'All right,' she said. 'I accept your apology. Mostly because, on the evidence of this' – she shook the poem – 'you're talented enough to get a pass.'

He didn't necessarily agree that talented people could go around being as creepy as they liked. But the future love of his life had given him a compliment, and he couldn't think straight. He grinned at her, then realised talented people probably didn't grin, and moderated it to a knowing smile.

Her eyes met his. *Gimlet eyes*, he thought. Not just because of their sharpness, but their colour, exactly like the cocktail, a green so pale it was almost yellow. They looked through him, searching for something he wasn't sure he contained. 'I tend to find collaborations flow better in more intimate surroundings,' she said in her low, musical voice. 'Why don't you come by my room tomorrow morning and we'll give it a go?'

He tried to look as if he wasn't exploding. 'Uh – sure. Absolutely. Here's my number.'

She typed it into her phone and gave him a missed call. As if by magic, Diana Dartnell's number appeared on his screen. 'F5, Whewell's Court,' she said. 'Trinity Street gate. Shall we say eleven? Text me when you're outside. I'll buzz you in.' She leaned forward, a breath of orange blossom and patchouli, and kissed

him almost imperceptibly on the cheek. 'Must go. Got to circu-
late.'

He watched her leave, his soul buzzing. He'd done it. He'd made
his future happen. But even as joy spread through him, he felt it
dull at the edges. He hadn't really done anything. He'd been a passenger, floating on the tides of fate, no more responsible for his
success than a message in a bottle that had happened to be found.

He knew one person who would give him credit. As he left the
theatre, he took out his phone and texted Esi.

Want an update?

YES

don't tease me, joseph greene

please tell me you unbroke the future

Don't tease me was too much of an invitation.

:-)

what is that

It took him a minute to understand what was confusing her.

An emoticon. Look at it sideways.
It's a wee smiley face.

oh my god

that is the best/worst thing I ever saw

why is everything about the past so stupid

Don't ask me, I just live here.

so that means good news?
what happened??

He was typing another teasing reply when his phone buzzed again, and again.

please

just tell me

I need to know

He felt a stab of guilt. He'd been too caught up in his own triumph to think about what this meant for her. Swiftly, he deleted his reply and typed another.

It went well. Really well. I'm invited
to her room tomorrow.

To practise in 'more intimate
surroundings'. Her words, not mine.

oh thank god

so what's the next step with my mum?

> You free to meet up? I've got some
> ideas, but we should talk.

A moment passed. Then:

:-O

> Is that a no?

it's a talking face. let's talk

> :-O means surprised.

who made you king of the little face pictures

talk where

He looked up from his phone to gauge where he was.

> I'm just coming back to college.
> Meet me outside?

too central

too many people

I told you, I'm trying to keep a low profile

He checked up and down the street. A group of girls in wedge heels were heading out for pre-clubbing drinks. A wild-haired professor was cycling towards the river, his dog trotting frantically to keep up. The tour groups, time traveller or otherwise, were long gone.

> It's not exactly jumping this time
> of night. Come on! Live a little!

I'm not here to live, I'm here to reset my life

but fine

give me 20 minutes

He waited outside the gate, vibrating with euphoria, until he saw her round the corner of Pembroke Street. As she came up the steps, he unlocked the gate and held it open.

She stopped. 'Wait, we're going *in*?'

'Aye. I want a beer, and it's cheaper than anywhere else.' He saw her hesitate. 'What's wrong? And don't say the butterfly effect. You work in a coffee shop. It's not like you never interact with people.'

'That's Mill Road. This is the university. It's different.' When he started to demur, she gave him a look. 'You're telling me I'm not going to be the only Black person in that bar?'

He thought about the two Black students he knew in the college. 'Well, Omar never comes to the bar, but Vanessa spends more time on the quiz machine than she does on her degree, so overall, odds are about fifty-fifty?' She smiled a little, but she still looked tense. 'You can't avoid the uni forever,' he reminded her gently. 'Your mum's here.'

'Exactly. She never felt like she fit in, and she was a genius. Compared to her, I've got no right to be here at all.'

'You're my guest.' He leaned back against the door, pushing it open wider. 'You have as much right to be here as anyone else.'

She bit her lip. 'Can we have a code word? If I say it, it means *I need to get out of here.*'

'Absolutely. What's the code word?'

Her eyes flicked up to the grand stone archway. 'Threshold,' she said with a smile, like she was making a private joke.

He held the gate open. She ducked through, humming uneasily under her breath. 'So,' he said. 'Don't you want the full story of how I swept Diana Dartnell off her feet?'

'If I say no, are you going to tell me anyway?'

'I'll give you the short version. I did everything you said, and it worked.' He looked up at the crescent moon, remembering the odd, hollow feeling that had descended on him afterwards. 'I mean, of course it worked, because it was always going to work.'

'Don't take this away from me, Joseph Greene. It worked because I'm amazing at romantic advice.' She looked sideways at him. 'And don't take it away from yourself. You listened, and you did what I told you. That can't have been easy.'

He led her down the arched tunnel towards the bar, feeling a little patronised. 'You think I'm incapable of following basic instructions?'

She looked surprised by his reaction. 'No. I just didn't think you'd want to.'

The cosy, old-man-pub atmosphere of the bar enveloped them. Esi wrinkled her nose. Joe experienced a moment of dislocation.

Smoking in pubs was going to be banned in Scotland in March –
his regulars had talked about nothing else all summer – but the
idea of his everyday reality being obsolete made him feel suddenly
ancient.

'We can go somewhere else,' he offered.

'It's fine,' she said, waving her hand in front of her face. 'I'm
getting used to it.'

He got the drinks – a beer for him and a blue cocktail for Esi –
and took them to a table in the corner. 'Cheers.'

'Cheers.' As their glasses clinked, an odd look crossed her face.
'What?'

She started laughing. 'I'm sorry. You have no idea how weird
this is for me.'

'Oh, this is weird for *you*? Me, I've had the most normal week
I can remember.'

She sipped her blue drink, winding a braid around her finger.
'I mean, I get that, but – look at it from my side for a second.
Like – who's a writer you had to study in school that you hated?'

'Walter Scott.'

'Who?' He opened his mouth. She waved a dismissal. 'Actually,
doesn't matter. Just think about how you'd feel if you were me, and
he was you.'

'That's who I am to you? Walter fucking Scott?' He groaned
into his pint glass. 'Jesus, I'm starting to get it. Walter Scott rocks
up in my coffee shop, ruins my day, steals my book, I give him a
makeover, he buys me a drink . . .' He looked up at her, horrified.
'Wait. Is this – is this creepy? Am I being a creepy old man?'

She laughed. 'No, you're fine. I get the concern, but – it's not
creepy.' She took a sip of her blue drink. 'Also, you're not an old
man. Not yet, anyway.'

'Thanks,' he said dryly. 'I feel so much better.'

'Want to know what the weirdest thing of all would be?' She rested her chin on her hand and gave him a sideways smile. 'If Walter Scott turned out to actually not be a total nozz.'

His heart leapt strangely. 'No, sorry. Too far. That's impossible.' Her words surfaced a thought that had been lurking in the back of his mind since he had met her. The look she had given him, as if he was the last person on earth she'd wanted to see. 'Why did you think I would be, though? Is that what future me is really like?'

She picked up a beer mat and started tearing tiny perforations around the edge. 'I don't know. Maybe there's no way to become a famous poet without turning into kind of a nozz.'

She said it offhand, like it was a neutral observation. He felt like she had slapped him, in some deep part of himself he had thought no one could reach. 'So I'm fated to become a bad person?' His voice shook. 'Why the fuck would you say that?'

Her eyes widened in alarm. 'Because I say the wrong thing. Always.' She shook her head wildly. 'I don't know future you. How could I? Future you is famous, and happy, and I'm—nothing. I'm nobody.' She stood abruptly, heading for the door. 'This was a mistake.'

Chapter Ten

He surged to his feet. 'Wait. I'm sorry. I just— You hit a nerve, I guess.' She stopped, but her eyes stayed fixed on the door. The conviction came to him before he understood it. 'You don't really want to leave.'

She turned on him in frustration. 'What are you talking about?'

'You didn't say *threshold*.'

She rolled her eyes, as if he'd caught her out on a technicality. Slowly, she came back to the table and sat down. 'Sorry I called future you a nozz. I only said it because you really don't seem like one now. And sorry about – that,' she added, gesturing at the door. 'It's what I do. I run away.'

'Oh, me too,' he said lightly. 'When I was ten, I made it as far as the harbour before I ran home.'

She hiccupped out a laugh. 'I made it halfway across London.'

He stared. 'You're serious?'

'I was twelve, not ten. But yeah.' She picked up another beer mat and started drilling a hole in it with a pencil someone had abandoned on the table. 'I wanted to get away from myself. So I walked, and walked, till I figured out I couldn't walk myself into being someone else. Then I called my dad to come and pick me up.' She slid one beer mat somehow inside the other, pulling it through to make a three-dimensional star. 'He was so angry. He kept saying he couldn't believe I'd done it. He didn't think I was that kind of person. I said I might not have been that kind of person before Mum died, but now . . .' She shrugged expressively.

He imagined a young Esi pacing across the sprawling map of London, trying to outrun herself. His heart contracted. 'Your dad . . .' He searched for the right words. 'He didn't mean you were a bad person. He was just scared for you.'

She turned the star in her hands, lost in the future past. 'I guess. He was always so protective, especially after what happened to my mum.' She dropped the star and looked up, eyes falsely bright. 'Anyway. The best way to fix it is to make sure we never have that conversation, because I'll never have run away in the first place. You were saying something about societies?'

He thought about asking if she'd talked to her dad before deciding that the best way to resolve a conflict was to make it unhappen. Then he remembered it was none of his business. 'Can you think of anything your mum might have been into? Music? Rowing? Bell-ringing?'

She shook her head. 'I told you. She was really academic.'

'I mean, this is Cambridge. There are some pretty nerdy societies.'

She sighed. 'Okay. Do you have a list?'

'There's one on the university website.' He finished his beer and stood up.

She looked at him in confusion. 'Where are you going?'

'To my computer. How else are we going to look at a website?'

She looked down at her phone with comic despair. 'Right. How else?' Before she followed, she doubled back to pick up the beer mat star from the table.

He led her up the staircase into the living room, where Rob was writing *TEN TONNE WEIGHT* on the side of a cardboard box.

'This is Rob. He's my roommate.' His brain went on, *This is Esi. She's a time traveller.* He decided to forgo that side of the introductions. 'Rob has this thing where he pretends to kill people,' he added, by way of explanation.

'Assassins. Yeah, I used to play it with my cousins,' said Esi, like it was a completely normal thing to admit to. She offered Rob her beer mat creation. 'Want this? You could use it as a throwing star.'

Rob looked up at her with delight. 'Legend. Thanks.'

They went through to Joe's bedroom. Self-consciously, he removed *Meant to Be* from the bed and straightened the covers. 'Sorry. I've only got the one chair.'

'That's fine,' she murmured, sitting down on the bed.

He closed the door and pulled up his desk chair. He started typing 'Cambridge University student societies,' then paused. 'Hang on. I'm overthinking this. What's her name?'

'Efua Eshun. And you're underthinking this. I've already searched her name. Trust me, nothing comes up.'

'Not even her MySpace? Or a GeoCities page she made when she was thirteen?' He registered her expression. 'I sound like a wizard muttering spells right now, don't I? What I mean is, it's weird. Is she a spy?'

She shrugged. 'Dad always said she was just a really private person.'

'Exactly what a spy would tell people.' He opened another website. 'I can try the facebook?'

'The . . . ?' She appeared to be fighting a laugh. 'The facebook?'

'It's like – a book of faces. They opened it up to Oxford and

Cambridge last year.' He searched. A few Efuas popped up, none with the right surname.

Esi leaned over his shoulder, her breath warm on his cheek. 'No. No, no, no.'

'Okay. Guess we're back to societies.' He brought up the list and turned the laptop towards her.

She peered comically at the buttons under the trackpad. It took her a while to figure out how to scroll. 'Some of these academic ones, maybe. Chess Club. Student Community Action – is that volunteering?' He nodded. 'The African Caribbean Society. The Christian Union.' She scrolled back up, then down again. 'Honestly, the rest of them seem – not serious enough.'

'Well, make a list of the ones you think are worth checking out. I'll find out when their next meetings are so you can crash them.'

'Crash them? How?'

'They usually happen in colleges. You can just walk in. No one's going to stop you.'

She smiled a too-bright smile. 'You sure about that?'

'What do you mean?'

'I already tried walking into a random college to look for her. The porters stopped me. When I couldn't show university ID, they told me to leave or they'd call the police.'

He couldn't believe it. 'Why would they stop you? You look like a student.'

She shook her head, gesturing at him. 'You. *You're* what a student looks like, according to this time and place.'

He felt like he had in the ADC bar: conscious of his sameness, guilty that it had taken him so long to notice. He had always been so focused on the ways he didn't fit in that he hadn't thought about all the ways he did. 'Okay. Then I'll come with you.'

She laughed. 'What, act as my white male shield?'

'Sure. Then we can lurk around asking about awards until someone kicks us out.' He shrugged. 'It's the least I can do. You helped me with Diana.'

She looked at him sideways. 'But if I was always meant to help you, then it's not like I had any choice.'

'Then I don't have any choice either.'

She smiled, brief and incandescent. For a moment, they just looked at each other. Then she coughed and stood up. 'I should go.'

'Threshold?'

'Threshold.' She touched *Meant to Be* where it lay on his desk. 'Good luck with her tomorrow. Not that you'll need it, obviously.'

A thought struck him. He opened the book to the page with the photographs. 'What if I show her?'

She looked at him like he had gone insane. 'The book of all your future poems about her?'

'No!' He pointed at the picture of her mum with Diana.

She shook her head. 'Too risky.'

'What's the risk? We're not sticking her face up all over town. We're showing it to one person, who clearly already knows her.' He looked up at her earnestly. 'It's our best lead. We'd be idiots not to use it. If they're still friends, Diana can lead us right to her. If not, we can still narrow down which college she's at.'

He saw her waver, the conviction that had led her this far softening under his words. For an uncertain moment, he wondered if he was doing the right thing. 'Fine,' she said. 'Ask if she knows her. But don't tell her why you're asking.'

He nodded. 'I'll be careful.'

She tapped the door frame, ducked her head, and left.

'So,' said Rob, waggling his eyebrows as Joe shut the living room door. 'I'm assuming that was Diana?'

Joe stared at his friend, completely thrown. 'What?'

'Diana,' Rob said slowly. 'The girl you wrote the poem about.'

'No. No, that was . . .' He stared at the door, wondering how Rob could have got the wrong idea so completely. 'That's Esi. She's – we're . . .' He didn't know how to describe what they were. Friends? Acquaintances? Reluctant coconspirators? 'She's not Diana.'

'Okay,' said Rob, in the voice that meant *Whatever you say, Greeney*. 'Well, she makes a mean throwing star.' He flicked it in Joe's direction.

In an uncharacteristic display of reflexes, he caught it. He turned it in his hands, thinking about Esi as she made it, her look of intent concentration. The way she felt unrooted, in his world but not of it. 'Don't get too attached,' he said, wondering who he was talking to. 'She's not sticking around.'

THE NEXT MORNING, he stood outside the gate of Whewell's Court, agonising over the most poetic way to tell Diana he was here. Finally, he settled for:

Here

Across the street, the Great Gate of Trinity was thronged with tourist crowds. Among them was a group of time travellers who had followed him from college. Vera was corralling them together, ushering them back towards King's. He was wondering why when he remembered the terms and conditions. *Time travellers may not follow the target into any private premises.* Shame, that they wouldn't get to witness his historic first rehearsal with Diana. Maybe later, he could arrange a special outdoor performance just for them.

The gate buzzed open. He slipped into the sudden quiet of the court, then climbed the staircase labelled *F* and knocked on the fifth door.

As he waited, a painting on the neighbouring door caught his eye. A forest of golden lines grew sideways through shades of black, varied and subtle as a monochrome rainbow. He wasn't sure what the picture was meant to be. The longer he looked at it, the more possibilities he saw: a sideways lightning strike; a reef of branching coral in a dark ocean; hundreds and hundreds of paths, branching out from one initial step.

Before he could work it out, the door in front of him opened. Diana, in a crisp white blouse and fitted skirt, her eyes cool and assessing. 'Train Boy!'

He winced. 'Am I ever going to live that down?'

'That depends. Can you impress me enough to make me forget?'

Her attention made him feel like the most important person in the universe. What should he say? *Yes* would be too arrogant, *no* too self-deprecating. He searched for a third response that would strike the perfect balance and also make her laugh, but too much time had passed, and he had to settle for mysterious silence.

'Well?' She was holding the door open. 'Are you coming in?'

He stepped inside. He had hoped the room would impart something of her essence, but he just saw a mess: books in tottering piles, clothes in silky heaps, copies of *Vogue Paris* spilling out of the blocked-up fireplace. In defiance of college regulations, the walls were covered with photographs from ADC shows and clippings from the theatre pages of *Varsity*. The muffled sound of a woman singing drifted through the wall. He was about to jokingly ask her if it was the muse when she said, 'I'd like to start by hearing you read the poem.'

His heart plummeted. 'Me?'

'No. The ghost of Lord Byron, who is standing directly behind you.' He actually turned to look before he realised she was joking. 'Of course, you. How else am I going to understand your poetic intent?'

But I don't know my poetic intent. He focused on the more immediate problem. 'I'm not an actor.'

'No. You're a poet. And if you're serious about being a poet, you need to learn how to perform your own work.' She sat down in an armchair, making a *get on with it* gesture.

There was no way out. He cleared his throat, focused on a neutral patch of carpet, and started reading. He tried to feel the words as he spoke them, but her attention was a searchlight, burning everything else away. When he reached the word *mouth*, he felt a blush rise up his throat. By the time he got to the word *tongue*, the blush had consumed his entire face. He cursed his past self for choosing this poem, when he could have picked a nice, safe one about beauty and moonlight. He stumbled through the last stanza, tripping over the words in his eagerness for it to be over.

When he dared to look at Diana, she was covering her eyes. 'Can I ask you something?'

Joe, whose brain was at this point one long scream, nodded.

'Did you actually write that poem?'

He froze. The last time she had asked him, he had avoided a direct lie. But if he kept dodging the question, she was bound to get suspicious. 'Yes?'

She clapped her hands like a gunshot. 'Then act like it!' She came to stand next to him. 'This is you right now.' She hunched in on herself, arms hanging like noodles at her sides, and mumbled nonsense syllables into the floor.

He stared at her, appalled. 'Fuck.'

'Indeed.' She straightened up, grace flowing back into her body. 'We need to sort out your posture first. Shoulders back.' She jerked him upright like a malfunctioning puppet. 'You have nice arms. Shame not to show them off. And when you speak, project. Your voice needs to come from down here.' She touched his lower belly with a light caress that made the blood rush from his head. 'And try not to look so *embarrassed*, for God's sake. You're a grown man, and you're acting like a preteen boy who accidentally read a romance novel.' She settled back into the armchair. 'Now,' she said, with a flourish. 'Try again.'

He had been imagining this moment since the message from Love Poems for Tomorrow had landed in his inbox. He had pictured himself bathed in golden light, watching his muse perform and falling desperately in love with her. Instead, he felt like his soul was being fed into a blender. He tried again. This time, he managed to keep his head up, but he was focusing so hard on what his shoulders were doing that he forgot how to say words. '. . . longaf – *long after* it all went dark,' he finished, sweaty and exhausted.

'Better,' said Diana, rising from her armchair. 'But given where you started, that's not saying much.' She circled him, fascinated. 'It's extraordinary. I've never seen anyone so uncomfortable in their own skin that they're actively trying to crawl out of it.'

He felt horribly seen, like a corpse cut open on a table. He wondered uneasily if this was love, and if so, how he could make it stop.

'Anyway. Progress,' she said brightly. 'Let's do this again next week.'

She was already turning away; he hadn't expected to be dismissed so fast. He fumbled in his pocket for the picture he had carefully ripped out of *Meant to Be*. 'I wanted to ask. Do you know this girl?' She turned, eyebrow raised, and glanced at the picture. 'Her name's Efua Eshun,' he added.

Her eyes showed no recognition. 'Doesn't ring a bell.'

'She has her arm around you,' he pointed out.

'A lot of people put their arms around me, Joseph. I can't always keep track.' She tapped herself in the photograph. 'I remember that dress, though. Very 2003. This picture's from first year.' Her eyes met his. 'I'm sure you met plenty of people in first year you couldn't place now.'

'Do you at least know which college she's at?'

'One of the hill colleges, maybe?' She headed for the mirror. 'Now, if amateur detective hour is over, I have a show to prepare for.'

He left her room feeling like a steak that had just been tenderised. Still trembling, he took out his phone and texted Esi.

> Showed Diana the picture of your mum.
> She says she doesn't recognise her.

what

I mean it's one thing if she said
they're not friends any more

but not recognising her? isn't that weird?

It hadn't seemed weird at the time. But then, Esi hadn't met Diana. She hadn't heard the airy unconcern in her voice when she talked about anything that wasn't her art. He decided to stick to the facts.

> She thinks she's at one of the hill colleges.
>> That narrows it down to three.

good detective work, Joseph Greene

He tucked his phone into his pocket, smiling. He couldn't help but be pleased with his progress.

Chapter Eleven

Diana was as good as her word. They met up again the next week, and the next, at which point she blessedly got tired of torturing him and started performing the poem herself. He had longed for the sublime experience of hearing his muse read the words she would inspire, but the reality was more odd than transcendent. Her approach to the poem baffled him: she lingered on words he would have passed over, made up her own rhythm completely at odds with his, skipped over the best parts in a breathless rush. He pushed back, tentatively at first and then firmly, heeding Esi's advice. *Treat her like a person.* And as he did, as he lost the urge to spontaneously combust every time she looked at him, he came to a disconcerting revelation: she wasn't really his type.

It wasn't how she looked. She was undeniably gorgeous, and anyway, his type had never been a set of physical attributes. He tended to go for girls who shared his sense of humour: self-deprecating, always ready to flip from sincerity to absurdity. Diana was funny, but in a dry, cutting way that knocked the breath out of him, leaving him powerless to respond. And when she was in earnest, it was deadly: she took herself and her art seriously, and upbraided him whenever he failed to do the same.

It troubled him. Why wasn't he falling for the great love of his life? When would he start feeling the way the poems described him feeling? The preoccupation dogged him as he crossed Magdalene Bridge on his way to meet up with Esi. Their hunt for her mum was going about as well as his romance with Diana. So far, they had attended meetings of the Law Society and the Engineering Society. Esi had spent most of her time being talked over, Joe had jumped to her defence and just made things worse, and they had left with no further leads on the award.

He looked over his shoulder. The time travellers who had been following him had stopped on the bridge. One had thrown a white rose after him, petals splayed wetly on the pavement. At the head of the group was Vera, wearing her usual tabard and an unusual look of concern. He didn't stick around to see what was bothering her. He crossed the road, hurrying up the hill until she and her group were out of sight.

Esi was waiting outside Kettle's Yard, a safe distance from the half-mile boundary. The sight of her made him smile: she was playing Snake on her phone, oblivious. He tapped her shoulder. 'Ready to search some colleges?'

'Joseph Greene!' She turned to him, beaming. '*So* ready. Look what I found on Burleigh Street.' She pointed at her hoodie, which said *CAMBRIDGE UNIVERSITY* in huge letters. 'Instant student, right?'

He shook his head. 'Only tourists wear those. It might as well say "I don't go to" along the top.' She looked crestfallen. 'It's fine. We'll just pretend you're a super-keen prospective student.'

'Prospective student?' She made a face. 'Pretty sure I'm older than you.'

He hadn't thought about it since they'd met. 'How old are you?'

'Twenty-one.'

'So will I be, in a month.' A thought struck him. 'When were you – when will you – will you have been—' He gave up. 'What is your year of birth?'

She smirked. '2023.'

'Okay, so you're . . .' He did some quick mental arithmetic. 'Minus eighteen. An anti-adult. That definitely makes me older.'

She sighed theatrically. 'Are we going to stand around all day doing time maths?'

'No, you're right. We should get going. The hill colleges are pretty far out of town.' She was hiding a smile. 'What?'

'Nothing. Just, whenever you say "far out of town", it means *fifteen minutes' walk*.' She shook her head. 'It's cute how you think Cambridge is a city.'

'What do you mean? It has a cinema!'

'Mmhm.' Her smile faltered as she looked ahead up the hill. 'So when you say *search some colleges*, what does that mean exactly? Are we going door-to-door?'

He caught an edge to her words. 'Would that be a problem?'

'Yeah. I don't want her seeing me.' With a jolt, he realised it wasn't just concern in her voice. It was fear.

'There's no need to go door-to-door,' he reassured her. 'The Porters' Lodge of each college has pigeonholes with all the students' names. We just need to check if hers is there.'

'Okay.' Her stride lengthened, her shoulders relaxing. She was always happier when she had a plan. He didn't want to ruin her mood, but he did need her advice.

'So there's something I wanted to ask you,' he began. 'As a romance expert.'

She looked at him with strange tension. 'Yeah?'

'How long does it take to fall in love?'

Her smile burst out. 'Really fall in love? Months, at least. Years. For the right two people, I don't know if that's ever finished.'

'Right. But – how soon are you supposed to know?'

She tilted her head, considering. 'I mean, if you really like someone, you pretty much know right away.'

'Oh,' he said heavily.

Her expression was pained. 'Please tell me this isn't about Diana.'

'Who else would it be about?'

'I don't understand,' she said in frustration. 'I got you through the hard bit, which was making her ever want to see you again. Now you're seeing her weekly. What's the problem?'

'I don't know,' he said, feeling ungrateful. 'She's just – she's really different from any girl I've been with before. Any girl I've even been interested in.'

She gave him an *obviously* look. 'She's the love of your life. She *should* be different, right?'

'I guess. It's just that spending time with her, it's not really . . .' He searched for a word to describe the antithesis of the constant stress of being with Diana. '. . . Fun.'

'Maybe you just need to relax. You're putting too much pressure on yourself.'

'How can I not put pressure on myself? She's my one and only! My soul's destination!' He tore at his hair. 'See, I think it's the opposite. I need to work harder. Treat it like revision. Note down her best attributes on index cards and memorise them. Write timed essays in praise of her beauty—'

She halted, turning to face him. 'With all due respect, Joseph Greene, stop your nonsense.'

He blinked. 'That's not very respectful.'

'It feels weird with Diana because your first meeting got messed up. If you'd met like you were supposed to, you wouldn't be overthinking it like this. You'd just be enjoying yourself. Like a normal person.' She indicated the *New Hall* sign on the corner. 'In there?' He nodded. She marched into the Porters' Lodge, humming the soft, repetitive tune she always hummed when she was anxious. She scanned the names, searching the *E*s, then shook her head. As they left, she glanced back over her shoulder, as if her mum might appear the second she stopped paying attention. The fleeting, instinctive movement broke his heart.

'All right, then,' he said, trying to distract her as they continued up the road towards Fitzwilliam. 'How do you think we were supposed to meet? In this hypothetical world where our first meeting got *messed up*. We don't have any friends in common. We're not on the same course. We're not at the same college. Our paths would never have crossed if it wasn't for the book.'

A dimple appeared in her cheek. Some part of her was enjoying the argument. 'What about this poetry thing you're doing? You would've met then.'

He hadn't told her the poem he'd submitted had been from the future. And he probably shouldn't. 'That *is* how we met, if you don't count the train incident. And it's not exactly been romantic so far. She's spent most of her time correcting my posture.'

She laughed. 'Then maybe you were supposed to have a classic meet-cute.' Her face went dreamy. 'Like, you were in a coffee shop and she bumped into you, and you spilled your coffee all down her, and she laughed, and you helped her clean it up, and you got to talking . . .'

'I don't think she would have laughed,' he cut in. 'Her clothes look really expensive.'

'Then maybe she spilled her coffee down you.' She eyed his current jumper, which featured a friendly badger. 'Would have done you a favour.'

He shook his head, repressing a smile. 'I still don't get it. What's so romantic about a coffee shop?'

'It's not about the coffee shop.' She stopped, arguing with herself. 'Or – I guess it is. It's a place where people's paths can cross. People who wouldn't have met anywhere else.'

'Like you and me,' he said. 'We met in a coffee shop.'

Her eyes widened. *Uh-oh,* he thought. He'd been so caught up in the flow of their conversation, the teasing give-and-take he'd get into with any girl he liked, that he'd forgotten who he was talking to – or rather, who he wasn't. She looked flustered, then annoyed. 'Don't ask for my advice if you're not going to take me seriously.' She marched ahead of him into the Porters' Lodge of Fitzwilliam. By the time he got to the entrance, she was already coming out, shaking her head. 'You said there's one more?'

'Aye. Just down the road.' They walked on, her silence tingling in the air like a thunderstorm. Before he could work out how to apologise, they had reached the blocky mass of Churchill.

She walked up to the pigeonholes, checked the *E*s, and turned away. He followed her back outside. She stood on the edge of the steps, hugging herself against the wind. 'I knew it. I knew Diana was lying.'

He didn't think that was fair. 'Come on. Why would she lie? She probably just remembered wrong.'

'Oh, so now you're defending her?' she snapped. 'I thought you didn't even like her.'

He stepped back. 'Jesus. Was it something I said?'

She laughed bitterly. 'Something you said? Oh, no. It's been deev, hearing you complain for half an hour about how the future love of your life is not your type.'

He was wrongfooted. 'Sorry. I didn't mean to—'

'You know how important this is, for both of us. Literally your only job is to let your destiny happen.'

'I've been trying,' he protested. 'But – I think the problem is, I have to *make* it happen. I just don't know how.'

She exhaled, her shoulders dropping. He sat down on the steps. After a minute, she sat down beside him. 'Here's a crazy suggestion. Have you tried asking her out?'

When she put it that way, it sounded simple. 'No.'

She patted him lightly on the back. 'Then maybe start with that.'

'"If this is love,"' said Diana.

She stood by the window that looked onto the court, a ray of pale sun turning her collarbones to sensual art. '"Then douse me in it. Set me aflame, set me . . ."' Midflow, she cut herself off. Her posture changed entirely, as though she were shifting selves. It was a compelling illustration of her craft, and, he had to admit, very sexy. 'Douse,' she said thoughtfully.

He coughed, trying to focus. 'Uh. Yeah.'

'In what sense?'

'I, uh—' He had forgotten what *douse* meant, and indeed the meaning of all words. 'What sense were you thinking?'

'Extinguish. As in dousing a candle.' Her elegant fingers made a snuffing gesture. 'So the poet is annihilated by love. Destroyed by it.'

He nodded sagely. 'Makes sense.' When she rolled her eyes, he protested, 'Look. What I intended when I wrote it – that's not the point.'

'Death of the author is very passé, Joseph.'

'I look forward to my immortality.'

She smiled a small, reluctant smile. 'Be serious.'

He tried. He was surprised to find he disagreed with her. 'I don't think I meant *extinguish*. I think I meant more like, uh, drench. So the poet is . . .' He tailed off, gesturing vaguely. He couldn't say it better than the poem already had.

'Soused in love,' she filled in, her voice low. 'Soaked to the skin.'

Their eyes met. *And this was the moment*, said the narrator in his brain, *that Diana Dartnell looked into Joseph Greene's eyes and knew—*

She dropped her head, with a soft exhalation that might have been a laugh. 'I looked him up, you know. McGonagall.'

She remembered his Halloween costume. He didn't know whether to be flattered or horrified. 'So you have a new favourite poet?'

She ignored his attempt at a joke. 'Interesting that you chose to dress up as a man universally acknowledged to be the worst poet of all time. Very psychologically revealing.' She fixed him with sharp attention. 'Laughing at your own ambition before anyone else can. A classic defensive tactic.'

He felt like she was running her nails lightly over his soul. He desperately needed to deflect. 'So why were you dressed as an angel?'

'We dress up as what we aren't.' A smile played around her mouth. 'That's the point, isn't it?'

He felt the jab at his hypocrisy. 'Or, it's a double bluff. You dress as what you really are, under all the pretence.'

She threw her head back in a delighted laugh. 'If you think I'm an angel, you obviously don't know me very well.'

The line came to him easily, like he'd always been meant to say it. 'I'd like to know you better.'

She raised an eyebrow. He caught the invitation to back off, to turn it into a joke, but he refused. He held her gaze until it was unambiguous what he meant.

She shook her head with a slight smile. 'Joseph, I have a boyfriend.'

The name came out by reflex. 'Crispin?'

Her eyes widened with the ghost of an expression he hadn't seen since that first disastrous night. 'How do you know that?'

Fuck. He flailed for an explanation that didn't involve him having read her future history. If they had been at the same college, or had any friends in common, it would have been easy, but what he'd told Esi was true: they existed in non-overlapping worlds. *What about the poetry thing?* At least once, those worlds had collided. He seized on it. 'Someone at the ADC mentioned him.'

The tension left Diana's body. She leaned back against the wall, crossing her arms. 'So you heard I was with someone else, then decided to make a pass at me?'

He threw up his hands. 'Okay. I'm sorry. If you're with him and you're happy, then obviously, I was out of line.'

Something happened to her face: a flicker of hurt, immediately sealed over by cold disdain. 'Yes. You were.' She marched to the door and flung it open. 'These rehearsals aren't working. I need to develop my own relationship with the piece. Alone.'

He couldn't believe how instantly he had ruined everything. He searched for something he could say to turn it around, but her words left no room for argument. He headed sheepishly for the door.

'Oh, and you should know,' she added icily as he left. 'Even if I weren't with Crispin, it wouldn't make any difference. You're really not my type.'

Chapter Twelve

He thundered down the stairs, his fury at Diana's words only slightly tempered by the fact that he had thought the exact same thing about her. But it didn't make any sense. They were destined to be together. Something was going to turn him into her type: he just had to figure out what.

He was reaching into his coat pocket for the book when he remembered where he was. He couldn't exactly whip it out and consult it in Diana's corridor. But he couldn't take it outside either: it was a quarter to twelve, inside visiting hours, and he didn't want to ruin his mystique with the time travellers. On impulse, he ducked into the nearest bathroom and locked the door. He sat in the dry bath and read through the Introduction, seeking out the most romantic thing he had ever done for Diana. As always, the book was frustratingly thin on details. He was about to give up when his skimming eye caught the phrase *fell in love with him all over again.*

'Oh aye. Here we go,' he murmured, leaning over the pages.

Greene's legendary devotion to Dartnell extended beyond mere words. Throughout their relationship, he showered her with extravagant gifts, like the surprise trip he arranged to a friend's

private island. 'It was incredible to be somewhere so secluded,'
Dartnell was quoted as saying. 'Like it was just the two of us,
alone in the universe. I fell in love with him all over again.'

Joe stared emptily down the plughole. Despite having been at
Cambridge for two years, he was yet to make any friends who had
private islands. It was so much easier to be romantic when you
were already rich and famous.

He pocketed the book and let himself out onto Trinity Street.
Twelve o'clock had come and gone; so had Vera and her latest group.
Still, he couldn't shake the feeling that someone was watching him.

'Greeney!' His nickname clashed so wildly with the Joseph
Greene he had just been reading about that it gave him whiplash.
He finally spotted Rob, waving at him from behind the postbox.

'What are you doing here?'

'Lurking. Word on the Assassin street is, Darcy's at Trinity.'

Rob looked very calm for a man about to face his nemesis.
'Wait. Darcy's finally your target?'

'No, not yet. Just trying to get the latest intel. My current target's at Sidney.' He headed for Green Street, beckoning Joe to
follow. 'Come with me. You might learn something.'

'I doubt that,' he said, but followed anyway. Being an Assassin
had given Rob an encyclopaedic knowledge of the city that Joe
could turn to his advantage. 'Can you think of anywhere in Cambridge that's really . . . secluded?'

Rob shot him a look. 'Creepy.'

'No, I mean like – somewhere to take a girl.'

'Not making it any less creepy.'

'You're not understanding. Deliberately. I want to take Diana
somewhere she's never been before.'

Rob led the way across the road – Joe cringed in anticipation of the inevitable bike – and turned up the narrow pedestrian alley of Sussex Street. 'There's this restaurant on Chesterton Road. It's quiet, intimate, the food is *incredible*—'

'That sounds like it costs money,' he interrupted. 'My overdraft's nearly maxed out. I need something free.' Looking up, he did a double take. Standing on the balustrade by the baked potato shop was Vera. She wasn't wearing her tabard; if she hadn't been staring at him with such intensity, he might not have recognised her.

He checked his watch. Twenty past twelve. She shouldn't be here. He felt an aggrieved impulse to march up to her and recite the terms and conditions. But something else was strange. No time travellers crowded onto the steps beside her: she was alone.

He had been staring at her for too long. With a look of alarm, she hurried down the steps and strode away. He watched her disappear into the crowd, wondering what had brought her here out of hours. Maybe she was a fan of his poetry. That might be what had drawn her to the job in the first place: the chance to use her position to get her own private tour. Whatever the reason, he was annoyed. Now he'd have to watch out for her every time he met up with Esi.

'Greeney?' Rob beckoned him in the opposite direction.

Joe followed him through an open gate into the back of Sidney Sussex College. 'So?' he prompted. 'Any ideas?'

'You could try the secret terrace.'

'What secret terrace?'

'The one you can get to from your battlements.' Rob stopped next to a window and peered inside.

Joe shuddered. 'By inching along a death-defyingly narrow ledge and shinning up a drainpipe?'

'Yeah. That one.' Rob pulled at the window. It swung open. 'Yes! My accomplice came through.' He turned to Joe. 'Give me a boost?'

He knelt, wincing as Rob stepped on his shoulder and climbed up through the window. He dropped with surprising agility and turned to help Joe through. 'Might not be a great idea. You're not much of a climber. Wouldn't want you ending up smeared across Trumpington Street as a patch of Greeney-flavoured jam.'

His old fear, that his life would amount to nothing but a page-six story in the *Courier*. 'It would be a really stupid way to die,' he agreed.

'Speaking of stupid ways to die . . .' Rob crouched over the bed-side table.

Joe came closer to see what he was looking at: an old-fashioned perpetual calendar, with dials for the day, month, and year. Rob scrolled through the final set of numbers until they read 2150. He picked up a pad and paper from the victim's bedside and wrote a note saying, *You have died of old age.*

'Wow,' said Joe. 'Genius.'

Rob clapped him on the shoulder. 'Let's get out of here before we get caught up in the time vortex.'

It turned out the time vortex was the least of Rob's worries. Someone was waiting outside the window, armed with a banana. 'Bang,' said the assassin lugubriously.

Rob looked disbelievingly at Joe. 'I'm dead.'

'What is it with you and bananas?'

'The banana was incidental. My accomplice sold me out.' Rob glared at his killer, who was taking a picture for posterity. 'I forgot rule one of the Game. Make yourself hard to find.'

Joe stared at his friend. 'So you're dead? It's over?'

'Respectively, yes and no. There's still the Lent Term Game, and the May Week Game. Two more chances to meet Darcy in the field and triumph.' Rob lifted his chin. 'I do not fear death,' he proclaimed, 'for my future is glory.'

'Is that a quote from something?'

'Yes. Rob Trevelyan, 2005.' He pointed at Joe. 'If you use it in a poem, I want royalties.'

Joe stared into space. *I do not fear death, for my future is glory.* There was something important here, unfurling in his mind like seaweed when the tide came in. Rob was dead. *Joseph Greene lives with Diana Dartnell in London.*

He had documentary proof that he would still be alive at sixty. He didn't need to worry about falling and dying, because he couldn't. Not for at least another forty years.

'Greeney?' Rob waved a hand in front of Joe's face. 'What's up?'

'Oh, nothing much,' he said distantly. 'I just realised I'm immortal.'

TWENTY MINUTES LATER, he stood on the edge of the battlements, ready to jump.

A voice like Dr Lewis's rang in the back of his mind – the way to be destined to live to sixty was not to throw yourself off any buildings – but he dismissed it. The book proved that whatever he did between now and then couldn't kill him.

Unless he was wrong.

He saw Esi in his mind's eye, looking down tenderly at her mum's picture. If she was right, there was no deterministic force, no hand of fate holding him back from plunging to his death. But if she was right, then his future was nothing but a possibility. He couldn't believe that. He needed it to be a fixed reality, even if he had to stake his life on it.

He gathered himself, counted to three, and leapt.

An instant of terrifying plummet. He was falling, nothing between him and the old, cold stones of the court below. His feet hit the ledge, jarring his knees. He scrabbled at the wall, gripped for a crack between the stones, and held.

He clung, sweating, gasping, feeling invincibly alive. He shuffled crabwise along the narrow ledge, grabbed the drainpipe, and shinned up, a preternatural strength animating his limbs. Hauling himself over the lip of the roof, he got to his feet and emerged onto the secret terrace.

'Terrace' was pushing it. It was a flat niche between tiled roofs, with a view of the edge of King's College Chapel crisscrossed by wires. The place felt like Cambridge folded in on itself, a portal to past and present and future all at once. It was perfect.

Shaking, he opened his phone and took a picture. He sent it to Diana with the message:

New rehearsal space?

She didn't reply. Not that day, not the next day, not the day after that. He was still forlornly checking his phone as he sat in the vaulted cellars of Clare College bar, waiting to escort Esi back from her African Caribbean Society meeting. She'd jokingly invited him along – *might be good for you, standing out for a change* – but they'd agreed it was probably best if he met up with her afterwards.

As the meeting broke up and the ACS members started to drift into the bar, he saw her, laughing easily in the midst of a group, her braids pinned up in a way that accentuated her cheekbones. She had swapped her usual sweater and leggings for a patterned black-and-white dress that looked like stark shadows in sunlight. It was like seeing a different person. He couldn't take his eyes off her as she excused herself and came to sit on the bench next to him.

'How did it go?' he asked.

She slumped, laying her head briefly on his shoulder. He felt a wave of electricity run through him. 'No joy?' he said with forced calm.

'She wasn't there, and I didn't hear anyone mention her. Was fun when I asked if the society gives out awards, though. They thought that was hilarious.' She looked over at the group she'd come in with, huddled by the jukebox arguing over song choices. 'Hard to remember they're all my dad's age in the future.' As the opening riff of 'Kiss' by Prince echoed through the bar, she rolled her eyes. 'Okay, maybe it's not that hard.'

He touched the badge on her shoulder bag. 'You didn't think about introducing them to The Swerves?'

She choked on a laugh. 'Oh yeah. I should have just got out the – the recording disk, and put it on the megaphone.'

'Gramophone? Come on. We have CDs, you know.'

'Sounds painful.' Her eyes went distant, her lips and shoulders moving minutely to the music, as if she couldn't help it. 'This is, like, my dad's party anthem.'

The joy in her voice was infectious. 'He throws a good party?'

'The best.' Her face lit up. 'Everyone comes round to our house – my aunties, my uncles, cousins, neighbours, friends – and we just eat and talk and laugh and dance together, all night. Till morning, sometimes.'

He looked over his shoulder, where the ACS meeting was turning into a free-flowing gathering, drawing in other students from across the bar. 'Looks like some of them might be up for that.'

He caught a flash of longing in her eyes, but she shook her head. 'Too late. I blew my cover. Someone asked me what I'm studying.' She looked seriously at him. 'Did you know, time science is apparently "not even a subject"?'

'Says who?'

'Some guy Adewale who seemed personally offended by the idea.' She drew in a long breath. 'I should've known this society thing wouldn't work out. I mean, Mum was an only child of Ghanaian immigrants. She felt so much pressure to do well here. Even if she'd been interested in anything outside of her studies, it's not like she'd have had the time.'

'Don't give up yet. We'll keep trying. And we can search more colleges too. She's got to be at one of them.' He felt strangely reluctant to change the subject, but he had no choice. 'In the meantime, we should talk about Diana. There's been . . . a development.'

She sat up, her face filling with dread. 'What did you do this time?'

'I tried asking her out. Like you said.'

'And?'

'And . . . she kicked me out and basically told me not to come back.'

Esi's head sank into her hands. 'Tell me what happened. And I mean everything. What you said, what she said, how she looked – I need all of it.'

He told her. She listened, silent and serious, her chin resting in her palm. Her dress fell off one shoulder, drawing his eye to the curve of her neck.

'Joseph Greene.' She clicked her fingers. 'Are you done? You just, like – tailed off midsentence.'

He blinked. 'Oh. Uh – that was it.'

She no longer looked existentially terrified, which he took as a good sign. 'Okay. So. There's a chance you haven't fucked this up completely.'

'Really?'

'You said you'd like to know her better. She answered by reminding you she has a boyfriend. That means she was already thinking of you romantically. And it sounds like she wasn't completely against the idea, until you talked about her and Crispin being happy.'

'Fuck.' He ground his knuckles into his forehead. 'I knew that was going too far.'

'No, no, it's good! It tells us a lot that she reacted that way. It means she's *not* happy with him, and she *is* interested in you on some level, even if she can't admit it yet.'

He sat back, baffled. 'I don't get it. She tells me I'm not her type, and you say that means she's into me. What would she have done if she really wasn't interested?'

She gave him a *that's obvious* look. 'She would have laughed.'

He shook his head. 'I am so glad you speak girl.'

'"I am so glad you speak girl." Joseph Greene, famous lover.' She drew in a breath. 'So, have you heard from her since?'

He held up his phone. 'I sent her this message right after. No reply.'

She squinted at the screen, then back at him, her eyes crinkling in disappointment. 'You just sent her that? With no explanation, no reference to anything she said?' She tipped her head back and addressed the vaulted ceiling. 'This. This is why it's so hard to be a woman who dates men.'

He tried not to focus on the soft hollow of her throat. 'Are men not better in the future?'

She laughed, her head dropping. 'You know what, I think it actually might have got worse. You at least are teachable.' She pressed her hands flat on the bench between them. 'Here's a test. Joseph Greene. What's the first thing we do when we've hurt someone through our actions?'

He narrowed his eyes. 'Apologise?'

'Apologise.' She patted him on the head. 'You get a gold star.' She tapped her fingers against her lips. 'Okay, how's this. "Sorry about before. You're beautiful, and I got carried away."'

'Bury a compliment in there. Nice.' He typed the message eagerly. 'What else?'

Esi closed her eyes and extended her hand towards Joe, like she was channelling him. '"Sometimes,"' she said, '"I get poetry mixed up with real life."'

He was indignant. 'That makes me sound like a psycho.'

'No. It makes you sound like a *passionate artist*,' she growled. 'Which is exactly who she wants you to be.'

He sighed and added it to the message. 'Okay,' he said, feeling like he was getting the hang of it. 'And now I say it won't happen again.'

'No!' She rapped the back of his hand. 'Bad poet!'

'What? You told me to say that last time!'

'This is different from last time. Last time, she didn't want your attention. This time, she does.'

He groaned. 'This is so complicated.'

'It's really not.'

He went back over the message, then held it up to show her. She scrolled through it and nodded. 'Send.'

He pressed the button and put his phone away, feeling like he had just survived an exam.

The ACS gathering had divided into an impromptu dance floor and an informal study group. Esi's head was turned over her shoulder, watching the talking, laughing students around the table. He could almost see the gap she saw, the person who should have been there but wasn't.

'Hey,' he said gently. 'Don't worry. We'll find her.'

She looked at him, her eyes huge in her solemn face. 'What if we don't?'

Chapter Thirteen

He didn't understand. 'We will. We've got months. Your mum might be some kind of reclusive spy genius, but – this is Cambridge. Like you said, it's barely a city. She can't hide from us forever.'

Esi was shaking her head. 'But that's the point. She shouldn't be this hard to find. And it got me thinking. What if it means you're right?' She dipped her fingers into a pool of spilled water on the table. 'What if I can't save her?'

He tried to find a way to say it gently. 'I guess – you go back home and you try to live with it.'

She made a soft noise. 'You sound like my dad.' Her finger drew the water out into a looping line. 'He told me not to come here. He thought it was a mistake.'

'He didn't think the past could be changed?'

'He didn't want me to change it.' She swept the water into curlicues, branching out like leaves from a stem. 'Course, he didn't just come out and say it. He had to tell me a story first. It's a Jamaican thing – they love to speak in riddles.'

He watched a fond, frustrated smile spread across her face. 'What was the story?'

'It was about a girl whose friend was drowning in a river. She jumped in to try and save her, but she ended up drowning herself.' She shook her head tightly. 'I told him, *I'm not going to drown. I'm saving her, then I'm coming back.*'

'And what did he say?'

She swept her palm across her drawing, smearing it into oblivion. 'He said, *Someone's going to step out of that river, but it won't be you.*'

He understood. 'He doesn't want you changing yourself. Even if it means bringing your mum back.' Tears were filling her eyes. He looked away, giving her a moment. 'He sounds like a good dad.'

'Yeah. Yeah, he is.' Out of the corner of his eye, he saw her wipe her tears away. 'I just miss him. His parties. His jokes. His stupid stories. His *cooking*. You know he learned how to cook all the Ghanaian food Mum used to make? Jollof rice, fufu. Because he didn't want us to forget that side of where we come from.' Her voice was warm. 'And my sisters – they're fifteen and seventeen now. They think they're so grown-up, but they're really not. They're babies.' She stared across the bar. 'I feel so bad about leaving them. Even just for a while. But . . .' She shrugged, helpless. 'I'm their big sister. I have to fix it.'

He didn't know what to say. 'Sorry,' she added with a sniff. 'Just – sometimes, it gets to me, being here.' She tipped her head up, as if to stop more tears falling. 'The loud cars, and the smoke everywhere, and the antique phones, and the stupid indie bands that all sound the same, and everything being – not what I'm used to.'

'You're homesick,' he said gently. 'It's not surprising. The past is a foreign country, right? You've got the world's worst case of culture shock, and you've been trying to deal with it alone.'

She made a strangled noise. He saw another tear fall, even as she brushed it away. He could read her discomfort in every line of her body: she didn't want to break down in front of him. He wanted desperately to make it better, but he didn't know how. Then, an idea came to him, bright as a new poem. It was stupid, and it would be bad for his overdraft, but it would be worth it.

'Come with me.' He strode off, giving her time to collect herself before she followed. At the college gate, he checked up and down the street for Vera, but the tour guide was nowhere to be seen.

Esi came up beside him. 'Where are we going?'

'You'll see.' He led her through the darkened streets to the run-down shopping precinct of Bradwells Court.

At their destination, she stopped, staring. 'What the hell is Laser Quest?'

They donned their vests and guns and entered the arena. He turned to face her in the flickering darkness. 'You said you miss the future.' He gestured around at the cardboard neon dystopia. 'Here it is.'

'I mean, yeah, it's uncanny,' she said, in a kind of hysterical deadpan. 'I could literally be in my house right now.'

'Including the body armour and laser guns?'

'Don't laugh, Joseph Greene. I told you I played Assassins.' She raised her gun. 'What I didn't tell you is, I play to win.'

She darted away. He ran after her, his heart pounding. Joy flooded his veins as he crept along the wall, transformed from a cardboard prop to a neon facade in a city of the future. He peered around the corner, looking for Esi. He would take it easy on her, since it was her first time. He'd let her get in a couple of shots to boost her confidence, then—

A noise blared in his ear. He jumped, the sad bleeps of his virtual death echoing from his vest. 'Hey!'

Esi, who had inexplicably ended up above him, waved and took aim again. He yelped and sprinted away to recover.

After that, he abandoned his chivalry and set his mind to taking her down. She should have been an easy target, in her patterned dress that fluoresced under the lights, but somehow his shots never hit her, as if she were a mirage, not truly there. He found himself with one life left, heart pounding, breath coming in hot gasps. He was staring ahead into the neon smoke, trying to see what was coming, when something rushed at him from the side. Before he could react, his gun was dangling from his vest and Esi's was pressed up against his temple.

'*Bang,*' she whispered in his ear.

A shiver ran through his whole body. He had trouble keeping his voice level. 'Laser guns don't go *bang.*'

'No. They go like this.' She pressed the gun point-blank to his chest and fired. His digital blood spilled out in a gush of bleeps. 'Pleasure murdering you, Joseph Greene.'

'Pleasure to be murdered.' He followed her as she sashayed towards the exit, wondering why he still felt like he was fighting for his life.

They tumbled laughing out into the cold. Esi struck a pose, blowing smoke from the barrel of an imaginary gun. 'They call me Poetkiller.'

'Poets are notoriously easy to kill. Byron died of a cold in Greece.' She laughed, her warm, chaotic laugh that set him off like a firecracker. 'Might as well call yourself Sheepkiller, or – or Lettucekiller.'

Her eyes squeezed shut, her hand pressed to her throat. 'Joseph Greene,' she gasped. 'How do you keep on surprising me?'

He grinned. 'Well, the bar was pretty low, given that you expected me to be the worst person in the universe.'

She raised an eyebrow. 'Problem is, every time you impress me, the bar's rising. Think you can keep up?'

He looked into her dancing eyes. He knew this feeling, his blood fizzing, the air between them pulsing with light. *Are we flirting?* She laughed, as if answering his unspoken question. *Yes.* And why not? They both knew it wasn't going to happen. So if they tiptoed around the edges of it happening, where was the harm?

Her attention flickered over his shoulder. Her face went slack. 'You okay? You look like you've seen . . .' *A ghost.* He knew, with a lurch of his gut, exactly who she had caught sight of in the crowd, even before she started running.

She ran with abandon, flailing and desperate as a child. Straining to look beyond her, he caught a glimpse of a slight girl in a puffy coat, the edge of a familiar cheekbone, a fall of straightened dark hair. He followed Esi out onto St Andrew's Street, crossing the road to a chorus of ringing bikes, up the slope behind the church that led into Lion Yard shopping centre. He caught up with her in the crowd of early evening shoppers, turning fruitlessly in circles.

'*Fuck.* She's gone.' Her eyes, wide and unseeing, glanced off his and back into the crowd. 'I lost her.'

A feeling coursed through him, leaving him trembling in its wake. He was disturbed to find it was relief. He was glad she hadn't found her mum yet, because once she found her, she would be one step closer to leaving, and he didn't want her to go. But he didn't want to see her like this, dulled and broken, the pain of a second loss written all over her. The two impulses warred inside him, tearing him gently to pieces.

'Hey.' He touched her shoulder. 'It's a good sign. We found her once, we can find her again.'

He had meant to cheer her up, but she met his eyes with blank desolation. 'I should go.'

'Let me walk with you.'

She didn't protest. She didn't talk at all, not on the way out of town up St Andrew's Street, not as they crossed the flat dark of Parker's Piece under the overcast sky. The feeling of being watched crept up on him again. He turned, but there was only a random drunk weaving along the path behind them.

Esi turned with him. 'Who are you looking for?'

'Vera.'

She frowned, not understanding. 'We're fine. It's way after five.'

'I don't think she's sticking to the terms and conditions anymore. I've seen her on her own, out of hours. Watching me.'

'Shit. She must be looking for me.' Her eyes met his in panic. 'Why didn't you tell me?'

'I didn't think it was important! I thought she might just be a fan.' It sounded stupid now he said it. The woman spent every day following him around: she must be utterly sick of him.

Esi searched the darkness, walking backwards past the Reality Checkpoint. She shook her head. 'I'm going to have to be so much more careful.' Another worry he'd added to her list. He thought with a pang of how much simpler her life would have been if she'd never met him.

They went on up Mill Road, a backwards retread of their first walk together. As they neared the café, her steps slowed. In the window, coffee bean fireworks exploded around more coffee beans that spelled out *remember*.

'Another Campbell classic.'

She didn't smile. 'Need to update it. Fifth of November was weeks ago.' She reached in her bag for a jangling ring of keys.

He looked at her uncertainly. 'Do you need to update it right now?'

'Oh. Yeah.' She turned, standing awkwardly in the doorway. 'So, this is where I sleep.'

He stared. 'What?'

'It's not so bad. There's a bathroom in the back, and turns out, sacks of coffee beans are actually pretty comfortable—'

'No. This – this is not okay.'

She sighed. 'Don't make a big deal of it. You sound like Shola.'

'Shola?'

She gestured at the counter. 'The girl I work with. She's a master's student at the uni. She found out I was sleeping here, and she offered me a room in her house share.'

'So take it! Or – or come and stay with me and Rob! We have a sofa, and college never checks if we have guests—'

'Joseph Greene,' she interrupted him, a little warmth returning to her expression. 'Much as I'd love to come live with you and your friend who kills people, that's not going to work. And I can't live with Shola either. I'd get tangled up in her life, and her housemates' lives, and I can't risk that. Remember, I'm trying not to leave a mark, except the one I want to make.' She shrugged. 'I don't officially exist. Better if I'm a ghost.'

But you're not a ghost. You're real, and you're alive, and you're allowed to take up space. He sensed it was something she wasn't ready to hear. He exhaled. 'Look. I'm heading home next week to stay with my family for Christmas. Far from Vera, far from your mum, far from Diana. Nothing that happens there will affect – well, anything, really.' He shrugged. 'Come with me.'

'Come *with you*?' Her voice cracked. 'Just – come with Joseph Greene to Scotland? Stay in Joseph Greene's house, with Joseph Greene's family?'

'Eat Joseph Greene's Weetabix. Pet Joseph Greene's cat. Whose name is Jeely Piece, by the way.' He tugged at his hair. 'Can we stop with the full name? It's starting to make me feel like I'm already dead.'

'You are, remember? I killed you like five times.' She leaned against the door frame, looking at him with a strange mixture of frustration and delight. 'You're an idiot.'

'I'm sorry—'

'Thank you. For today. And for the offer. I – I'll think about it.' She leaned forward, sudden as a bird, and gave him a kiss on the cheek.

He stood back, swaying. They looked at each other. He smiled, and she laughed.

'Do you want to—' he started, then his phone buzzed in his pocket. He pulled it out. 'Shit. It's Diana.'

Chapter Fourteen

Love the new rehearsal space.

Let's give it a try.

He showed Esi. In the glow of the screen, her face held a strange despair. 'Now?'

'This is the first time she's texted me in four days. If she wants to meet now, I meet her now.' He looked to her for reassurance. 'Right?'

She let out a breathless laugh. 'You can't keep asking me for help with her.'

He gazed at her in half-seeing panic. 'I should meet her there. But – no. She can't get there without me. And – shit. It'll be dark. And not in a romantic way. In a walking-off-the-roof-to-our-deaths sort of way—'

'Oh my God. Stop. Just – text her saying you'll meet her nearby. And wait here.' She unlocked the café and disappeared inside. He heard her rummaging about in a drawer as he composed a message asking Diana to meet him outside college. 'Candles.' Esi emerged with a heap of them, dumping them awkwardly into his arms. 'Put them everywhere. You can't overdo it.'

'Okay.' He distributed the candles between his pockets and ran a hand through his hair. He hadn't put goop in it, but it was too late now. 'Is this – do I look—'

She met his eyes. 'You look fucking beautiful,' she said with perfect sincerity. 'Go.' She turned him around and shoved him gently in the back.

He ran. He ran down Mill Road under the thinning clouds, patches of star-studded black showing like glimpses of reality through a dream. He ran away from how he was feeling, torn up and remade, all his raw edges showing. He ran towards Diana.

She replied as he got back to college.

Be there in ten.

He pelted up the stairs to his room, grabbed a lighter that one of his smoker friends had left on the battlements, and scrambled to the secret terrace. In the dark it was otherworldly, a floating raft under an ocean of stars. He lit the candles and melted their bases, sticking them down in clusters that hopefully evoked a romantic grotto on a private island and not the Phantom of the Opera's lair. He slid down the drainpipe, side-hopped along the ledge, leapt back onto the battlements, and crashed into the living room, where he was dismayed to find Rob sinking face down into the sofa.

Vibrating with urgency, he hovered by his friend's head. 'What's up?'

'Darcy just won the Michaelmas Game. Confetti grenade again.' Rob rolled over, his face a picture of misery. 'My nemesis is officially a Master Assassin.'

Joe felt for him, but he also felt the pressing need to get him out of the room within the next minute. 'You can still win in Lent. Or

May Week.' He sat Rob up, giving him a hearty clap on the back. 'Go on. Get back out there. Grab your best rubber band and – and murder the shit out of someone.'

'I can't,' Rob explained as Joe heaved him to his feet. 'I'm dead, remember? The rules clearly state that dead people can't kill anyone, unless they join the Police . . . Why do I feel like you're trying to usher me out of the room?'

'Because I am,' he admitted. 'Diana's coming over.'

'Oh. Right. Glad things are going well for one of us.' Rob headed morosely down the stairs. 'Should you need me, I'll be drowning my sorrows in the bar.'

Joe sprinted past him, ran round the edge of the court, and burst through the college gate. Waiting outside was Diana, in a military-style jacket paired with an absurdly skinny scarf.

'Joseph.' She eyed him, obviously judging his dishevelled hair and the fact that he was gasping for breath.

'Diana.' He held the gate open and gestured her through.

She didn't ask where he was taking her. She walked beside him, her body carrying a strange tension. He felt a stab of guilt. He had seen her message as a victory, another step on the path towards his future. He hadn't thought about how she might be feeling, or what had happened to make her contact him after four days of silence.

At the foot of his staircase, he turned to her. 'Are you okay?'

She looked more amused than touched. 'Ha. You're very sweet.' She pulled her scarf tighter. 'All the way to the top?'

He nodded. She took the stairs ahead of him, then waited demurely by the door while he unlocked it. 'So this is your set?' He nodded. She cast her eye over the carpet stains and the cheap wine, Rob's tally of kills tacked up above the fireplace. 'If this was all a ploy to get me into your bedroom . . .'

'Not into. Through,' he said, opening the window and climbing out.

She followed him onto the battlements. Steadying herself in the wind, she looked out over the lamplit hush of the college court. 'Not bad.'

'We're not there yet.' He leapt across to the ledge. 'This way.'

She looked at him sternly. 'Are you sure this is safe?'

'No. It's incredibly dangerous.' He reached out, offering her his hand. He was surprised to see that it was perfectly steady. 'But I know for a fact that neither of us is dying tonight.'

She stared at him across the plunging gap. Then she looked down, with a tiny shake of her head, as though rebuking herself for being impressed. 'All right.' She climbed up on the edge of the battlements. She swayed once, twice, and leapt, landing lightly beside him. 'Okay,' she said huskily. 'Where now?'

'Follow me.' He strode confidently along the narrow ledge towards the drainpipe. The third time, it was almost becoming routine. He had forgotten it wasn't routine for Diana.

He didn't see her fall. He only heard a shriek, high and shattering. He lunged for her, grabbing the drainpipe with his other hand almost as an afterthought. She caught his arm and he pulled her in. She clung to him, her body pressed against his, her breath loud and panicked in his ear.

'Shit. Fuck. Shit.' She was shaking, waves of near-death running through her. He held her close, feeling her heartbeat drown out his own.

'I've got you,' he said, shocking himself with his own calm.

She disentangled herself from him carefully, like someone unhooking their life support. 'Let me guess,' she said as if nothing had happened. 'We're going up the drainpipe.'

'We don't have to,' he offered. 'We can go back.'

She chuckled, a low, rolling sound in the dark. 'Oh, no, Joseph. It's far too late for that.'

She stepped neatly around him and started climbing. He heard her gasp while he was still halfway up. By the time he emerged, she was framed in the gap between the two roofs, staring out at King's College Chapel.

He couldn't help grinning. 'You like it?'

She turned to him. In the candlelight, her face was more than beautiful: it was as if the soft, golden glow was coming from inside her. 'How long did it take you to set this up?'

He shrugged. 'Five minutes. Nine, if you count climbing here and back again.'

She leaned over his shoulder to look at the drop. 'You weren't afraid. Not even when I almost fell.'

He shook his head, acutely conscious of her closeness. 'You weren't going to fall.'

She looked at him curiously. When he didn't elaborate, she went to sit between two clumps of candles that formed a natural stage. 'I don't understand you, Joseph.' She leaned back on her hands, arching her neck. 'You write with such conviction. And the way you talk sometimes, it's as if you have this – this unshakeable belief. But you don't seem to actually hold that belief inside you.' She examined him, candlelight chasing shadows across her face. 'It's as if it comes from the outside, somehow.'

'Oh, it does,' he said, aiming for an echo of her dry tone. 'A time traveller told me I'm going to be a famous poet. That's the only reason I believe it.'

She shook her head with a tiny smile. 'So. If you're not afraid of heights, what *are* you afraid of?'

He stared up at the darkness, waiting for his eyes to adjust and reveal the stars. There was nothing to be afraid of anymore. Fear came from not knowing, and he knew everything. It was a strangely empty feeling. And, he realised, it was a lie. He was still afraid, but he didn't know what he was afraid of. Images swirled in his mind. The infinite paths in the painting on Diana's neighbour's door, one of them marked out for him. Esi's palm swiping water across the table, unmaking her art like she wanted to unmake her life.

'I'll tell you what you're afraid of.' He felt the burnished weight of Diana's attention. 'You're absolutely terrified of making a fool of yourself.'

He laughed, the surprised, gut-punch laugh that comes with recognising a truth. That was it, after all: the dark mirror of his desire to be great, that he might put his soul on display and find it judged worthless. He knew now there was no danger of that; still, he couldn't shake the lingering terror. 'Fair enough.'

'It's not funny, Joseph.' She hugged herself against the cold wind that made the candles flicker. 'Fear can be a good thing, up to a point. It keeps you sharp, keeps you striving. But too much fear can paralyse you.'

'I know.' He came to sit down next to her. 'That's why I haven't finished a poem since I got to Cambridge.'

She frowned at him. 'Except for "A Taste of Stars".'

He froze. The honesty of their conversation had caught him: he had been talking to her like she lived in his head, as if he didn't have anything to hide. 'Aye, except that one,' he said, trying to sound normal. 'I guess the competition motivated me.' She was looking at him strangely. He could taste his own lies, sour and electric on his tongue. He cleared his throat. 'What about you? What are you afraid of?'

She looked out into the dark. 'I'm afraid of waking up one day in my thirties and realising I missed my chance.'

He stole a glance at her profile, serious in the low light. His heart filled with the knowledge of who she would be, of how completely her future would realise her hopes. He smiled. 'You're not going to miss your chance.'

She looked at him under her eyelashes. 'Did your time traveller tell you that?'

He shook his head, gazing at her. 'I don't need a time traveller to tell me that you're going to be a star.'

She drew in a heavy, shuddering sigh, as if he had given her a wonderful gift. 'Do you ever just want to be . . .' She looked down at her hands. 'More than you are?'

'Yes,' he said, his soul singing with it. 'Every second.'

She leaned against him, a touch so brief he could have imagined it.

They sat side by side, looking out at the roof of King's Chapel, the stars above dimmed by the floodlights. The moment was everything he had imagined Cambridge to be. It should have been glorious, transcendent, but he was so conscious of its significance that it felt like he was watching it happen to someone else.

Diana's phone buzzed, and kept buzzing. 'Fuck.' She didn't need to say that it was Crispin. He read it in the tension of her shoulders as she pressed the phone to her ear and turned away. 'Yes.'

A man's voice, low and indecipherable. She said, 'You're really asking me why?'

A pause, then a questioning tone. She sighed. 'Well, the thing is, Crisp, when you say those things, it makes me not want to be around you.'

The voice went softer, coaxing. She closed her eyes. 'Okay,' she breathed. She hung up and stood, swaying. 'I have to go.'

He got awkwardly to his feet. 'Let me walk you back.'

She gave him a wry smile. 'Don't worry, Joseph. I'll be careful, since you think my future is worth sticking around for.' She studied him, a cool, evaluating gaze that made him feel like he was under a microscope. 'Are you doing anything for New Year?'

'Uh. No. I mean – I'll be at home.' He should have made something up – who in their right mind admitted to having no plans for New Year beyond getting drunk with their parents?

'Sounds depressing.' She held out her hand. 'Do you have a pen?'

'What kind of question is that?' he asked, producing one from his jacket pocket.

She smiled. 'Ready to poeticise at a moment's notice.' She took the pen, then his hand – hers was icy cold – and wrote on it in prickly letters. He looked down as an address in London materialised on his skin. 'Come to my party.'

'Okay,' he said, trying to sound like he wasn't bothered. Worried he'd overdone it, he added, 'Thanks.'

'It's the very least I can do,' she said archly. 'You saved my life, after all.'

He laughed. 'Not sure it counts if I'm the one who endangered it in the first place.'

'Oh, it counts.' She kissed him on the cheek, then dropped over the edge of the roof.

He touched the place where her lips had met his skin. He felt it burning long after she had gone.

Chapter Fifteen

They pulled up at the house in the afternoon drizzle. Behind them stretched the brown winter fields; ahead, a cluster of low-roofed houses lay between them and the sea. Joe stepped out of the car, tasting the salt in the air. Strange, the things you only noticed once you'd left.

'Guess I understand now why you think Cambridge is a city.' Esi stretched, arching her neck as Joe's dad got their bags out of the boot. 'You going to show me around?'

'Got thirty seconds? That should be enough to cover the highlights.'

His dad dumped their bags inside the front door. 'I'm afraid Joe doesn't have thirty seconds. He's going to be too busy catching up on his reading. Turning that 2:2 into a First.'

The 2:2 was a lie. In fact, he'd scraped a Third, one step away from failing. The knowledge of his predestined 2:1 made him weak with relief. But he needed to moderate expectations. 'A First's not going to happen.'

'Not with that attitude.'

'No, I mean it. It's metaphysically impossible for me to get any higher than a 2:1.'

Esi gave Joe's dad a look. 'I keep telling him, the future's not set in stone. If he just *tries*, he can do anything.'

Joe's dad shook her hand. 'You can come back anytime.'

'Joe!' His mum flew down the stairs, enveloped him in a hug, then immediately pushed him away to look at him. 'Oh, darling, you're skinny as a rake! What are they feeding you down there?'

'I'm feeding myself, Mum. I'm an adult.' He took in his parents, his mum's freckled face sporting new wrinkles, his dad's posture a little more stooped. Since he'd moved away, he'd started to notice them ageing secretly in the gaps.

He became conscious of the way Esi was watching, with a wounded softness he couldn't bear. Her mum didn't age. She was frozen in her memory, forever as she'd been when she last saw her.

Joe's mum turned to her. 'You must be Esi,' she said warmly. 'I've heard so much about you.'

Her eyes widened in alarm. 'Really?'

His mum laughed. 'All good things! Come on in.' She ushered them inside, where she gave Esi a lightning tour of the ground floor, then immediately dispatched her and Joe on a mission to the village shop.

As they headed down the road, he looked sideways at her. He had been surprised she'd said yes to his offer: surprised, and delighted, and a little anxious, in a way he couldn't explain. He had half expected her to change her mind. Now, here she was, walking beside him on the streets he had run down as a child, hugging herself against the sea wind he'd been missing. Realities were colliding, and it made everything feel unmoored.

He felt the shy, restless flicker of her attention. 'Was that your poem on the wall of the downstairs loo?'

'It is, indeed, an original Joseph Greene,' he said dryly. 'I won a national contest with it while I was in high school. That's why it's on display.'

Her brow furrowed. 'But – in the loo?'

'It's their way of showing they're proud of me, but also turning it into a joke in case anyone thinks they're *too* proud of me.'

She shook her head. 'I've been here two minutes, and I already feel like I understand you better than I have for the past two months.'

'You mean that's not how your family does it?'

She laughed. 'Yeah, not exactly. One time I came second in my class in school, and my dad wouldn't shut up about it. He was telling strangers on the street. Posting about it on' – her cheek dimpled – '*the facebook*. And it was never *Esi came second in maths, isn't that great.* It was, *My daughter came top in the entire school! In every single subject! She's a future genius!*'

'Maybe he's right about that.'

She rolled her eyes. 'And maybe you're a future comedian instead of a poet.'

They reached the village shop. He bought the tattie scones and butter his mum had asked for, then found Esi in the back, browsing the tiny DVD rental section. He was shocked to see tears in her eyes. 'What's wrong?'

'Nothing. Just . . .' She pointed at one of the DVDs. 'That was my mum's favourite when she was a teenager.'

He took it down. It was a romantic comedy starring Meg Ryan, but not one he'd heard of. 'Have you ever seen it?'

She shook her head. 'Dad had the thing that plays the tapes, so we could watch some of her old Nollywood collection. But we didn't have anything to play her – discs, or whatever.'

'Your dad has a VHS player, but not a DVD player?' She stared at him blankly. He shook his head. 'Doesn't matter. Let's rent it.' Her blank look continued. In a series of gestures, he explained. 'We pay some money. We take this home. We watch it. We bring it back.'

'Like, the physical object?' She burst out laughing. 'That's hilarious.'

'How else would you rent a film?'

'I'm not telling. It's too much fun watching your prehistoric brain try and figure it out.'

They walked back by the scenic route, taking one of the crooked lanes that ran down to the sea. By the harbour, a knot of lads were laughing and spitting into the water. Joe's guts froze with a stale fear he couldn't reason away.

One of them looked up and saw him. 'Aye, it's Alfred Lord Tennyson! How's the poetry?'

Esi looked between the lads and Joe. 'You know them?'

He lifted his hand, walking on. 'Aye. That's the lads from school who used to shove my head down the toilet.'

'Why?'

'Oh, a million reasons. I was quiet, and weird, and I wrote poetry.'

'I don't know. Some girls are into that. Not me, obviously.' She nudged closer to him, taking his arm. 'But they don't need to know that.'

One of the lads whistled. The rest laughed. Joe understood what she'd done, and his heart tingled with sudden warmth. 'It didn't start because of that,' he added. 'At the beginning, it was because my dad's English.'

She looked incredulous. 'Is it that big a deal?'

He snorted. 'Ask my grandparents. They were ready to disown Mum when she told them who she was marrying.'

She laughed. 'Same story with my mum and dad. Her side is African, his side is Caribbean, it's a whole thing. But their families got over it. Eventually.'

'Did you get grief about it at school?'

'Not really. It's not such a big deal in my generation.' She looked back over her shoulder. 'Who's Alfred Lord Tennyson?'

'Victorian poet. They call me that because . . .' He closed his eyes. 'Because that's what I said when the teacher asked us to name our favourite celebrity.'

'Oh my God.' She leaned into him, shaking with laughter. 'That's so adorable I can't accept it.'

He took her down to the beach, yelling his tourist spiel over the howling gale. She bent to examine a pile of seaweed, draping strands of it into spirals, her braids whipping around her head. He watched as she worked, building up layers that started out as nothing but turned incrementally into a woman's face, calm and pensive, her hair a profusion of Afro curls.

'Your art,' he said. 'It's really good. You should do something with it.'

She looked up at him, amused. 'First time I've heard that. My dad was always like, *Esi, nice picture, but shouldn't you be studying? No one gets paid to draw.*'

'Aye, sounds familiar.' He smiled. 'Did you point out some people do get paid to draw?'

'So that's what you're saying I should do with it? Try and sell it?'

'Not necessarily. Show it to folk. Give them something to remember.' He thought again of the statue of Byron in the Wren Library, gazed at by seven generations of watchers.

'But I'm not doing it for anyone else. I'm doing it because it's fun. And because . . .' She looked up, as if searching for words in the overcast sky. 'I like making things that didn't exist before. Things only I could make. Even if I'm the only one who ever sees them.'

It felt like listening to himself three years ago. Where had it gone, that joy in just creating, without obsessing over what people would think, whether it would impress them enough? Could he ever get it back?

She shivered, turning to the lashing grey waves. 'It never stops, does it?'

He laughed. 'The sea? No, customarily the sea doesn't stop.'

'How do you get used to it?'

'It becomes a part of you, I guess. When I first moved to Cambridge, I used to sit holding a glass to my ear, just to feel less homesick.' He closed his eyes, letting the sound pass through him. 'Then I realised, it's not really here I miss. It's the fact I grew up here. All the versions of me it remembers.' He understood, as he was saying it, what it meant. 'We're all time travellers. Just, most of us don't get to go back.'

They climbed the hill to the house, grimacing into the wind. He dropped the supplies on the kitchen table. A strangled meow announced the arrival of his grumpy fifteen-year-old cat, who padded in and rubbed his head against Esi's ankle.

'Hi there . . .' She stopped short. 'What did you say its name was?'

'Jeely Piece.' He bent down to knuckle the old tabby's head. 'It means jam sandwich,' he explained.

She gave him a dead-eyed look. 'You're meant to be an entire famous poet, and you can't even name a cat right.'

'In my defence, I was five.'

'Mmhm.' Her cheek trembled with suppressed laughter. He dropped his head with a grin.

His mum came into the kitchen and started tidying the shopping away. 'Joe. Are you going to show your guest her room, or are you going to make me look like a bad mother?'

'Jesus. Fine,' he protested, and ushered Esi up the stairs to his sister's room. 'Kirsty's staying with her girlfriend for Christmas, so it's all yours.'

She sat down on the bed and looked around at Kirsty's walls: pages torn from rock magazines, moody charcoal drawings of the harbour in winter. 'Your sister's cool.'

'Hence why she's the one with the girlfriend.'

She batted his arm with forced casualness. 'Just wait till New Year. Catch Diana at midnight, and the rest is history.'

He felt a lurch like a skipped heartbeat. He thought of Diana on the roof, bathed in candlelight, the glowing mirage of King's Chapel behind her. Here, in the ordinary mess of his sister's bedroom, it seemed like an image from another reality.

Esi was looking down at her hands. 'How's it going with her?'

'I guess – I'm starting to get to know her. Sometimes, I can imagine how it might feel to be in love with her. But I'm not there yet.'

Her voice was carefully neutral. 'If you keep comparing your feelings to how you think you're supposed to feel in the future, you'll never get the chance to feel how you feel right now.'

'But the future's the only thing we have in common,' he protested. 'The one time we were really talking, really connecting, it was about who we're meant to be. It felt like she was finally taking me seriously.' He sat down on the bed, exhaling. 'Or maybe she was just impressed that I took her night climbing.'

'You took her what?'

'Night climbing. You know. Shinning up drainpipes to get to secret bits of the college roof. Like that picture I showed you.' She was looking at him as if he had entirely lost his mind. 'Anyway, I was trying to re-create this romantic moment in the future where I take her to a private island. Clearly, that's not an option right now, so—'

She interrupted him. 'How did you know about that?'

'It was in the book.'

She stood up, eyes wide in alarm. 'You shouldn't be trying to impress her using stuff from the book. You're not meant to know any of that yet.'

This again. He sighed. 'I know you're worried I'm going to change the future. But I'm not changing it. I'm making it happen.'

'You know I don't believe that. And anyway, that's not the point.' She shook her head. 'It's wrong. It's – manipulative.'

He felt the accusation like a blow. 'I'm sorry. Weren't you the one helping me manipulate her into liking me?'

'Making you look good. Telling you how not to be a nozz. That's one thing.' Her gaze closed him in. 'Using stuff you know about her future that she doesn't know herself? That's something else.'

He looked up at her, arms crossed, an angel of judgment. He searched for a reason he'd done it, a good reason that would prove he was in the right, but the truth was, he didn't have one. He had seen a way to get what he wanted, and used it. He felt a stab of shame. But it was too late to take it back. The whole shaky edifice of his and Diana's relationship was built on the foundation of a poem he hadn't written yet.

She said it quietly. 'Are you going to tell her?'

His heart skipped a beat. Esi didn't know about the poem. Did she? 'Tell her what?'

'About the future. Are you ever going to be honest with her?'

He imagined Diana opening *Meant to Be*. He imagined her looking up at him, eyes bright with accusation. He shuddered. 'Esi, she'd be furious. You need us to get together, right?' Reluctantly, she nodded. 'Well. If that's going to happen, I can't tell her.'

'Guess you're right. Doesn't mean I have to like it.' She sighed, rubbing her face. 'We should focus on getting you ready for the party. What are you planning to wear?'

He shrugged. 'Clothes?'

Life came back to her expression. 'Come on. Let's see what we have to work with.' She took his arm and marched him across the landing.

'Didn't we already do the makeover scene?' he protested.

'A makeover isn't a onetime thing, Joseph Greene. It's an ongoing process of becoming.'

'Aye, right.' In his childhood bedroom, he saw every embarrassing detail through her eyes: the single bed with the cuddly Nessie tucked in; the skeletal rabbit head on his *Donnie Darko* poster; the pictures of his baby cousin sticking her fingers in his mouth.

Thankfully, Esi was focused on the contents of his wardrobe. 'No. No. Oh my *God*, no. What? No. Wait.' A screech as she pulled every hanger but one to the front. '*Yes.*'

His kilt outfit, complete with Prince Charlie jacket and waistcoat. It had been hanging there undisturbed since his cousin's wedding two years ago.

She ran her hand over the blue-and-green squares. 'Is that your family tartan?'

'Kind of. Clans are supposed to go down the male line, but my dad doesn't have one, being English and all. That's my mum's.'

'Matriarchy. I like it.' She pulled it from the wardrobe, almost dropping it when she discovered how heavy it was. She hefted it and hung it on the wardrobe door. 'You're wearing this to the party.'

'No!'

'Come on. Kilts are ving.'

'Ving?'

She rolled her eyes. 'You need me to spell it out for you? The Scottish thing is a major selling point! There are a billion romance books about the sexy laird, or whatever.' She coughed, looking self-conscious. 'I mean, not like I've read any of them. Just – you know. I'm informed.'

Joe, who was experiencing some confusing sensations, tried to focus on what she was asking. 'Fine. I'll wear my kilt. On one condition.' He cleared his throat. 'You come with me.'

'Come with you?' She looked dubious. 'I'm not going to stand next to you whispering lines in your ear.'

'No, nothing like that. Just – I'd feel better if you were there.'

It was simple when he said it, but her reaction – a look of soft surprise – made him feel suddenly vulnerable. 'What about her?' she said. 'Do you think she'll be there?'

It took him a moment to realise who she meant. He remembered the photograph, her mum and Diana arm in arm. 'You still think Diana was lying about not recognising her?'

She shrugged. 'I don't know. But if there's a chance she was . . .' There it was again: the fear, like a ghost behind her eyes.

'Look. If we go, and she's there, we'll learn something. But I don't want you to do anything you're not comfortable with.'

Esi nodded. She looked back at the kilt, an uncertain smile on her face. 'Okay. Let's do it.'

THEY HAD A DVD night, huddled on the old sofa with a blanket and Jeely Piece, who had decided Esi's lap was his rightful place. They started with her mum's favourite film, which was a romantic comedy about a woman from modern-day New York falling in love with a time traveller.

'Mum was into period romance,' Esi explained as the Duke of Albany fell screaming through a time portal. 'Guys in breeches and *yes, my lady* and all that. Me, I always went for more contemporary stuff.'

He looked sideways at her, radiant in the dark. 'You realise what you call contemporary is now science fiction?'

'Stop it,' she complained. 'You're making me time-sick.'

He tried his best to follow the plot, but the warmth of Esi against his side was pleasantly distracting, and the film's time-travel mechanics were confusing at best. 'Wait, so . . . he's going to be the inventor of the lift?'

'Elevator,' she corrected in a decent American accent.

'The elevator. And – because he's travelled into the future, elevators in New York are just – randomly malfunctioning?'

'Don't look at me. I don't know how real time travel works. Why would I know how fake time travel works?'

They kept watching. 'So she's just going to stay with him in 1876?'

'Looks like it.'

'What's she going to do? I thought she was this high-powered career woman!'

'What's she *not* going to do? Think about it. She could invent everything a hundred years early. Move the future onto a better path.'

He looked at her fondly. 'Of course you'd say that.' For a moment, the tension of the real argument between them hung in the air.

She gave a tiny shrug. 'Or, you know. Maybe she decided the past has some good points.'

He smiled and looked back at the screen.

'Okay,' he said as the film ended. 'I'm sorry to say it, but my level of respect for your mum has dropped substantially.'

'Come on. This came out when she was—' She flipped the box and counted. 'Sixteen. No one has good taste when they're sixteen. I mean, judging by that poster in your bedroom, you were into movies about zombie rabbits.'

He was indignant. '*Donnie Darko* is not a film about zombie rabbits.'

'Prove it.'

They watched *Donnie Darko*. Esi sat in silence, a delicate furrow on her brow, until the credits rolled. 'Okay, that made no sense.'

'I know, right? I didn't get it till the fifth time I watched it.' He swivelled to face her. 'So. Donnie realises he was supposed to die when the plane engine fell in his room. He didn't die, and that's created a divergent universe, which is causing a paradox and breaking reality. So he goes back through a wormhole into the original universe and makes sure he's in his room when the plane engine falls, so he can die like he's meant to and set things right.'

She was staring at the screen. 'Why do time-travel stories always end with putting things back how they were?'

He shrugged. 'Maybe it's comforting. The idea that there's one way things are meant to be.' He felt her stiffen. Too late, he realised how it sounded. 'Sorry. I didn't mean—'

'You did, though.' She turned to him, serious in the screen's muted glow. 'And I get why you want it to be that way. You're meant to end up with everything you ever wanted.'

He tipped his head back against the sofa. 'And I get why you want the past to change. *Need* it to change.'

'We don't have to change your future, though.'

He stared up at the ceiling, fear wound tight inside him. 'I just – I still don't really believe it's possible unless it's inevitable. Does that make sense? Me succeeding – it feels so unlikely that if it doesn't happen the exact way it always did, it won't happen at all.'

She didn't reply. He heard her breathing, and felt her warmth against him, but he didn't dare to look at her. He had known since the start that they had different ideas about how time travel worked, but he had never let it bother him. Now, for some reason, he desperately wanted them to be on the same side.

He tilted his head towards her. 'Maybe we're both wrong. I mean, Rob's always telling me physics is much weirder than we can imagine. Time travel could work differently from how either of us thinks it does.'

She met his eyes. 'It doesn't matter how it works,' she said softly. 'There's no way both of us get what we want.'

He tried to think around it, like a tricky essay question, but she was right. There was no world where his future was fixed and her mum's past could change. They would have to keep on as they were, working together but apart, in parallel but untouching universes.

She got up, dislodging Jeely Piece. Her warmth against his side was gone. 'Night, Joseph Greene.'

'Night,' he said, and watched her disappear into the dark.

Chapter Sixteen

Three weeks slid away like sand through his fingers. Too soon, he was at the kitchen table on their last evening, and his dad was raising a glass to Esi. 'Thank you for coming to the ends of the earth.'

'It's been lovely to have you,' said his mum. With a conspiratorial smile at his dad, she added, 'It's great to see Joe so happy.'

'Mum,' he protested.

She beamed at him, watery-eyed. He recognised that look: it meant she was tipsy enough to sincerely express her feelings. 'We're just so proud of you. And, Esi, you should be proud too. Getting into Cambridge, staying the course – it's a huge achievement.'

It was the cover story they'd decided on. He hadn't questioned whether it was a good idea until he saw the way she was looking at his mum, with fragile intensity. 'Thanks. I . . .' Her voice wobbled. 'Sorry. I have to—' She got up, her face a mask of tears.

He followed her out to the hall, where she was pulling on her borrowed boots. 'Where are you going?'

Her voice was choked. 'I need to be alone.' She walked out, closing the door behind her.

He went back to the kitchen. 'She's fine,' he said, rubbing his face. 'She just needs some time.'

His mum and dad looked at each other. He knew what they were thinking: that this was some kind of lovers' tiff. The thought made him irrationally angry.

'It's starting to rain,' his mum said, looking anxiously out of the window. 'Did she take a waterproof?'

'No.' He tried to ignore her reproachful look. 'Mum, she'll be fine. She's from London, she's not soluble.'

His mum steered him to the door and put a spare raincoat in his arms. 'Find her,' she said, and pushed him outside.

He pulled up his hood against the smirr of rain and headed down the street. He was too late to follow her, but there weren't many places she could have gone. His feet led him, as they always did, down to the sea.

He found her on a bench beside the harbour, looking out into the rolling grey dark. Her hoodie was soaked, clinging in wet patches to her skin. Wordlessly, he handed her the spare waterproof. She pulled off the hoodie and slid her shivering arms into the sleeves.

'I'm sorry,' he said. 'I know you wanted to be alone, but Mum was about to disown me if I didn't come and check on you.'

Her face crumpled. 'It's just hard. Seeing you with them, both of them. How much they love you. How proud they are of you. It's like you've got everything I lost.'

'Your dad's proud of you. And your mum would be too, if she could see you.'

A sob shook her. 'No, she wouldn't. She'd be so disappointed in me. She was so smart, so successful, and I – I'm nothing. I'm going nowhere.'

He finally understood: the real reason why she was so afraid of her mum seeing her, why she wanted to intervene without leaving a mark. 'What are you talking about? You're literally trying to change the world. That's more impressive than anything I've ever done.' He leaned towards her. 'Not to mention, you've also managed to do the impossible and impress my parents.'

Her voice wobbled. 'Only because they think I go to Cambridge.'

'That's got nothing to do with it. Trust me, they've complained about plenty of my uni friends. But they love you.' His heart thudded strangely as he went on, 'They'd want me to marry you tomorrow, if it wasn't obvious that you're way out of my league.'

She huffed out a laugh. 'I'm not out of your league. You're out of my league. You're' – she cast him a sideways glance – 'surprisingly hot, and you're funny, and you're kind, and you're destined to be with a gorgeous famous actor.' She shrugged violently. 'I'm just – broken.'

He tried not to focus on the *surprisingly hot*, which was making him feel all kinds of things, and stuck to what was important. 'Has anyone ever said that to you?' he asked gently. 'That you're broken?'

'Not *to* me.' She took in a great sniff of the sea air. 'But I heard my dad talking to one of my aunties, not long after it happened. He said . . .' She swallowed. 'He said when he looked at me, he couldn't see his little girl anymore. It was – it was like he'd lost her.'

He reached for her. He couldn't help it: he wrapped his arm around her shaking body, as if he could hold her together. 'Esi, no. He was worried about you. He wasn't saying – he didn't mean—'

She shook him off, eyes flashing. 'What do you know about it? You weren't there! You were an old man in a mansion somewhere. And when I go back, that's all you'll be again.'

He shifted along the bench. He felt the distance between them, inches and decades and the incommensurable gap between one soul and another. 'How's it going to work?' he said quietly. 'When you go back.'

'I told you, I don't know—'

'How do you hope it's going to work?'

'I guess . . .' She stared ahead at the dark ocean. 'I'll go to the wormhole. I'll step through. And – I won't be me anymore. Or, not this me. I'll be the new me. The one I was meant to be.'

He took in her face, familiar to him after these weeks of spending every moment together: the curve of her cheekbone, her generous mouth, her curious eyes that lit up when an idea struck her. He couldn't imagine another Esi. She was so specific, so herself, that any alternative version of her dissolved into nonexistence. What part of her would change? Her wide-eyed enthusiasm? Her flashes of sarcasm, like sparks flying out from a low fire? Her quiet moments, when she seemed to go somewhere else, arriving back with a self-conscious shiver and a smile? To him, in that moment, the loss of any of those seemed like a tragedy.

'Someone's going to step out of that river,' he said, remembering her dad's story.

She gave him a strange, heartfelt look. 'But it won't be me.'

'So, if you're right, then once you go back – you won't remember any of this. Your time in Cambridge. Me. This conversation. It'll be like none of it ever happened.'

'I guess not.' She looked at him sideways: a low, lingering glance, as if she was trying to memorise him.

He felt a wave building inside him, powerful as the sea, deep with unknown currents. He let it carry him to his feet. 'Come on. If we don't get back soon, Mum's going to call the coastguard.'

They slopped in, shedding their dripping waterproofs in the

hall. Up in his room, he peeled off his wet jeans and boxers and groped in the drawer for his pyjamas.

The door of his room opened. Before he could cover himself, he heard Esi scream. 'Oh my God! Sorry!'

He pulled on his pyjamas, swearing. She was gone, and the door was firmly closed. He laughed in delayed, breathless panic, waited until he had stopped shaking, and went to knock on her door.

'Come in,' she said in a high, strange voice.

She was sitting on the bed, wearing Kirsty's skeleton pyjamas and a faded peach silk headwrap. Her face was glowing, and she was having trouble meeting his eyes.

He cleared his throat. 'Sorry about that. I'm decent now. What – uh, what did you want?'

She looked down, fiddling with the blanket. 'I wanted to say thank you. You didn't have to invite me here. I don't know if it was a good idea to come. Maybe it wasn't. But – I had fun.' A wild laugh burst out. 'Also, now I've seen Joseph Greene naked.'

He puffed out his chest. 'And nothing will ever be the same.'

'Oh, I don't know about that.' She smiled wickedly. 'Like you said. What happens in Scotland stays in Scotland, right?'

He didn't get a lot of sleep that night. He lay in bed, acutely aware of her just across the landing, thinking about the few steps between her room and his.

He rolled over, groaning into his pillow. It was never going to happen. With an effort, he turned his thoughts to Diana. He imagined her in London, frozen in place at the door of her house, as if her life were on pause until he arrived. When he finally fell asleep, he dreamt of Esi writing her name on his hand, over and over, in endless spiky lines.

*

THE NEXT EVENING, they stood outside the door of a snow-white town house in Chelsea. Joe was trying to look casual, which was difficult when wearing full Highland dress. Esi was radiant in a white gown she had found in a St Andrews charity shop that looked distractingly like a nightie.

'You look really ving,' he said gallantly.

She looked like she was going to explode. 'Please don't ever try and use that word again.'

He grinned, enjoying her discomfort. 'This party's going to be deev. Can't wait to get rashed.'

She tugged at the hem of her dress, eyeing the grand houses that lined the street. 'This is a bad idea. I'm not supposed to be here. On multiple levels.'

He turned to her. 'Hey. If you want to go. Anytime. You know what to say.'

She met his eyes. 'Threshold,' she said as the door was opened by a tall, pale man with fashionably shaggy hair.

He stared at each of them in turn. 'I have no idea who you are, which means you're Diana's problem. DI!' he bellowed over his shoulder. 'Your Scottish stripper's here!'

'Um – we brought—' Esi held out the wine.

He looked at the label with barely concealed disdain. 'Oh, you shouldn't have.' He took the bottle and turned smartly away, shoes clicking on the marble floor.

Joe hardly had time to process that he had just met Crispin when Diana swept into the doorway dressed in blue, looking like the goddess of twilight. He had forgotten the presence she had, a palpable aura that seemed to pull everything in the world towards her. Now, faced with her, he was literally breathless.

Esi was staring at him in alarm. *Say something.*

'Uh. Hi,' he said suavely. 'I – Joseph Greene? The, uh – the poetry—'

Diana shot Esi a look, as if to say, *What are we going to do with him?* 'Yes, I know who you are, Joseph.' She took in his outfit with unmistakable appreciation. Her attention shifted to Esi; her face flickered, a moment of confusion, then she held out her hand. 'Diana. Lovely to meet you.'

In the future, Esi must have seen the face before her on screens and billboards, lit up larger than life. He'd wondered if she would be starstruck. But she took Diana's hand calmly, head high, almost in challenge. 'Esi.'

He felt them quaking, the three of them, on some faultline. Then a dog rushed out of nowhere and shoved its nose under his kilt.

Diana laughed. 'Oh, I'm sorry. Chamberlain has a tendency to get – amorous.' She grabbed the dog by the collar and yanked him backwards. 'Come and find me later,' she called to Joe as she left. 'We should talk.'

He straightened his kilt, his heart rate returning to normal. 'Sorry. I think I blacked out. How did that go?'

'She liked the kilt.' Esi was watching Diana leave, a strange tension in her shoulders. 'And if it doesn't work out with her, you're in there with Chamberlain.'

He gave her a grim look. 'I'm going to dedicate my book of dog poetry to you.'

'Aww. I'm touched.' Fragments of posh chatter echoed down the high-ceilinged hallway. 'You should go after her.'

Her words said one thing, her body another. He had never seen her look so uncomfortable. His heart cramped. 'Not until we've done the tour. When else will you get a chance to see inside Diana Dartnell's childhood home?'

'My lifelong dream.' She took his arm, her posture relaxing.

The house was huge. They passed through room after room, elegant and strangely impersonal. Most were empty: the party guests had congregated in the kitchen, where the marble-topped island clinked with bottles. Through the French windows loomed the dark outline of a garden.

'No sign of your mum,' he commented, scanning the crowd.

She let out a strangled laugh. 'Yeah, even if Diana does know her, I don't think she'd have made the guest list. I just overheard someone saying their dad's an earl.'

He sorted through the bottles. Half of them were liqueurs he'd never heard of. 'Would a drink help?'

She shook her head. 'I need to stay alert.'

'Yeah, think I'll pass too. Remember the last time I talked to Diana when I was drunk?' He got what he wanted: a small, reluctant smile. 'Look. Here's a plan. We'll talk to some people. We'll find someone who's not completely fucking awful, and I'll leave you with them while I talk to Diana.'

She took a breath, steeling herself. 'Okay. Let's do it.'

Half an hour later, the two of them were huddled in a corner next to a table full of desserts. 'Let's just go,' he said around a forkful of admittedly excellent pavlova. 'I can catch up with her back in Cambridge.'

'No. We're staying. This is your big night.' Esi put down her empty plate and picked up another. 'But if I'd known this was just going to be a roomful of people bragging about their skiing holidays, I would've let you come on your own.' She took a bite. 'Mmm. Try this one. It's like – burnt oranges with honey.'

He leaned in to take her fork in his mouth. Their eyes met, and a thrill like lightning went through him.

'Fuck, that's amazing,' he said, exaggerating to distract from the pounding of his heart. What was wrong with him? He was acting like a sixteen-year-old. 'At least her desserts are good. Even if her friends are terrible.'

'Not all of them.' She pointed at a tall man with floppy hair. 'Jonty was all right.'

'You're just saying that because his dad's an earl.'

She gave him a peculiar look. 'A what?'

'An earl.'

She grinned. 'Airrul,' she said happily.

'Sorry. Euuhl,' he corrected himself in his best attempt at her accent.

She grimaced. 'You're making me sound like the King!'

'The *King*? You're making me time-sick again. Also, the monarchy still exists in 2044?'

'One of many not-great things about when I'm from.' She stared into the crowd, shaking her head. 'It's like they're all trying to convince each other that they're the most impressive person in the room. But no one's listening, because they're too busy trying to do the same.'

He followed her gaze, worry sprouting in his chest. 'Are these the people I'm going to have to hang out with once me and Diana are together?'

She shrugged. 'Maybe they're Crispin's friends. Some people are like that. They base their whole personality on whoever they're dating. Once she's with you, she'll get better taste.'

He tried to imagine Rob and his other friends in this glimmering palace, the chat about Klosters and the stock market replaced by stupid in-jokes and *Lord of the Rings* references. He couldn't make it fit.

He had meant to try again, let Esi take her chances with Jonty and go off in search of his destiny. But somehow it was easier to stay in the corner with her, laughing at the party and at each other while everyone around them got drunker and drunker. At one point, a man in a tailcoat stumbled directly into him, pulling back with exaggerated slowness until he registered the kilt. 'Och aye the fucking *noo*!!' he yelled, before blundering away into the crowd.

He and Esi looked at each other. He wasn't sure who started laughing first. He only knew that he couldn't stop, that he was leaning against her and gasping, tears in his eyes, an ache lodged deep beneath his ribs. He found himself just watching her, in the soft light of the ridiculous chandelier: how her smile made her face come alive; how in this room full of brittle facades, she felt like the one real thing.

She was shaking his shoulder, her face lit with alarm. He tuned in to what she was saying. 'It's nearly midnight! You need to talk to her!'

'Shit.' He turned to look for Diana. There she was, in the midst of the crowd, flanked by a tall shadow. 'I can't.' He felt almost relieved. 'She's with Crispin.'

'So we get him out of the way.' Esi leaned into him. 'Here's the plan. We get close to them. Then I shove you.'

'Shove me?'

'Shh. Trust me. I read a scene like this once in a romance novel.' She mimed with her dessert fork. 'I shove you, you crash into Crispin, his wine goes all over his fancy shirt, he has to go and get changed. Leaving you alone with Diana.'

He blinked at her. 'That's – actually a decent idea. Things are getting messy enough that it's not going to look deliberate.'

'Right. Let's do it.' She forged determinedly through the crowd.

He followed her, thrumming with apprehension. She steered him into place, hands firm on his shoulders. 'Ready?'

He stared into her eyes, unable to look away. *No*, he thought, *no, I'm not ready*, but her face was taut with dread, and he would have done anything to make it better. 'Ready.'

She shoved him, surprisingly hard. He tripped, sprawled, and careened into Crispin, who whisked his glass out of the way at the last moment.

'Christ,' said Crispin, giving him a dirty look. 'Steady on.'

Joe gaped at Crispin, then at Diana, not understanding how the plan could have gone wrong. In his panic, he did the only thing he could think of. *Complete the plan.* He grabbed Crispin's glass and dashed the wine down his pristine white shirt.

Diana gasped. 'Joseph, what on earth—'

Crispin stared down at the blood-red stain spreading across his torso. Then he looked up. For an instant, Joe was utterly certain Crispin was going to hit him. He could already feel the blow, and worse, the humiliation, like he had felt at school, that he was nothing and no one, and the universe would not step in to save him.

Instead, Crispin turned to Diana, two spots of high colour in his cheeks. 'Look, Di. I don't care if you want to slum it with provincials. Just keep them away from me.'

'Slum it?' Her laugh was glacial. 'What exactly are you implying?'

'I'm not implying anything. Like I said, I don't care. I just wish you wouldn't embarrass yourself like this.' He tugged at his sodden shirt in disgust and stalked away. Diana shot a murderous look at Joe before flouncing after him.

Esi looked even angrier than Diana. 'Threshold,' she said icily, and marched through the French windows into the garden.

He followed her out into a clear night, lit by London glare and an impossibly thin crescent moon. She whirled on him. 'What was that?'

'I – I don't know!' he stammered. 'That man has the reflexes of a cat! What was I supposed to do?'

'Walk away? Make another plan? Now you've just made yourself look like a complete psycho!' She paced away and back, until she was in his face again, her eyes bright with fury. 'Do you even want Diana? Because you don't act like it.'

He stared at her. In the cold and the adrenaline, it came on him like a rush: the truth he had been pushing away for weeks now. *I want you.* 'No,' he said, his voice unsteady. 'I don't.'

She was so close to him, barely a breath between them. Her gaze flicked down to his mouth. 'Joe,' she said, half-alarmed and half-wanting, and he barely noticed that she hadn't used his full name. All that could fit into his head was how badly he wanted to kiss her.

He pulled her close and she was warm, an ember burning in the cold garden. Her mouth was soft, her fingers hesitantly exploring his neck, as if she were just beginning to believe he might be real. He crashed headlong into the moment, not thinking of the future, thinking of nothing but her, the impossible sensation of her tongue sliding against his, the way she tasted like tangerines and honey. They kissed like time was running out, because it was, closing the window in which this wasn't-happening-couldn't-happen-was-never-meant-to-happen, narrowing to their hands and their mouths and the tiny, panicked sound she made as she pulled away.

They stared at each other. Esi was breathing hard, her eyes wide, her face stricken. Without a word, she turned and fled back inside.

Chapter Seventeen

'So,' said Dr Lewis, facing him down from her armchair. 'How was your break?'

He stared at her, wondering how best to sum it up. *Oh, it was great. I utterly failed to seduce my future lover. Instead, I assaulted her boyfriend and ended up kissing someone else.* A thrill of guilt ran through him. Not just *someone else*. Esi.

They had spent the rest of the party avoiding each other. He had awoken the next morning, surrounded by strangers on the floor of Diana's basement, to a single text:

staying in London to get my hair done

He couldn't have imagined a more transparent excuse to get away from him. He had sent a vague, pleasant reply, and spent the two weeks since in a spiral of self-loathing. He was supposed to be Joseph Greene, famous romantic, obsessively devoted to one woman for eternity. The kiss felt like a betrayal, not just of Diana, but of his future self.

Dr Lewis was looking at him expectantly. He cleared his throat. 'Uh, yeah, it was good. Can we just . . .' He gestured at his essay.

'Fine by me. I was trying to ease you in with small talk.' She leafed through his essay, which looked like it had been recovered from the corpse of a shooting victim. 'Page three. You cite the text as if it supports your argument, but if you'd bothered to read the footnote, you'd see that the author was actually making the opposite point. Attention to detail has never been your strong suit. But this is sloppy, even for you.' She took off her glasses. 'Answer me honestly. Did you do any work at all over the break?'

He didn't want to lie to her. Part of him was convinced she had a sixth philosophical sense for it. He shook his head.

She exhaled. 'Okay. This is going to scare you, but I think you need to be scared.' She put her glasses back on. 'You are running out of time. I'm serious. If you keep on like this, we're not talking about a 2:2, or even a Third. You are not going to graduate.' She leaned forward, gazing at him earnestly. 'Is that really where you want to be? Three years of your life gone, with nothing to show for it?'

An old, cold terror rushed through his veins. The nightmares where his parents turned away from him, where the whole pub heard the news and started pointing and laughing. A small voice protested that he couldn't fail. He was going to graduate, with the 2:1 that was printed in black and white in the book of his future. But he couldn't see a path that led him there, any more than he could see a path that led him to Diana. 'Can I ask you something?' he said. 'Not about philosophy.'

'Everything's about philosophy.' When he stared at her beseechingly, she shook herself. 'Sorry. Sometimes I have trouble turning it off. Go ahead.'

He looked down at his hands. 'When do we become who we're meant to be?'

She looked at him as though she were pondering a tricky logic problem. 'In my experience, there's no single moment of becoming. We're always works in progress.' She leaned back in her chair. 'Want my advice? Don't think about who you're going to be in twenty years' time. Focus on what you can do this week, then next week, then the week after. That way, you'll be in a good position by the time June comes around.'

June, when he would sit his final exams. June, when Esi would disappear from his life forever. He wondered miserably what she must think of him. She had almost got over her bad first impression, even started to think he was a good person. And then he had kissed her, recklessly and impulsively, when they both knew he was destined to be with Diana. He had let a month of enforced proximity amplify a crush he should have been getting over, and in a moment of vulnerability, he had unleashed his stupid infatuation on the last person in the universe who had asked for it. He had disrespected her, he had ruined their friendship, and, as far as she was concerned, he had put her mission in jeopardy. He wouldn't blame her if she never wanted to see him again.

'Mr Greene?' He started. Dr Lewis was carrying her sousaphone case. He wondered for a confused second if she was about to whip it out and play him a motivational anthem, but she ushered him impatiently towards the door. 'Time's up. I have band practice.'

He tripped down the stairs in a daze. He had sleepwalked his way through the entire supervision, his body on Dr Lewis's sofa but his mind elsewhere. He wandered vaguely into the post room. The porters had emailed him saying his pigeonhole was overflowing and he needed to clear it out. He sorted through the miscellany of gifts: three more white roses in varied stages of wilting, a notebook, and a snow globe of the Eiffel Tower. He binned the roses, left the snow globe in a blank pigeonhole, and pocketed the notebook. That one at least might be useful.

The gifts had pushed something else to the back. He reached in to pull it out. It was a mug that, disconcertingly, had his face on it. Underneath was a quote in flowing italic letters: *If I knew what I meant, I wouldn't need to write poetry.*

'A flagrant violation of the terms and conditions,' he muttered. He imagined the time traveller who had left it returning triumphant through the wormhole, boasting that they'd given him the idea for the quote. He felt faintly annoyed. He would have liked the chance to come up with it himself.

He turned the mug in his hands. A nudge in the direction of his future.

He sat in the window seat and tried to draft a text to Diana. What did you say to someone whose boyfriend you had deliberately spilled wine all over? There was no emoticon for this situation. He thought of Esi, and the last barrier of resistance inside him crumbled. He needed her help, even if he was the last person she wanted to see.

Outside the gate, Vera and her usual crowd were lurking. He didn't spare them a glance. He took a circuitous route, walking out of town up Trumpington Street until the gasps and mutters faded behind him. As he crossed Lensfield Road, he cast a surreptitious look over his shoulder to see them on the other side, caught behind their invisible boundary. He double-checked that Vera was shepherding them back towards the wormhole, then headed on in the direction of Mill Road. As he came out onto the narrow, busy thoroughfare, he felt a fizzing apprehension that kept building until he walked into the coffee shop and saw her.

She was serving a customer, looking down with a guarded

smile. Her braids were finer and longer now, hanging past her shoulders. When she moved her head, silver-and-blue threads woven into them subtly caught the light.

He stared at her helplessly. His attention must have been loud, because she looked up and met his eyes. For a moment, she looked like he felt: lost, vulnerable, happy and sad at the same time. Then she shook her head minutely and waved him away. He retreated to a table in the corner. He opened his new notebook and stared at a blank page until she came over.

'Did Vera follow you?' She was looking anxiously out of the window.

'No. I was careful.' He looked up with an unsteady smile. 'You really did get your hair done.'

She tilted her head, arms crossed. 'You thought I was lying?'

Yes, because we kissed, and you ran away, and I thought you were making an excuse to avoid talking about it, but now it looks like you were telling the truth, so my only possible conclusion is that it meant nothing to you. Which is perfect. I should be relieved. I am relieved. He swallowed all of that and said instead, 'It looks nice.'

She touched her hair self-consciously, then looked annoyed at herself for doing it. She crossed her arms again. 'What are you doing here?'

'I need your help.'

She laughed, a short, angry sound. 'Because I've been such a great help so far.'

'You have, though. She'd never have spoken to me again if it wasn't for you. But I'm running out of time. The poetry thing's on Valentine's Day. Less than a month away. After that's done, I won't have an excuse to see her anymore. Unless—'

'Unless she decides she wants to keep seeing you.' Despair flickered across her face. With a resigned sigh, she sat down opposite him. 'Have you been in touch with her since New Year?'

'No. What would I say? I made myself look like a complete bampot.' He put his head in his hands. 'I don't know how to walk this one back.'

'So don't.' She lifted her chin. 'You're going to have to act like you meant it.'

He winced. 'Can I not just say I had a spasm?'

'No. You cannot just say you had a spasm.' Was that reluctant fondness he could see in her eyes? 'Pouring wine all down her boyfriend is a dramatic gesture. It says, *I want you, and I don't give a fuck who knows it, or what the consequences are*.' Hearing those words from her mouth sent his thoughts onto another track entirely. After a moment, she seemed to become aware of it. She looked away. 'What I mean is, if you can sell it to her like that, then it might change how she feels about you.'

He tried to focus. 'So what do I do first? Text her asking if we can talk?'

'No. Pretend nothing happened. Text her saying you want to meet up and rehearse. She'll say yes, because it'll drive her crazy wondering what's going through your head. Then, when you meet, she's going to bring it up. She'll ask why you did it. That's your cue. Passion blah blah blah, jealousy blah blah blah, you can't think straight when it comes to her.'

'"Passion blah blah blah,"' he intoned, hand on his heart. 'Sure it's not you who's the poet?'

Her face lit with a smile that she immediately repressed. 'One day my genius will be recognised.'

It felt so good, so normal, to be laughing with her again. A glimmer of hope lit in his chest. Maybe he hadn't irreparably broken everything.

'Okay.' He composed a quick text, showed it to Esi, who nodded her approval, and sent it. He felt immediately lighter. 'Right. Now that's done, let's sort out the next steps for finding your mum. There's all the societies we haven't tried yet—'

'No.'

He took in her closed expression, her clenched fists. 'You don't think the rest of them are worth a shot?'

'I do. But I can check them out on my own.' More quietly, she added, 'It's not a good idea for me to be around you.'

Ringing filled his ears. She did hate him, and the worst thing about it was, he couldn't blame her. Mechanically, he got up. 'Okay. I understand. I – I'll just go.'

'I'd better go too. Before my fascist manager fires me.'

The other barista was talking to the manager, her body angled to block the view of Joe and Esi's table. He remembered her name. Shola. 'Say yes.'

Esi blinked in confusion. 'What?'

He gestured. 'To Shola. About moving in with her.'

'I told you, I can't—'

'Affect the world. I know. But I know the real reason. You don't want to let anyone close to you, because you've got this idea of yourself as something temporary. Just waiting to be replaced.' The pain was crystallising into a terrible clarity. 'But you deserve a home, and friends, and a life. You do. Even if you don't believe it.'

She gazed at him, something complicated in her eyes: warmth, regret, and a flash of anger. 'I'm not here to stay, Joseph Greene.'

The weight of his full name fell between them like an impassable barrier. 'I know,' he said, and left.

When he got back to college, Rob was in the living room, whistling as he smeared the rim of an envelope with jam. 'Contact poison,' he explained.

'Did I ask?' Joe eyed the growing pile of envelopes beside him. 'Are all of those for Darcy?'

'For anyone, potentially. The Lent Game doesn't start for another twelve days. I'm just building up my arsenal.' He looked up. 'You all right, Greeney? You look like you just got shot in the feelings.'

'Yeah. I – uh – things are rough right now.'

'With Diana? Sorry to hear that, mate. Look on the bright side, though. Emotional agony makes for great poetry.'

'Sure,' Joe said emptily, as his phone buzzed. He wasn't sure why he was surprised to see a message from Diana. Her reply had been inevitable: just like him, she didn't really have a choice.

Absolutely. My place, next
Friday. Usual time.

He could almost hear her saying it, in her cool, detached tone that gave nothing away.

Rob gave him a questioning look. 'Was that her?'

'Yeah. Yeah, she's – she wants to meet up.'

'Great!' His roommate smeared jam carefully around the rim of another envelope. 'That's all sorted, then.'

Joe stared out of the window. 'Aye,' he said. 'All sorted.'

Chapter Eighteen

Next Friday. Ten days away. He could have taken Dr Lewis's advice and filled the time with work. But he had so much to catch up on that getting started seemed impossible.

It shouldn't have been so hard. The Joseph Greene who did the work to get his promised 2:1 undoubtedly existed. He would have to turn into him any day now. But like the poet who stared out from his mug as he drank endless procrastinatory cups of tea, that successful version of him felt increasingly distant from who he currently was.

To distract from all the ways he was failing to live up to himself, he overprepared for his meeting with Diana. He went over and over the script Esi had suggested until the future felt like it had already happened. On the day, he woke tingling and nauseous. He put on an actual shirt, and made an attempt at applying goop to his hair, but the effortless swoops Esi had crafted were impossible for him to re-create. He gave up and headed for the door, doubling back to pick up *Meant to Be* from under his pillow.

As he waited outside Whewell's Court, he felt the slim weight of the book inside his jacket, a talisman anchoring him to the future. No time travellers were watching: Vera had led them back to the wormhole earlier than usual. He tried not to let the change in routine worry him, but these days, every little thing struck him as a harbinger of disaster.

He had texted Diana as soon as he arrived, but she had obviously decided to keep him waiting. Someone pushed past him, holding up their card to open the gate. Joe caught it before it closed and slipped inside.

He climbed her staircase and knocked on the door. After two minutes of ostentatious shuffling – he resisted the urge to knock again – she finally opened it.

'Joseph. How wonderful to see you.' At the sight of her, luminous in a black cashmere sweater, his annoyance evaporated. 'Can I get you a cup of tea?' Before he could accept, she added sweetly, 'As long as you promise not to throw it all over me.'

Apologies leapt to his tongue like frogs in a fairy tale. He brushed them away. *Act like you meant it.* 'So that was just a line?' he asked, leaning nonchalantly in the doorway. 'You're not actually offering me tea?'

She put her hands on her hips. 'No, I'm not offering you tea! You poured wine all down my boyfriend!' When he failed to wither under her glare, it shifted into curiosity. 'What exactly were you thinking?'

He remembered what Esi had told him to say. *Passion blah blah blah, jealousy blah blah blah.* He couldn't do a convincing performance of those, not yet. But when he thought about the Crispin in the book, the misery hidden in the few terse words describing their marriage, it already made him furious. 'I was thinking about how he doesn't deserve you.'

She sighed. 'Joseph, respectfully, you don't know anything about mine and Crispin's relationship. What are you basing this on? An overheard phone conversation, and the fact that he called you my Scottish stripper?' She waved a dismissive hand. 'Sorry about that, by the way. It was uncalled-for. But hardly proof that he's some sort of storybook villain.'

'I'm not saying that. I'm saying he takes you for granted. And if you get back with him, it's only going to get worse.'

'Get back with him?' She affected a look of confusion. 'Sorry, I wasn't aware we'd broken up.'

Not yet. He was getting ahead of himself. Time to get back on script. 'Look. You're right. Maybe I should have thought about it, taken a step back. But the truth is, I can't think straight when it comes to you.'

She smiled a rich, exulting smile. 'Is that so.'

Hating himself a little for having said it, hating her a little more for liking it, he nodded.

She came closer, invading his space. He flinched – he couldn't help it – and she laughed. She slid her arms around him. 'Is this what you want?' she asked curiously.

His heart was hammering. *Finally, here it was,* said the narrator, *the fateful moment when muse and poet would—*

She raised an eyebrow. 'Is that a book in your pocket, or are you just pleased to see me?' She reached inside his jacket.

'No. Not a book.' He stepped back. Panic flooded his veins. If she saw, it was all over. Her picture, her name on the cover—

'Joseph. I'm an English student. If I've learned nothing else from my degree, I hope I can at least reliably identify a book.' She made a playful grab. 'Why are you being so cagey about it? Is it pornography?'

He danced away, letting out a nervous laugh. 'Yes, it's a hard-back book of porn. What am I, a pervy Victorian lord?'

'Perhaps. You do have a certain timeless charm.' She pinned his arm with a surprisingly strong grip. 'Let me see it!'

Desperate, he burst out, 'It's a philosophy textbook!'

She made a face like she'd smelt something rotten. 'Well, that killed the intrigue stone dead.' Sighing, she went to stand by the window. 'So. Shall we get into it?'

'Sure.' As she began to recite the poem, his phone buzzed. He looked at the screen, and his heart thudded. A string of messages from Esi: the first time he'd heard from her since he'd left the café ten days ago.

Just saw my mum go into Trinity

porters didn't stop her

must be her college

Diana was reaching the end of the first verse. Surreptitiously, he texted back:

Can't be. Diana would've recognised her.

He turned the phone over in his hand, waiting for her to reply. Midway through the second verse, Diana paused. 'That ambiguity again. "Igniting what is to come."'

'Mm,' he said. 'Interesting.' His phone buzzed again.

Unless she was lying

When would she get over that idea? He was typing a reply when another message came through.

Can we just check?

Diana tapped the windowsill. 'Did you mean setting it going, or burning it all down?'

He stared at his phone. Raw, hurt replies ran through his mind. *Thought you didn't want to see me anymore. Oh, so now you need me?* But she was asking for his help, and he couldn't imagine a world where he would refuse her.

Course, he typed. Meet me outside the Great Gate at 5:30. I'll do a Vera sweep before.

'Joseph!'

He looked up, guilty. 'Yes?'

'Igniting.' She was glaring at him. 'Initiating? Destroying?'

He shrugged. 'Both.'

'I know it's both,' she snapped. 'That's what ambiguity is. I want to know what you meant by the ambiguity.'

To give himself time to think, he gazed poetically out of the window. An image flashed into his mind: his own brooding face, a quotation inscribed below. 'If I knew what I meant,' he said, 'I wouldn't need to write poetry.'

She rolled her eyes. 'Very profound. Give it a few years, they'll be printing that on T-shirts.'

'Mugs, actually.' His phone vibrated. He looked down, heart in his throat.

Ok

When he looked up, Diana was watching him. 'What did she say?'

He was about to correct her misapprehension when he realised that something in her manner had changed: she wasn't angry anymore. She was intrigued. The idea that he might be interested in someone else actually made him more appealing to her.

He tucked the phone into his pocket, a dull ache spreading through his chest. 'She said yes.'

He waited for Esi outside the Great Gate. She was late, and that made him worry that she'd changed her mind, that she'd decided to do this alone. He shifted from foot to foot under the skeletal trees, his breath smoking in the chill. By the time he saw her hurrying towards him, her shoulders hunched, her head downcast, it was nearly six and he was freezing. 'I said five thirty,' he pointed out.

She looked over her shoulder. 'I've been watching you for the last half hour. I had to be sure Vera's not tailing you.'

He bristled. 'I told you I was going to do that.'

'Yeah, and I decided to double-check. The stakes are higher for me than they are for you.' She avoided his eyes, heading for the Great Gate. 'Let's get this done.'

He could hear her humming her nervous tune as they entered the Porters' Lodge. He checked the Es: a single column of names, interspersed by a couple of dropout blanks. Esi cast up and down them, tender, impatient. Her face fell. 'She's not here.'

He hadn't expected anything different. Still, he couldn't bear the heartbreak in her eyes. 'Let's just do this. Come with me. We'll search all the other colleges.'

'What's the point?' Despair filled every line of her body. 'So I find out which bubble-within-a-bubble she's at. How does that help me?'

'It gets you a step closer to knowing where she lives. Even better, it gives you a way to contact her. You could leave her a note.'

'Saying what? *Beware the twenty-third of June? If someone tries to give you an award, don't accept it?*' Her face was taut with misery. 'I don't have enough details to be specific. And a vague note's worse than nothing. It might make her do anything. Send her off on a whole new path.'

Her words sank through him, seeding an awful realisation in his gut. 'It's worse than that.'

She looked at him in alarm. 'What do you mean?'

'See this award – what if it's something she has to put herself in the running for? You could give her the idea. Send her on the path that leads to her death.' He knew he should stop talking, but the thought was unfurling in his mind and he had to follow where it was leading. 'Maybe what you do when you come back here – maybe it doesn't stop the accident. Maybe it causes it.'

The horror in her face was too much. 'Why would you say that?'

He stepped back. 'I don't know, okay? It just occurred to me.'

'It occurred to you. So of course you had to share it, because you're Joseph Greene, and every random thought you have is gold. What am I even supposed to do with that?' Her eyes fixed him with fury. 'You're Mr Destiny, aren't you. Mr Meant to Be. According to you, it's going to happen no matter what I do. I leave her a note, she dies. I don't leave her a note, she dies. I tear the universe apart with my bare hands and put it back together, it doesn't fucking matter. She still dies.'

'Esi—' he began, reaching for her, but she drew away.

'The way you think time works,' she said, her voice shaking. 'I hate it.'

He gazed at her, miserable, aware somewhere in the depths of his being that he was beginning to hate it too. 'I'm just saying. Maybe trying to fix yourself isn't the answer.'

'Oh, and I'm supposed to listen to you?' she lashed out. 'You think sleeping with one out-of-your-league woman is going to turn you into a version of yourself you actually want to be?'

Her words didn't hurt right away. He felt a lurch in his stomach, a premonition of pain to come. 'Wow,' he said quietly. 'Okay.'

The porter was eyeing them over his newspaper. Joe touched Esi's arm – she shied away – and followed her outside. Snow was falling, turning to slush the instant it hit the cobbles. 'Look. I meant what I said. We can go college-to-college, right now. You can decide once we find her—'

'*We* aren't doing anything. I told you. I don't want your help.' She emphasised each word with her fist in her palm. 'Don't you get it? I can't do this. I can't just – stand here and talk to you like it's normal, like I'm not aching, like I'm not dying inside.' Her face was wild with an emotion he couldn't read. 'I've spent enough of my life wanting something I can't have.'

He had a beating awareness, her face close to his, of what she meant. There was a moment, trembling and fragile as a bubble, where he could have said something. But his future lay heavy on his tongue, and he stayed silent.

She caught her breath. 'I wish I'd never met you,' she said, and walked away.

Chapter Nineteen

*M*r Destiny, aren't you. *Mr Meant to Be.* The words followed him through the next two weeks, as he sat under Dr Lewis's glare in two more disastrous supervisions, as he walked the streets with an ache under his ribs and a gaggle of time travellers following behind him like starstruck ducklings. He and Diana met up for two more rehearsals. He was starting to wonder if they were overpreparing for what was, after all, a recital of a twenty-two-line poem. A voice like Esi's murmured, *She's just using the rehearsals as an excuse to spend more time with you.* The thought should have excited him: as the time ticked down towards Valentine's Day, the moment he had been longing for drew closer. But instead, he found himself resenting it. Why should they have to fall in love to a deadline? Why couldn't they come together spontaneously, at their own pace, like normal people?

'Joseph.' He looked up. They were at the end of another rehearsal, and Diana was watching him with soft concern. 'What are you thinking about, my love?'

My love. She had started calling him that, with no apparent irony. He tried not to read too much into it: she probably did the same with all her actor friends. *My sweet, my darling, my dear heart's beloved.*

She touched his shoulder. 'Tell me.'

There was a question in her eyes, one he couldn't quite translate. *And this?* said the narrator uncertainly. *Was this the moment when Joseph Greene and Diana Dartnell would—* He interrupted. 'Are we maybe overdoing it with all these rehearsals? It's just a poem.'

She gave him a look of affronted surprise. 'On the contrary. I don't think it's possible to overdo it. Your poem is perfect, and it deserves a perfect performance.' She kissed him lightly on the cheek. 'Let's meet up again on the thirteenth, shall we? Last chance to get it together.'

She was more right than she knew: that final rehearsal had to be when it would happen. He tried to look forward to it, but it felt less like anticipating a date and more like being an actor in some strange pantomime. They would both perform their parts, they would kiss when the stage directions told them to, and the future would play itself out.

He left Whewell's Court. Vera stood alone and tabardless across the street, watching him with narrow concentration. He ignored her and took out his phone, looking in vain for a text from Esi. After their disastrous conversation, he had sent her a message to apologise, but she still hadn't replied. He was still weighing up whether he should try again when he arrived in front of his door and found a box.

It sat at an awkward angle in the hallway, as if it had been dropped there by someone in a hurry. More alarmingly, it was emitting scuffling sounds.

Cautiously, he opened it. Inside was a tiny kitten, looking up at him out of round blue eyes.

Under the kitten was a folded note with his name on. He carefully lifted the kitten's paw to extract it.

Joseph Greene,

Hi. I love you. I know this is breaking the rules but I don't care. There's a poem you're going to write about Diana and a cat, and I want it to be this cat. So look after her please. Thanks and I love you and bye,

Beryl (if you could call the cat Beryl, that would also be amazing)

He stared into the middle distance. He imagined a moment in the future, him and Diana at home, bathed in the glow of mutual adoration. As she leaned down to caress the cat, inspiration would have struck. But not anymore. Now, he would recognise the moment as a scripted cue. Any chance of writing the poem in a spirit of genuine inspiration was gone.

He ripped up the note and dropped the pieces in the box, surprised at the strength of his anger. He had accepted that he would never truly write the poems in the book. They were an artefact of physics, their origin as incomprehensible as time travel itself. But he had consoled himself with the thought that there were other poems, maybe even better ones, still left open for him to write. This careless gift had closed them down by one more.

Still, he couldn't exactly leave the kitten in the hallway. He shut the box, tucked it under his arm, and unlocked the door.

In the living room, Rob was filling a balloon with rice. 'Great news, Greeney,' he said as Joe shouldered the door closed. 'Darcy's been eliminated! Squashed by a boulder someone dropped out of a window. Means I've got everything to play for.'

'Brilliant. Happy for you.' He put the box down gently on the sofa. It meowed.

Rob cocked his head. 'I'm sorry. Did that box just—'

'Meow? Yes.' He took a moment out of his intense existential suffering to enjoy Rob's bafflement. 'I'm experimenting with making a cat that's both alive and dead.'

'Classic misconception,' said Rob, pressing his ear to the box. 'The point of Schrödinger's cat was to show the absurdity of the Copenhagen interpretation of quantum mechanics. Under a many-worlds interpretation, reality splits in two, and the cat in each universe is simply alive or dead.'

Joe opened the box. 'Looks like we're in the universe with the alive cat.'

The kitten looked up reproachfully. Rob lifted it and held it next to Joe's face. 'The resemblance is uncanny.'

'Don't get attached. I'm taking her straight to Cats Protection.'

'No!' Rob held the kitten close, until she squirmed out of his arms and jumped down to the sofa. 'We're keeping her.'

'We can't keep a kitten. We're not allowed. It's in the student handbook.'

'Byron kept a bear in his room,' Rob pointed out. 'He didn't care about the student handbook.'

'He deliberately kept a bear because the student handbook said he wasn't allowed to keep a dog. That was in 1806. They've tightened up the wording since then.' His thoughts returned to the ripped-up note and the pit of despair it had sunk him into. 'Also, I'm not Byron.'

'Not yet. But you need to act like the poet you want to be, not the poet you are.' Rob scratched the kitten's ears. 'Where did you get her?'

'Oh, the usual. Through a wormhole from the future.'

Rob laughed in a *very funny, Greeney* sort of way. 'Doesn't look very futuristic.'

'Turns out kitten technology isn't going to change that much.' He tickled her under the chin. She purred and pushed against his hand.

'Does she have a name?'

'I'm reliably informed that I'm terrible at naming cats.' His heart cramped, remembering Esi's repressed laughter as she looked down at Jeely Piece rubbing against her ankle. 'Definitely not Beryl,' he added resentfully.

Rob stared at the cat, who stared back. 'Bear.'

Joe couldn't help smiling. 'See what you did there.' He took the kitten and looked into her watery blue eyes. 'Bear, Jeely Piece is going to murder you. If the porters don't get to you first.'

Rob scoffed. 'I'm an expert at concealment and subterfuge. The porters won't notice a thing. Can't help with Jeely Piece, though. That cat is a law unto himself.' He looked up at Joe hopefully. 'Can I use her as an attack animal?'

'What would that involve?'

'Oh, just throwing her at people. Gently,' Rob added, seeing the look on Joe's face.

'Absolutely not. Is that the real reason you called her Bear? Like writing *GUN* on a banana?'

'It was a multipurpose name. Anyway,' said Rob, with an air of changing the subject, 'how are you doing? Isn't your poetry thing soon?'

'Tuesday.' He couldn't believe it was nearly here. He had thought that by now, he would have become a different version of himself: more certain, less confused, closer to the man on the cover of the book. But if anything, he felt like he had got further away. He was caught in the void between who he was and who he was meant to be, no longer firmly anchored to either.

'You don't seem very excited.'

Joe rubbed his knuckles against Bear's tiny ears. 'I don't?'

Rob laughed hoarsely. 'If I'd told you four months ago you'd be having one of your poems read at some fancy literary event, I think your head would have exploded. I'd still have been cleaning bits of Greeney off the walls.'

He thought about explaining that the poem wasn't really his: strictly speaking, it was no one's, because it had appeared by magic from the future. But as usual, he suspected Rob would be more interested in the physics of how that could possibly have happened than in the ways it was turning Joe's life upside down. He rubbed his eyes, feeling the future boxing him in: the mug in his pigeonhole, the cat on his doorstep, his union with Diana looming closer and closer, nothing either of them could do to actively choose it. 'Do you think all our actions are predetermined?'

One of his favourite things about Rob was that you could ask him a question like that, with no context whatsoever, and he wouldn't even blink. 'Oh yeah. Physics-wise, it's pretty likely.'

'How do you cope with that?' He searched for an example that would make Rob care. 'Like, you've been trying to murder Darcy since your duel in first year. What if you knew it was never going to happen? Would you still keep trying?'

Rob looked at him like he was insane. 'Of course. Because it's not just about the outcome. I'm in the Guild because I enjoy it. I love making weapons, I love staking out a target, I love the chase and the kill and writing up the report. I'd do it all, even if I knew it'd come to nothing.'

Joe felt like he was trembling on the edge of a profound truth. On impulse, he checked his phone: still no reply from Esi. 'And what if you knew the opposite?' he said. 'That you were certain to win? What would you do then?'

Rob shrugged, as if it was perfectly straightforward. 'I'd pretend I didn't.'

Joe went into his bedroom and closed the door, wondering vaguely if Rob might be a genius. He took *Meant to Be* out from under his pillow, dropped it into his desk drawer, and slammed it shut. No more voice of the narrator. No more idea that a narrator even existed. He would go to Diana and meet her on her own terms, here and now, and he would see what was going to happen.

Chapter Twenty

' " **H**er tongue, a dart, a star, a" – shit.'

The final rehearsal wasn't going well.

Diana broke off for the fifth time in five lines. 'This isn't working. It's flat. Isn't it? It's flat, and boring, and it's going to send the audience to *sleep*. Fuck. Joseph, why am I making such a hash of this?'

'It's not you.' He tried to think of what he'd say if he didn't know the future. 'Maybe it's the poem.'

'It's not the poem, you idiot genius. And it's not me. I'm wonderful. It's something between the poem and me.' She waved her hand airily back and forth. 'I'm not connecting with it. There's something missing.'

He tried to restrain his panic. 'You're having this revelation a day before the event?'

'Better a day before than a day after.' She paced across the room. 'We need to shake things up.' She whirled on him, grabbing his arms. 'Let's go punting!'

He stared at her. 'It's February.'

'You're Scottish.' She let him go and headed out of the door.

He followed her onto Trinity Street, trying not to think about where fate might be manoeuvring them. They were just two people, going on a spontaneous, completely insane boat trip. He registered Vera at the corner of his eye, but he refused to look at her. No time travellers today, no future. Just him and Diana.

She took him to the supermarket, where she bought a punnet of strawberries, a bottle of gin, and a pack of paper cups. Then she marched him down to the river, where she negotiated a discount self-hire punt simply by raising her eyebrow. When the overawed employee had shown them to their boat, she settled back on the cushions like a queen.

He laughed at her from the dock. 'Oh, so I'm driving?'

She looked at him over her sunglasses. 'If you'd rather, I'm happy to send us round in circles.'

'You've been at Cambridge two and a half years, and you haven't learned how to punt?'

'I've had better things to do.'

'That's convenient.' He took the pole and stepped onto the rocking platform. He hadn't done much punting, but he had overheard enough of Rob's rants about technique to absorb the basics. *Keep the pole close to the boat. Drop it straight down, not at an angle.* And finally, and most importantly, *If the pole gets stuck, let it go.* He lifted it hand over hand and dropped it, steering them smoothly out from the dock.

'Very nice, Joseph,' she drawled with an approving smile. 'A man of many talents.'

'Poetry and punting. At this rate, I'll be rich enough to retire by forty.'

She laughed appreciatively. She slopped gin into a paper cup and raised it. 'To being carried away in boats by strange men.'

Her tone was undeniably flirtatious. He could laugh it off, but he had learned enough about Diana to know that his natural reaction was rarely right. He needed to confront her, see her bet and raise it. 'How does Crispin feel about you getting carried away in boats by strange men?'

With her sunglasses on, he couldn't tell where she was looking. 'He adores me,' she said as they drifted under the low arch of Silver Street Bridge. 'Nothing can change that.'

Joe tried to maintain a stoic, manly pose, which was tricky when he had to bend almost double to avoid losing his head. 'He doesn't act like he adores you.'

She scoffed. 'Crispin doesn't act like he adores anything. He's basically incapable of any external expression of emotion. But he still has feelings. They're just – buried, under a deep layer of trauma and manly nonsense.'

'Wow.' He straightened up as they emerged into the pale sunshine. 'He sounds like a real catch.'

'Very funny.' She took off her sunglasses, draping her arm picturesquely along the side of the boat. 'But the point is, Crisp's not a bad person. He's just – broken. His parents shipped him off to boarding school when he was eight years old. It's no wonder he can never really be vulnerable in front of anyone.' Her eyes darted up, and he felt the tingling shock of her attention. 'And before you say it – no, I didn't board, but my parents were so emotionally absent it might actually have been easier if I had. At least that would have been consistent.' A laugh, brittle as lightning. He thought of the dazzling vacancy of her parents' house in London, a little girl sitting alone in all that empty splendour. 'Neither of us has ever really known love,' she mused softly. 'So we perform our version of it for each other.'

He let the pole trail in the water, the wooden crossbeams of the Mathematical Bridge receding behind them. 'You're saying you're both broken in the same way.'

'You and your way with words.' She glanced up at him fondly. 'But yes. Maybe that's not enough for a relationship, but it's better than nothing.'

'Is it?' He steered them on past Queens', the wind sending the boat briefly astray. 'Wouldn't you rather be on your own than with someone who can't be himself around you?'

Her smile didn't reach her eyes. 'Nice idea. But that's not going to work.'

'Why not?'

'I need to be adored.' She stared across the empty lawn of King's, fingers clenching unconsciously on her cup. 'It's not something I'm proud of. But it's a fact. It's as if part of me is afraid I won't exist if no one is looking.' She took a sip of gin, wincing. 'I suspect that's the reason I act. Why else would I feel the need to seek the admiration of complete strangers? I was deprived of affection in childhood, so I seek it out elsewhere. Insatiably. Pathologically.' She shrugged. 'Simple cause and effect.'

They drifted towards the triple arches of Clare Bridge. He steered left, laughing under his breath.

She eyed him mistrustfully. 'What?'

He shook his head. 'Nothing. Just – do you really think you can explain yourself like that?'

'Oh yes.' Her face was deadly serious. 'There's always an explanation for people like us.'

'Us?'

'Us.' She gestured back and forth between them. 'You're not immune, Joseph. You have another form of the same disease. Pouring your heart out on paper and offering it up to strangers isn't normal behaviour. Just like my compulsion to be admired. You can always trace it back to something. Usually in early childhood.'

He felt himself adopting a defensive curl. 'Speak for yourself. My parents are great.'

'Well, bully for you.' She raised her cup in a sarcastic toast. 'But mark my words, there'll be something. Some way they failed you that you're not even conscious of.'

Without wanting to think about it, he thought about it. It was easy enough to play her game, point to small moments in his past and diagnose them as the source of something greater. The way his dad had laughed when he'd first said he wanted to be a poet. The poem his mum had hung like an in-joke on the bathroom wall. All the little ways they had undermined his ambition in the hope of shielding him from ridicule, or themselves from disappointment. But he didn't want to think like that, turning well-intentioned care into damage. 'Can't think of a single thing,' he said breezily.

She crossed her arms. 'Really. You're telling me your dad's not a classic dour, borderline-alcoholic, perpetually disapproving Scot?'

'*Dour* rhymes with *sure*, not *shower*.' He looked past her down the river. 'And no. He's not even a Scot.'

'Oh?' she said with a flicker of interest. 'What is he?'

'English.'

He regretted telling her as soon as he saw her eyes widen. 'Aha! There it is.'

He shoved the pole against the riverbed. 'There *what* is?'

'The explanation.' She clasped her hands. 'An outsider in your own home, marked out as different, never truly belonging. Bullied and excluded, you—'

'Why do you assume I was bullied?'

She snorted. 'Please, Joseph. You project wounded puppy to a distance of a hundred metres.' She dunked a strawberry in her cup, sucked the gin out of it, then ate it. 'So,' she continued, licking juice off her fingers. 'You were bullied. Which completely torpedoed your self-esteem. Then – let me guess. A teacher took an interest in your poetry, encouraged you? And you achieved some big external milestone, something that finally made you feel like you existed?'

He remembered: the envelope, the foiled certificate, the giddy, disconnected joy, like he had discovered a door leading out of himself into a bright golden world beyond. 'I won a national poetry contest,' he said miserably.

'QED,' she said, and took a sip of gin. 'The rest is history. Or it will be, someday.'

He should have been focusing on the breeze dancing in her hair, the rosy undertones of her porcelain skin, the way her eyes picked up the hint of green in the water. But he was annoyed, not so much by what she was saying as by her obvious delight in finding what she thought was the key to him. He didn't like the feeling of being made into a puzzle box for her amusement. 'But that can't be all there is to it. I was already writing poetry before any of that. It's been part of who I am since forever.'

'But you probably didn't feel the need to impress anyone with it until life put a hole in your heart.' She shivered, turning towards the golden cloisters of the Wren Library. Inside, Byron lounged on his shattered temple, the human being he once was perfected into marble. 'There's no help for it, Joseph. Artists aren't people. We look like people, and we can sometimes pretend to be people, but any chance of actually being people was burned out of us long ago.'

He was almost sure he disagreed. But her words had a terrible pull. She made not being a person sound so wonderful: a tragic, glamorous calling, inevitable for both of them from the moment they were born. And wasn't that what he had always wanted: to be more than he was, to escape the daily mess and awkwardness and humiliation of being himself?

The immaculate grass of St John's Meadow spread out to their left, the eagle on the gate staring fiercely in their direction. Diana stood up, setting the boat rocking. 'My turn,' she announced.

He adjusted his stance to steady himself. 'I thought you were too busy and important to learn punting.'

'That remains the case. But, much as I was enjoying the view – I'm getting cold.' She lurched elegantly down the boat. He offered his hand, and she took it, stepping up until they were sharing the narrow platform. She clutched at him to steady herself, and before he knew what was happening, they were twined together, her leg sliding between his, her hand cold on the back of his neck. With a strange hunger, she said, 'You've known it, haven't you? Love. Or something like it.'

His heart thundered with a peculiar mixture of excitement and apprehension. *This was it. The moment*— No. No narrator. If this was happening, he was making it happen. He leaned in, close, closer—

Diana drew back, a smile in her sharp green eyes. 'Who is she?'

The question sent him into a panic he didn't understand. His mind screamed with obscuring static. 'Who?'

'The girl you wrote "A Taste of Stars" about. The girl you were kissing.' She looked at him under her eyelashes. 'More than kissing. We all know what you were doing putting *come* at the end of a line, after all that buildup.'

He felt himself blush. He had read the poem a hundred times, but he had never really understood it until he had heard her perform it: the line breaks breathless, the rhythm urgent in a way that had invaded his dreams.

She was enjoying his discomfort. 'So?' She pressed herself into him, gimlet eyes and warm juniper breath, and he was undone by the nearness of her. *You*, he thought. *She's going to be you.*

But he could never tell her that. The realisation broke the moment. 'That's between me and her.' He handed her the pole and sat down.

She was watching him with a strange, thoughtful expression. He laughed, pouring gin into a cup to cover his self-consciousness. 'What?'

'Remember what I said about you not being my type?' She hauled the pole out of the water at an angle that would have made Rob weep. 'Maybe that's not such a bad thing.'

It was hardly a declaration of love. But it still made him feel like she had given him something precious, foiled and inked and marking him out as chosen. He settled back against the cushions with a smile he found it difficult to hide.

As he did, a figure on the riverbank caught his eye. Vera. She was alone, watching them from the grass, a look of alarm on her face.

'Right. Here goes.' Diana dug in the pole, setting the boat spinning. Vera lurched out of sight. By the time they were pointing in the right direction again, she was gone.

The sight of her had shaken him. He would have found it hard to forget. But Diana's punting was so terrible that he couldn't concentrate on anything else. He sipped neat gin for courage as she steered them unerringly in circles, crashed into the bank, then another boat, then narrowly avoided braining herself on the

Bridge of Sighs. He was consumed with secondhand embarrassment, but it was clear she didn't care. She rode each misadventure with blithe unconcern, tossing her hair with a smile, pivoting into a flawless impression of a punt guide that made him laugh so hard he got gin up his nose. By the time they were zigzagging towards Magdalene Bridge, he was both mildly drunk and also, impossibly, enjoying himself.

Diana launched the punt diagonally across the river, prompting one of the professional guides to swear under his breath and change course. Joe felt something pulling their boat back. 'What's happening?'

'The pole's stuck. As the actress said to the bishop,' she said with a dirty chuckle.

He laughed, less at the joke than at her exaggerated amusement. She winked cheekily and half turned, making an ineffectual effort to tug the pole free. The boat was still moving forward, and she was leaning farther and farther back. Rob's third rule of punting pushed its way into Joe's tipsy brain.

'Diana,' he said, sitting up. 'Let go of the pole. Let go—'

She didn't let go. He watched, helpless, as the boat went one way and the pole went another, and Diana followed the latter into the cold grey water.

She surfaced with a shriek, arms flailing. 'Fuck! Fucking *fuck* that's cold. Oh Jesus fucking Christ.' A tour boat drifted past, a little girl watching in fascination as her dad clapped his hands over her ears.

'Hold on,' said Joe. 'I'm coming.' He tried to use the paddle to row the boat towards her, but it was like trying to steer a bus by blowing on it. He leaned out, grabbing the floating pole and swinging it out towards her. She clutched the end and he pulled her in, reaching into the freezing water to help her clamber into the punt. She crouched, dripping, on the wooden slats, hair plastered across her forehead, as far from the polished, perfect actress on the cover of *Meant to Be* as he had ever seen her.

'I told you to let go of the pole,' he said.

Diana was convulsing. He thought for a terrifying second that she'd gone into shock. Then she took in a shaky breath, and he realised she was laughing.

'As the bishop said to the actress,' she gasped, then rolled onto her back, drenched and hysterical, eyes squeezed shut against the grey winter sky. He had never seen her like this, all awareness of herself gone, given up entirely to what she was feeling. He felt a lurching swoop, less a sensation than a premonition: this was the woman he was going to fall in love with.

They landed at the docks by Magdalene Bridge. He requested a blanket, which she draped around her shoulders like an ermine. They walked back towards Trinity through the tourist crowds. Diana was soaked, shivering, river weeds in her hair. A couple walking past laughed under their breath; a group of children sitting on the wall by St John's were staring, mouths hanging open. Joe would have been mortified. But Diana walked on like the street was a red carpet, head held high, wearing the weeds in her hair like a diadem. He understood: by turning her humiliation into a performance, she made it about something outside herself. None of it could touch her.

She led him up the stairs, past her neighbour's painting that looked now like a lightning strike, frozen at the moment of impact in a world turned sideways. In her room, she came into focus: a queen no longer, but a girl he could see and touch, her wet dress clinging to her body. She grabbed a towel and headed for the shower. 'Don't go anywhere,' she said, in a husky, commanding voice that gave him the shivers.

He was left alone in her room, feeling like a spring wound up to an unbearable compression. He tried to calmly peruse her walls: the noticeboard covered with reviews of her shows, the pictures of Sarah Bernhardt arranged into a shrine above the fireplace. Every detail was an arrow pointed to her future, lit up with how fiercely she wanted it.

'I think I figured out what's missing.'

He turned. She stood, naked under a towel, her collarbone and her bare shoulders a speechless poem. The scent of her damp skin drove every other thought out of his head.

His voice came out hoarse. 'Did you?'

'To understand your poem, I need to know it from the inside. Feel what you were feeling.' She stepped closer, sliding her arms around his neck. 'Can you show me?'

Her words were hesitant, but her expression was certain: she had no doubt about where this was going. With plunging realisation, he understood that she had choreographed this moment, from the punting trip to falling in the river to bringing him back here: all of it a performance, painstakingly crafted to seduce him. He should have felt manipulated. But all he could feel was a kind of amused relief. All his worry about being a pawn of fate, about acting out a prewritten script, when it was Diana who had been quietly pulling the strings all along, manoeuvring him exactly where she wanted him. And that in itself – to be wanted, so frankly and so confidently – took his breath away.

She doesn't really want you, whispered a traitorous voice. *She wants the man who wrote the poem.* But that man wasn't in her arms, her fingers trailing across his neck, making questions of *if* and *might* and *should* seem impossibly abstract and faraway. He was here with her, and even if the person she was interested in didn't really exist yet, he could pretend to be him for a while.

'Yes,' he said, and kissed her.

Chapter Twenty-One

He awoke on the morning of Valentine's Day in Diana Dartnell's bed.

Really, he was half-in and half-out of it. In her sleep, she had sprawled diagonally across the single mattress, consigning him to a precarious strip on the edge. One of his legs had dipped to the floor, and the other was cramping.

He sat up, stretching until the pain faded. He was naked, and his muscles ached, and his stomach was churning with a strange unease. Other than that, he didn't feel fundamentally different: a night with his muse hadn't magically transformed him into someone else. Esi's words came back to him, cold and bitter. *You think sleeping with one out-of-your-league woman is going to turn you into a version of yourself you actually want to be?*

The churning in his stomach intensified. He should tell her: he owed her that much. He reached for his phone, abandoned with his jeans on the floor. She still hadn't replied to the message he'd sent her nearly three weeks ago. He typed:

> You don't have to worry about the future
> anymore. Diana and I are together.

He stared at the screen for some minutes after sending, waiting for her to reply. What would she say? *Thanks? Good for you? Enjoy?* Each option seemed more absurd than the last. But the idea that she wouldn't respond, that their relationship would end with angry words and a string of unanswered messages, seemed the most impossible of all.

When it became apparent she wasn't going to reply anytime soon, he dropped the phone and turned to Diana. She was still sleeping, mouth open in unfamiliar abandon. At the base of her neck, he spotted the purple bloom of a love bite. A memory rushed back – his mouth on her throat, unsure if he was being passionate or just trying to act like someone passionate. Either way, she had seemed to enjoy it.

He pulled on his clothes, then went to the sink and washed out his mouth, smearing some toothpaste around with a finger. He couldn't imagine Diana Dartnell wanting to kiss someone with morning breath.

He sat back down on the bed, intending to gaze at her adoringly until she woke up. Five seconds later, the fire alarm went off.

She bolted upright, hair over her face, eyes half-open. 'Oh God. What time is it?'

'Half ten,' said Joe, who had hoped for his first words of the morning to be more poetic. 'Uh – the fire alarm's going, should we—'

'Ignore it. They test it every Tuesday.' She leapt out of bed, in delightful disregard of her nakedness, and crossed the room to the sink. She splashed water on her face and started brushing her teeth.

He hovered behind her, not sure where to look. 'I was wondering if I could take you out for breakfast,' he shouted over the shrilling alarm. Belatedly, he realised he probably couldn't afford any breakfast place she would want to be taken to.

She spat into the sink. 'That's a lovely idea, but I'm afraid I've arranged to meet my fellow actors for brunch. It's tradition on show days. We get together and drown our nerves in Buck's Fizz.' She looked critically at her reflection, spotted the love bite, and efficiently applied concealer until it disappeared.

The alarm cut off, leaving behind a loud silence. He watched regretfully as she got dressed. 'I could come with you?'

She did something with her hair that miraculously transformed it from a tangled mass to a neat bun in the space of ten seconds. 'They're not really your sort of crowd, Joseph. You'd be terribly bored.' Seeing his face fall, she tutted and came over to him. 'My poor puppy,' she said, stroking his cheek. 'Don't worry. This is not me shamelessly using you for inspiration and then dropping you like last week's news. Although God knows, enough of your lot have done that to their muses over the centuries.' She kissed him, soft and lingering. 'Let yourself out. I'll see you tonight.' She blew a kiss over her shoulder and left.

He stood motionless, as if all his energy had left with her. He was shaking, still nauseous, and he didn't know why. He and Diana were together; he had taken the first step on his path into the future. So why did he feel so utterly lost?

As he was pondering the answer to that question, a muffled sob came through the wall. He froze, listening. Diana's neighbour was crying.

It wasn't the first time he had overheard someone falling to pieces. It was part of the texture of Cambridge life, like punting or Formal Hall or black-uniformed men appearing out of nowhere. But that didn't make it any easier to listen to. Should he knock on her door, check if she was all right? Walk away, leaving her to have her breakdown in peace? He was still frozen in indecision when the crying stopped. A moment later, he heard something else: quiet at first, then rising and strengthening until it vibrated through the wall. She was singing.

The tune was familiar somehow. It stuck in his head as he descended the stairs and came out onto Trinity Street, the cold wind chasing away the afterglow. He checked his phone. No reply from Esi. Did she resent him for sleeping with Diana? Was she judging him for not telling his muse the truth? Each imaginary reason made him angrier, until he was so furious with the Esi in his head that he started talking to her out loud. 'You can't be annoyed with me for doing exactly what you wanted,' he muttered as a woman walking past shot him a puzzled look. 'You're the one who kept saying I had to—'

A bike bell rang, high and piercing, right by his ear. He turned to realise he'd narrowly escaped being run over.

He stepped back, nerves jangling like an echo of the bell. The predestined bike accident. He had forgotten, but it was still coming, pedalling inexorably towards him over Cambridge's cobbled streets, bound to hit him at some point between now and the summer. He rubbed his right leg with an anticipatory grimace. He'd have to hope Diana was into scars.

The churning in his stomach followed him, past Indigo café, where he and Esi had first made their deal, through the market square to the pavement where she had dropped the book, back to the river where she had watched him drift away, his future in his hands. Finally, resignedly, he headed back to college. The grey day was turning greyer, the invisible sun already sinking behind the rooftops. Something was missing, and he couldn't put his finger on what. It was only when he reached the gate that he realised.

He turned, scanning the street behind him. No time travellers. No Vera. He had been walking out in public for most of the day, but he hadn't seen a single visitor from the future.

A chill passed over him. He tried to reason it away. Maybe Vera was on holiday, or the wormhole was having some scheduled maintenance. But the absence of his future fans, on this of all days, felt like a bad omen.

He went on up to his room and checked his email. A message from Dr Lewis, blank, the subject line a question mark. He swore and checked the date: he had missed his weekly supervision. He sent a quick reply telling her he was ill. Guilt prickled at him, but he dismissed it. No use regretting what couldn't have been otherwise. He would get started tomorrow, and the 2:1 would follow as it was written.

He got dressed in the clothes Esi had picked out for him, that day in the charity shop on Burleigh Street, her eyes lighting up with surprise as he stepped out from behind the curtain. He stood in front of the mirror and carefully applied goop to his hair, trying to mimic the way her fingers had teased him into a better version of himself. When he was finished, it almost looked right.

'Thank you,' he said, not to her, but to her absence, following him about like an accusing ghost. He peered into the mirror, seized by the uncanny feeling that he was looking at two people: Joseph Greene the poet, brilliant and in love and a bit of a nozz, and Joe, unsure and heartbroken, trying his best to look the part.

He started out of his room, then doubled back. He opened the drawer where he had dropped the book, intending never to look at it again. Now, with the time travellers gone, he needed his future with him. He slipped it into his coat pocket and left.

As he came out of the staircase, he almost bumped into someone. Dr Lewis stepped back, eyebrows raised in surprise. 'You're looking well,' she said mildly. 'Going somewhere nice?'

Her words were painfully neutral, but he could see the disappointment in her eyes. 'Yes. All better. Sorry,' he mumbled, and fled.

At the ADC, he was directed backstage. Actors were clustered in one wing, and poets in another. As the compere strode out and the show began, Joe looked apprehensively out at the audience. Surprisingly, the room was packed: poetry didn't usually draw this kind of crowd, but no one could resist a love-themed event on Valentine's Day. In the front row was Rob, so overdressed in a bow tie and tails that he seemed to belong in another universe. Joe scanned the crowd for Esi, but of course she wasn't there. *She never liked your poetry*, said a bitter voice in his head, but his heart knew that wasn't why she was avoiding him. She had told him, the last time they had met. *I've spent enough of my life wanting something I can't have*. He felt again the rush, somewhere between wonder and terror, when he had understood what she meant. A trail of tiny moments, leading to nothing spoken: only a kiss that should never have happened, and a longing he had seen in her eyes, even as she told him to stay away.

'And now we have "A Taste of Stars" by Joseph Greene, performed by Diana Dartnell.'

She swept out from the opposite wing in a burgundy dress that fell off one shoulder, swathing her body in silk. At the sight of her, he lost his breath. He couldn't believe he had shared her bed, woken to see her dishevelled and unguarded, brushing her teeth naked to the jangle of the fire alarm. That Diana had been a person, flawed and vital. This one was an idea, blazing and perfect, untouchable as a mirage. Applause greeted her entrance: not the rapturous ovations that awaited her in the future, but a smattering of whoops from her small circle of fans.

The room fell silent. She cleared her throat. In the glare of the spotlight, the love bite he had given her last night was obvious. He felt his cheeks flame. Had she forgotten to reapply her concealer? Then her fingers self-consciously brushed her collarbone, and he realised: she hadn't forgotten. She wanted the audience to see it.

She cast a glance sideways, meeting his eyes. Her smile would have felt like a secret, if she hadn't been bathed in lights with two hundred people staring at her. He remembered what she had said, standing inches from him, shoulders bare, lips parted. *I think I figured out what's missing.* She was using their night together as material for her performance. For a moment, he was indignant. What had happened between them was private: what right did she have to share it with the world? Then he realised with uncomfortable recognition that he was no different. In the future, he had already cut her into fragments, reassembled their moments together into boasts of his own brilliance. How could he blame her for doing the same?

Besides, it was working. She read the poem beautifully, with a conspiratorial intimacy like she was alone with every single person in the room. Listening, he felt his self-consciousness fall away. He wasn't the poet, agonising over what people would think: he was inside the poem, in a way he never had been before. He closed his eyes and let himself feel it.

this:
my mouth
and hers, no words,
no sight, no light, just heat—
her tongue, a dart, a star, a catalyst

a kiss we cannot
live inside, a house
already on fire, embers
filling our mouths, igniting
what is to come—

but this, this:
there is nothing after this

if this is love
then douse me in it:
set me aflame, set me spinning
out in the universe,
bearing
only the memory
that we were this:
a once-burning thing,
so bright it kept them staring
long after it all went dark.

A pause, a breath; her eyes closing, her head dipping, as the theatre detonated with applause.

Not the polite golf clap that had greeted the other poems: this was real, a thunder of roars and whistles, two hundred people's delight and wonder and surprise, and it was all for him. But he barely heard it. As the words of the poem sank through him, his mind went wild with images: lights cutting through smoke, the sea crashing against a winter beach, the taste of tangerines and honey. *You've known it, haven't you?* Love, the burn and pull of it, the feeling of being caught in a moment you never wanted to leave – but it wasn't his night with Diana that he was remembering. It was Esi: her hands, her mouth, her smile, her laugh. Her kiss.

The shaking, stomach-churning uncertainty that had filled him all day transmuted into perfect clarity. He loved Esi. He wanted to be with her, even if it was temporary, even if it was doomed. He wanted to taste every moment they could possibly have before it was over.

Chapter Twenty-Two

He was still reeling with the revelation when Diana swept offstage, pulling him into her arms. 'Hear that?' she said breathlessly in his ear. 'That's for us, my love. You and me.' She was trembling, her breath hot on his skin. 'I know a secret storeroom backstage. Let's go and celebrate.' She kissed his neck.

He disentangled her arms from him and stepped back. He had a second to register her dismay, another second to take it back, explain it away before it was too late. Both passed. 'I can't do this. I'm sorry.'

He rushed out onto the stage and down the steps, causing a commotion in the audience as he ran up the aisle towards the exit. He pushed through the glass door of the lobby out into the frigid night. He ran on, turning down Sidney Street, scattering smug Valentine's couples in his wake. He pelted across the frosted grass of Parker's Piece and crossed Gonville Place without waiting for the lights. Ahead of him was Mill Road and the coffee shop and Esi, and every moment he spent without her was another moment wasted.

He wasn't sure what happened. One second he was striding across the road. The next, he was on the ground, ears ringing, a searing pain in his leg.

He sat up, lightheaded. Nearby, a cyclist was swearing. Joe watched through the stars floating in his vision as they got back on their bike and wobbled hastily away.

Well, he thought. *At least that's over.* He rolled up the ruin of his jeans to examine the blood running down his left leg. The wound looked deep enough to scar. But something wasn't right. He felt it in his gut, a wrongness he couldn't yet define.

He scooted backwards to the pavement, yelling in pain, and fumbled *Meant to Be* out of his pocket. In the fuzzy light of the streetlamp, he turned to the page with the photographs. There he was, grinning and dishevelled, bandages swathing his right leg.

He was trying to reason his way out – *maybe I'm supposed to have two accidents, this is Cambridge, bikes crash into people every day* – when he saw it. In the bottom right-hand corner, a detail he hadn't noticed: a date, stamped on the photograph by the camera that had taken it. 13.02.06.

The thirteenth of February. Yesterday. But that photo had never been taken. The accident it documented had never happened. Here, on the printed page, was definitive proof that the past had changed.

Ringing filled his ears, like the fire alarm from this morning was still happening. What came through it, strangely, was the voice of Dr Lewis. *Attention to detail has never been your strong suit.* He stared blindly at the last picture, the one of him and Diana as thirtysomethings, still looking newly in love. He had never bothered to read the caption. What could it say that wasn't already clear from the way they were gazing at each other? Now, his hands shaking so badly he almost couldn't focus, he read it. *Greene and Dartnell on 22nd May 2018,* it said. *The day they first met.*

He stared across the road into the empty darkness. 'We're not supposed to meet for another twelve years.'

It all fell into place. Vera starting to follow him after she saw him outside Diana's rooms. The look on her face when she'd caught them together. The time travellers' absence, stark as the silence from a broken clock. He had unwritten his future, his glorious, perfect future, and now it was gone forever.

Horror filled him, tinged at the edges with self-loathing. The truth had been right there in the book, hidden behind the questions he should have asked as soon as he read it. Why was there no photograph of him and Diana together as students? Why did the Introduction skip over their university years as if they were irrelevant to their love story? He had read that they had both studied here, and his assumptions had done the rest: that Cambridge was where successful people met, that his future had to start right now. Dr Lewis again, speaking in his ear. *You have a tendency to make leaps of logic that aren't justified by the evidence.* He stared down at the book, searching for an excuse, a way that this could not be all his fault. His eyes landed on Diana in her first-year dress, her arm around Esi's mum.

Esi. He seized on the thought of her like a drowning man reaching for a lifebelt. She was the one who had pushed him off his destined path. Worse than that, she had taken his hand and led him further into the wilderness, claiming all the while that she was setting him back on track.

He got to his feet with a roar of agony. He limped his way along Mill Road, the pain in his leg nothing to the torment in his soul. The coffee shop lay ahead of him, the focus of all his rage: love and betrayal drawn together into a vanishing point.

The art in the window had changed. Now, it was a Valentine's Day display, ringed with coffee bean hearts. Two figures were locked in an embrace under a thin crescent moon. He stopped in his tracks. A fingernail moon, a breath away from new: the same moon that had looked down on him and Esi in Diana's garden, on the kiss that was never meant to happen.

He couldn't think about that right now. He hammered on the door. He waited, then hammered again. Nothing. He was resolved to keep hammering until daybreak when he realised: Esi was trying to be a ghost. Of course she wouldn't open the door to a random stranger. He got his phone out and texted her with shaking hands.

It's me. Open the door. We need to talk.

After a moment, she appeared from the back. Her expression was soft, expectant, like she was both terrified and excited to hear what he had to say. He thought of the original reason he had come here, and his heart twisted in his chest.

She unlocked the door. 'What are you . . .' She caught sight of his leg, and her eyes widened in alarm. 'Joe, you're bleeding.'

'Yes, I'm bleeding! I'm bleeding from the *wrong leg*!' He barely even registered that she had used his first name.

She stepped back. 'What are you talking about?'

He barged past her into the darkened coffee shop. 'I'm talking about the future,' he said, turning to face her. 'I'm talking about what was meant to be, but isn't going to be anymore. Because of *you*.'

She was silhouetted in the light from the window; he couldn't see her expression. 'What . . .'

'Pretend not to understand. That's fine.' He paced towards her, and she turned into the pale light. 'You've been helping me get together with Diana. Right? That's what we've been trying to make happen since we met.'

'Yes,' she said uncertainly. 'Isn't that what you wanted?'

Either she didn't know, or she was a better actor than he had ever suspected. He refused the first possibility, too angry to let it in. 'No. I wanted my future. The one that's supposed to happen. And in that future, Diana and I don't meet until we're thirty-three.'

He saw the thoughts flying across her face, chasing implications. 'Wait. You're saying – you're saying we've changed the future?' Her brow furrowed, then lifted, light coming into her eyes. He saw that joy, and for a terrible, unworthy moment, he hated it.

'Yes. You were right. Are you happy? You get what you want. Congratulations. I just don't see why you had to fuck up my life in the process.' He hated how the words sounded even as he said them. 'Did you hate my poetry that much?'

'No!' Her face was open, desperate. 'I didn't know, okay? I would never have tried to help you get with Diana if I'd known.'

She was telling the truth, and he knew it. But he was a wound-up coil of rage, and that anger needed to get out. 'What do you mean? It's right there in the book!'

'I didn't read it! I told you, it was a free gift! I'm only here to save my mum. That's all.' Terror flashed over her face. 'Shit. Shit! The whole point was not to make any other changes. If Diana's future has changed this much, then the effects could be huge—'

He laughed, ecstatic to find a real reason to be angry with her. 'Aye, let's focus on you right now. Never mind that this whole time, I've been blithely setting my existence on fire because I thought my future was guaranteed. I nearly threw Diana off a roof because I thought we were both immortal! Fuck, I could have killed her!' He buried his face in his hands. 'I could have killed myself.' That last part should have hit harder, but losing his immortality barely registered when weighed against the only future he had ever wanted.

'I never told you your future was fixed. That's on you.' He could see her mind racing; she was still thinking about how this affected her. 'You have to make this right. Break things off with Diana.'

He started laughing. 'Oh, I'm way ahead of you. I did that before I even found out.'

Relief flooded her face, until it was replaced by confusion. 'What? Why?'

He thought of his previous self, running here in joy and terror to tell Esi he was in love with her. It felt like a vision from another universe. 'I . . .' She was looking at him with strange expectation. He shook his head, sinking down into a chair. 'It doesn't matter now.'

She sat down next to him. 'It doesn't mean it's over. You can meet her again in the future, when you're supposed to.'

He kept shaking his head. 'Maybe that would have worked four months ago. Maybe it would have even worked two days ago. But not now.' He drew in a breath that turned into an embarrassing sob. 'That future's gone, and it was all I had. I stopped working on my degree. I'm going to fail, and go home with nothing, and everyone'll know I was never good enough.' He pressed his eye sockets until he saw patterns, spinning out to infinity. 'I'm fucked.'

'You're not fucked.' Tentatively, she touched his shoulder. 'You're still *you*. You still have the talent, the potential. Even if you don't get back with Diana, you can still have a future.'

She was trying to make him feel better. He didn't want to feel better. He wanted to set himself on fire. He stood, shaking her off. 'I don't want "a future". I want my future. Mine. The one with my name on it. The one I had, before you came along and took it away.'

She rose to her feet, slow and deliberate. He had thought he had seen her angry before. He had been wrong. Her real anger didn't look like his, hot and blustering. Hers was cold, and it froze him to the heart. 'You came in here that day,' she said. 'You talked to me. You followed me to town, you stole the book, and you went and talked to Diana. You. No one else.'

His mouth worked silently. 'Okay. Fine. I talked to you. But you – you talked back. You couldn't resist, could you? Oh, here's that fucking nozz Joseph Greene, let's make a crack about his poetry. I should have known right then that you didn't give a fuck about my future—'

'"My future. *My* future",' she mimicked him. 'Tell me something. What makes it yours?'

He stared at her, lost. 'What?'

'Why should you be entitled to it, just because you had it before? Why shouldn't you have to work for it, and risk, and doubt, just like everybody else?'

Her words undid something in him, something so deeply rooted he had never even realised it was there. It hurt, like being a child and watching a longed-for balloon disappear into the empty sky. The hurt had something underneath it, something important, but he wasn't ready to face it yet. Right now, he just wanted to push the hurt outwards onto the person who had caused it. 'You told me when we met that you were a bomb crater. But you're worse than that. You're a bomb. You came into my life and you exploded it to fucking smithereens, and you don't even have the honesty to admit that's what you did.' He shook his head, trembling. 'You tried to warn me. Guess I should have listened.'

He got what he wanted. Her expression splintered, and her proud, upright posture sank, as he hit the heart of her vulnerability. 'And I should have walked out as soon as you came in here. I wish—'

'—we'd never met,' he filled in. 'That's what you do, isn't it? Wish things had never happened, instead of facing up to them. Rewrite history, instead of finding a way to move on.' He walked to the door, turning back to face her. 'I've never been real to you, have I? This whole time, you've treated me like nothing but an obstacle to your plan. But I'm a person, Esi. I exist. Here and now.' He hit his chest, wishing she could feel it. 'You can walk away. Jump into that river and come out of it as someone else. Overwrite me and you like we never met. But we did. It happened.' He swallowed, wondering why his voice was shaking. 'I'm not going to forget.'

He wasn't sure how it had happened, but he wasn't talking about his future anymore. Somehow, through the rage and the hurt, he had circled back to the reason he had first meant to come here.

She walked up to him, until they were as close as they had been that night in Diana's garden. He stared into her dark, red-rimmed eyes, unsure if she was about to kiss him or shove him away.

What she did was worse than either. Her voice trembled as she said, 'I can't wait to forget you.'

She reached past him and opened the door. He turned and left, the pain in his leg surging back, his eyes filling with stupid, needless tears. As he passed the window, he saw Esi sweeping away hearts and couple and moon, scattering them to fragments as if they had never been.

Chapter Twenty-Three

He staggered down Mill Road, blinded by tears, his leg throbbing with a hot, angry pulse. He should have been concerned about that, and about the way he was starting to feel, lightheaded as if he'd had too much whisky on an empty stomach, but he couldn't see past the aching void where his future used to be.

His phone was buzzing insistently; someone was calling him. If it had been anyone but Rob, he wouldn't have answered. 'What?'

'Where are you?' said Rob over the hum of a crowd. 'I'm surrounded by thesps and poets and I can't see you anywhere.'

Joe stared bleakly at the night-lit curve of the swimming pool. 'I'm on Mill Road.'

'Mill Road? Why are you on Mill Road?'

'I don't know,' he said miserably. 'Why is anybody anything?'

'You sound sad. Why are you sad? Everyone was clapping for you, Greeney. They really liked your poem. Isn't that literally your main life goal?'

'I'm bleeding,' he said, reasoning that *I had an accident* would be an easier explanation than *I was wrong about time travel*.

'You're bleeding?' Rob sounded amused. 'Were you set upon by critics?'

'No. A bike crashed into my leg.' He looked down at the gory mess of his shin. 'The wrong leg.'

Rob's tone shifted. 'Greeney. Listen to me. Sit down where you are. No, actually, lie down, and prop your leg up on something. I'm coming to get you.'

Joe felt inexpressibly relieved that someone had taken his fate out of his hands. He crumpled where he was and rested his head on the pavement. People walked around him. Some of them laughed. But it didn't matter: nothing mattered. He stayed where he belonged, in the gutter.

When Rob found him, he made a very un-Rob-like sound. He called a taxi to take them to hospital. At the hospital, Joe had stitches, after which the doctor gave him some strong painkillers and advised him to avoid strenuous activity for a while.

'That won't be a problem,' said Rob, 'he's a poet,' and he and the doctor had a good chuckle while Joe stared at the floor, wondering if he was actually anything at all.

It was midnight by the time they got back to college. Rob helped Joe up the stairs, and deposited him ungently on his bed. 'Your phone's ringing.'

He hadn't noticed. He got it out of his pocket – maybe it was Esi, calling to say she was sorry, and he could say he was sorry too, and they could go back to how it was – and saw the name on the screen.

He looked up at Rob in horror. 'It's Diana.'

'The stunning and talented actress you're in love with?' Rob gestured at the phone. 'She's probably worried about you. Aren't you going to pick up?'

The painkillers were kicking in. Everything felt pearlescent and ethereal, and he saw a way out, quivering like a mirage in the distance. 'No,' he said. 'I'm going to do the opposite.' He rejected the call, then blocked Diana's number. He placed the phone carefully inside his shoe, then slumped down in bed, muttering to himself. 'I have to undo it all. Reverse it. Go back to where I was. Then the future can happen, just like it was meant to.'

Rob patted Joe's head reassuringly. 'Sounds like a plan, Greeney. Sleep well.' He closed the door, leaving Joe in darkness.

HE DREAMT OF forking paths in a garden. Every time he reached a junction, he split in two, watching another Joe walk decisively off while he lingered, lost.

When he finally woke, he was exhausted. He blinked up at the ceiling. For a blessed, quiet moment, he had no idea who or when he was. Then it all came back to him: first, the pain in his leg, then, the memories. The caption of the photograph in the fuzzy light. The shattering realisation that everything he'd done to fulfil his destiny had only been pushing it further off course.

We're not supposed to meet for another twelve years. He wanted to kick against it, scream that it wasn't true, but part of him had recognised the truth of it the instant he spoke the words. It made sense of so much. The feeling he'd had since he first spoke to Diana, that they weren't right together, that they were too different to make any sense. The nagging conviction that in a universe without time travel, they would never have met. Because they weren't supposed to meet: not now, not as they were. They were supposed to meet when they were different people, twelve years of experience shaping them into the right fit for each other. He would have come to her clean, all his embarrassing mistakes nothing but stories to share with her, instead of scars across their personal history. Cambridge would have been a shared reference point, instead of two separate worlds that just happened to occupy the same physical and temporal space.

But now, this jagged, mistaken attempt at a relationship whose time hadn't come would haunt any future they tried to build. When her eyes met his across a room, she wouldn't see an intriguing stranger. She would see Joe, who had convinced himself he was in love with her and then rejected her.

It hit him with full, crushing force. He would never feel the love described in the poems. He had lost that chance, and in doing so, he had unmade them, scribbling over their perfection like a toddler with a box of crayons. Now, they were a relic from a lost reality. The future he had thought was waiting for him was gone, and there was no way of getting it back.

The enormity of the disaster was too much for him to process. He remembered what he'd said to Esi, the judgmental words he'd thrown at her about rewriting history. They sounded so hollow to him now. If there had been a wormhole he could walk into that would reset everything, he would have done it in a heartbeat.

Wincing, he reached down inside his shoe to retrieve his phone. He had blocked Diana's number, as if that would have the same effect as rewinding time to before they had met. But it had still given him a measure of relief.

A mad impulse seized him. Maybe if he offered the universe a symbolic walking-back, an undoing of everything he'd done since meeting her, then destiny would take pity on him and give him another chance.

He sat up, pivoting his leg off the bed. He was still dressed in the clothes he'd worn to the poetry reading, one leg of his jeans cut off above his bandage to make absurd half shorts. He wriggled disgustedly out of them and flung them in a corner. He got dressed in his old, shabby clothes, the jeans with holes in, the jumper Esi hadn't known what to say about. He took another dose of painkillers, hoisted the crutch they'd given him at the hospital, and made his slow way down the stairs.

He undid everything he could think to undo. He gave the shirt he'd bought with Esi back to the charity shop and threw the ruined trousers into a Burleigh Street bin. He went to the street corner where he'd first seen Diana, where he had spoken the words of a poem that would never be written. Now, he spoke them in reverse, then walked solemnly backwards towards college, to the baffled amusement of the watching tourists. No time travellers: they were gone. 'Nothing to see here,' he muttered as he climbed backwards up the steps. 'Not anymore.'

He revisited everywhere he had been with Diana, each backward step taking him into a better world, a world where he hadn't ruined everything before it had even begun. He hired a punt and poled his way backwards from Magdalene Bridge to the Mill Pond, nearly falling in several times, until the punt guides started working him into their patter, talking about the superstitious things Cambridge students did to keep from failing their exams. He really should have climbed out to the secret terrace and backed his way along the ledge to the battlements, but he was no longer immortal, and dying while undoing something reckless felt even stupider than dying while doing it.

Finally, weary and aching, he walked up King's Parade in the darkness. He propped himself up outside the door of Whewell's Court and waited.

By the time someone opened the door and he slipped in after them, it was almost midnight. He climbed up to Diana's room, the stairs creaking, his leg screaming. He paused outside her door. He wanted to focus on the ceremonial moment of undoing, but his attention kept drifting to her neighbour's painting: the endless bifurcating paths, like his dream, the path that ended in his future obliterated now by a fire he had set himself.

He should leave. If Diana was home, she could open the door at any second. He began to manoeuvre himself backwards down the stairs.

He was navigating the tricky corner when he bumped into someone coming up. He was so terrified it might be Diana that when he turned and saw it wasn't, he forgot to pay attention to anything else. He registered a girl with wide, surprised eyes, her hair tied up under a red silk headwrap. She looked vaguely familiar. He wondered if he'd seen her coming out of the ACS meeting with Esi. She seemed to be on her way back from a late-night study session in the kitchen: she was holding a mug of hot chocolate, a pile of political science textbooks in the crook of her other arm. She was looking at him like he was certifiably insane.

'Sorry,' he said. 'Didn't see you there.'

'That might be because you were walking backwards.' Her voice was low, her tone precise. Her brow furrowed delicately. 'Why?'

'That's a good question.' He gestured up the stairs. 'I'm unvisiting Diana Dartnell.'

She nodded slowly, as if this made complete sense. 'I should have realised Diana would have something to do with it.'

His heart thudded. He didn't want one of Diana's friends telling her he'd come looking. 'You know her?'

'Sort of.' Her eyes darted up the stairs. 'She's my neighbour.'

'Neighbour. Right.' The painting, the soft singing, the crying through the wall, reassembled into the person standing in front of him. He smiled, like he had bumped into an old friend. 'Is that your art on the door?'

She tilted her head up. Something about her manner, shy but assured, caught at him. 'Yes.'

He had stared at the painting so many times that he couldn't resist asking. 'What's it about?'

She rolled her eyes. 'Come on. Isn't it obvious?' As he flailed, a smile broke across her face. 'No, I'm messing with you. I don't really know what it's about. I just made it.' She gave a small half shrug. 'I guess you get to decide.'

Having to decide for himself felt overwhelming. He wished she could have just told him.

They hovered a step apart. She shifted her grip on the stack of books. In the middle, he spotted a slim paperback that didn't belong. White script on a pink spine. *The Earl's Wilful Wife*.

She saw him looking, and drew the stack defensively up to her chest. On the folder underneath, a coffee spill had made a dark splodge. She had drawn around it, turning it into a starry, cross-hatched portal.

'Excuse me,' she said.

He was lost in the melody of a familiar song, his head buzzing with echoes. 'Yes?'

She looked awkward, then annoyed. Her expression smoothed over with a practised sigh, like she spent a lot of time hiding how she was feeling. 'No, I mean – *excuse me*. You're in my way.'

'Oh. Sorry.' He moved abruptly to the side, forgetting his injured leg. He swore silently.

She shook her head and walked past him, laughing. 'Bye, Backwards Boy.'

Her laughter followed him around the curve of the staircase. He lurched down, step by frantic, burning step, until he reached the entrance, the list of room numbers and names stark on the wall in white on black. There, below *F5: Diana Dartnell*, an empty row he hadn't noticed, the glare of his muse obscuring everything around her. He looked closer. Black tape, stuck carefully to the wall. He peeled it back. Underneath, there she was. *F6: E. Eshun.*

Chapter Twenty-Four

'Oh,' he said aloud, feeling deeply, transcendently stupid.

He left Whewell's Court and crossed the road, waiting by the Great Gate until a column of late-night revellers spilled out and he could slip inside. In the Porters' Lodge, he went back to the column of *E*s, the blank pigeonhole he'd passed over, assuming it belonged to a student who'd dropped out. For the second time, he peeled back the tape covering Efua's name. Her pigeonhole was empty, except for a blank notelet that read, *With Deepest Sympathy*.

He staggered back, the pain in his leg surging with the rhythm of his pulse. Why was her name covered up? Clearly, she hadn't dropped out; he'd just seen her in her staircase, carrying textbooks back to her room. He couldn't shake the feeling that it meant someone didn't want them to find her. His thoughts went to Vera, standing watch outside Whewell's Court. Had she somehow figured out why Esi had come to the past, covered up Efua's name to stop her changing the future?

He reeled in his spiralling thoughts. It didn't matter. Vera was gone. What mattered was that he knew where Esi's mum was, and he had to tell her.

He limped back to college in the frozen dark. He couldn't face her directly, not with the things they'd said to each other still lying between them raw as open wounds. But there was no way he could keep this to himself. Even though he didn't want her to leave; even though the thought of her overwriting herself made him feel sick to the stomach. This was more important than what he wanted.

He ripped a leaf from his notebook and sat down at his desk. At the top of the page, he wrote her mum's room number: *F6, Whewell's Court.*

He meant to leave it at that. But given her last words in the café, he doubted he'd get the chance to speak to her again. If he had something to say to her, he had to say it now.

He didn't set out to write a poem. He just thought, and wrote, and the words turned gradually into a poem, because that was the only honest way to tell her what he was feeling. He wrote, without thinking about whether it would be good, about whether anyone other than Esi would ever read it. He thought only of her, and what he wanted her to understand: all the things he hadn't been able to tell her, because his fear and his pride and his obsession with the future had got in the way.

When he was happy, when the shape of it was a close enough match to the shape of his heart, he tore a new sheet of paper from his notebook and copied it out clean.

F6, Whewell's Court

I found her. And in her, I found
you:
your eyes,
your laugh,
your sometimes-wickedness,

your love of casual, accidental beauty,
your love of love, and your defensiveness
at being seen to love it—
you, alive
in her;
her, alive
in you.

That little girl was never lost.
She grew up, turned into
a butterfly,
a hurricane,
a traveller with her mother's eyes
who danced through years
like they were moments,
unwound the springs
of time itself
to save the one she loved.

We are more than what made us,
and our paths through time
are never straight lines.
The footprints you leave
will stay,
even if you unmake
the one who made them.
Through all my broken, overwritten days,
I will remember:
not who you were meant to be,

but you, as you are,
on a rain-swept beach,
shivering, laughing, alive.

He folded the paper in half. On the outside, he wrote her name.

He walked: one last, agonising walk through the cold to the long, straight road that led from the university out to reality. The window of the café was empty. A light was on in the back; through a half-open door, he caught a glimpse of Esi moving. He hovered, torn by the compulsion to talk to her. But the poem was better than he was: he didn't want to hobble it with his embarrassment and his explanations and his excuses. He had to let it speak for itself. He posted it under the door and turned away to limp his slow way home.

THE NEXT MORNING, his leg hurt too much to get out of bed. Two mornings after that, his leg felt better, but despair had settled on his mind, weighing him down. For days, he left his room only to forage from his dwindling stock of food, until he was eating a heel of bread coated in the wipings from an empty pot of jam. Bear broke off from washing to stare at him judgmentally.

'Why don't you go back to the future,' he said sourly, and rolled over to stare at the wall.

Finally, Rob barged into his bedroom and flung open the curtains. 'Greeney. Get up. You're coming with me.'

He cringed away from the daylight. 'What? Where?'

'Queens'. Got a target there.'

He pulled the covers over his head. 'I'm not in the mood to help you pretend to murder someone.'

'Of course you won't *help*. You're deeply unqualified. We'll be lucky if you don't get us both killed.' Rob pulled the whole duvet off Joe's bed. 'But I refuse to let you sit and stew in whatever's bothering you. You need to rejoin society.' He sniffed the air and wrinkled his nose. 'Correction. You need to have a shower first.'

Washed and dressed for the first time in days, he followed Rob outside. A dense fog had descended, colleges looming out of it like spectres from the past. As they crossed the river, he looked out at the ghostly timbers of the Mathematical Bridge. He remembered drifting under it with Diana as she spoke about Crispin, feeling for the first time like he was seeing her real self.

Crispin. He had thought how odd it was, that she would leave him for Joe only to turn around and marry him later. But she wasn't going to leave him. She was going to stay with him and get engaged to him and walk open-eyed into two years of misery with a man who couldn't tell her he loved her. Even if the future could change, Joe doubted a fling with a provincial nobody would be enough to throw that off course.

He followed Rob into Cripps Court, a 1970s block that sat across the river from Queens' original fifteenth-century court like the aftermath of a time-travel accident. Rob unzipped the bag he was carrying and pulled something out.

'Why are you brandishing a poster tube?'

'It's a sword. Clearly.' Rob indicated the base of the tube, where *SWORD* was written in neat black letters. He put a finger to his lips and started climbing the stairs.

Joe followed wearily, his leg aching, up to the third floor. Rob crept along the corridor, poster tube held high, and took up position behind the second door. As he followed, Joe tripped on the doorstop and banged his bad leg on a fire extinguisher. *'Fuck.'*

The second door flew open. Something hit Joe's jumper, and he fell back instinctively against the wall. It took him some time to register that he had been shot.

The assassin lowered his water pistol, staring at Joe. 'Who the hell are you?'

Rob looked from Joe to the assassin and back with an expression of utter devastation. 'You killed Greeney! Now it's *personal*,' he growled, and launched himself at Joe's assailant, who retreated hurriedly back into his room.

Joe looked down at the spreading wet patch on his jumper. So this was what it felt like to be dead. It wasn't as bad as he had expected: in some ways, it was a relief. Joseph Greene the poet was dead already, his ashes blown to the wind. A water pistol to the chest seemed a fitting way to mark the end of all his hopes and dreams.

Rob emerged from the target's room, the front of his hoodie dark with water.

'Jesus,' said Joe, momentarily distracted from his own predicament. 'Are you okay?'

'No, Greeney. I'm dead.' Rob thwacked the poster tube against the floor in frustration. 'That's what tends to happen when you bring a sword to a water pistol fight.'

Joe stared over Rob's shoulder, his mind still turning on wormholes and second chances. 'Maybe you could go back in time and fix it.'

Rob laughed. 'Not in this universe.'

As usual when Rob talked about time travel, Joe was immediately confused. 'You mean because time travel isn't possible in this universe?'

Rob was too preoccupied by his death to answer. 'The worst thing is, it scuppers my chances of getting a PhD.'

'What are you on about? You're the most likely person to get a PhD I know.'

'Not that kind of PhD. Paranoia Hardened Death-Master. It's the title awarded to Assassins who win the Game twice. Now there's only the May Week Game left, so it's Master Assassin or nothing.'

Joe was barely listening: he only heard the end of the academic year rushing down on him, inexorable as time itself. His guaranteed 2:1 was gone. In its place was a blank sheet of paper, and the fact that he hadn't done any serious work since before the Christmas holidays. He could have been making an effort – unlike the rest of the book's broken promises, this one was in his power to fix – but he hadn't been able to bring himself to try. If his original future was gone, he might as well have no future at all. He saw it bleakly laid out before him: moving back home, where his failure would become a running joke, working in the pub and paying rent to his parents until he died and was utterly forgotten.

The cold air chilled the wet patch on his jumper as they came out onto Silver Street. Rob stopped on the bridge, leaning over to watch a lone punt drift into the fog. 'Greeney, what's up?'

Joe hunched his shoulders. 'What do you mean?'

'You had your big moment, then you ran away and got yourself run over, and since then you've basically been a shut-in.' Rob looked at him, puzzled. 'What happened? Was it something with Diana?'

He shuddered against the cold. There were so many ways he could describe what had happened with Diana, but only one that Rob had enough context to understand: that moment backstage, when he had stepped out of her arms and turned away. 'She invited me to a sex cupboard and I said no.'

'Right,' said Rob slowly. He rubbed his face. 'I'm sorry, why exactly did you say no to the sex cupboard?'

'Because I was in love with someone else.' He closed his eyes, swallowed, let the truth come out. 'I *am* in love with someone else.'

'And you can't be with that person because . . .' Rob left the question hanging.

She had told him a hundred times. She was a ghost, already drowning in a river of her own choosing, and she didn't want him reaching in his hand to help her out. 'She's not staying.'

'Ah.' Rob picked up a loose chip of stone from the bridge and threw it in the river. 'It's Esi, isn't it?'

Joe gaped at him. 'You saw us together *once!*' Months ago, at the very beginning, when he had barely known himself. 'Was it that obvious?'

Rob chuckled. 'Yeah, Greeney, it was obvious.' He reached into his bag and took out the throwing star Esi had made, turning it admiringly in his hands. 'And I don't blame you. Nothing more attractive than a woman who can craft a weapon.'

'She also wiped the floor with me at Laser Quest,' he said miserably. 'It was really hot.'

'Oh, mate,' said Rob as if he'd witnessed a bereavement. 'I'm sorry.'

'It's okay.' He took in a long breath. Talking to Rob didn't stop it hurting, but it made the hurt cleaner, like exposing a wound to the air. He blinked back tears, feeling stupidly grateful for his friend, who didn't know anything about his future, but had come to his show anyway because he wanted to support him. 'I never asked. What did you think of the poem?'

Rob paused. 'Do you want me to be honest?'

He felt a lurching terror. 'Go on,' he said lightly.

'It wasn't very – you.' Rob wrinkled his nose, searching for the words. 'It was like you were trying to be someone else.'

That's because I was *someone else. Will be. Would have been going to be.* It was just as well he couldn't tell Rob the truth: verb tenses weren't really up to it. 'Aye,' he said. 'I think you might be right.'

They fell silent, staring out into the fog. A group of blazered drinking society types passed behind them, talking loudly about the lucrative finance jobs they were going to walk into after graduation. Dr Lewis again, resonating in Joe's mind. *I see too many students here who think they know the future.*

He had thought he was so different. But his future as a poet had never been something he had really questioned. He had always thought it belonged to him by right, even in the days when it seemed the world didn't want him to have it. He had never considered the possibility that it might not happen, not because of any great injustice, but because of a hundred arbitrary reasons, fate and chance and chaos and simply not being good enough. *Why should you be entitled to it, just because you had it before?* The words Esi had thrown at him in the darkened coffee shop, the words he hadn't been ready to hear. Now they unfurled inside him like a bruise, painful but right. The world didn't owe him anything. He owed back the sum of what he had been given: the chance to be here, to strive, to try.

He apologised to Dr Lewis. He poured himself into his degree, both because he had a future to salvage and because he hoped the dry, abstract work of poring over philosophy would help him to stop thinking about Esi. He was coming out of the faculty library, his rucksack weighed down with books, when he saw someone familiar lurking behind one of the building's concrete stilts.

He stopped dead, his heart in his throat. He must have been mistaken. But he wasn't, because it was Vera, out of her official tabard, lounging against the pillar with her arms crossed.

He stared at her, not bothering to hide his astonishment. Any minute now, she would drop his gaze and hurry away. But she didn't. Instead, she walked right up to him. 'Hello, Mr Greene,' she said. 'Think it's time we had a chat.'

Chapter Twenty-Five

'**A** chat,' he said slowly, to buy himself time to figure out how she could possibly still be here.

'Yeah.' She glanced over her shoulder. 'Mind if we walk and talk? I'm on a deadline.'

He looked down at his leg. 'As long as we can walk slowly.'

She led the way through the car park, watching him limp after. 'So how much do you know about what's going on here?'

He snorted. 'I know your leaflet's a load of shite.'

'Leaflet?' A wave of alarm crossed her face, followed by a wave of resignation. 'You've seen the book.'

He had to be careful. He couldn't risk sending her after Esi. But she was hardly the only time traveller who had broken the rules. 'One of your clients left it in my pigeonhole. Under a mug with my face on.'

Vera buried her face in her hands. 'Uggh. This is really not a one-person job. I keep *telling* them that, but they're all like *opening wormholes is expensive, Vera*, and I'm like *well, maybe you shouldn't be opening so many of them*, and then they say *but we need to maximise our return on investment, and you do such a great job—*' She sidestepped to avoid one of the plane trees that erupted out of Sidgwick Avenue like inconvenient giants. 'I knew something wasn't right. You were off your expected pattern, almost from the start. You weren't in the places you should have been, and then you *were* in all these places you never should have gone . . .'

His mind boggled. 'How do you know my past to that level of detail?'

'Because it's my job. Anyway. After I saw you hanging around outside Whewell's Court, I started to worry. Lucky I was on my own when I saw the two of you out punting together. Imagine if I'd had a group with me. Joseph Greene and Diana Dartnell getting cosy on a boat when they're not even supposed to be a thing yet? Makes it hard to maintain that whole *can't change the past* line.'

He latched onto one word, glinting in the midst of her tirade like a star through the darkness. 'Yet?' He limped to catch up with her. 'So on the other side of the wormhole, me and Diana still get together?'

She frowned, as if she didn't understand the question. 'Of course.'

'Right. Otherwise you wouldn't be here.' The implication blossomed in his mind. His future was still possible. It might not be guaranteed anymore, but Vera's presence meant he could still get there by another path.

'I mean, if you ask me, I always thought she was wrong for you. I've got to know you a bit with all this following you around, and to be honest, she doesn't seem like your type.'

'Really,' he said distantly.

'Not much of a fan of the poems either. No offence.'

'None taken.' He was surprised to realise he meant it. After all, it wasn't as if he had written them.

'I used to run the Byron trip. Now *there's* a poet.' Her eyes went dreamy. 'You've seen the statue of him in the Wren Library? Doesn't measure up when you've met the real thing. The *presence* that man has . . .' She tailed off, blinking. 'Sorry. What was I talking about?'

It took him a while to remember. 'How you saw me and Diana getting cosy on a boat.'

'Right. Obviously, I immediately advised my bosses to shut the trip down.'

'Shut the trip down?' He thought of Esi, still hoping to climb out of the river into her new self. 'You mean, close the wormhole?'

'We can't close it. No one knows how. Yet another trade secret we're not keen to have leak out.' She disappeared for a moment as they split up to round another tree. 'No, usually, we just seal them off to the public. Which was my recommendation in this case. But my bosses feel we haven't yet recouped sufficient value from this trip. The schedule says we keep it open till the end of June. We take a break while you're doing your exams – we're not monsters – then we open up again and get a nice flurry of visitors around graduation.'

That was going to be awkward if he didn't graduate. 'So keep it open,' he said, trying to ignore the lurch in his stomach. 'Why do you care what I think? It's not like I ever agreed to this anyway.'

She laughed. 'Oh, you agreed to it. Or you will, in the future.' He imagined his future self signing away the rights to his past, and felt a wave of resentment. What a nozz. 'But if we're going to keep this trip open, we need your help.'

His leg was starting to ache. He stopped on the narrow pavement, leaning against the wall. 'What kind of help?'

'I'm not asking you to stop seeing Ms Dartnell. If that's really what you're into, knock yourself out. But if you could keep it to private locations during time travel hours – that's nine to five – then I would really appreciate it.'

She was tense awaiting his answer, as if it really mattered. 'What if I say no?'

'Then the trip gets shut down, the wormhole gets sealed off, and I get fired. Because fixing this fuckup is now apparently a condition of my continuing employment. And I really, really need to keep this job, for reasons I don't care to explain to you right now.' She took a breath. 'So? What do you say?'

She didn't know that her concern was completely unnecessary: he wasn't with Diana anymore. But either way, it didn't matter. Esi needed the wormhole kept open, so he would promise whatever he had to. 'Fine.'

'Thank you. Wow.' She looked almost as surprised as she was relieved. 'You know what, I didn't expect you to actually help me out. In the future, you're kind of—'

'A nozz,' he said tiredly. 'I know.'

'Seriously, though. I owe you a favour. If there's anything I can ever do for you, let me know.'

He couldn't help asking. 'The people who come on your trips. Do any of them ever try and stay?'

'Some people get the idea in their heads, yeah. We've got one on this trip, actually. Gave me the slip early on and still hasn't reappeared.' She shrugged. 'Doesn't bother us, as long as they don't interfere with the target. It's all covered in the terms and conditions. We just say their future was always in the past.'

It meant Esi was safe, as long as he kept away from her. He felt a pang of bittersweet relief. But Vera's words made him imagine something else: a future where Esi didn't go back through the wormhole. A future where she stayed. The consequences spiralling out from that decision felt immense enough to knock the

world off its axis. 'But if you let people stay in the past, they're going to affect everything. They could change the future completely.'

Vera wrinkled her nose. 'Not *the* future. *A* future, maybe.' He
didn't understand the distinction. Maybe if you were used to everything being rewriteable, it made your idea of time less absolute.
She clapped him abruptly on the shoulder. 'Anyway, I've got to
run. Thanks, Mr Greene. I appreciate it.'

He sketched an awkward half bow. Seconds later, he had no
idea why. Something about being called Mr Greene, probably.
'You're welcome. Sure I'll see you around.'

'Soon.' She darted a glance at his leg. 'Although we'd better wait
till that's healed up.'

'Thanks. That's very considerate.'

She shot him an odd look as she jogged away.

He went to sit on the grass behind Queens', watching the post-
lecture wave of students pass down Silver Street. For so long, he
had thought his future was guaranteed. Then he had thought it
was hopelessly lost. In truth, it was neither. Vera had come from
a future where he and Diana were together, where he was still famous for his poems about her. He felt a strange, tender awe, that
their connection was powerful enough to survive everything he'd
done to destroy it. But nothing was set in stone: with one wrong
step, that future could disappear.

He had wanted his life to feel less scripted, for his decisions to
truly be his own. Now, he'd got what he wanted, and the result was
that he felt paralysed, too afraid to move forward.

WEEKS PASSED. HIS leg healed. The first time he stepped out of
college and saw the time travellers across the street, his insides
melted with relief. But it didn't last. Instead, it sent him into an

anxious cycle, obsessively checking his pigeonhole for gifts, terrified of finding it empty in case some random action had thrown
his future off course. His borrowed confidence was gone, and he
didn't know how to get it back.

His pigeonhole wasn't the only one he kept checking. Each day,
he stopped by Trinity Porters' Lodge and went to the one labelled
Eshun, E. The tape was gone, her name clearly visible, as if he had
imagined it ever being hidden. The contents were unremarkable:
a random flyer, a cupcake, a letter with an official college stamp.
Nothing that looked like a note from Esi. She must have held back,
too afraid of consequences she couldn't control. It was so like her
that it made his chest hurt.

On the last day of term, he was working on an essay when a
message popped up in his MSN window. He opened it, expecting
Rob demanding tea, but instead, there was a request from a new
contact:

butterfly_hurricane@hotmail.com has added you

He stared at the email address, not daring to hope. He accepted
the request and waited.

hi

Nice email, he typed, fingertips buzzing. Is that a quote from
something?

just some poet
you won't have heard of him
he's pretty underrated

He laughed as a host of yellow smileys filled the window.

> no more stupid punctuation faces
> I feel so free
>
> How did you even find me on here?
>
> Rob told me to add you
> bumped into him when I was
> following my mum
> he said this is the best way to reach
> you when you're in hermit mode

He remembered what he'd told Rob, leaning over the bridge and staring out into the fog. His heart quaked with vulnerability. How much did she know?

> we should talk
> can we meet?

He checked a street map, tracing a half-mile radius around King's Lane.

> Do you know Hodson's Folly? It's on Coe
> Fen, just upriver from the boundary.

A pause.

> ok
> meet you there in half an hour

It would only take him fifteen minutes. Still, he set off straight away, walking with jittery purpose. The Folly was an odd, roofless ruin that looked like a miniature temple, perched on the edge of an island on the river. He sat in the windowsill facing the water and waited.

He heard the gate open, and the soft sound of her footsteps. Then she was there, sitting down on the windowsill across from him. He felt the time since he had seen her collapse and expand simultaneously, as if he had just limped out onto the darkened street, as if centuries had passed since they had spoken. She looked different. Her dress was vibrant red, her hair coiled into twists that bounced as she turned to look upriver. 'How's your leg?'

'Better, thanks.'

Silence hung in the air between them. It had been easier, somehow, to type words to her disembodied self as if nothing had happened. Now, faced with her, he could only think of how badly they'd hurt each other.

She looked down at her hands. 'Saw a few time travellers hanging around outside your college the other day. Guess your future's not broken after all.'

He cleared his throat. 'I spoke to Vera. She says I'm still with Diana in the future.'

'Course you are,' she said with a shaky smile. 'You're meant to be.'

Their eyes met for an instant before he looked away. 'Anyway, you're safe. Vera's not going to be looking for you, unless she sees you with me. I told her all this' – he gestured, vaguely indicating the whole disaster – 'was someone else's fault.'

She laughed with a touch of bitterness. 'We both know that's not true.'

For an instant, he was back there in the darkened coffee shop, the expression on her face burnt into his mind. 'I'm sorry for what I said. About you being a bomb.'

She didn't flinch. 'You weren't wrong,' she said quietly. 'I did kind of explode your life.'

'I did most of the exploding. You just lit the fuse.' He scrubbed his hands through his hair. 'And you weren't wrong either. The future in the book – I was acting like it was mine by right. But it never was. I could lose it tomorrow. I could have already lost it.' He imagined going back to college and finding his pigeonhole empty, the spot across the street abandoned. Terror coursed through his veins.

Esi was watching him with fond frustration. 'You're still stuck on that book. Like your whole future's getting marked against it. But whatever comes next, it's brand-new. A load of blank pages. What you end up writing on them – it won't be the same.' She shrugged. 'It might even be better.'

He stared past her at the trees on the riverbank, new leaves rustling in the wind. 'Huh. I didn't think about that.'

She smiled. 'Yeah, well. Creating a better future is sort of my whole thing.'

A better future without you in it. He focused on her, as if his attention could hold her to the here and now. 'How's that going?'

'I've been following my mum. Every chance I get. And I get a lot of chances.' Her brow furrowed. 'It's weird. She was so hard to find before. But whatever she was hiding from, it's like she's not afraid of it anymore.' Her expression turned curious. 'How did you find her?'

'Funny story. She's Diana's neighbour.'

Her eyes widened. 'Come on. That makes it even weirder that she said she didn't recognise her.'

He grimaced. 'I don't want to speak ill of my once and future muse, but – given the kind of person she is, it's really not that weird.'

She smiled reluctantly. 'It's actually kind of hilarious. That whole time you were rehearsing, she was literally next door.'

'I know. I'm such an idiot. I even used to hear her . . .' He stared at her, finally making the connection. 'That tune you hum sometimes. I heard her singing it. She'd been crying, just before. It was like she was trying to make herself feel better.'

She shook her head in wonder, her eyes filling with tears. 'It's a Twi song, from Ghana. Nana used to sing it to her, and my mum sang it to me and my sisters. I sing it to myself whenever I need to calm down. I can't believe she did . . .' She paused, revising her thought with a trembling smile. 'I can't believe she does the same.'

He tried to put himself where she was, to conjure the strange, time-piercing depth of what she must be feeling, but his imagination couldn't grasp it. 'What's it like, seeing her?'

A troubled look crossed her face. 'It's not easy. Sometimes I see what a hard time she's having, and there's nothing I can do to fix it. But – she has fun too.' A smile broke through. 'One time, I was waiting outside Whewell's Court, and she and her friends came out all dressed up in old-timey gowns. And she's part of a club that meets up to watch Nollywood movies. I snuck in the week they watched *Keeping Faith*.'

He smiled, caught up in her enthusiasm. 'Is that a good one?'

'The best. I must have watched that tape a hundred times

growing up. Genevieve Nnaji and Richard Mofe-Damijo have such amazing chemistry. The way they look at each other, the way they make each other laugh . . .' She met his eyes and looked away, suddenly bashful. 'Anyway. I just lurked in the back. I wish I could have sat and watched it with her.'

'Why didn't you?'

'Because I can't risk her seeing me.' She gave him a look. 'I know what you're trying to do. You're not going to change my mind.'

He adopted an innocent expression. 'What are you talking about?'

Her eyes saw right through to his heart. 'I read your poem, Joe.'

He felt a wave of crushing embarrassment. He had laid himself bare for her, more vulnerable than when she had walked in on him naked in his bedroom. 'Oh God. I'm sorry I wrote a poem. I know you hate my poetry. And I didn't want to make it about me, I just – I wanted to tell you, and the only way I knew how to do that was—'

'I loved it,' she said simply. 'The way you see me – I . . .' She seemed to run out of words. She just looked at him, her gaze soft, her lips parted.

He sensed a chance to say something, to finish the conversation he'd meant to have with her on that terrible Valentine's night. But he recognised now the selfishness of the impulse that had driven him there. It wouldn't have been fair, to offer her a conditional fragment of his future; any more than it would have been fair of her to say yes, when the person saying it wouldn't exist for much longer.

She seemed to recognise the same truth at the same time. She dashed a tear away, her voice shaking. 'Anyway. It was good. Way better than Classic Joseph Greene.'

'I know, right? Fuck that guy.' She laughed, and he laughed too, all the tension melting out of him. 'And I can't think of a greater honour than inspiring your email address.'

She made a face. 'I didn't want to get one. Felt like putting down roots. But Shola insisted. She said I need to stop living in the past.'

'Little does she know.'

'I moved in with her, by the way.' Her glance warned him not to make a thing out of it, even as fondness warmed her voice. 'Big mistake. She has the worst taste in music. And she makes jollof all wrong.'

'And there I was thinking I'd have to invite you up to mine again for the Easter holidays.'

She smiled. 'You're going soon?'

'Wednesday.'

'Say hi to your mum and dad for me. And Jeely Piece.'

'Jeely Piece is about to get the shock of his life. One of the time travellers left me a kitten. Her name's Bear. I'm taking her home with me.'

'Your cat names are not improving.'

'That one's actually Rob's fault.'

She nodded, as if that made sense.

He settled back against the windowsill, a ray of sunshine lighting up the space between them. It felt so good to be with her here and now, all their angry words behind them. In an instant, he knew what he needed to say. No flowery words, no grand declarations, just the truth. 'I missed you.'

She looked up at him sharply. Then she smiled. 'Yeah. I missed you too.'

'I'll be back at the end of April.' He shrugged. 'Come and see me sometime.'

She swallowed a laugh. 'What, waltz up to your college in full view of your future fans and their tour guide?'

'There's a back gate. Text me when you're there. I can get Rob to come and let you in. Vera'll be none the wiser.'

'Okay.' She closed her eyes, turning her face to the sun. The breeze rippled the river, set her hair dancing. It kindled something inside him, fragile as a new leaf. It felt like hope.

HE ARRIVED BACK in Cambridge on a spring day in late April, wisteria blooming on college walls in purple profusion, the sky streaked blue and white with scudding clouds. He checked his pigeonhole: two white roses, three scribbled notes of devotion. He threw them away without reading them. He hadn't earned them yet, and in any case, the details weren't important. It only mattered that they were there, a promise of better to come.

The only non-time-travel-related correspondence was a flyer for the college May Ball, which was happening on the twenty-third of June. The day Esi would be leaving. He dropped it in the recycling. It wasn't like he could afford a ticket anyway.

He climbed the staircase to his rooms and unlocked the door. The window of the living room was open, the curtains flapping in the breeze. He was alone with the blank page of his final term at Cambridge. He closed his eyes, reeling with the terror of how to fill it.

Through the silence rose a sound: a light, deliberate tread, far-away at first, then climbing closer. Outside his door, the footsteps stopped. He heard a breath, shallow and urgent, then a soft sound, like someone placing their hand against the wood.

He turned, wondering why his heart was pounding, why his neck was prickling with superstitious dread. He walked to the door and pulled it open.

Standing there, her fist raised to knock, was Diana.

Chapter Twenty-Six

His first reaction was panic. She wasn't meant to be here. He had dismissed her, first to an unwritten past, then to an unstable future. And yet here she was, on his doorstep, taking her fate into her own hands.

'Joseph.' He had caught her before she had time to compose herself. The vulnerability on her face made her look like a stranger.

'Diana.' He stepped back, as if he hadn't already stepped back from her in every way he could. 'What are you doing here?'

She laughed breathlessly. 'What else was I supposed to do? I would have called first, but . . .'

But he had blocked her number. To him, it had been a gesture, part of his grand symbolic walking-back of everything. Now, he thought about how it must have been for her: cut off with no explanation, left to imagine a reason why. He had told himself she wouldn't care, that he meant nothing to her. But the look in her eyes told him that had been a self-protecting lie.

She moved past him, brushing his arm. Her scent caught him, and time collapsed, sending him back into every moment they had shared. He was in her bed, kissing her neck, her fingers tangled in his hair; he was under a streetlight, reciting another man's poem, transfixed by her cool green eyes. He was in the darkened wing of the theatre, taking her hands, pushing her away.

She turned to face him. 'I'm not quite sure how to do this. I've never actually been rejected before. God knows Crisp likes to leave me hanging, but he's never strictly said no to me.'

She was comparing him to Crispin. He felt ill. 'Diana. Look. It's not y—'

'Please don't demean me with clichés. Whatever is between us, I think it deserves more than *it's not you, it's me.*' Her gaze dropped. 'Besides, I rather suspect it *is* me.'

Shame crushed him. 'Don't say that—'

'Please. Let me speak.' She took a breath. 'I live my life wearing a mask. Most people never get to see behind it. But you – I let you see me, and then you walked away. Do you understand what that did to me?' Tears of fury shone in her eyes. 'I'm supposed to be the one who decides when something's over. I'm not supposed to be the one moping, and pining, and turning up at your door like a lost puppy.' She laughed, cracked and human. 'I'm rather pissed off about it, actually.'

He wanted to tell her the truth, that seeing her real self was the closest he had come to falling in love with her. But he had broken this once before by rushing it, and he didn't want to do it again. 'I'm sorry,' he said. 'For how I treated you. I should have given you a proper explanation. I just – I don't think we're ready.'

'Ready for what?' Her eyes widened in half-amused perplexity. 'I'm not asking you to marry me, Joseph. Or to swear your eternal devotion. I'm asking you to be with me, here and now.'

Should he say yes? Was this how it could happen, in the new world he'd accidentally created? He was still caught in a spiral of consequence and second-guessing when she added, 'I've left Crispin, if that makes a difference.'

He felt it like a tremor. Diana wasn't supposed to leave Crispin. She was supposed to marry him. 'Why?'

She shrugged. 'Because you were right. I deserve better.'

He heard the echo of what Esi had said by the river. He was still measuring everything against the book, even after he'd shoved it under his bed and tried to forget about it. But this wasn't the Diana from the book. This Diana was real, and she was here, and for some insane reason, she wanted to be with him.

He wasn't sure. But maybe he wasn't supposed to be sure. Real relationships weren't written down ahead of time. You might look back and think you were always in love, but that could just be your future self telling a story. It might really have felt like this, a paralysis of indecision, a teetering between outcomes. The world where he told her *no, not yet*, and she walked away. The other world, this world, where he took her in his arms and kissed her.

AFTERWARDS, HE LAY with her head resting on his chest, her fingers dancing lightly across his shoulder. 'Let's just stay here,' she said softly. 'Pretend the rest of the world doesn't exist.'

He felt like he was watching from somewhere high above, a spectator on this moment. It made him feel like a voyeur. 'I'd love to,' he said, kissing the top of her head. 'But I have to make a plan for how not to fail my exams.'

She looked up at him reproachfully. 'Really? You're turning me down for philosophy?'

When she put it that way, it sounded insane. But he had already wasted enough time acting like his future was guaranteed. 'I'm not the only one with finals,' he pointed out. 'Don't you need to revise?'

'What's the point? I have one plan for my life, and it doesn't rely on me getting a good degree. I'm not going to waste my time trying to be something I'm not.'

'But that's not the only possible future,' he argued. 'Why not have a backup plan?'

'Because that would mean part of me had already given up.' She propped herself on her elbow, looking at him earnestly. 'This life I'm chasing, Joseph – it's all or nothing. I'm not going to make any choice that takes me further away from it. I'll choose my art. Every time.'

He felt like he was looking at her from the other side of a glass wall. He wanted to live in her world, where art was all that mattered, and everything else was subordinate to that one consuming purpose. But he suspected her world came with a hefty financial cushion from her parents if she didn't turn out to be employable.

'Anyway, I can take a hint. I'll leave you to your darling books.' She climbed over him and started getting dressed.

He sat up, feeling guilty. 'Let me walk you out.' He threw his travel-worn clothes in the corner, put on whatever was at the top of his suitcase, and made a token effort to fix his hair.

In the mirror, Diana was looking at him with something like alarm. 'What on earth are you wearing?'

He looked down at the little boats and trees decorating his front. 'A jumper?'

She pulled a face. 'It's not very you.'

It was a stark reminder that for as long as she had known him, he had been pretending to be someone else. 'Actually, it is,' he admitted sheepishly. 'I was only wearing all that fancy stuff to try and impress you.'

She slid her arm into his as they descended the stairs. 'I see. And now you've impressed me, that's it? You're just going to stop making an effort?'

Her tone was teasing. 'Och, I don't know,' he said with a smile. 'Maybe I'll buy another shirt.'

'A whole shirt,' she said, mock-amazed. 'I'm a lucky girl.'

A wave of relieved fondness ran through him. Maybe this could work after all.

As they approached the gate, the Chapel clock was striking two. It reminded him of something, but he couldn't nail down what, until he pulled the door open and saw Vera and a tour group waiting across the street.

Time travel hours. He swivelled, flattening himself against the door.

Diana looked at him curiously. 'First you kick me out, now you're not letting me leave?' He took her arm and marched her away from the gate. 'Where are we going?'

'Back gate. It's handier for Trinity.' It absolutely wasn't. He would just have to hope Cambridge's maze of streets was sufficiently confusing to obscure his lie.

'Joseph.' She stopped him as they reached the tree-lined shade of the Bursar's Garden. 'Are you trying to hide me from someone?'

He winced. 'Would you believe me if I said no?'

She crossed her arms. 'What are we talking about here? Another girlfriend?'

The word *girlfriend* momentarily short-circuited his brain. Diana wasn't his girlfriend. She was his one true love, his muse, his destined— He cut himself off. He wasn't supposed to be thinking about the book. 'No! Just – someone who doesn't think we should be together.'

'How intriguing. So this . . .' She stepped close, twining her arms around his neck. Her voice dropped to a whisper. 'This is a secret?'

His breath caught. He nodded.

She looked over his shoulder, then drew him down for a stolen kiss. 'I rather like it.'

HE SPENT THE next two weeks oscillating between the library and Dr Lewis's rooms, trying to climb out of the academic hole his past self had dug him into. In the moments between, he gradually adjusted to Diana Dartnell as his girlfriend, who he kissed and slept with and took out on dates, although never during daylight hours. The fact that they had to sneak around gave the whole thing a thrill of the forbidden. Part of him enjoyed the irony of feeling that way about a relationship that was sanctioned by fate itself.

And he was writing about her. The poems came to him in fragments, inexplicable as the gifts in his pigeonhole. Only after piecing them together and reading them back did he understand what it was like to be with her. It was a strange, backwards way to fall in love with someone. But maybe that was how it had to be with him and Diana. The poems had come first: reality could only do its best to measure up.

There was just one problem, which he had been successfully pretending wasn't a problem until Rob had the temerity to bring it up.

'So when are you going to tell her?'

Joe looked up from revising Hegel. Rob, as usual, was knitting. He'd come back from Easter break with a huge circle made of black wool, and had been adding to it ever since. 'Tell who what?'

'Campbell.' Rob's acceptance of Esi into their inner circle had been sealed when he'd started calling her by her surname. 'About you and Diana.'

He affected a casual tone. 'You think she'd care?'

Rob barked out a laugh. 'You know she'll care. That's why you haven't told her.' His phone buzzed. 'Speak of the devil. I'll go and let her in.'

Joe stared into the void of Rob's knitted circle. Over the holidays, he and Esi had talked endlessly, late-night MSN conversations that had kept him up till the small hours. But since he'd returned, a distance had grown between them. He reminded himself that he didn't have the right to be upset about it. In less than two months, she would be leaving. Diana was his future, and Esi's was on the other side of a wormhole.

It was hard to keep that in mind when the door opened and there she was, in a green-and-yellow dress that made her look like spring come to life.

Rob led her to his circle. 'Feast your eyes. This is how I'm going to take Darcy down.'

'Amazing.' She looked at the circle, then up at Rob. 'What is it?'

'It's a black hole.' A manic grin lit his face. 'Once inside the event horizon' – he tossed the circle into the air above Joe's head. It landed, draping him in darkness – 'the unlucky occupant gets turned to spaghetti.'

Joe clawed his way out, feeling his hair go static. 'There's no way you're allowed to use this as a weapon.'

'Course I am. I got approval from the Umpire before I started knitting.' Rob looked eagerly at Esi. 'It's genius, right?'

She looked sceptical. 'I don't know. Feels like you're overthinking it.'

'Of course I'm overthinking it! Two years I've been preparing for this duel.' He jerked a thumb at Joe. 'Blame him. He took my attack animal away.'

'Because I'm not letting you throw my kitten at some confetti-wielding psychopath!'

Rob and Esi shared a look. For a moment, Joe felt intensely left out. He wished he and Esi could have that easy camaraderie again. But maybe he was rewriting the past; maybe things between them had never been so simple.

'Anyway,' said Rob. 'Got to go. Revision supervision.' He looked meaningfully at Joe. 'I'll leave you two to catch up.'

He left them alone with their silence, full of all the things they hadn't said to each other. Joe hurried to break it. 'How's it going with your mum?'

She sat down on the sofa, tucking her feet up. 'I feel like I know everything about her life at this point. All her friend groups, all her lectures, all the societies she's in. But I've still got no idea about the award. And the twenty-third is six weeks away.' She bit her thumb. 'Any ideas?'

'One. But you're not going to like it.' She looked at him questioningly. 'You could talk to her.'

'No. No way.' Her face was half-wondering, half-terrified. 'What would I even say?'

'Tell her about the award. Say she needs to refuse it. Or don't mention the award at all. Just tell her not to come back to Cambridge on the twenty-third of June 2031.'

She gave him a look that was so characteristically her that it made his heart ache. 'Why would she believe me? I'm just some random stranger.'

'You don't have to be.' He took her in, the curve of her cheek-bones, the shy confidence of her bearing, all the ways the girl on the staircase had rhymed with her. 'You could tell her who you are.'

'I can't.' He thought he knew why: her old fear, that her mum would be disappointed in her. But she didn't look afraid. 'I can't do that to her. It'd be too much. Imagine knowing all that about your future. You'd end up second-guessing every decision you made. It could ruin your whole life.'

His stomach twisted. 'Aye. Imagine.'

A flash of guilt crossed her face. 'Shit. I'm sorry.' She touched his arm, a fleeting moment of contact before she drew back. 'How are you doing?'

This was his chance to tell her. *I'm with Diana.* But he couldn't. It would open up the box of unspoken things they had silently agreed to keep locked up until she left. 'Yeah. I'm writing, and – it's good.' Better than good. Last night, he had read over the poems he had written since getting back together with Diana. They were the best he had written in his life. They weren't good like the poems from *Meant to Be*; they were good in a way that felt like him, but better. Something vital had been missing, and now it was there, burning through the words, turning them incandescent.

Her face lit up with honest joy for him. 'That's great.'

It *was* great. He was with his true love, and he was writing good poetry, and thanks to the work he'd put in over the past two months, he might not even fail his degree. So why wasn't he happy?

He was still dwelling on it a week later, arm in arm with Diana, walking down the floodlit grandeur of King's Parade. They had just finished dinner at a restaurant where the waitress had stood staring at him for a good thirty seconds because he hadn't realised he was supposed to taste the wine.

'I don't get it,' he argued now, as Diana leaned into him, resting her head on his shoulder. 'Why should I have to check if their wine's any good? Isn't that their job?'

She laughed, a low chuckle that resonated through his body. 'It's a perfectly normal part of wine service, Joseph. If anyone had taken you to a decent restaurant before . . .' She straightened up. 'Shit.'

'What?' He looked ahead, madly expecting to see Vera, but striding up the street towards them was Crispin. As he passed, he shot Joe a glare. Diana held her head high and acted as if she hadn't seen him.

'Do you know he asked me to marry him?' she said in a neutral voice after he had gone. 'I might have said yes, if it wasn't for you.'

The weight of everything he knew and she didn't settled on Joe's shoulders. 'Engaged at twenty-one,' he said distantly. 'Old-school.'

'Crispin's very old-school.' She went on, talking about his insistence on opening doors for her even when it was actively inconvenient. Joe tried to listen, but his mind kept drifting to the Diana he hadn't met, who had married Crispin at twenty-one and lived to regret it. He imagined how it must have felt for her, to go through that and then meet someone new, someone entirely unexpected. He remembered the picture of the two of them on the day they met, the look of helpless adoration in her eyes. Whatever happiness he could give her now, he wasn't sure it could compare.

'I also thought I might take the opportunity to run naked through the town centre,' she said lightly.

'Mmm,' he said, nodding, then, 'What?'

She gave him a strange, sad smile. 'It's all right, Joseph. I chose to go out with a poet. The fact that you're elsewhere half the time is part of the deal.'

He put his arm around her in apology. He wondered if it would always feel like this: like he was looking back at her through the wrong end of a telescope, trying to reconstruct a love made out of fragments. A white rose, a feather, a snow globe of Paris. Scribbled copies of poems that had been unwritten. Even if he could write a new version of that love, it would never belong just to the two of them. He had already turned it into art.

He walked her up the stairs to his room. At the door, she pulled him back against the banister and drew him into a kiss. He felt a shadow of how it was for her: the passion, the intensity, the in-the-moment thrill of it. He tried to join her there, but he was a universe away.

Behind him, the door opened. He waited for Rob to make a disparaging comment about public displays of affection. Instead, there was a silence that felt like ice water on his neck.

He turned. In the doorway was Esi, wearing a look that twisted his heart.

She didn't speak. Before he could say anything, she ran past them down the stairs.

'Well.' Diana craned over the banister. 'At least now I understand why you've been hustling me out of the back gate like a criminal. You've been trying to spare her feelings.'

His mind was a whirl of static. 'What are you talking about?'

'She's clearly in love with you, Joseph. I saw it at the party. Do you think I'm blind?' She touched his back gently. 'Go after her. You need to sort this out.'

He didn't stop to think about what she'd said. He ran down the stairs, taking them two at a time, and pelted out of college into the night. He caught up with Esi on Pembroke Street, by the arched tunnel that led into the New Museums.

'Esi. Wait. Let me explain.' She walked away from him into the tunnel. He followed. 'Vera told me it was fine as long as I kept it secret. And I have. No one's seen us. It's not going to affect the trip.'

She turned, misery written on her face. 'That doesn't make any sense. Why would they let you be with her now when their whole business depends on you getting together later?'

He didn't want this resigned, wrenching sadness. He wanted her to be angry with him. 'You tell me! You're the one who's obsessed with changing the future! But only in the way that suits you, right? The rest of us have to stick to the script, so we don't mess up your plan.'

She let out a despairing laugh. 'Do you really think that's what this is about? You don't belong to me, Joe. I don't get to decide what you do with your life.'

She was inches from him, backed against the wall of the tunnel. He didn't want to give her a way out. He wanted to make her say it. 'So what is it about?'

She tilted her chin up, meeting the challenge in his gaze. 'Why are you with her?'

The tremble in her voice betrayed what she was really asking. He answered that question as well as the one she had spoken. 'Because she wants to be with me.'

She looked down the tunnel with a heartbroken smile. 'And have you been honest with her?'

'Yes. I'm not pretending to be someone else anymore. I'm being myself—'

'You know what I mean,' she interrupted. 'Does she know the truth?'

'No. Of course she doesn't.' All the turmoil of how he'd been feeling for the past month rose up inside him. 'Do you know what it's like, to try and be with someone when you've read the book of your relationship? It's never enough. Because you're not comparing it to reality. You're comparing it to something perfect. Something that never existed.' He gazed at her, desperate to make her understand. 'I don't want her to have to feel that too.'

'That's not how relationships work. You're in it together, or you're not in it at all.' She fixed him with a look that knew him inside out. 'Do you really think you can spend your whole life like that? With her, but not with her? Measuring every moment against a future she doesn't even know exists?'

He knew the answer. But he knew what that answer meant. If he broke up with Diana a second time, she wasn't going to forgive him. She would be gone, and his future would be gone with her.

Esi must have read it in his eyes. She lowered her head with a soft exhalation. 'I thought you were better than this.'

The words echoed down the tunnel, ricocheted back to strike him in the heart. By the time he had recovered enough to take a breath, she was gone.

Chapter Twenty-Seven

'So? How are you feeling? Are you ready?'

He stared unblinking at Dr Lewis. This was his final supervision, the day before the start of his exams. 'No. Yes? Maybe.' He rubbed his tired eyes. 'I don't know.'

'It's common to feel that way at this point. You just need to let go of the outcome, and do the best you can.' She settled back in her armchair. 'You've really impressed me this term, Joe. Of course, no result is guaranteed. But you should be very proud. You've done the work. Now you can focus on the future.'

He tried to feel proud, but he couldn't feel much of anything. Esi's words were still ringing in his ears. *I thought you were better than this.*

Dr Lewis peered at him. 'What's up?'

A sudden lump in his throat. He swallowed it. 'I guess – I'm finding it hard to get excited about the future.'

'It can feel a little abstract sometimes. You know what always used to help me?' She drew an arc in the air as if she were opening a portal. 'I used to imagine my future self, coming back to tell me who she had become.'

He almost laughed. He thought of Joseph Greene the poet, stepping through the wormhole with a smug smile and a copy of *Meant to Be*, and felt physically ill. 'What if I don't like my future self?'

'Then that's a sure sign you're on the wrong path.' She clapped her hands, making him start. 'Invent a new one! That's the point! The future is nothing but the sum of all our present moments.'

The idea was terrifying. To walk up to Joseph Greene, celebrated poet, and decide not to become him. To take a different path. 'But what if my new future's not as impressive?'

She scoffed. 'Who cares?'

'Easy for you to say. Your future was being a professor at Cambridge.'

She gave him a sly look. 'Do you know why I play the sousaphone?'

A complete non sequitur. He stared at the instrument's looping coils in desperation. 'Because it's a symbol of infinity?'

'No! Because it's *fun*. It's loud, and it's silly, and it's like wearing a musical hug. It makes me happy.' She got to her feet, signalling that the supervision was over. 'You're twenty-one, Joe. Find what makes you happy. Wherever that leads, you can't go wrong.'

He left her rooms and walked out into the court. The spring breeze whipped through his hair, swirling the grass into unpredictable patterns. He thought about destiny and desire, and the gap between a life and a work of art. He thought about the version of himself he wanted to be.

He went up to his room and reached under his bed for the book. He leafed through it one last time: the Introduction, with its top-down, distorted view of a life turned into an idea; the poems, strange and distant now, like set texts for an exam he had failed and forgotten. He slid it into the inside pocket of his jacket and went to find Diana.

He knocked on her door, but she wasn't home. He sat on the floor outside to wait for her. He looked up at Efua's painting, the shining gold paths through a rich, uncertain sea of black. He had thought one path was marked out for him. When he'd realised he had strayed from it, he had scrambled for the one that looked closest, a shortcut heading in the same direction. But in truth, no path had his name on it. He wouldn't even see the path until he was at the end, and that was how it was supposed to be: not a fast-forward to the finish, but a hopeful, purposeful wandering, one faltering step at a time.

'Joseph? What are you doing here?'

He got up. Diana stood at the top of the stairs, just back from a show, the roses in her pale skin hidden by flawless make-up, her eyes kohl-dark and infinite.

'We need to talk,' he said, and hated it as he said it, the way it flattened the complexity of what lay between them to a cliché.

He saw her flinch, the mask briefly slipping. 'Well,' she said in a low voice. 'That sounds rather ominous.'

He could still change his mind. Whatever it was in him that responded to her, the part of him she made sing, desperately wanted to. Maybe she really was his one true love. Maybe, by doing this, he was losing the chance of writing the best poetry of his life. But the words came out, as if the choice had already been made. 'This isn't working. I'm not happy, and I don't think I'm making you happy either. I don't listen to you, and I'm distracted all the time. And the truth is—'

'You're in love with someone else.' She said it with soft resignation. When he looked puzzled, she laughed. 'I told you. I'm not blind.'

'That's not all.' He reached into his pocket for the slim, innocuous shape of the book. 'I've lied to you. Or at least, I haven't told you everything.'

He offered her *Meant to Be*. She looked down at it with confusion, then with shock. She grabbed it, turning to the back, then to the inside cover. He watched her flick through, eyes darting, breath coming fast. It was intimate and a little disturbing, like looking through a wormhole at his past self.

She looked up at him, searching his face for answers. 'What—'

'It's real,' he told her. 'Or, it was. But the future can change. We've already changed it. For starters, we met twelve years early.' He leaned in to kiss her cheek. 'Read it. Then call me if you want to talk.' He went back down the stairs, leaving her alone with her heart's desire.

THE NEXT MORNING, his exams began. As he left college, the time travellers' usual spot across the street was deserted. His gut plunged with the finality of his decision, until he remembered: Vera had told him the trip would be suspended until his exams were over. He tried to focus on what Dr Lewis had told him. *Let go of the outcome. Do the best you can.*

Two weeks passed in a blur of urgent scribbling and constant low-grade terror. Finally, he came out of his last exam into the blinking sunshine. Champagne corks were popping, three years of pent-up anxiety spilling out into hysteric laughter. The hard part was over. May Week beckoned, seven days of parties and day drinking, but to him, it was nothing but a clock counting down to when Esi would leave.

He hadn't spoken to her since the night she had found out he was with Diana. There was so much he wanted to say to her. He wanted to thank her, for showing him a truth about himself he couldn't have recognised alone. He wanted to tell her he loved her. He wanted, more than anything, to ask her to stay. But there was no way she would say yes. She was already set on forgetting him; there was no need to make it any harder.

His phone buzzed. He looked down, heart in his mouth, but the message wasn't from Esi. It was from Diana.

I want to talk. Meet me at Byron's Pool.

He followed the river to Grantchester, past the sounds of drunken picnics and punters falling in the water. The pool wasn't easy to find; he got lost in an orchard, then had to ask directions from a man who looked like he had stumbled out of the nineteenth century. Finally, he found the wooded trail and followed it down to the river.

Diana was sitting on a jetty in cropped trousers and a white blouse, hugging her knees. Beyond her, the river broadened out into a grey basin, matted with weeds and algae. He wondered if in Byron's day, there had been a concrete weir covered in warning signs. The reality was so distant from the green, shaded idyll in his head that he wasn't sure he'd come to the right place.

Then he realised. That was the point. The reality and the idea were two separate things: you had to live one, even if you were striving to become the other. He thought of himself seven months ago, staring up at Byron's statue, overawed by an ideal he could never live up to. But Byron couldn't live up to it either. This pool was just a place, and he had just been a person: a rich, aristocratic person, who had felt at home enough in Cambridge to make a joke of it, but no more essentially a poet in himself than Joe was. The statue crumbled, revealing nothing but a young man in deep water.

He sat down, rolling up his jeans to dip his feet. Diana looked sideways at the crooked line running across his shin. 'Nice scar.'

'It's on the wrong leg. But thanks.' He focused on the water, the sun glinting off the ripples in the grey. 'I'm sorry. I told myself I was sparing you the burden of knowing the future. But that's not my decision to make.'

'No. It isn't. But I understand.' She saw the relief on his face, and laughed. 'Oh, don't get me wrong. I'm furious. But I understand. Probably better than anyone. I know what it's like to focus so single-mindedly on what you want that you stop thinking of other people as people.' She said it lightly, with a self-deprecating air, but he felt the accusation and, worse, the justice of it. 'Did you know, all this time, that you were changing the future?'

'No. For a long time, I thought I was making it happen.' It was hard to believe, now, his arrogance, his conviction that time would work in the way that suited him best. 'By the time I realised, it was too late.'

She smiled wryly. 'Well, this certainly makes sense of a lot of things. I kept seeing people following me around. Odd-looking people. Like someone might come to a 2000s dress-up party in fifty years' time, you know? And this bored-looking woman in a tabard who kept ushering them away.'

'That's Vera,' he said. 'She's the tour guide.'

'Vera?' She made a face. 'I suppose it has to come back in fashion sometime.'

'They shouldn't have been following you. My future self might have sold the rights to my life, but that didn't include the rights to yours.'

She smiled. 'I didn't mind. I'll have to get used to it, after all, if

I get where I want to go.' She lifted her hand. 'Speaking of which. Aren't you going to congratulate me?'

He looked at her, puzzled. She sighed and pointed to the huge diamond that he had failed to notice adorning her ring finger. 'I'm engaged.'

He still didn't understand. 'To who?'

'The Duke of Devonshire,' she said, in such perfect deadpan that for a confusing moment, he believed her. She rolled her eyes. 'Crispin, you loon.'

'Why?' He stared at her, appalled. 'You don't have to marry him. Surely that's one good thing to come out of all this mess.'

'Of course I have to marry him. Because I do.' She took *Meant to Be* out of her bag and laid it on the jetty between them. 'It happens. On the way to where I'm going.'

He looked down at the book, then up at her, the frozen black-and-white face and the living one, shade-dappled and intent. 'But – none of that has to happen now.' He drew his feet out of the water and swivelled to face her. 'You can do anything. You can be with someone else, or not be with anyone, or you can have a harem of guys you see on a rota. You can move to Borneo, or become a lion tamer, or – or freeze yourself in a cryogenic tank and wake up in the future.' He laughed in hoarse desperation. 'The possibilities are infinite. I know that's scary, and I know you've built yourself around one idea of who you're supposed to be. But that doesn't mean it's the only version of you that could ever exist.'

She looked at him steadily. 'Joseph. I've been perfectly clear with you who I am, and what I want. Did you think I was lying? Or did you think I wasn't sure?' She shook her head, throwing a twig into the water. 'My whole life, I've been sure about exactly one thing. Other possibilities don't interest me.'

He watched the twig float in place, pushed and pulled by invisible forces. 'But – think of everything we changed. We're on a different path now, for better or worse.' He tried to say it gently. 'Diana, your future in *Meant to Be* – it might not even be possible anymore.'

'I know that,' she snapped. 'I'm not an idiot. But given that I still want it, what should I do? Pretend I'm walking blind, stumbling through the rest of my life? Or use what I know' – she laid her palm on the book – 'to make sure I don't change anything else?'

His mouth moved helplessly. 'But Crispin – he doesn't have to be part of that future. He's not the reason for your success.'

'Do you know that for certain?' She held his gaze, challenging, until he looked away. 'Wanting to be an actor is an insane dream, Joseph. Success is balanced on the slimmest knife-edge. If I do succeed, a lot of it will be down to luck.' She frowned into the deep water. 'I can't be sure that Crispin is part of that luck. But I can't be sure he isn't. Maybe he introduces me to someone. Maybe the experience of being married to him turns me into the right person to play some crucial role. I don't know. But the best way of reaching that future is to follow the path that already led me there.'

It sounded like what he had said to Esi, huddled on the sofa in his parents' house, before his life had been upended by a bike crash and a kiss. He wanted to tell Diana that she was wrong, that he knew better now, but she wasn't him: she hadn't been through what he had been through, and even if she had, she might have learned something completely different.

She tapped his arm. 'Don't feel sorry for me. I never wanted to be a person, remember? Much less a happy one. My sights are set elsewhere.'

He stared out at the river. He imagined Byron on his back, weeds tangling his feet, something tugging him down to the green depths. *I'll choose my art. Every time.* It made sense, in a twisted way he wished he didn't understand. It was a choice he might have made himself, once upon a time. In another universe, perhaps he had. An image transfixed him, sudden and dizzying: the two of them sitting by the river, overlaid a hundredfold, a thousandfold, their outlines trembling with a million potentials.

She held out the book. 'Here you go. It's yours, after all.'

He took it. He ran his hand over the cover, thinking of the first time he had seen it, falling out of Esi's bag onto the street; of the uncloseable gap between then and now. 'It's not mine,' he said. 'I stole it. But the person I stole it from doesn't want it.' He handed it back. 'And I don't need it anymore.'

'They're very beautiful. The poems.' She looked down at her own face, austere in black and white. 'When I read them, I see her. The me I want to be.'

Her words should have made him feel something: joy, pride, satisfaction. But he didn't feel any of those things, because it wasn't about him. He had no more ownership over the poems than he had over Diana herself. 'So keep them.' He shrugged. 'It's you I would have written them for.'

'All right.' She tucked the book into her bag. With a wry smile, she added, 'You can keep the photo.'

He didn't understand. 'What photo?'

'The one of Efua and me.'

Everything rearranged in his mind, an optical illusion flipping from one state to another. 'You do know her.'

'We were friends in first year. No dramatic bust-up, if that's what you're thinking. We just grew apart. Different priorities, you know.'

He thought of what Esi had told him about her mum: academic to the exclusion of all else. Meanwhile, Diana never read anything she wasn't about to perform. It made sense. 'So why did you lie?'

'She has her reasons for not wanting to be found. I might not understand those reasons, but I try to respect them.' She got to her feet. 'If I'd known it was her daughter looking for her, I might have made an exception.'

He felt ashamed; she was more perceptive than he'd given her credit for. He was running through the reasons Efua might not want to be found – that she had a stalker, that she was in witness protection – when Diana cleared her throat. 'Well. See you in twelve years, I suppose.'

He stared up at her. 'What are you talking about?'

'Our fateful meeting. Our great love.' She tilted her head. 'Are you saying it's not going to happen?'

'It can't. Not anymore.' He laughed. 'I've spent the past seven months trying to live up to those poems, and it's impossible. If we'd met like we were supposed to, if our lives had come first and the art had come second . . .' He shook his head. 'But it can't work the other way around.'

'Maybe that's how you feel right now.' She looked down into the opaque depths. 'But in twelve years, you might change your mind.'

He looked her in the eyes. 'I won't.'

Her voice was wry as she walked away. 'You sound very sure, for someone who believes in infinite possibilities.'

He turned to watch her go. He wanted to say something, a final line of the unfinished poem they had been writing together, but perhaps this was how it was supposed to end: her shape receding into the woods, her fate left open.

HE HAD MEANT to sleep in the next morning, but his exam-tuned nerves woke him at half past eight. He lay for half an hour trying unsuccessfully to get back to sleep. Then he sighed, got dressed, and went downstairs, going out of habit into the post room.

In the doorway, he stopped. For the past two weeks, his pigeon-hole had been empty. Now it was full again.

He crossed the room and sorted through the contents with trembling hands. A white rose. A snow globe of Paris. A scribbled note. He unfolded it. *Joseph Greene. Thank you for teaching me about love.*

He dropped everything on the floor and ran to the front gate. He opened the door a crack, peering out into the street. There they were, in their usual spot: Vera and her tourist huddle, craning anxiously towards the entrance.

He pushed the door closed and backed away, his guts churning. What did it mean? Was Diana right? Were the two of them inevitable? Or was he going to live out the same love story, write the same poetry, about someone else? Both possibilities seemed completely insane.

'Greeney!' Rob came out of the Porters' Lodge, beaming. 'Incredible news. Just spoke to my mate who's on the May Ball committee, and he told me Darcy's going to be attending. Guess Trinity was too pricey for her.'

Joe blinked at him. 'Her?'

Rob looked confused by his confusion. 'What, you assumed she was a man just because she has a male pseudonym? It's 2006,

Greeney. Women can be soulless killers too.' He rubbed his hands together. 'She thinks she's getting the PhD, but my black hole's going to get her first.'

'PhD?'

'I told you,' Rob explained with exaggerated patience. 'Paranoia Hardened Death-Master. The award you get for winning the Game twice.'

'Award?' He felt like a radio tuning back in, static shrieking into coherence. 'Sorry. When's the Ball?'

'A week from now. Twenty-third of June.'

It all came together in his mind, like a clump of inexpert stitches knitting into a black hole. Darcy, short for The Deadly Mr Darcy. *Mum was into period romance.* Rob's number one rule of the Game. *Make yourself hard to find.* The sympathy card he'd found in Efua's pigeonhole, a few days after Darcy had been 'killed': an Assassin friend's idea of a joke.

He reached into his pocket for the picture he'd ripped out of the book. Mechanically, he unfolded it and showed it to Rob.

His roommate looked up at him, puzzled. 'Why have you got a picture of Darcy with Diana?'

He put the picture back in his pocket. He knew what the award was. And he knew how to stop her from winning it.

'Greeney?' Rob was watching him with concern. 'You okay?'

'Sorry. Got to go,' he said, and sprinted out of the gate.

Chapter Twenty-Eight

He was heading for the coffee shop when he realised the time travellers were following him. He cursed and changed course, careering down Tennis Court Road. By the time he came out at the other end by the chemistry department, Vera and her crew were far behind. Still, he played it safe, weaving through a maze of backstreets that confused even him until he finally found Mill Road almost by accident. He turned in a circle to reorient himself, ran in a weaving zigzag through the pavement crowds, and burst into the café, heart pounding.

Esi wasn't there. Standing behind the counter was Shola, her colleague and now housemate.

'Hi, Joseph Greene.' She was looking at him with strange familiarity, as if she knew more about him than he knew about her. It didn't make sense. Shola wasn't a time traveller. Then he realised the more obvious explanation: Esi had talked to her about him. The thought was simultaneously thrilling and terrifying.

'Hi. Uh – is Esi here?'

She shook her head, setting her beaded earrings swaying. 'It's her day off.'

Friday. 'Shit. Do you know where she might be?'

'Try our house.' She pointed out the window. 'Cross the road, second left, end of the street. Blue door.' She winked at him. 'Try not to get run over.'

A little disturbed, he thanked her and followed her directions to a narrow house at the end of a terrace. He rang the doorbell. After a few minutes, Esi opened the door. She looked sleepy and vulnerable, in Shola's Homerton MCR T-shirt and her own silk headwrap – the same headwrap, he realised now, that he'd seen her mum wearing, faded from red to peach. He tingled with the strangeness of it. It was easy to forget she was a traveller from a place that wasn't on any map, a place she would soon be returning to.

She looked at him, a hundred conflicting emotions warring on her face. 'You,' she said, like the universe was about to end and it was all his fault.

He took a breath. There was so much he wanted to say to her, but he had to start with what was important. 'Darcy's your mum. Your mum is Darcy.'

She rubbed her temples. 'Sorry, you're going to have to run that past me again.'

'Rob's nemesis! The Deadly Mr Darcy. That's your mum's Assassin name. She and Rob are going to have a duel at my college May Ball on the twenty-third of June. If she beats him, she gets an award. For winning the Game twice.'

Her brow furrowed, then cleared. 'You'd better come in. Tea?' She headed back to the small kitchen.

'Aye, that'd be great,' he called. Music was playing, a woman's soft voice twining around complex beats. The living room was a cosy nest of mismatched sofas and slanted bookshelves, the walls plastered with photographs of Shola and her housemates. The most recent batch prominently featured Esi: laughing in the canopied basement of a club, cooking with Shola in the kitchen, their housemates acting as judges in what appeared to be some kind of rice-off.

She brought the tea, looking marginally more awake. 'You're sure about this?'

'Hundred percent. I showed him the photo. He said it's her.'

She shook her head in wonder. 'So all this time, Rob's literally known her?'

'More than that. He's been actively hunting her down. We just never thought to ask him, because – you know. Assassins.'

Her face lit with realisation. 'That's why she was so hard to find. The whole time we were looking for her, she was in the Game.'

'Until February. Rob told me Darcy got killed. That's why she let her guard down. She wasn't playing anymore.' He smiled. 'You used to play, right? Something else you have in common.'

She sat down on the sofa, tucking her legs underneath her. 'But it's just a stupid game. How could it be that important to her that she'd come back for the anniversary twenty-five years later?'

'Maybe she had different priorities than you thought.' The phrase chimed with something in his memory. 'Shit. Diana knew.'

She looked up at him sharply. 'What?'

'You were right. She was lying. They were friends in first year. She pretended not to know her because your mum didn't want to be found. Diana said she didn't understand her reasons, but she'd still respect them.'

Esi shifted on the sofa. 'I guess that's nice of her. Annoying for me. But nice.'

'We're not together anymore,' he said hurriedly.

He caught her relief before she tried to hide it. 'Oh?'

'I broke up with her. You were right. It wasn't fair not to tell her the truth. I gave her the book.' Her eyes widened. 'I wouldn't worry about it disrupting anything,' he reassured her. 'She's planning to stick to it word for word.'

She looked down at her hands. 'So she thinks you're still going to get together in the future?'

'Yeah. And the weird thing is, it looks like the future agrees. The time travellers came back this morning.' A troubled look crossed her face. He thought he knew what was worrying her: the idea of the future correcting itself, converging back to its original path. 'Hey.' He touched her arm. 'It doesn't mean we can't save your mum.'

She met his eyes. The troubled look lingered, as if that wasn't all she had been thinking about. 'Yeah,' she said after a moment. 'And now we know how.'

He nodded. 'We have to help Rob win.'

AN HOUR LATER, they were assembled in Joe and Rob's living room. Rob was in the armchair, looking uneasily up at Joe and Esi, who were flanking him like prison guards. 'What's happening?'

'See this duel with Darcy?' said Joe. 'I can't overstate how important it is that you win it.'

Rob laughed. 'I mean, obviously I agree. But why do you care? You've never been invested in how I do in the Game before.'

'This is bigger than you, Trevelyan,' said Esi sternly. 'This is about setting history right.'

He looked up at her, baffled. 'Again, I agree. But you don't need to worry about it. I've got it covered.'

'No. You haven't.' Joe paced away, exhaling. 'Whatever you were planning, it's not going to work.'

'How do you know?'

At the same time, they both said, 'We know.'

Rob looked between the two of them. 'Why are you being so intensely weird?'

Joe turned to Esi. 'Something needs to be different.'

'Different from what?' Rob asked plaintively.

'From how it was going to be.' He scrubbed his hands through his hair, trying to dislodge an idea. 'We need a new variable.'

'I'm a new variable,' Esi offered. 'So are you, if you've never cared about the Game before.'

She was right. He whirled back to Rob. 'You once told me non-Assassins can be – what's it called . . .'

'Accomplices?' Rob laughed. 'I'm not letting you be my Accomplices. If you get yourselves killed, that makes me Wanted, which means—'

'We're not going to get ourselves killed. We'll just – be there, watching, waiting for her to make her move. And then, at the crucial moment—'

'We can distract her.' Esi's smile dazzled him.

Rob was less pleased. 'You both need to explain to me what the hell is going on here.'

'Later,' said Joe. 'Right now, you just need to trust us.'

Rob stared at him, like he was weighing their years of friendship against his heart's desire. Finally, he sighed. 'Okay. Fine. I accept your mysterious and frankly unnerving offer of assistance. But that means you and Campbell both need to be at the Ball.'

Esi looked at Joe in alarm. 'Aren't the tickets really expensive?'

'We can work for half of it. Get into the other half for free.' He shrugged. 'A lot of people do it. It's the only way to get in, if you don't have a spare hundred quid lying around.'

'Completely normal university,' Esi muttered.

'Okay. Darcy's working the first half, so I'd need you two to do the same.' Rob was out of bewilderment and into strategy mode, steepling his fingers. 'I'll talk to my mate on the committee. He can sort you out.'

Joe met Esi's uncertain, hopeful eyes. 'It's a plan.'

THE TWENTY-THIRD OF June. The date had been circled in red on the calendar of his mind for so long that it felt like doomsday had arrived.

He had spent the first five hours of the Ball serving champagne cocktails to a never-ending stream of his beautifully dressed peers, who had treated him as if he were invisible. Now, as the Chapel clock struck eleven, he was on the other side, dressed up in his kilt outfit, part of the privileged crowd. The champagne cocktails had run out; the only drink left was beer in a plastic cup. He drained it and dropped the cup in a bin, thinking wryly how the evening summed up his Cambridge experience: half-in and half-out of it.

He and Esi had been assigned to different stations, so he hadn't yet seen her. Rob had given her his key so she could use their room to get changed. He waited near the entrance of the staircase, watching the coloured lights sweep over the college's limestone walls, the past and the future colliding.

And then he saw her. His breath caught. Her dress was floor-length, gathered at the bodice, pale blue with a violet overlay that picked up the delicate shimmer of her skin. Her hair was done up in a complicated, sculptural arrangement, tiny flowers studded all over like stars. Forget-me-nots. His heart ached at the irony. 'You look fucking beautiful.'

She lowered her head, a smile blooming across her face. 'Burleigh Street charity shops came through again.'

He offered her his arm. She took it, and they walked across the grass under the lights as though they belonged there. He kept stealing sideways glances at her, taking in her proud, upright stance, her serene expression. He remembered how she'd been at Diana's party, self-conscious, hiding in the corner. She must be feeling even more out of place here, but if it bothered her, she was refusing to let anyone see it. She was coming into herself, and it was incredibly sexy to witness.

He reminded himself to focus on the task at hand. 'Has Rob found her yet?'

'No.' She looked around with an intent, sweeping gaze. 'I'm not going to lie. It feels weird that I'm here to help him kill her.'

'A fake death to prevent a real one,' he reminded her as his phone buzzed. He opened his sporran and took it out, Esi watching with amusement. A message from Rob. 'He wants us to check the dining hall.'

They headed up the steps into the high-ceilinged space. Up on the dais, the ceilidh band was announcing the last dance to four long rows of swaying guests.

Heart beating strangely fast, he turned to Esi. 'You know, the most efficient way to search a room is to join in Strip the Willow.'

She gave him a knowing smile. 'Really.'

He held out his hand. She took it, and he led her to the top of the group of dancers.

'I don't know the steps,' she protested as the band started up.

'See that guy?' He pointed to the caller. 'He's literally going to be yelling them out.' As the familiar music filled him, he whooped and grabbed her arms, spinning her round and round until she threw back her head with laughter.

They spiralled down the line, dancing with a new partner every few beats, always coming back to each other. He made a token attempt to look for Efua, but the truth was he couldn't keep his eyes off Esi. She was on fire, matching him step for step, putting her own spin on the moves he'd known since he was a child. They kept dancing, as the ceilidh band gave way to an Outkast song that sounded like it was from the future, Esi moving with sweet abandon, her cheeks glowing, completely at one with herself. He wanted to forget why they were really here. He wanted to stay with her in a vibrating, endless now.

And then, over her shoulder, he saw her. Efua. She wore an elegant green gown, her hair twisted up into a bun with an ornamental wooden comb tucked into one side. He was wondering if that was her weapon when she took something out of her clutch: a small blue parcel made of tissue paper.

'Confetti grenade.' He touched Esi's arm and pointed. They followed her out of the dining hall, down the steps, across the lawn towards the chocolate fountain. At the front of the queue was Rob, oblivious. 'Fuck. Chocolate fountains. His one weakness.'

Esi grabbed his arm. 'She's going to get him any second.'

'Time for a distraction.'

She let out a nervous laugh. 'Maybe we should have actually planned this.'

His mind raced. 'Your mum's into romance, right?'

'Joe,' she warned him, but they were out of time. He took her hands and pulled her back with him, until they were standing between Efua and Rob. He tried to channel what he'd learned from Diana, her absolute confidence when she was playing a role, her disregard of what anyone watching would think of her.

'I told you,' he said, projecting his voice to the crowd. 'She means nothing to me.'

Esi's eyes widened as she caught on. She drew herself up in queenly affront. 'Then why were you kissing her?'

'I thought I was in love with her. But I wasn't. I was in love with the idea of being in love with her.' He wasn't sure when it had stopped being a performance and turned into the truth. 'She wants to be a work of art,' he said simply. 'I want to be happy.'

Her voice was softer now. 'And what makes you happy?'

He pulled her close. She came willingly, sliding her arms around his neck, staring into his eyes. *It's not real*, he reminded himself as his heart pounded, as her lips parted. They were only doing this so she could get what she wanted and go.

He tore his gaze away from her, looking over her shoulder. Efua was watching them open-mouthed, a hand on her heart. Behind her, Rob crept the last few steps and draped the knitted circle neatly over her. 'Death by gravitational singularity,' he explained, then chivalrously helped to extricate her from it.

'Really?' said Efua, fighting her way free. 'You got approval from the Umpire for this?'

'She's a physicist too,' Rob admitted. 'That probably helped.'

Efua carefully extricated the last strands of black hole from her comb and slid it back into place. 'Congratulations, Entropy,' she said, grudgingly shaking Rob's hand.

He grinned. 'I told you. It's going to—'

'Get you in the end,' she completed wearily. 'I know.' Hope flickered across her face. 'Wait. Isn't there a theory that people could survive falling into a black hole?'

'Absolutely,' said Rob with an enthusiastic grin. 'There's so much we don't know. Which is why I also made sure to coat my hand in contact poison.' He showed her his palm, which he had painted ultramarine blue. 'Belt and braces, you know.'

She shook her head. 'Guess we're even.'

'Good Game, Darcy.'

'Good Game.' She turned away, dropping her confetti grenade back into her clutch.

Rob ran up and enveloped Joe and Esi in a crushing hug.

'Congratulations, Master Assassin,' said Joe, laughing.

Rob kissed first Esi and then Joe resoundingly on the cheek. 'I love you both. Now go. Have fun.' He pointed back at them as he walked away. 'And don't forget, you still owe me an explanation.'

'Absolutely,' called Joe, waving.

'Are you actually going to tell him the truth?' Esi murmured.

'Aye, I think so. He deserves it.' He watched Rob run into the embrace of his Assassin friends. Efua was sitting nearby, her smile wavering. He leaned in to speak in Esi's ear. 'What about her? She looks like she needs cheered up.'

She turned to him, so close he could kiss her, a look of awed terror in her eyes. 'What if I change her future?'

'That's the point, isn't it?' He shrugged. 'Change her next five minutes. Make them better.'

She gave him a wide, full-hearted smile. Hesitantly, then with resolve, she walked over.

Efua looked up and made room for her on the bench. He didn't want to eavesdrop, but as the conversation around them ebbed and flowed, he couldn't help overhearing fragments.

'Your hair looks amazing,' Esi said.

'I was worried about it raining. Didn't realise it'd have to withstand a black hole.' They both laughed. 'Yours is incredible. Where did you get it done?'

'At home. My housemate has a gift. Took her hours, but at least I got to catch up on the latest about this librarian she has a crush on.'

They laughed again, their voices subsiding into a murmur. He watched Esi, how her nerves gave way to smiles, how she gradually leaned in, like a compass drawn to the north.

'So you're really into Assassins?' he heard her ask.

Efua nodded. 'Trying to survive here, it's – intense. I just sometimes need to let it all out by killing people, you know?'

Esi laughed – God, he loved her laugh, the way her eyes screwed up in joy, an unshed tear spilling to the ground. 'Yeah. I get it.' She looked at her mum with trembling hope. 'So? Did you survive?'

'Oh, I more than survived.' A smile broke across her face. 'I found my people. I made this place my own.'

Their voices lowered again. As she listened, Esi looked up at him and laughed, her face glowing. He just gazed at her, knowing he probably looked like a lovesick idiot, but not really caring enough to stop.

She stood up, her voice rising again. 'You're amazing, by the way. You should know that.'

Efua looked up with delighted surprise. 'So are you.'

They embraced, holding each other tight. Esi said something in her ear before she walked away. Efua watched her leave with a puzzled smile.

Joe took in her face as she came back to him, shining with deep, fierce joy. 'Did you tell her who you are?'

She looked back over her shoulder, waving. 'No.'

He looked at her curiously. 'So what did you say to her?'

She smiled, tears glinting in her eyes. 'I told her everything's going to be okay.'

Chapter Twenty-Nine

They left college. He could have asked her to stay, spend the rest of the Ball with him, but it would only have been delaying the inevitable. They headed for King's Lane, where her steps had always been taking her. Fireworks trailed in neon colours across the sky, like a celebration happening in another universe. As he watched the starbursts reflecting in her eyes, she slid her hand into his.

They walked along like lovers, not like two people who should never have met and were about to end up on opposite sides of a cosmic portal. He tried to hold on to her lightly, but the feeling of her hand in his was a torment: an apology that meant nothing, a promise there was no way she could keep.

'So help me visualise it,' he said, feeling like if he didn't say something, he would fly to pieces. 'You step through, and then – what? What's on the other side?'

She walked slow and swaying, her hip brushing against him. 'There's a gift shop. And an exhibition, about you and your poetry and Diana.' Still waiting for him in the future, no matter what he had decided. The idea sent a chill through his heart. 'There's also a statue.'

He stared at her, his train of thought completely derailed. 'A statue?'

'Yeah. A giant statue of you doing this.' She posed briefly with her chin on her fist, her expression comically serious.

'Jesus. Really?' Once upon a time, the image would have thrilled him. He remembered a young man in a library, staring up at a poet made of stone. It made him feel ashamed, and relieved, and a little sad.

They turned left down the grey concrete alley of King's Lane. Esi stopped opposite a blank patch of wall. He squinted. 'Is it invisible?'

She smiled sadly. 'I told you. There's a password.'

He was desperate to delay her. 'Do Shola and your housemates know you're leaving?'

She shook her head. 'They think I'm going on holiday. I booked leave from work and everything.'

The silence of the unspoken descended. Too much to say, and too little time left to say it. She let go of his hand. 'This is where I walk away.'

The words weren't new. His vision doubled. A different Esi, anxious and unrooted, facing him on a crowded street. He knew what he had said then, what he was supposed to say now. *Okay.* But the new version of Esi overlaid her, a hundred times more familiar and complicated and beloved, and he refused to let her go.

With his heart in his throat, he said, 'You don't really want to leave.'

A smile of recognition trembled on her face. 'What are you talking about?'

Another echo: the two of them in his college bar, her storming out, him asking her to stay. He began to understand. There was no past that was separate from the present. All their moments collided into this one, forming their path as they walked it. He smiled back at her. 'You didn't say *threshold*.'

A hole opened up in the universe.

He saw it out of the corner of his eye: a gap in reality, wrong as a galaxy trickling through an hourglass. Slowly, he turned his head to look at it. His eyes refused to focus: whatever the wormhole really looked like was beyond his mortal senses to process. What he saw was a fractal disc, radiant with silver light, that was both sinking into and surging out of the wall. If he shifted his head an inch to the left or right, it disappeared.

'Fuck me,' he breathed.

'You guessed the password.' Esi was gazing through the portal, as if she could already see herself on the other side.

The door was open: all she had to do was step through. Urgency gripped him. 'Esi. Wait.' He touched her arm, drawing her attention back to him. 'Listen to me. I mean it. I don't think you want to do this.'

Her expression was indefinable: hope and longing and fear, all woven together until he couldn't tell which one was uppermost. 'But this is the whole reason I came here,' she protested. 'To fix my future. To fix myself.'

'No. You came here to save your mum, and you've done that.' He stepped forward, taking her hands. 'And you're not the same person you were when you arrived. I've seen you start to let people in. I've seen you start to take up space. Is that why you didn't say goodbye to Shola? Is there part of you that's maybe thinking about changing your mind?' He barely dared to ask the question, so afraid of what the answer might be. 'Do you really still want to be someone else?'

Her eyes pinched shut. He could almost see the decision tugging her in opposite directions, towards a long-cherished dream or an uncertain future. He had no right to tip the scales: he was afraid of saying too much, of inviting a rejection that would hurt worse than any he had experienced in his life. Maybe he should hide his feelings, let her do what she would have done if they had never met. But they *had* met, and made a million tiny changes to each other, and she deserved to know how he felt about her, regardless of what she decided to do with it.

He cleared his throat. 'Also, and this really shouldn't sway your decision either way, but – I'm completely in love with you.'

It was amazing, how easy it was to say. No need to agonise over the right words, to hide behind the constructed facade of a poem. He was just sure, as he had never been before.

Joy flooded her face. Then doubt moved in to replace it. Her mouth moved wordlessly. 'But you and Diana – you're meant to be.'

'Maybe. But you know what? I've had it with *meant to be*. You and me, we're the opposite of meant to be. We're barely even supposed to breathe at the same time. But here we are.' He caressed her face, trying not to hang the universe on how she leaned in to his touch. 'And I know, I'm being selfish. "Hey, I love you, give up your dreams and stay with me in the nineteenth century, where phones still have physical buttons and you have to look at the internet on a computer."' She laughed, bowing her head. He tilted her chin up until she met his eyes. 'But the truth is – I don't want you to forget me.'

'I don't want to forget you either. I want to remember it all. How I fought so hard to save her, and I did it. How I made a life here.' She shook her head wildly. 'I don't want someone else to come out of the river. I want it to be me.'

His heart kindled with hope. 'So stay.'

'I can't.'

The two words he had least wanted to hear. The ground dropped out from under him. 'You don't feel the same.'

'It's not that! Fuck, I love you, I've loved you for an embarrassingly long time, but – Joe, my whole family is through there. I can't just abandon them.' She buried her face in her hands. 'I can't stay. And I can't go.'

'Listen,' he said, simultaneously trying to process that she had said she loved him. 'We've never really known how this works. All this time, we've just been hoping. Imagining what we want to be true. The only way to really find out is to walk through.' He offered his hand. 'Together.'

She gazed at him, terror written on her face. 'What if I forget you? Or – what if you can't even go into the future? What if it causes some kind of paradox and you disappear?'

He contemplated the weight of what she was saying. Not to be the famous poet Joseph Greene. Not to be any Joseph Greene at all: to vanish from existence, hand in hand with the woman he loved. He shook his head wordlessly. 'I don't care. I'm not letting you do this alone.'

She made a strange sound, between a squeak and a hum. Then she leapt into his arms.

She kissed him with hot, bottled-up fury, like she had been waiting all this time to give herself permission. He staggered back against the wall, taking the warm, living weight of her, gasping into her mouth. He kissed her, and kissed her, and if this was the way his world would end, it was an ending he could live with.

They broke apart, staring at each other as if they could pour a lifetime into the space of a moment. Hand in hand, they turned to face the wormhole. 'I love you,' he said.

'I love you,' she said, and they walked together into the future.

Splintering light, and a magnetic hum in his ears. The universe stretched, shuddered, broke into kaleidoscopic fragments. For an instant, he saw the wormhole as it really was, and his mind flew open, like a gale blowing through a shattered window.

Then he was on the other side, under the soft glow of security lights, looking up at a statue of himself.

They had dressed him in a loose shirt and knee-length breeches, as if they couldn't imagine a poet wearing modern clothes. The pose was exactly as Esi had shown him, down to the self-serious expression on the lifeless face. He had gazed up at the statue of Byron so many times, but he had never imagined what it would be like to see himself turned into a symbol of deathless art. It turned out the answer was *extremely uncomfortable*. He averted his eyes, taking in the rest of the exhibition: panels with quotations in foot-high italics, photographs of him and Diana blown up to larger than life. A hologram of the two of them kissing, the same moment of tenderness repeated again and again until it became uncanny.

'You didn't mention the hologram,' he murmured to Esi. Then he remembered. They were on the other side of the wormhole: she might not be his Esi anymore.

He turned to her in panic. She stood by his side in her shimmering dress, forget-me-nots studded in her hair. But her expression was blank, confused, as if what she was seeing made no sense to her.

'Esi.' She looked at him with glazed incomprehension. His heart froze. He didn't know how to ask her. 'Are you – did you—'

She shook her head. 'I didn't change.' Before he could process his relief, she gestured at the exhibition. 'None of it did. You're still going to end up with her. Nothing you just said made any difference.' Her eyes shone with furious tears. 'It means you were right all along. Any changes we think we've made, they don't matter. Whatever we do, we end up in the same place.'

'No. No way.' His heart rebelled. He jabbed a finger up at the statue. 'I'm not turning into that fucking nozz—' The words caught in his throat. He walked closer. There, on the right shin, subtle but undeniable: a scar.

Esi's eyes followed his to the statue, then down to his left leg. Below the hem of his kilt, his own, fresh scar showed like a reversed reflection.

They looked at each other. Without speaking, they ran through the exhibition. All of it was familiar, like a story told and retold to death: the quotations from the poems in *Meant to Be*, the photograph of him and Diana on the day they met, the look in their eyes, the precise angle of their heads tilted towards each other.

'It's all exactly the same as the book,' he said in disbelief. 'It's not like the changes don't matter. It's like they never happened.'

'But how?' Esi asked him, bewildered and terrified. 'How can the past change and the future stay the same?'

Not the *future*. A *future*. Vera, shooting him an amused look. The Retroflex logo, the shadowy second *R* branching off from the first. Rob peering into a cardboard box, trying to explain Schrödinger's cat. *Under a many-worlds interpretation, reality splits in two.* He looked back at Esi, revelation thundering through his veins. 'Because it's not the same future.'

'What?' Her eyes were wild. 'What are you talking about?'

'Vera told me. She said Retroflex doesn't change the future. They change *a* future.' He walked out of the exhibition, back to the wormhole. Where it met reality, the edges splintered, warping the straight lines of the brickwork into forking paths. 'Whenever I've asked Rob about time travel, he's gone off on a tangent about parallel universes. Or, I thought it was a tangent. But this is what he was talking about.' He shook his head in wonder. 'When you first went through the wormhole, you didn't just step into the past. You stepped into a whole new universe. We can change the future of the new universe – we already have – but the future of the original universe stays the same.'

Her voice trembled. 'So what does it mean?'

There were a hundred ways he could answer that question. But he knew what she needed to hear. 'It means you saved your mum, in my universe. And it means you get to keep being yourself in this one.' She drew in a great, shuddering breath. He took her in his arms. As he held her close in that dark, glowing space, he realised it meant something else too. The Joseph Greene in this universe was a different Joseph Greene, one whose life was already written. None of this – the exhibition, the statue, the absurd, thrilling immensity of it all – was in his own future. He took it in, and with a bittersweet pang, he let it go. 'And it means we were both wrong.' He stepped back, taking her hands. 'There was never any one future, to break or be bound by. There's infinite futures. All of them are real. All of them will happen. We just have to choose which one we want to happen to us.'

He hadn't realised he was asking her a question until he found himself breathless, waiting for her answer. She looked like she was about to speak. Then a sound came out of the darkness behind her.

She turned, sliding close to him. 'What was that?'

Behind the statue, a shadow was walking towards them. As it came out into the light, he was astonished to see that it was Vera, wearing a high-waisted dress that made her look like she'd just stepped out of a costume drama.

She stared at the two of them in utter confoundment. 'What the fuck are you doing here?'

Chapter Thirty

He looked her up and down, the rumpled muslin of her empire-line dress, the ringlets coming loose from her chignon. 'What are *you* doing here?'

'This is my workplace, remember? I'm allowed to be here. Unlike you.' She marched towards him, nodding in passing at Esi. 'Ms Campbell. My October fugitive. You're going to have quite the NDA to sign.' She took Joe by the shoulders and turned him round. 'But first things first. Time to send Mr Greene back where he belongs.'

'Wait!'

Vera turned back. She took in Esi's outstretched hand, the look of anguish on her face. 'No way.' She laughed aloud, looking between her and Joe. 'You're together?'

He broke out of her grasp and ran to Esi, taking her hand. 'Yes.'

Vera whistled in admiration. 'Now that is something. Congratulations. You're the first Joseph Greene to actually surprise me.' Joe, who was still adjusting to the idea of there being two of him, reeled anew at the thought of there being more. 'But I'm sorry. I still have to send you back. If anyone sees you on this side, it's going to play havoc with the official narrative. And maintaining the official narrative is a non-negotiable part of my job.'

'So find another job!' he said in desperation. 'One that doesn't involve lying to people!'

She shook her head. 'I told you. I need to keep this one.'

'Why?'

Esi had been fixing Vera with quiet attention. Finally, she spoke. 'Because she's with someone in the past.' Confusion briefly crossed her face. She corrected herself. 'One of the pasts. Why do you think she's here at midnight, doing the Jane Austen walk of shame?'

He turned back to Vera. He wasn't an expert on period fashion, but he knew enough to roughly place what she was wearing. Early 1800s. Cogs turned in his mind. *'No.'* Esi looked at him questioningly. With strange vertigo, he explained, 'She used to run the Byron trip.'

Esi looked askance at Vera. 'Seriously?'

'Oh, you're judging me?' Vera put her hands on her hips. 'Clearly I'm not the only one with a thing for dead poets.'

Esi looked uncomfortable. 'Mine's not dead.'

'Neither's mine. He's on the other side of a wormhole that's been sealed off from public access. And since I have no desire to move to the early nineteenth century, I need to keep this job so I can visit him.' She took hold of Joe's shoulders again, jerking him forward. 'So. On you go.'

He struggled against her grip, racking his brain for how to reason with her. 'Can't you just persuade your bosses to tell the truth?'

She sighed impatiently. 'The truth isn't marketable. People want to see Joseph Greene because he's special. One of a kind. If there are a million Joseph Greenes, if we can call another one into existence by opening a glorified door, then – he's not special anymore.'

He dug in his heels. 'But you know better than that. Your Byron, he's not replaceable. He means more to you than the original, because of what you've been through together. Because of the experiences he'd never have had if it wasn't for you.' He turned in her grip, straining away from the wormhole. 'We're real, all of us. Everyone you bring into existence by opening these glorified doors.' He looked over her shoulder, meeting Esi's eyes. 'Your trip broke my future. But it gave me a new one when it brought the two of us together. All I'm asking is for you to let me live it.'

Vera's grip slackened, but she didn't let go. She glanced at the spinning hologram of the other Joe and Diana. 'I'm not going to lie. I do love the idea of messing with that.'

He seized on her hesitation. 'Exactly! You never thought me and Diana were right for each other.'

'You know what it's like,' Esi added. 'To meet someone you never expected. Someone who makes you feel lucky that you're alive at the same time.' She looked at Vera, pleading. 'We deserve a chance. Like you and Byron deserve a chance.'

Vera's expression softened. 'George,' she said. 'I call him George.' She closed her eyes. 'Fine,' she said to Esi. 'I can get you an access chip, let you come and go even after this trip's over. As long as you keep it discreet. But you . . .' She looked back at Joe, pitiless. 'This is the last time you step foot on this side of the wormhole. I mean it, Mr Greene. No loopholes.'

He saw his own anguish reflected on Esi's face. It was better than permanent separation, but it wasn't the future he had been hoping for. He had wanted to be with her, not just as a brief, conditional holiday from her real life. He had wanted more, all the foolish things lovers promise each other: a lifetime, an eternity.

She came to him, took his hands. 'I need to talk to my family.

Sort some things out. But I'll be back.' He nodded, wondering helplessly how this had happened, that they had run out of time again.

Her hands slipped from his as Vera turned him round. 'Don't get any ideas. I'm changing the password as soon as you step through.' She shoved him, and he stumbled back through mind-melting infinity, out into the dark alley of King's Lane. When he turned, there was nothing but a brick wall behind him.

THE WORLD HE had come back to was different from the world he had left. May Week was over. Everyone was waiting, for exam results and graduation and the beginning of the rest of their lives. Joe was waiting too, but for something else: the opening of a hole in the universe, familiar footsteps echoing down a narrow lane.

Rob asked him where Esi was. He told him she was on holiday, in a tone that warned him not to push it. He tried to do what everyone else was doing, which was drinking a lot and making extravagant plans for the future, but it was no use. He ended up in King's Lane, sitting across from the invisible wormhole, throwing words at the wall in the hope that one of them might be the new password.

'Deev,' he tried. 'Ving. Nozz.' He searched his memory for one of the complicated physics words Rob used when he talked about time travel. 'Quantum.' The wall remained stubbornly a wall.

A drunk-looking man walked past, giving Joe a funny look. 'Fucking students.'

This was hopeless. He levered himself to his feet and went back to college to keep waiting.

Two more days passed. Exam results came out. He got a 2:1 after all. He stared up at his name on the noticeboard outside the Senate House, feeling a strange lack of surprise.

Rob stood beside him. 'You always said you were going to get a 2:1.'

'Aye. I did.' Was his destiny reasserting itself? Or was a 2:1 just the natural combination of doing next to nothing for half the year and spending the other half scrambling to catch up?

'Don't overthink it, Greeney.' Rob patted him on the back. 'The Assassins are having a last-chance social in Grantchester Meadows. Go and find us a good spot. I'll get some drinks and meet you there.'

Joe walked out of town along the river. Time travellers tailed him as far as Lammas Land, then lingered at the boundary, dwindling into the distance behind him. In three days' time, he would graduate, and they would vanish, the last relic of a future that was no longer his. To be honest, he was looking forward to it.

He walked on through the quiet streets of Newnham, out onto the rolling green fields that led down to the water. The grass was studded with groups of third-years, exulting and despairing, futures temporarily on hold. The cloak-and-dagger flag of the Assassins fluttered in the early evening breeze. He spotted Efua among the crowd, but she was the only one he recognised, and being introduced as Backwards Boy would only invite awkward questions. Instead, he went to sit alone by the riverbank, feeling strangely suspended, as if life was happening somewhere else and he was on a train waiting to get there.

His phone vibrated. Rob always got lost on the way to Grantchester. He was preparing to type *LITERALLY JUST FOLLOW THE RIVER* when he saw the message was from Esi.

His heart seized. Could a Nokia 3210 breach the barrier between universes? It didn't seem likely. Hands trembling, he opened the message.

:-G

He frowned, tilting his phone.

> What is that?

my disappointed face

because you're not here to meet me

Emotions warred inside him: excitement that she was here, dread that she would soon be gone again. He tried to keep his reply casual.

> I wish I'd never taught you about emoticons.

?:-/

that's you

> Why does my hair look like that?

you tell me

where are you?

> Grantchester Meadows. Follow
> the river south. If you see cows,
> you're on the right track.

ok

there soon

He turned to face the path. It would take her at least half an hour to walk here, but he didn't want to miss a single second.

He felt her coming before he saw her. She was wearing a bright red summer dress that lit her up like a conflagration. Her hair was loose and full, framing her face in spiralling curls. He gazed at her like she was the sun and he had spent three days in a darkened room.

She stopped, then turned: she was looking for him. He got to his feet and waved her over. The smile that lit her face when she saw him was a wonder and a heartbreak all at once. He wanted to go to her, take her in his arms and kiss her. But he couldn't see past the knowledge that this was only temporary: soon, she would be leaving, going back where he couldn't follow. 'So you talked to your family?'

She nodded. 'I thought everything would've fallen apart without me. But honestly, they were fine.' Her smile returned, deepened. 'It was so good to see them. I talked to my dad. Like, really talked. I think he finally gets why I had to come here. And my sisters – I told them about Mum. What she's really like. Not just the idea they grew up with.'

He couldn't help smiling back. 'That's brilliant. I'm happy for you.'

'Sorry it took me so long. I figured I should give them some time to adjust to the news.'

He didn't understand. 'What news?'

She lifted the bag he hadn't noticed hanging off her shoulder. 'That I'm moving here.'

His heart cracked with joy. But his brain wouldn't let him believe it. 'I thought you were going to do what Vera does. Live in your universe and just – come and visit me sometimes.'

Her eyes were soft. 'I don't want to be a visitor in your life, Joe. I want to be part of it. And I can still see my family. Every week, if I want to. They're only a wormhole and a train ride away.' She held up her arm, showing him a tiny scar on the inside of her wrist. 'Vera gave me an access chip, so I can always get back.'

He shook his head, the last tendrils of doubt dissolving. 'You don't have to do this for me.'

'I'm not just doing it for you. It's like I said to my dad.' She looked back over her shoulder, as if she could see all the way to the wormhole and beyond. 'That's where I'm from. But here . . . here's where I became myself.'

Finally, urgently, he crossed the space between them. They kissed, not the frantic maybe-goodbye of the last time or the dreamlike unreality of the first, but a warm, deep kiss, full of hope and desire and trembling possibility. He stroked her cheek. 'Welcome home.'

They sank down on the grass, hands joined, heads tilted together. He just gazed at her, his impossible love, who had appeared one day in a coffee shop and led him into a whole new universe.

She raised an eyebrow. 'I know that look. You're overthinking something.'

'I was trying to remember what I thought of you when I first saw you. But I can't. It's like everything I feel for you now has travelled back in time to that moment. I can't see the past for the present.'

'It's not like that for me,' she said dryly. 'I remember exactly what I thought when I first saw you.'

'Really?' he said, trying not to sound too interested.

'Yes.' She repressed a smile. 'I thought, *Here's that fucking nozz Joseph Greene.*' He lunged for her, tickling her mercilessly. She giggled, mock-pushing him away. 'Then I thought, *Uh-oh. He's cuter than I expected.*'

'That statue clearly didn't do me justice.'

'It's not funny!' she protested. 'You really weren't supposed to be this much of a problem for me. Just – walking in, with your big blue eyes and your stupid jumpers and your surprisingly-not-being-a-nozz.' She murmured in his ear. 'Ruining all my plans.'

Her low, warm voice made him shiver. 'I'm sorry. You're right. It's not funny.'

She sat back. 'You know what the hardest part was? Convincing my dad I'm not making a huge mistake. To him, you're just some old white guy I used to complain about having to study. I was trying to explain how it is between you and me, but he wasn't getting it. Until I showed him your poem.' Her lashes lowered. 'He said, *Here is someone who really sees you and loves you.*'

It still terrified him, that he had laid his feelings bare before he was ready to say them out loud. But if it could communicate his love for her across universes, it had been worth it. 'I'm sorry I won't get to meet him.' He turned over her wrist, kissing the tiny scar. *No loopholes.* Whenever she travelled into that other future, she had to go there alone.

A hundred worries crowded into his mind. What if Vera lost her job? What if the company shut down, the access chip stopped working, and Esi was trapped on the other side? With an effort, he pushed those thoughts away. He had spent enough of his time fixating on what might or might not happen in the future. He focused on her here, now, in the golden light: her soft breathing, her pensive expression. He followed her gaze to its target. Efua, relaxing in the grass, tipping her head back with laughter.

'What is it?' he asked gently.

Her brow furrowed. 'We think we saved her, but – how can we know for sure? The wormhole only takes me to the future of the universe I came from. I wish there was a way to go to the future of *this* universe.'

He felt himself smile. 'There is.'

She looked at him uncertainly. 'How?'

He kissed her softly. 'We travel there,' he said. 'One day at a time.'

She rested her forehead against his. 'It's funny. For the longest time, I thought I didn't need to plan for my future. I'd become the me I should always have been, and she'd have all the answers. Now, I guess it's on me to figure it out.'

He put his arms around her. 'You could apply to uni.'

She made a face. 'Here?'

'Only if you want. I know this place thinks it's the centre of the universe, but it didn't invent the concept of higher education.' He smiled. 'I mean, anywhere that'd give me a 2:1 is clearly not a reputable institution.'

Her eyes lit up. 'Seriously? That's amazing! Knew there was a reason I brought this.' She reached into her bag and took out a bottle of sparkling wine and two mugs. It wasn't until she'd opened the bottle and started pouring that he noticed one of the mugs had his face on.

She grinned and mimicked the pose, propping her chin on her fist. '"If I knew what I meant, I wouldn't need to write poetry,"' she declaimed, in a surprisingly good imitation of his accent.

He couldn't repress a grin. 'Where did you find that? I chucked it out.'

'And I rescued it.' She sipped from her own mug, raising an eyebrow. 'Might be worth something someday.'

He snorted. 'I doubt that.'

'Why? Did you stop writing?'

'No. But – I don't know. What I'm writing now, it's so different from the poems I was writing about Diana. I've got no idea if it's any good.'

'Does it make you happy?' He nodded. She smiled, the wide, generous smile he'd fallen in love with. 'Then it's good.'

'Greeney! Campbell!' Rob swooped down, clanking with bottles. 'See you got started without me.'

Esi took out another mug and poured him a drink. 'Cheers.'

'Cheers.' They clinked their mugs together. Before Joe could drink from his, Rob grabbed it, squinting at the image on the side. 'Why are you drinking out of a cup with your own face on?'

Joe looked down at the mug, then up at Rob. A reasonable explanation completely failed to come to him.

Rob took the mug from his unwilling hand. He inspected it, then turned to Esi, eyes wild with speculation. 'Campbell. Is this your doing?'

She blinked at him, the picture of innocence. 'What are you talking about?'

'I've been gathering evidence for a while.' Rob started counting off on his fingers. 'You treat technology like a personal insult. You don't understand contemporary slang. You wear normal clothes like they're a costume. And now you've somehow come into possession of a picture of Greeney where he is visibly decades older?' He shook his head. 'There's only one possible conclusion. You're a—'

'Master Assassin!' someone was yelling across the grass. 'All Master Assassins, come and assemble for your photo!'

Rob hovered, torn between the present moment and posterity. 'We are resuming this conversation the instant I return.'

Esi watched him go, shading her eyes. 'So we're telling him?'

'Guess so. Hope you weren't enjoying talking to Rob about anything other than quantum mechanics.' Joe frowned, watching his friend take his place in the lineup. Rob, who had got a First in physics apparently without even trying. Rob, who was the most likely person he knew to do a PhD. 'Who invented time travel?'

Catching his meaning, she shook her head. 'Not Rob.'

'Maybe not in your universe.'

She sent a wicked smile in Rob's direction. 'You think knowing a time traveller might give him a head start?'

Their eyes met. She laughed, and he slid across to her, embracing her from the side, inhaling the scent of her. How absurd, that he had thought he needed to be in love to write great poetry. Now he was in it, he knew he could never capture the fundamental wordlessness of this feeling, that any time spent not touching her was a tragic waste of seconds. He buried his face in her neck and made a soft, frustrated sound. 'I'm so in love with you.'

He felt her smile. In a teasing voice, she said, 'You going to write a poem about it?'

'Maybe later. Right now I have better things to do,' he said, and fell back with her onto the grass, giving in to the glory of the present.

Acknowledgements

This book is a time traveller. I started the first version in 2008, two years out of undergrad, living in a shared house off Mill Road in Cambridge. I finished the final version in 2024, married with two kids in Edinburgh. One of the reasons it took so long was because much of the revision process happened while I was also attempting to raise said tiny humans. So my first thanks go to those who literally or figuratively held the baby: my husband, Christos; my parents, Liz and Pat; and my mother-in-law, Afroditi, who twice came all the way from Greece to take care of everything so I could write.

Next, my huge and undying thanks to the editors who worked on this book over its long journey into print: in the US, Julia Elliott; in the UK, Natasha Bardon, Jack Renninson, Vicky Leech Mateos, and Rachel Winterbottom. I feel very lucky to have benefited from the insights of all these incredibly smart and perceptive people, who enabled me to gradually turn a total mess into something book-shaped. Thanks also to Chloe Gough for fantastic support throughout. On the agenting side, thanks as always to Bryony Woods, who never complains when I insist on writing weird, complicated books that cause immense problems for me and everyone around me, and to Alli Hellegers, for being the best possible advocate I could have in the US.

For research, thanks to Dr Louise Owusu-Kwarteng for her paper (https://doi.org/10.5153/sro.4265), which was very helpful as an introduction to Esi's background, and for putting me in touch with the wonderful Ebony Owusu-Nepaul, whose feedback has contributed in so many ways to making this book stronger. Huge thanks to Ebony for sharing both her lived experience and her critical insights to help me enrich Esi's character and do her journey justice. Thanks also to Nia Howard for her thoughtful review of the manuscript that reminded me to centre Esi's joy as well as her struggles, and the brilliant anthology *Black Joy*, edited by Charlie Brinkhurst-Cuff and Timi Sotire, which helped me think about ways that joy might manifest for her. Any mistakes that remain are my own. Thanks also to Philippa Pearson and Richard Ames-Lewis, who kindly answered my questions about St Bene't's Church in the 1800s, although the scene in question unfortunately ended up on the cutting-room floor. Maybe in a future book!

Cambridge in 2005–2006 is a lost city, accessible now only through the wormhole of memory. Special mention to Indigo and to CB1, coffee shops I frequented during my gown and town days respectively. Thanks also to my undergraduate supervisors, particularly Chris Tilmouth and Sarah Cain – sorry it's a time-travel rom-com, not a PhD thesis, but I hope the mind-expanding impact of your teaching is visible nonetheless.

I've been surprised by the number of early readers who have thought I invented Assassins. To clarify, it's real, and is still going strong at Cambridge and many other universities. I never played it, but have drawn from the Guild's excellent and entertaining online archives (https://assassins.soc.srcf.net/index.html), with some tweaks for story purposes (yes, I know the May Week Game doesn't work like that).

Anyone familiar with the songs of Frightened Rabbit, particularly 'My Backwards Walk' and 'Head Rolls Off', will recognise their impact on this book – another of the 'tiny changes' Scott Hutchison made during his too-brief time on Earth.

https://tinychanges.com/.

Thanks to the ESFF community, both in Edinburgh and across the world. Particular thanks to Julie Leong, without whom this book might still have been untitled. Thanks and love to my friends and family, especially to Hannah Little, who was enthusiastic about this book before anyone else was; to my dad, for ensuring I imprinted on Douglas Adams at a young age; and to Christos, for always being happy to brainstorm plot points with me. Sorry I still haven't taken you to Formal. And to A. O. and J. E. – when you grow up, I hope you feel free to be whoever you want to be.

Finally, to the friends I made between 2003 and 2006, whether or not we're still in touch: thank you for the tea, the cider, the arguments, the river swims, the fires, the shoes lost and found, and the laughter. This book is for you.

About the Author

Catriona Silvey is the author of *Meet Me in Another Life*. She was born in Glasgow and grew up in Scotland and England. After collecting an unreasonable number of degrees from the universities of Cambridge, Chicago, and Edinburgh, she settled in Edinburgh where she lives with her husband and children.

Visit her online at catrionasilvey.com

Discover more by

CATRIONA SILVEY

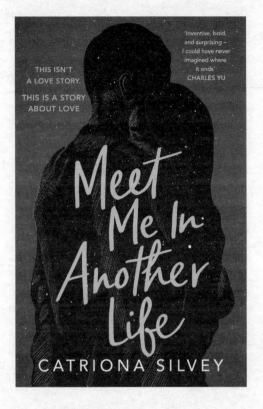

'Inventive, bold and surprising . . . Builds in suspense and
emotion, revealing itself page by page, layer by layer.
Cleverly constructed and highly entertaining.'
CHARLES YU

For fans of *The Invisible Life of Addie LaRue* and *Life After Life*,
a poignant genre-bending debut novel about a man and woman
who must discover why they continue to meet in different versions
of their lives – a thrilling and imaginative exploration of the
infinite forms of love and how our choices can change everything.